MAD SCIENTIST JOURNAL PRESENTS

utter
FABRICATION

HISTORICAL ACCOUNTS OF UNUSUAL BUILDINGS AND STRUCTURES

Edited by
Dawn Vogel and
Jeremy Zimmerman

Mad Scientist Journal Presents
UTTER FABRICATION:
Historical Accounts of Unusual Buildings and Structures
Edited by Jeremy Zimmerman and Dawn Vogel
Cover Illustration and Layout by Scarlett O'Hairdye

ISBN-13: 978-0-9977936-7-3
ISBN-10: 0997793678

table of CONTENTS

Foreword.. 3

"Every House, A Home" provided by Evan Dicken 7

"Heart of the City" provided by Ian M. Smith.................................. 23

"The Orpheus Well" provided by Dorian Graves................................ 33

ART BY LUKE SPOONER 57

"Кориолан (Koriolan)" provided by Alexander Nachaj.................... 59

"A Pocket Guide for Mistress Horne's Home for Weary Travelers"
provided by Gwendolyn Kiste 83

"Can't Be Locked Down" provided by Alanna McFall........................ 89

"Thump House" provided by M. Lopes da Silva 103

"Stand not Between a Cat and his Prey"
provided by Christine Lucas 125

"Outlier" provided by Julian Dexter 147

ART BY RAY MCCAUGHEY 153

"Kingsport Asylum" provided by Diana Hauer................................ 155

"Oshima" provided by Nyri Bakkalian 181

"The Safe House" provided by Georgie Hinojosa 185

"The Language of the Mud" provided by Betty Rocksteady 205

"The Girl Who Gives Me Sunsets" provided by Ali Abbas 213

"Hum" provided by Audrey Mack... 223

ART BY SCARLETT O'HAIRDYE... 229

"Remnants" provided by Timothy Nakayama 231

"Caution" provided by Lyndsie Manusos 257

"Visitor's Guide to the Waterfalls of Froskur National Park"
provided by Kathryn Yelinek 279

"Sector 5" provided by E. R. Zhang... 283

ART BY KRISTEN NYHT... 295

"The High Cost of Answers" provided by Michael M. Jones............ 297

"The More Things Change" provided by Carolyn A. Drake............. 313

"Memories of Farrowlee Beach" provided by S. E. Casey 335

About the Editors 352

FOREWORD

It can be hard to pin down the origin of some ideas. Dawn may have a different thoughts on it, but for me, the seed of this anthology starts with a giant drill named Bertha. Washington state has been working on boring a tunnel under the Seattle waterfront to replace an elevated highway. For this purpose, they had a giant drill custom built and shipped from Japan.

To put it mildly, it had an inauspicious start. Not far into the project, Bertha hit an object that damaged the drilling blades. Because of the way the drill worked, they couldn't tell what it had hit until they dug down from above in order to investigate.

Being huge nerds, we started to speculate on what sort of supernatural or extraterrestrial thing it could be. And whether that could be a future anthology. Which brings us to this book.

There are other things we love that have influenced the vision for this book. *House of Leaves, Neverwhere, Welcome to Night Vale, Nobilis, Doctor Who, Fallen London.* But for me, I think of that political scandal around a giant drill and what may possibly lurk in unusual places.

Yours,
Jeremy Zimmerman
Co-Editor

note

THESE STORIES *are fictional. Any similarity to real people is coincidental. Though they have a narrator that has a bio, the true authors are the ones listed as having "provided" the story.*

THANK YOU

THIS BOOK WOULD NOT BE POSSIBLE IF NOT for the generosity of our Kickstarter and Patreon backers. In particular, we would like to recognize the contributions of Adam R. Easterday, Adam T Alexander, Aimee Brooks, Alexandra Summers, Amanda D., Amanda L'Heureux, Amanda Robinson, Anders Smith, Andrea Parker Megivern, Andrew Cherry, Anne Delekta, Arinn Dembo, Ben Bernard, Brenda Yagmin, Carmen Maria Marin, Carrie Emmerich, Catherine Warren, Cathy, Chris Battey, Chris Newcomb, The Christiansen Family - Janene, Thomas, Daniel & Ethan, Christy Schmidt, Danielle Hinz, Dave Eytchison, David Ameer "Godzilla" tavakoli, David Young, Don Ankney, Dusty Wallace, Elizabeth Vann-Clark, Erik Scott de Bie, Erin C, Erin Hawley, Ernie Sawyer, Gavran, Gertjan, Ian Chung, Isabel Church, J.P. Brannan, Jäger Hein, Jacob Carson, James Do Hung LEE, Janka Hobbs, Jeanne Edna Thelwell, Joe B. Rixman, Joe Saul, John Davies, John Nienart, K. Kitts, K.G. Anderson, Katherine Nyborg, Kenda Salisbury, Kendra Petkau, Kenneth Zich, Kevin Varley, Kirstie Olley, "Kit Kindred; or the diabolical Dr. Kindred. whatever. I'm not your boss.", Kristen Nyht, The Ladies Jess, Laura Wilson-Anderson, Laurie J Rich, Linda Cottrell, Marina Belli, Marlo M., Mary Argent, Megan Awesome, Melissa Pritchard, Michael Deneweth, Miche Connor, Michele Ray—Queen of TMI, Mike Kenyon, MISSY COOK, Mitchell R. Dillard, Mr. DC, Murray writtle and Emma Sansone, Nathan Crowder, Noelle Salazar, Pamela Cobb, Patti J Oquist, Quentin Lancelot Fagan, Rainy Day Kitty, Raven Oak, Rebecca Hartsock, Rich Stoehr, Richard B, Sanford Allen, Sarah Grant, Seth Blumberg, Solomon Foster, Squirrel and Moose, Stephen Acton, Stephen Jack Cullen, T Kunkel, Tod McCoy, Torrey Podmajersky, Trystan Vel, and Vivian Smith.

every house, A HOME

An account by Natalie Na-Yeong Park,
AS PROVIDED BY EVAN DICKEN

"I guess nobody wants haunted houses, anymore." Derek checked his reflection in one of the Cape Cod's filmy windows, teasing his hair back to mussy perfection. He glanced back at me. "That was a joke, Natalie."

I gave him my best approximation of a smile.

He blew out a long puff of air. "Never mind."

The house wasn't haunted, which was a shame. A ghost or two would be just the thing to calm it down. The Cape Cod was faceless, without history or meaning. Sandwiched awkwardly on a scrubby half-parcel between two mid-century colonials, it felt out-of-place and forgotten. A decade ago, the lot had probably been wild, but some developer had come along and crammed a factory home where it had no place being. I even recognized the model: *Sea Breeze.* There were maybe a hundred in Columbus—same light-blue vinyl siding, same asphalt shingles, same fake shutters, same concrete porch with the same three white-painted pillars. It shouldn't have had a *feel*, let alone a personality.

"I just don't get it." Derek brushed by me to tug the "Open House, Sunday, 1-4pm, PRICE REDUCED" sign from the freshly replanted lawn. "Two bed, two bath, decent schools—a good starter house. It's these millennials, they're all about apartments and lofts nowadays."

"That isn't it." I kept my response short, clipped, careful not to get lost in exposition. Instead of relating an article I'd recently read about how millennial housing choices were related to finance rather than preference, I knelt on the lawn, squinting at the row of boxwood bushes in the front bed. Derek's landscaper had just put them in, along with a layer of red mulch and a couple perennials for accents. Not a bad job, but I could already see the resentment building—leaves beginning to brown, shoots of crabgrass and shepherd's purse poking through the beds.

Derek came back up the walk to join me. I noticed he kept a good ten feet between us, like he was afraid I might lunge at him. It was hurtful, especially since I'd been working with him for years, but I knew better than to say anything. People think because I have trouble reading emotions that I don't have any of my own.

I'd never been comfortable around others, or them around me—too many expectations. Every word was a potential pitfall, every exchange fraught. I never knew what would set someone off. *Places* though, they didn't expect anything from you except to be.

"Well?" Derek asked after maybe a minute.

"Well, what?"

"Aren't you going to—?" He twiddled his fingers at the front door. "—*feng shui* or whatever."

Another terrible joke. Another terrible smile. "I'm Korean, not Chinese. And you know that's not what I do."

He winced. "At least have a talk with it and figure out—"

"Can't talk to houses."

"Then talk to *me.*" Derek's expression might have been sad or angry, I never could tell the difference. "It's what I'm paying you for."

"It's a starter house." I stood to run my hand along one of the pillars, glossy paint cool and smooth beneath my fingertips. I could feel twenty, maybe thirty years of young families passing through, building equity.

"Two years on the market. *Two.*" Derek waved a hand at the property. "And three months since the last showing. New lawn, new roof, new kitchen. I'm dying here, Nat."

"If only." I pressed my forehead to the front door.

"What?"

"Nothing." I stepped inside. The house felt hollow—art prints, fake flowers, couches, chairs, accent rugs not quite hiding the fact the house didn't need anyone, didn't *want* anyone.

"Christ, will you look at that?" Derek pushed by me to scowl at a pile of shattered dishes. All the cupboards were open, their contents spilled onto the kitchen floor "Goddamn poltergeist. That's what it is."

"No such thing." I flicked the light switch. A dozen recessed bulbs flickered briefly to life only to die with a series of faint pops.

"I *just* replaced those." Derek pressed a hand to his forehead. "And before you ask, it's *not* the wiring. Hemi was in here all last week. She checked every connection, every lead, every—"

He kept talking, but I wasn't listening. I'd learned long ago it was unproductive to tell people like Derek to shut up, even when they were obviously babbling, so I just wandered upstairs.

There was nothing. A bathroom, a small closet, a little pull-down ladder leading up to the crawlspace, two bedrooms with canted ceilings, empty of not just furniture but of memories. The house had no bones, no reason to be anything more than a pile of lumber. And yet, I could feel its bitterness in the way the flooring didn't creak under my feet, the carpet that felt rough rather than inviting, the spreading water stain on the right front wall of the master bedroom.

Usually, cleaning a house was relatively simple—replacing the floor in the room where a child had lost their innocence; a wall punched and patched by an abusive husband; a set of new cabinets instead of the ones that held the vodka that turned mom nasty; a fresh coat of paint on the wall that once held wedding photos of the divorced couple. Bad memories could settle anywhere. Even a few strong ones were enough to sour a home.

And yet somehow, despite barely the lightest dusting of history, this house *hated*.

Derek was down in the foyer, trying to kick some loose molding back into place.

"I need to stay." I stepped onto the upstairs balcony.

"What?"

"In the house." I went down, careful not to touch the railing I was sure would give way under the slightest pressure. "I need to stay here."

He made a sad-angry face. "I'm not insured for residents."

There was no point in replying. So I didn't.

"Goddamnit," he said as the molding came loose again. "How long?"

"Don't know."

"You can fix this?"

"Don't know."

"Is it going to cost me extra?"

"Same price."

"You're the expert, I suppose," he said in a way that made me think he meant just the opposite. "Keys are on the kitchen counter. Any longer than a month, and I'm going to start charging rent."

"No, you won't."

Shaking his head, he left. Just like the house, and I, wanted him to.

It takes time for a space to become a place. I'd never quite pinned down at what point during the gradual accretion of events and memories that houses became more than the sum of their parts, but I'd put down enough supposed hauntings to have developed a feel for when a place had turned. And the Cape Cod had *turned*.

Something had happened here, I just needed to find out what.

A pair of deer stared at me from the backyard as I made my breakfast of tea and instant oatmeal. There were no tables in the house, so I went out on the back porch to eat. The deer should've run, frightened by the bang of the screen door as it slammed shut behind me, but they only stared, chewing acorns from the big pin oak and watching me in a way that seemed vaguely threatening. Neither had horns, but I didn't know enough to tell if they were does, fawns, or whatever male deer are called—I couldn't remember.

There were no pets buried in the yard, no dark secrets hidden in the tiny patch of lawn backed by a wooded ravine. The morning light made stained glass of leaves just beginning to turn, forest smells threaded with hints of frying bacon, toast, eggs from the houses to either side. Somewhere, beyond the woods or maybe in it, a child's shriek dissolved into laughter.

It was quite pretty, actually.

I'd gotten about two bites of my oatmeal when the deer charged. One second they were flicking their ears, quiet as could be, the next they were bearing down on the porch, heads lowered and hooves churning the new sod. If I'd run, I probably could've made it back to the house, but I just sat there, spoon in hand, staring open-mouthed as they leapt onto the porch.

The bigger one knocked me from my chair and probably would've given me a good stomping if I hadn't managed to roll under the little pressboard table. Hooves hammered on the table, little flecks of glue-covered wood raining down on me as the top bent and cracked.

I screamed, they screamed. Not that I was afraid—it was more a reaction. The whole thing was too surreal, too *sudden* for real fear.

One of the deer stamped down close enough to my hand that I could feel the porch flex beneath me. I flinched back as a foreleg broke through the top of the table, the deer's shrieks turning from furious to terrified as it flailed around. I leaned back to brace my feet against the table legs, then kicked out. Deer and table tipped over the edge. There was a hollow thump as they hit the grass a few feet below, then a wild cracking tearing as the deer fought to kick free.

I scrambled back, expecting the other one to kick at me, but it just stood, watching as I fumbled at the glass sliding door—which was locked, of course. I pulled myself up and turned slowly, hands clenched in tight fists at my sides.

The deer were back in the yard, a ruined table and a smear of bright blood on one of the deer's front legs the only indication of the attack. They stood silently, muscles trembling as I edged along the porch. Their eyes were strange, like glass gone all filmy and finger-smudged. Just before I slipped around the side of the house, one dipped its head as if to acknowledge our shared confusion, then they turned and leapt back into the trees, crackling down into the ravine to disappear from view.

Bucks. It came to me—male deer are called bucks.

My stomach felt light, my arms and legs loose and shaky like I'd just stepped off a roller coaster. I made my way around front to retrieve the extra key from the fake rock by the front porch. The twin window panes in the front door made me think of the deer's eyes, the wood frames positively vibrating with tense energy, but whether it was the coiled wariness of a predator or the nervous regard of prey I couldn't tell. It was like looking into someone's face, strange constellations of emotion as foreign as the Hangul Mom had taught me as a child.

It was unsettling that I couldn't read this place, frustrating that it was as closed to me as everyone else, sharing in that secret language of expression and context I never could seem to parse.

"What are you doing, Nat?"

I turned, startled, to see Derek just at the edge of the porch, grinning, although I wasn't sure why. Dully, I realized I'd been standing there for quite some time, the key held so tight it left a red imprint on the flesh of my fingers when I relaxed.

"Are you okay?" he asked, but didn't come up onto the porch.

"I'm going downtown to do some research." I brushed by, tossing him the key. "The table out back is broken."

"What the hell? You're supposed to be—"

I slipped into my car and shut the door, cutting off the last of Derek's words. He motioned for me to roll down my window, smile becoming strange as I backed out onto the street and drove away. It didn't matter what else Derek had to say.

We both knew what I was supposed to be doing.

My apartment was on the north side, twenty minutes out of my way along I-270, but worth it for a shower and a change of clothes in a place that didn't want me gone, didn't want anything as a matter of fact. I hadn't put much effort into decoration, purposely so—my apartment's blankness was the mental equivalent of white noise.

The space had come fully furnished, to which I'd added a few small touches—one of Mom's watercolor landscapes above the TV, an IKEA bookshelf for my photo albums, and a ratty futon left over from my college apartment. Other tenants painted their walls and doors, but white primer suited me just fine.

Sometimes it was nice not to be anywhere.

A long shower left me feeling, if not exactly calm, then clean, at least. I tossed some clothes into my suitcase, and, on a whim, Mom's watercolor and a couple albums from the shelf. If I was planning on living in the Cape Cod, I might as well make a show of it.

Like always, I couldn't resist paging through the travel albums before I packed them away, luxuriating in photos of the London Eye at night, the brightly painted houses of old San Juan, the bronze Tian Tan Buddha on Lantau Island, the way the autumn leaves accented the deep blue tile and cherry wood of Changdeok Palace. It was easy to imagine myself back in London, or Puerto Rico, or Hong Kong, even Korea—although the last had been less of a vacation and more of an obligation—stealing away from distant relatives to go sightseeing, biting my lip as yet another "aunt" introduced me to a friend with a son about my age.

"Why don't you take Chang-ho, he can show you all the sites?"

"Seongsan? Oh, Na-Yeong, you don't want to go *there*, too many tourists."

But I *had* wanted to go. As much as other people were like sand in my shoes, the places they lived had the most character. Once, while wandering the hills south of Athens, I'd found a mound that used to be a palace, or a forum, or maybe a battlefield—it was hard to tell—but that was one of the few exceptions. In my experience, people tended to be where people were, and ignoring others had never been hard for me.

It wasn't until my cell buzzed that I realized I'd spent the better part of an hour with my albums. I picked up the phone to silence it, then saw the call was from Dad and decided to take it. "I'm busy."

"Me too," he said. It was our joke, not a funny one by any means, but we always *did* seem to call each other at the worst times.

"Season almost done?"

"Almost." It was late September, the school year in full swing. Not many homes sold in the winter, and most of my clients had already packed it in for the year.

"Any plans?"

"Flights to Ireland are cheap." I could hear some rattling in the background—Mom washing plates, her head cocked to listen. It was strange for Dad to call me. "Am I on speaker?"

"No," he lied. But the rattling stopped. "You might want to think about coming home for a week or so. You remember Ms. Kim's daughter, Sam? Well, she's getting married in November and well, since you were so close as girls, I figured you might want to go and then maybe stay for a few—"

It wasn't that I wasn't listening, I was. It was just that I already knew everything he was going to say. It seemed Mom was still mad about Korea, but apparently hadn't given up trying to get me to settle down with someone, preferably a Korean someone, ignoring the fact she'd moved to Cleveland, Ohio, to marry a doughy German-Irish ESL teacher.

I picked up her watercolor, examining it as Dad rambled about the goings-on in the neighborhood—who had moved where, who was having babies, a new kayak he'd bought. The painting was of a long mountain range picked out in blacks and grays; points of red, yellow, and orange around their base hinting at a forest in full autumn finery; the peaks reflected in the lake below so carefully rendered it was impossible to tell what was water and what was sky.

For a moment, I could almost *feel* the place.

"Hey Dad, could you put Mom on?"

"Uh, I don't know if—"

"Please."

"We just want to *see* you, dear. It's been a while," he said softly. There was a crackling on the other end, then Mom's clipped voice. "Na-Yeong, you should really consider—"

"That painting you gave me. Is it *from* somewhere? I mean, did you base it on a real place?"

There was silence for a moment. When Mom spoke again, her voice was softer, almost hesitant. "The landscape? Ah, no, just my imagination."

That was odd. Photos could capture a place in ways that art, filtered through a human agent, just couldn't. I shouldn't have been able to feel anything from Mom's painting. Just like I shouldn't have been able to feel anything from the Cape Cod.

I thumbed the phone's screen back to life. "I need to go."

"But, you haven't—"

"We'll talk later. I promise." I hung up.

I drove to the Hall of Records downtown. I'd been right about the Cape Cod, a few young families, none staying more than a handful of years. I checked the microfiche archives for reports on the area, but it'd been nothing more than a cow pasture before the developers bought it. For the sake of completeness, I searched the earlier records for any mention, thinking it could've been a Wyandot village or the site of some pre-Columbian mound. I found nothing and left the Records Office more than a bit embarrassed once I realized I'd wasted hours trying to discover if the house was situated on an ancient Indian burial ground.

Derek was gone when I got back to the Cape Cod, but the key was back inside the fake rock. I took my stuff inside, moving plastic flowers to make way for my albums and replacing one of the half-dozen framed stock photos with my Mother's painting. The wall looked much better, if a bit bare. I'd have to see if Mom had any more.

The house didn't seem upset by the changes, but I decided to give it some space anyway. After checking there were no deer, I went out onto the back porch and sat for a while. The evening was cool, but not uncomfortably so—what Dad always called "sweater weather." Still leaves framed a sky that went from purple to hazy black, all but the moon and the brightest stars obscured by the diffuse glow of the city.

I sat back, drinking in the cool quiet of the place. For the first time since I'd arrived, the Cape Cod seemed calm. Not because, but rather in spite of me, almost as if it were enjoying the evening as well.

When I woke up, my albums were on the floor, pages bare and photos spread all over the dining room. There was a quiet wariness in the air, a feeling as if someone were watching me through the big picture window behind the couch. I picked the pictures up, starting at every creak and rustle, even though I was reasonably sure the house wasn't going to fall in on me. Then I stood at the counter and slowly slotted the photos back into place.

If this was a battle of wills, the house needed to see that it hadn't rattled me.

A crash from the main room startled me midway through recapitulating my London trip. I'd forgotten about Mom's painting, but when I rushed in, it was still hanging on the wall. The crash I'd heard was the house divesting itself of the rest of Derek's stock photos.

That made me grin. Whatever the house was, it had good taste, at least.

In the kitchen, my phone rang. I walked over, noticed Heather Paquin's name on the ID, and let it go to voicemail. Heather was another one of my clients, a thin, talkative little woman who prided herself on "communication," which was another way of saying she refused to e-mail or text despite me having asked her many, many times. Still, she was a decent enough realtor, and paid well, although not as well as Derek.

Heather had recently become the listing agent for a mid-century colonial near Goodale Park in the Short North and was having a hard time finding buyers when other similar houses in the area had practically sold themselves. I smiled at the thought of homes picking their residents. If only. I'd found plenty of places with influence, weight, but none with intention, well, not until the Cape Cod, at least.

I texted Heather my response and headed downtown. My phone buzzed, I let it go to voicemail, listened to the message, then texted her, again. It was a testament to her desperation that she actually texted me back—details peppered with a swarm of emoji.

The Short North wasn't far from downtown, so I swung by Heather's colonial to find her waiting out front, smiling. Heather was always smiling, but it didn't mean anything.

She repeated everything she'd already told me on the phone, hands fluttering like startled birds as she showed me around the house. It was old and well lived in, fresh paint and new hardwood floors not quite concealing the deep bones of the place. A lot of laughter in the main room, bright, but frayed around the edges like the pages of a favorite book. Sadness circumscribed the place, melancholy already yellowing the pale trim around the floor and making the rooms seem close and claustrophobic.

"Who died?" I had to go down into the basement to feel it, but the heavy oak floor beams practically *ached*.

"It's not a murder house, if that's what you're thinking."

I sighed. Why did realtors always jump straight to ghosts?

Heather gave a little flick of her chin. "The father of the last owner. Cancer, poor thing. Left the house to his daughter, but she lived here for almost eighty years. Passed away in her sleep late while visiting family, but you probably already knew that."

I hadn't, but it didn't matter.

It was easy to find where the father died—on the screened porch out back, in a chair overlooking the garden. Mostly because he was still there.

Some people think I see ghosts. I don't. It's more a *feeling*, like sitting on a park bench just before sunrise on a summer day, basking in the quiet stillness of the place before the crowds come rushing in, and realizing that someone has sat down beside you, or maybe that they've been there all along.

It's not frightening once you understand that ghosts aren't people any more than the image of an actor is that person. They can affect the world just like a performance can make someone laugh, or cry, but there's no awareness in it, no intentionality. Only the living can imbue somewhere with meaning, with memory. We can't help it, in fact.

"It's a beautiful garden." I said, palms pressed to the screen. It was late in the season for flowers, but the backyard was still a riot of crocuses carefully bounded by dogwood, maple, and pine. It made me wonder how the back of the Cape Cod would look with a few deep beds, nothing gaudy, maybe some heather or white chrysanthemums to offset the changing leaves.

"I thought so, too," Heather said. "It's been a real pain to keep up."

It came to me then, like a missing page slipping into place. "You need to make the porch a room."

"What?"

"It was an addition, at the end. So he could see the garden." I paced around the porch, trying not to talk too fast. "She missed him, seventy-nine years, and she still missed him, *that's* what it is. They were apart, you see. Father and daughter, house and garden, the porch is the bridge. You need to make it part of the home."

"But." There was the little chin flick, again. "It is."

"No, it's still *outside.*"

"Fine, okay." Heather's smile might have been practiced, but even I could see it was fake.

"If you want to sell this house, turn the porch into a room." I didn't realize I was standing too close to Heather until she took a quick step back.

"I think I missed a call." She took out her phone, glanced at it. "It's a client. Sorry, I've got to take this."

I nodded and walked away. It would be a shame if Heather didn't change the porch, but I'd done all I could. Still, the melancholy had settled on me, clinging like damp to my skin, my clothes, following me all the way back to the Cape Cod.

My photos were out again, spread over the entire house. It took most of the afternoon to find them all—in cupboards and behind dressers, wedged up under the crown molding or between the toilet seat and cover. I'd just about gotten them all when the windows banged open, letting in a wind that set my photos fluttering like trapped moths.

It was too much.

The Cape Cod just wasn't worth the commission. I snatched up my suitcase, stuffing my albums and photos inside along with the few changes of clothes I'd brought. The front door slammed behind me, but I didn't care. I'd call Derek tomorrow and tell him he was best off leveling the Cape Cod and building something new.

He would never sell it.

This house would never be a home.

It wasn't until I stepped into my apartment that I realized I'd forgotten Mom's painting. Cursing, I hopped back into the car and drove back to the Cape Cod. Once this was over, I'd take a long vacation—Ireland, Japan, maybe London again—I certainly had enough money saved up.

My phone buzzed, another call from my parents. I thumbed it silent, then saw I'd missed two others from them.

The Cape Cod was a rough shadow in the dark, squatting on the lot like a sullen child. I hadn't left the lights on, so I had to stumble across the uneven brickwork and on to the porch. The front door stuck in its frame until I gave it a hard yank. It opened so quickly I almost tumbled off the porch.

Of course, none of the lights worked.

There was a flashlight in my car—one of the many things Mom had harassed me into buying.

The painting was gone.

It got to me in a way I couldn't quite put into words, so I had a good shout, stomping from room to room as I searched. The house seemed surprised, at first, then it gave my anger right back, glass rattling in the windows, floorboards creaking like a home ten times its age. I shoved furniture around, tipped over bookcases and dressers, even used a kitchen knife to pry off the fake shutters so I could look behind, but Mom's painting was nowhere.

I didn't need to look outside to know the deer were back.

At last, I found myself glaring up at the pull-down ladder that led to the crawlspace above the master bedroom. The Cape Cod's hostility was almost a physical weight, pressing down on me as, teeth gritted, I yanked the ladder down and climbed.

Mom's painting wasn't the only thing in the crawlspace. The trembling beam of my flashlight found other things: a faded soccer jersey, a plush lion, a set of crayons, chipped pint glasses cut with various brewery logos, and more—a museum of suburban detritus, carefully arranged and preserved.

I could feel them then, a dozen families, maybe more, each just passing through on their way to a *real* home. No wonder the house had gone feral.

I sat back, hands pressed into the prickly insulation. I'd gotten it all wrong. The Cape Cod hadn't been dismantling my albums, it'd been *looking* at them.

I'd thought of the Cape Cod as a home, when really it was another person sitting on the bench beside me, enjoying the view. I looked at it and saw only how it was different from other houses, how I could make it like them. But it couldn't, no more than I could be like everyone else. I took a slow breath, feeling like a hypocrite. "I'm sorry, I didn't know."

I knew what I had to do.

I climbed down, texted Derek, then called Mom back.

"I'll come up for Sam's wedding, but I'm not staying," I said, feeling a strange flutter in my chest. "You and Dad should come to Columbus instead. Stay with me for a week or two."

"In your apartment? We'd be—"

"No, I just bought a house." I glanced around, feeling the Cape Cod tense. "Sorry, I've got to go. We'll talk soon." I leaned in, adding, almost as an afterthought. "Love you both."

Then I went through my albums, slowly, taking time to describe each place in detail—the look, the sounds, the smells, the *feel*. It took the better part of the night, but nothing interrupted me.

"I have to go to my apartment." Normally, you couldn't talk to homes, but I wasn't sure about this one. "I need to get my things. But I'll be back soon with more photos."

The front door closed behind me, wary as a stray dog. It didn't bother me. I'd get to know the place, eventually.

I had my entire life, after all, and eternity after that.

NATALIE NA-YEONG PARK is a real estate consultant with dozens of clients throughout Central Ohio. In 2012, *Realtor Magazine* named her one of its "Top 100 Closers," and in 2015, she was profiled by *Inman News*'s "Unbelievable Secrets to Success" column. In her spare time, Natalie enjoys travel, having visited over twenty different countries in the last ten years.

By day, **EVAN DICKEN** studies old Japanese maps and crunches data for all manner of fascinating medical experiments at Ohio State University. By night, he does neither of these things. His fiction has most recently appeared in publications such as: *Apex*, *Beneath Ceaseless Skies*, and *Daily Science Fiction*. Feel free to visit him at: evandicken.com, where he wastes both his time and yours.

heart of
THE CITY

An anonymous account,
AS PROVIDED BY IAN M. SMITH

There's a skyscraper in lower Manhattan that you cannot get to. You'd recognize it, maybe—it's in the skyline, depending on where you shoot. Superheroes and aliens have flown past it in movies. It's a middling tall mid-century building, unoriginal in scale or ornamentation, not mentioned in any of the architectural books or sightseeing guides. Just another anonymous stroke on the canvas of the city. Unexceptional.

But if you try to walk to it, you'll never find its base. It's always just out of sight, around a corner. It's tall enough that you can get glimpses of the upper floors as you walk the glass and concrete canyons of the city, all the way from Battery Park to Times Square, but I have walked them all, many times over. I've never been closer than a few blocks away.

I am—was—an architecture grad student at NYU. Second semester, Dr. Hawsler tasked us all to do a critique of a building in the city—one that none of his students had ever critiqued before. Hawsler has had tenure for roughly a thousand years, and even in a specimen-rich environment like New York, the pickings for noteworthy buildings were getting slim. It had become an informal competition each year to turn up some gem like a forgotten Gwathmey apartment or an immaculately preserved example of a Welsh Craftsman.

I'm from Iowa, graduated a Hawkeye. NYU waitlisted me for the program, and I had just about given up hope when I got a letter saying that a spot had come open. I leapt at the chance and hastily arranged an overpriced sublet in Greenwich Village.

New York City. Architectural Mecca. I woke up every day in shock that it was actually happening. But the reality of the coursework and competition quickly set in. Somehow everyone knew that I was the guy that just squeaked under the wire. They all thought I'd scrub out. And that first semester, I thought I might too. Every week I felt like I was producing the best work of my life, and every week my scores dipped lower. Everything after Thanksgiving was a blur of black-market Adderall and high-octane coffee and countless hours hunched over in the studio. I stayed off the academic probation list, but only just.

Seeing Mom at Christmas really drove it home. She was so proud of me, so worried for me alone in the big city, so quietly desperate for me to come home.

I just couldn't. I had to get ahead somehow. Had to find an edge. I wanted to blow away all my classmates and impress Dr. Hawsler with my discerning eye and keen critique. But every time I thought I had found the perfect subject, I checked Hawsler's database and some other precocious prick had already critiqued it.

My room has a window, but the view was mostly just the concrete gray of the next building. When I lay in my bed with my head against the wall, I could just manage a perspective that afforded me some blue sky. It was there that the building first caught my eye. I probably never would have noticed it, except that it was framed so nicely in the narrow patch of view between the window frame and the fire escape. For months, I had fallen asleep staring at it, its top floor twinkling with amber light, but I'd never really seen it. Now that Hawsler's quest was paramount in my mind, it shone like a beacon. I didn't know it. I hadn't seen it in my perusal through Hawsler's archive. Maybe this was the find I'd been looking for.

I set out a little early next morning, intending to find it on the way to class. While I am a relatively novice New Yorker, I have already put a lot of city miles under my boots. By my reckoning, the building should stand on one of the funny little diagonal streets near Crestview Park. I zigzagged the neighborhood, sure that I'd reach it soon, but even as I doubled back on my path the third time, I was no closer. The building was nearby but never on the same street as me. It danced just beyond my reach behind awnings and oaks and brownstone conversions.

I was late to class. I tuned out the lecture as I scrolled through pictures of the city, catching glimpses of it in the background. I couldn't find its name or its address. But I saw it. There in Hell's Kitchen. And another at the south end of Tribeca.

There were two pictures taken from the top of the Empire State Building, both looking roughly south, both with that damned building clearly visible blocks apart.

I couldn't fathom broaching this subject to any of my classmates, certainly not to the professors. What was I supposed to say? "Excuse me, Kate. Have you seen this building? I seem to have misplaced it." Or "Dr. Hawsler, I think there's a building moving around Manhattan." That was the first time I considered the possibility that I had just cracked. I mean, there had to be a logical explanation, and at this point, that was seeming like it was the most probable. And if I was legitimately unable to tell reality from fantasy, I preferred to keep that to myself.

I hailed a cab outside the school, showed him the clearest picture I had, and asked him to drive me to that building. He glanced at it for a second, and his eyes glazed over. "You got an address?" he growled in a thick Bronx accent.

"No, just this picture."

"I'm not running a tour bus here. Give me an address or get out of the cab." His eyes were wide, and there was a bulging vein on his forehead. I decided not to push the topic.

For a week, I hardly left the streets except to eat. I walked Manhattan up and down, following the building. I snapped pictures on my phone whenever I caught it at a particularly extreme angle.

I pointed it out to people. No one knew what building it was or where it was.

I dipped into my already perilously low savings and got a ticket on one of those touristy helicopter tours of New York. The poor pilot kept trying to point out the Statue of Liberty and the Brooklyn Bridge, but I just asked him to fly a grid over the city as low as he could. Thirty minutes circling lower Manhattan, but I never once saw the building from above.

I hailed a cab from the helipad and slumped in the back seat, letting the stale pine air freshener and faint aroma of last night's drunks fill my head. The turbaned driver caught my eye in the rear-view mirror. "You take the helicopter, yes? A good day for a beautiful city."

I grunted something affirmative.

"I drive these streets every day for thirty years. Still beautiful. Where do you go now, please?"

I needed to take a break from the search. But if I went home, the building would still be taunting me out the window.

"NYU, please."

"You're a student, yes? My son went to NYU. Very good school. You are what? Law? Medicine?"

"Architecture, actually."

"Ah! A city builder, yes? Very good. You want to go straight there, or did you want any more sightseeing along the way?"

His smile was infectious. "No, no. Straight there is fine. Unless… I've been looking for a building. Would you be willing to help me find it?"

The driver's grin broadened. "Of course, of course! What building do you seek?"

I pulled my phone out of my pocket, brought up the picture and held it up into the front seat for him to see. He glanced over at it, and a sudden tremor shook his body as his eyes went wide. He jammed on the brakes and dropped into Park in the middle of the street, eliciting a cacophony of horns from behind us. His mouth popped open, and he made a small choked noise. He turned to me, terror etched into every contour of his face.

"You got an address?" Gone was the lilting accent, replaced by a harsh growling Bronx. He did not blink.

"Wha-what?" I stammered. "Are you alright?"

Another shudder rolled through him. "I'm not running a tour bus here. Give me an address or get out of the cab."

His words did not match his expression at all. His eyes were pleading, his knuckles white where they gripped the seat in front of me. I slid toward the door. "What's going on?"

His jaw clenched, and the skin around his eyes tightened. Then he blurted out, "I'm not running a tour bus here. Give me an address or get out of the cab." Same cadence. Same inflection. Same surreal disjunction between face and voice. Tears formed on his lower eyelids. My hand found the door handle, and I stumbled out of the cab into the street.

As soon as my feet hit the ground, he gasped and pressed both his palms to his eyes, blinking rapidly. He squinted at me for a split second, as if I was an alien or a nightmare made flesh. Then he quickly shifted into Drive and squealed away.

In the distance, the late afternoon sun glinted off the copper trim on the roof of the building. I decided I'd walk home. Usually when I pursued the building, it danced and eluded me. But as I walked south toward my apartment, it loomed, unmistakably present through every urban vista. I couldn't tear my eyes from it, and believe me, I tried. As the sky darkened toward dusk, it seemed to fill the skyline, large in a way that defied even New York expectations.

When I finally made it home, there was an envelope lying on the floor just inside my apartment, with my name written in a formal script.

I picked it up with shaking hands and drew from it a single sheet of paper. The letterhead bore a logo that looked like it had been designed by M.C. Escher—it was unmistakably the building, but as the lines ran down to an abstracted cityscape, they took on a different perspective, merging with the lines of other structures and leaving only emptiness where the base of the building ought to be. Underlining the logo in a line of light, round font were the words "SERTAPHAS TOWER." The sheet was blank beneath that except for three handwritten lines:

> *Your Presence is Requested this Evening*
> *Transportation will be Provided*
> *Formal Attire Required*

I glanced at the clock. It was already after seven. I sat down hard on a stool, staring at the letter in my hand, trying to coax any additional meaning out of it. I googled Sertaphas and got no hits. Nothing but seraphs and serifs. Through the window, the top floor of the building twinkled merrily at me. There were no more answers to be had here. I pulled my roommate's special-occasion Scotch from the top of the fridge and poured a heavy three fingers in a glass, then drained it in two long pulls. I hesitated a moment, savoring the burn on my palate and in my sinuses, feeling the liquor move through my system like a flow of magma. And then I went into my room and changed into my suit.

I had no idea what "transportation provided" meant, but I wasn't entirely surprised when a black luxury car pulled up to the curb outside my building as I walked through the door. The driver stepped out of the car, wearing a suit that clearly cost several times what mine did. He walked quickly around the front and opened the door for me. He didn't say anything, but his eyes sought mine. They were bloodshot and disturbingly dry, giving them a wholly unnatural dull matte appearance. His posture was rigid. His mouth opened a few times, but no sound came out. I got in the car.

The windows were heavily tinted, making it difficult to see anything but lights passing by the window. I don't know that the driver made it more than a block without making a turn, and I soon lost all bearing on where in the city we were. The car pulled to a stop, and my door swung open almost immediately. A gaunt older man in a bellhop's cap stood holding the door open with his eyes closed, his features serene as if he was asleep. I stepped out of the car, and he shut it firmly behind me.

I didn't recognize the street. It was clean and clear of all life except the two of us. There were adjoining buildings, but no lights on, no music spilling out of windows. I could see cars passing by a block away, but none turned down this avenue.

Sertaphas Tower maintained the same understated class in its entrance as it did in its profile. There was a black awning trimmed in gold stretching out from the doors, and all the metal work was polished brass.

The doorman gestured to the entrance and strode ahead to open the door for me. All his movements were stiff and mechanically precise.

The lobby was a perfect study in mid-century modern class, all the austerity of Bauhaus tempered by the concession that each object was intended for actual human use. The doorman entered behind me and walked briskly to the elevator, pressing the button and once again retiring to a posture of resigned repose.

The bell rang, and the doorman once again gestured for me to enter. I hesitated and looked him over again. I had been wrong—his eyes were not shut. In the light of the lobby, I could see they were dried and pale as his skin, the weak faded blue of his irises and the outlines of pupils completely occluded by cataracts.

I stepped into the elevator, and the doors shut behind me. There was only a single button. I pressed it, and the elevator glided into motion. It felt like a swift ascent. My ears popped and then popped again. There was no way the Sertaphas was this tall.

The doors opened onto an unfinished floor: stub walls dividing the building into quarters—exposed ductwork, naked support beams, and bare concrete stretching to a plane of glass looking out over the city. I walked to the window and looked down at New York City, the tracery of lit streets winding between the twinkling behemoths of other skyscrapers. The city I knew from a thousand movies in childhood and a thousand wanders in the last few months. I reached out to touch the glass with the tips of my fingers. The view was south facing, and there was a nice tableau of Wall Street and the Ground Zero memorial and Lady Liberty sparkling in the harbor. It was all so beautiful.

I walked my way west, leaving streaked fingerprints on the otherwise unmarred glass. I turned the corner to take in the Jersey Shore, walked north to drink in the electric Mecca of downtown, and when I had my fill, circled around looking across the East River at Long Island and Brooklyn. It was incredible—a perfect view of the city in all respects. I wish I had stayed longer.

There was no sign of any other human, and after waiting a good while, I decided to return to the lobby to see if I could find any answers about what this place was and who invited me here.

I returned to the elevator and pressed the lone button. Much to my surprise, the elevator went up a floor instead of back down. The doors opened onto another unfinished floor, but an unfamiliar sight out the window—New York City was a ruin. Streaked lines of devastation radiated out from Central Park, buildings toppled or gutted, the black scoring of fires written across all the eye could see.

Nothing moved, nothing remained intact. The city I loved had been scrubbed from the face of the planet.

I doubled back to the elevator, desperate to undo this destruction. I hammered on the button and ascended one floor.

This New York was much more densely developed, the whole of Manhattan grown to downtown levels, and a sea of advertisements covered the roofs of the buildings, all written in Japanese.

I have seen New York an untamed jungle, a pre-Industrial settlement, a grid of identical perfectly rectangular buildings, flooded, grown over with vegetation, covered in ideograms I've never seen before, walled off, and burnt to a cinder. Every time I press the button, I go up another level and am presented with some other permutation of this landscape.

There is no food here. No water. There are no stairs and no other exits. There is only the elevator and the glass and the infinite ways that New York can be other than the way I knew it.

I found a skeleton yesterday. It was curled into the fetal position in the corner looking out over a New York of billowing smokestacks and smog. I am unwilling to accept that fate.

I am looking over a New York now that is the closest I have seen to the one I left. The signs are in French and the Hudson is black as tar, but it is the cityscape I knew.

I don't know if the window will break, and even if it does, that I will be allowed to leave. But if I am, and if some citizen finds my mangled body clutching this notebook: Treasure your world. All others are foreign and terrifying. And for the love of god, leave the Sertaphas Tower a mystery.

AUJOURD'HUI, LE CORPS d'un homme non-identifié a été trouvé sur la 5e avenue, rendant les voisins et la police locale perplexe. Le médecin de l'institut Médico-légal a déterminé que la mort avait été causée par un traumatisme important, due a une chute, mais la sévérité des blessures indiquaient qu'il avait achevé la vitesse terminale, ce qui suggérait qu'il était tombé d'une hauteur d'au moins 550 mètres.

Plus bizarre encore, l'homme tenait un bloc-notes rempli dans un langage intraduisible ayant une vague ressemblance à un dialecte Saxon qui n'était plus utilisé depuis plus de 1.500 ans. Les autorités fédérales ont été notifiées et l'enquête continue.

(**TRANSLATION:** The body of an unidentified man was found on 5th Ave today, baffling local police and neighbors. The coroner determined the cause of death to be blunt force trauma caused by falling, but the severity of the injuries indicate that he had reached terminal velocity—suggesting that he had fallen in excess of 550 meters.

More puzzling still, the man was clutching a notebook filled with an untranslatable language that seems to bear closest resemblance to a Saxon tribal dialect that went extinct 1,500 years ago. Federal authorities have been notified and the investigation is ongoing.)

IAN M. SMITH spends a great deal of time staring into space. Sometimes, after staring into space for a particularly long while, he writes things down. This was one of those things. Another is his novel, *Trace*, which some very smart and attractive people have said quite kind things about.

He lives with his best friend in Seattle, Washington, along with a handful of freeloading roommates: two kids, two cats, and a dog. He is rather happy with his life, though he'd be happier if the patriarchy was demolished. But who wouldn't, right? Right.

The
ORPHEUS WELL

An account by Catherine Florence,
AS PROVIDED BY DORIAN GRAVES

1968.

My first big report for the *Valley Herald* newspaper coincided with the first time I went to the Orpheus Well. Rumors had circulated ever since the first classified ad appeared with promises to return lost loved ones, but no one believed it, not then. That's why they sent a rookie out. Me.

It was far enough from town that no gray marred the thousand shades of green in the meadows and trees. The dirt driveway was marked with a simple wooden sign, and the location itself held only three things: a small white cottage, a large field that was full of flowers and surrounded by cedar trees, and, at the edge of that field, a well of piled stone.

"Welcome, welcome to the Orpheus Well. Are you Ms. Florence?" A man strode from the porch of the cottage, smiling softly as he extended his hand. Back then, a mop of blond hair hid his sun-kissed face and water-blue eyes. All I remember of his clothing was the shabby corduroy jacket.

"I am, but I was never one for formalities; call me Catherine. You must be Mr. Morgenstern." We shook, my grip stronger. "Quite an advertisement you've got. Promising to return any and all loved ones. But it sounds like you're more than a mere marriage counselor, aren't you?"

"Nothing of the sort. I merely maintain the well." He waved to the pile of stone. It didn't look like anything special. "Would you like to know how it works?"

"Throw in some pennies and make a wish?"

He didn't chuckle so much as rumble, a noise that didn't fit his soft voice. "Not quite. It is simple, really. All one must do is walk to the well, think about the lost loved one, and place a hand in. And that's where the magic comes in."

"Magic?"

Mr. Morgenstern did not extrapolate. Instead, he gestured toward the house, and another woman came out. She was mousy, with wispy brown hair and an oversized yellow jacket. She handed my host a tea-cup with a quiet thank you, then stepped to the edge of the flowers. She turned toward us, waiting.

Then Mr. Morgenstern nodded, and the woman crept past the petals. She twitched and looked to the trees whenever she moved, zig-zagging instead of moving in a straight line. At one point, about halfway through, she stopped. And after a moment of staring at the trees, she bolted.

"That is Mrs. Mills. She has frequented the well for a while now. The walk is a good deal more harrowing for her than it would be for a first-time visitor like yourself."

"What is she running from?"

"That, only she can see."

The shadows of the trees jittered; I passed it off as a trick of the light. But the mousy woman collapsed onto the well, panting as she gazed behind her. Her eyes were almost feral. But soon enough, she regained her composure and dipped her hand in. She muttered to herself, and I wondered if she spoke names or prayers.

An old man climbed out moments later. He smoothed back his nearly bald head, white hairs damp. The man embraced the mousy woman. The shadows of the trees retreated as Mrs. Mills helped the old man step out of the well.

Mr. Morgenstern cleared his throat. "And that's all there is to it. Make it to the end, and bring back one lost loved one, no questions asked. You can go through as many times as you wish, but the journey is more perilous each time."

I kept my gaze on the man in the well. "He was in last week's paper. In the obituaries."

"And now, he walks and smiles once more. Truly marvelous, is it not?" My host left my side for the moment to congratulate the couple, who wrapped their arms around him and cried through their thanks. Hand in hand, the two left, Mrs. Mills wrapping the yellow jacket around Mr. Mills.

"Now, Catherine, would you like to try?"

I didn't have anyone in mind to bring back. It wasn't that I hadn't lost anyone, but I was still skeptical. I believed myself to be a victim of a trick that the proprietor and the Millses were in on, and I was determined to prove I was smarter than that. Yet that first step was the most difficult to take. The path looked so inviting and simple, even after watching Mrs. Mills scurry through it. Surely the trick wasn't that simple?

I crushed a flower under the heel of my new shoes; I would've worn something flatter if I'd known I might have to run. Nothing jumped out at me. I was safe. I continued on, never taking my gaze off the well.

Mr. Morgenstern was correct in saying the first time was easiest. Any fear I felt was anticipation and wondering what in the shadows had caused my predecessor to scurry so. I jumped at the twitch of a branch; it was only a crow. It tilted its head like a child as I passed.

The Orpheus Well was warm to the touch, the water inside murky and still. Unable to see the bottom, I had no idea how deep it went. It was perfectly plausible that there was a hidden entrance so Mr. Mills could sneak in, climb out when a hand reached in, and escape his mistaken death. Yet I could think of no reason why they would perform such a ruse. I brushed the water with my fingertips, sending ripples along the placid surface. A memory flashed through my head of a dog I once had, Sparky, licking my fingertips to taste the leftover Popsicle juice one hot summer. His death, when he was run over later that year, was my first experience with such loss. I whispered his name.

I retracted my hand, but the water continued rippling. It bubbled as if boiling, and the next thing I knew, I was splashed as something broke the surface. It shook. It pawed at the stones and tried to jump up, but to no avail. I grabbed the collar and pulled, and once it was out, I looked. A yellow lab sat at my feet, tail wagging, tongue panting. A worn leather collar and rusted nametag read "Sparky," and the address of my childhood home back in Connecticut.

When we returned to Mr. Morgenstern, he handed me a leash. "The dogs often come without those," he told me. "I trust you are satisfied, and can vouch for the validity of the well? Such a report in the paper would do wonders for business."

I nodded, too tongue-tied with disbelief. Sparky licked the proprietor's hands as I attached the leash. I waved when we left, but I had to sit in the car for a minute before driving away. Sparky rested his head on my shoulder, as he did so many years ago.

My boss was never going to believe me.

1970.

My boss had not believed me, at first. He'd asked me if I'd eaten anything at the well, concerned that Mr. Morgenstern was an unscrupulous devil who'd poisoned my food. Sparky was not enough evidence, so my boss went to the well himself, along with two other reporters as witnesses. Three left, and six came back: my boss, his uncle, the other two reporters, one little girl, and the fattest orange cat I'd ever seen.

The resulting article transformed the town.

By my second visit to the Orpheus Well, the town's population had doubled. We rarely had obituaries anymore, and those that were published included a note about the survivors deciding not to brave the well. This usually only occurred for the elderly who'd lived full lives, or the lost and destitute who had no family or friends to brave the well for them. The one exception, a teenage boy whose well-to-do parents refused to revive him for suspicious reasons, became a scandal I reported on frequently. Funerals became parties instead, often ending with the deceased being walked into the celebration by whichever loved one had brought them back.

Those were not the reasons why, two years later, I drove down the freshly-paved driveway to the Orpheus Well. I shivered as I stepped out of the car; it was winter then, the flowers replaced with frost and the branches of the surrounding trees bare. Mr. Morgenstern strode over to meet me; he looked much like I'd seen him when we first met, save that he wore a home-knit scarf from one of his more frequent visitors.

"Why, Ms. Florence—excuse my manners, Catherine—what a pleasure to see you again. I do owe you so much for your coverage."

"Just doing my job. And it's Mrs. Lowndes now."

"Congratulations. Marriage is a springboard for many exciting changes in one's life." He walked me toward the little white cottage, neither of us wanting to stay in the cold too long. "And how is Sparky? Still an excitable young hound?"

"Indeed—it's like he never aged. I'm impressed you remember his name."

"Catherine, I remember the names of all who visit and leave this place. But enough about me—are you here to walk to the well again?"

I shook my head as we reached the steps of the porch. "I'm here for another interview, if you don't mind. After all the visits you've had these past couple of years, we wanted to know your thoughts on the matter." I pulled out a pad of paper that had suggested questions jotted along its lines. "I tried to call you ahead of time, but I couldn't find a listed phone number."

"I am not in possession of a phone. I'm afraid I have difficulty speaking to my clientele if it is not face-to-face." He smiled softly, as if it were possible for him to be shy.

He opened the door for me like a gentleman. The cottage was clean, with plenty of simple furniture for the increasing number of guests. It was odd that no one else was around; when I asked, Mr. Morgenstern told me that he'd closed for the day. "I had a feeling that something of import would happen this afternoon, not meriting interruption, so I have told all other visitors that I am preoccupied. And here you are for an interview; my instincts continue to prove uncanny."

He offered me tea. I asked him how long he'd been with the Orpheus Well. "As long as I can remember, I have stayed with the well, managing its upkeep and transportation."

"Seems like it'd be hard to carry." I remembered how deep it seemed when I looked in, so murky that maybe there wasn't a bottom to it after all.

"You'd be surprised. And before you ask, yes, it means the well will not be here forever—though I foretell that we will stay for a number of years yet."

We continued the interview over tea, boiling in contrast to the winter outside. Mr. Morgenstern told me he was pleased with the swell of visitors, and how the well existed to help humans—and the occasional animal, like Sparky—live as long and full of lives as possible. He would not reveal how the well worked its magic, nor anything about his own past. I had expected as much; I was not the first reporter to ask. Without enough to pad out a whole article, I asked him the most complex question in my arsenal—Why?

He laced his fingers together and brought them to rest on his lap. The corners of his lips twitched. "I just like to bring joy to others. The bliss of those reunited with their loved ones, the erasure of grief and pain… that's more than enough for me. And it costs me nothing, so I have no reason to charge anything. I wouldn't like to think of myself as a greedy person, after all."

"You're the least greedy person I know."

"How you flatter me."

I jotted down his answer, the scritch-scratching of my pencil filling the air. I looked to the well as I gathered my thoughts. I swore I saw something stare back from the shadows.

Though it wasn't on my list of questions, that moment prompted me to ask, "What happens to those who don't make it to the well?"

Mr. Morgenstern pressed his fingers together until they resembled a steeple on the verge of collapse. "That, only they know. Many run from what they see. Others run from the guilt, feeling they have failed. Were you to keep someone from enjoying life, wouldn't you feel shame as well?"

I thought back to the teenage boy whose parents hadn't brought him back, had pleaded that no one else try. The case was still ongoing, but one of the parents let slip that the boy had a "condition," and they wouldn't dare force him live through it—though the boy had seemed in perfect health. I wondered, not for the first time, if the boy had agreed to such terms, and what condition could be so horrible that it wasn't worth trying to live through.

I thanked Mr. Morgenstern for the words and tea. He thanked me for the company. As he escorted me back to the car, I couldn't help but look at the well once more. Like all around, it was cold and alone.

1973.

I tripped and skinned my knees on the driveway. I didn't see who helped me up, and my instinct was to swat them away. I had to make it to the well.

"Give her space. Catherine, what a surprise—whatever is the matter?"

I couldn't see Mr. Morgenstern through the hot tears in my eyes. It was an early spring night, crisp and clear. I trembled where I stood, the clothes I'd tossed on nowhere near enough to combat the cold. I was offered a handkerchief, but refused to take it.

"My… my baby. He stopped breathing." Five months old. Fine that morning, dead who knew how long. Sometime while my husband and I slept. I didn't know how or why. Those details weren't important anymore. "Please. I need to bring him back before he gets cold."

"Before he… very well. Right this way." Hands placed a coat over my shoulders and led me to the field. The Orpheus Well glowed a faint white in the moonlight—strange on reflection, for it was a new moon that night. "Do take a moment to breathe before you start. You want to walk with a clear head."

Already, my shoes were growing damp. I shrugged the coat on and wiped my face with one sleeve. I saw that it was Mr. Morgenstern's corduroy jacket, and that there was one other woman ahead of me on the path. She took a slow approach to the well.

The air froze my lungs with my next breath. I broke into a run.

The path to the Orpheus Well did not look long by any means. Yet I swore the run would get me there in minutes, but I was barely halfway before I had a stitch in my side. The other woman was still ahead of me. Closed flowers hung their heads as we passed, and shadows grasped at our dew-coated feet.

I almost stumbled again, but caught myself. The well seemed to be mere yards away. The other woman was almost there. She reached out a hand, as if she needed only three more steps to touch the stones. She took one step. Two. Her head twitched the slightest degree to the left, to the trees.

"Oh God." I barely caught the terror in her voice before she fled into the darkness past the well. I lost the sound of her footsteps, but swore I heard something growl behind me. I told myself it was the paranoia talking, even as my second wind carried me into another sprint. The air at my neck was suddenly warm. I tripped again. My fingers brushed against rough stone as I fell.

Nothing. No noise, no heat. I pulled myself to my feet and looked around again. The fields were aglow in the light of a missing moon. Mr. Morgenstern stood at the path's end, arms crossed. Nothing else.

Assured, I placed my hand in the well's waters. It seemed to bubble against my wrist. "Howard Lowndes," I whispered, imagining the baby I'd left in the crib when I went to bed that night. His bright blue eyes, his gurgling laugh as he clutched his tiny toes.

Something bobbed against my hand. I dipped my other hand in to pick up the bundle in the water. Little Howie opened his eyes, regarded me curiously. He reached a hand to me and cooed.

The field was as short as I expected on the walk back. The other woman never returned. I thanked Mr. Morgenstern, let him hold my child as I shrugged the coat back off and returned it.

"Glad I could help." Mr. Morgenstern handed me Howard back, shuddering as he took the coat. "It's time for me to close up for the night. Never could handle the cold too well."

Once I got home, I held Howie tight the rest of the night. My husband found me the next morning, asleep, baby warm in my arms.

1979.

I was busy decorating the Christmas tree when the phone rang. Sparky barked to inform me, tail wagging as I passed. He stood next to Howard, who was working on his holiday cards, crayons in hand and tongue sticking out in concentration. I answered the phone, hoping it was my husband letting me know he'd be off work early.

It was my boss. "Catherine. I know this is sudden, but I need you to report on the mayor's speech tonight."

"Isn't Johnny supposed to cover that one?"

My boss groaned, the phone translating the noise as static. "Was. He went to the well last night—said he was going to bring back his sister-in-law as a Christmas gift for his wife. Not only did he not come back this morning, but his wife's skipped out too. Haven't heard hide nor hair of 'em."

"I see." The longer the well went on, the more frequent this became. Whenever someone failed the well, their already-returned loved ones disappeared too, with no warning. Where they went and why, we'd yet to figure out. But Johnny, he'd braved the well a few times already—including once for his wife.

"Kurtis is at work right now, sir, but he should be back soon. But you know I can't leave Howard alone."

"I do, and that'll be fine. The speech isn't for another six hours anyway. Plenty of time, I'm sure." My boss paused before adding, "You know, we'll need someone to fill Johnny's position. And you may be a woman, but your articles have been top-notch ever since your first on the well. If you don't mind a few extra hours of working instead of playing housewife… think about it. Consider it your holiday gift from yours truly."

I kept thanking him even once I hung up the phone. Howard looked up at me and I told him, "Mommy might have a better job soon. Would you mind making another card, Howie?"

"Sure, Momma!" Howard, ever the little artist, showed me the plethora of cards he'd already made for relatives and family friends. The crayons were bright against the construction paper. But there was one card that stood out with sharp red paper. It had a white house, many green flowers, a tower of circles, and one figure in a black suit.

"Howie? Who's this for?"

"Mr. Morgy." He pointed to the tower. "That's the well, see? And his house."

I looked closer at the picture—the resemblance was there. There were even trees in the background, with patches of black between them to resemble shadows. The coloring was splotchy, leaving red spaces in the shadows—almost like glowing eyes.

"I'm sure he'll love it, honey. Now, we need one more for Mr. Abernathy—"

Only later did it occur to me that I'd never taken Howard to the Orpheus Well, not since I'd brought him back. He should not have remembered it.

1982.

"I regret to inform you that something's in the woods."

Mr. Morgenstern eyed me with his usual cool smile. His blond hair was slicked back, revealing those eyes almost the color of frost. But the corduroy jacket, and even the scarf, remained after all those years.

I continued. "Something chased me. It's not just nerves or anything. I saw it." I tightened my grip on the wrist I held. A car crash starting to sound like a murder, and the victim's family had disappeared upon attempting the well; I'd taken it upon myself to bring the victim back to finish the article. I never let my stories hang with no ending.

"Animals do live in the woods, Catherine. But tell me, what did you see?" Mr. Morgenstern prompted as we walked to the house. I had already requested using one of the rooms of his cottage to interview the young woman I'd rescued.

Even though the event was so recent, I had to push my thoughts to recall it. "It was large. Dark. And fast, quite fast. I'm amazed I escaped it. A wolf, perhaps? Or coyote?"

"You sound uncertain."

I hated to admit, but I was. My suggestions were to convince myself, but even so, some of the details didn't add up. I'd caught sight of an extra set of legs, for one thing. And for another, I saw fire. Flames coated the creature's feet, danced along its back, trailed from its mouth. But the path to the well was unmolested, still bright and vibrant from the recent rain.

"I… I have more pressing matters to attend to," I told him, lifting the hand of the girl I held. She was a small thing, watching the world with the eyes of a bird. "I just thought I should let you know. Might want to get it checked out. Especially with the disappearances happening more frequently."

Everyone knew at this point what happened when one failed the well, but not how or why. This should have lessened the well's popularity, but few were the folks who could ignore the chance to save those they loved. Being a savior was practically an addiction.

Mr. Morgenstern nodded and stroked the beard he was starting to grow. "Catherine, do recall our first meeting. Do you remember why I told you Mrs. Mills ran?"

Mrs. Mills. I hadn't heard that name in a while. She and her whole family left town a long time ago. I thought back to her pulling her husband out of the well. Remembered her mousy hair, her twitching gaze as she bolted through the flowers. Recalled my own naivety; was it really over ten years ago?

"She ran from something only she could see," I repeated. And I savored the words on my tongue, realizing but not wanting to believe.

I shoved the thoughts into the back of my mind and prepared for the interview.

1984.

The town's population fluctuated. Many moved in, hearing the wonders of the Orpheus Well and wishing to try it themselves. But just as many left, and it wasn't just from folks disappearing after a failed run to the well.

No, when something good happens, no one can believe its sincerity. Rumors spark, and then they catch flame.

The prominent theory was that the people who came back returned not quite right. They became darker, the gossips said, a fundamental part of them changed. Some grew silent, others raucous during their second chance at life. Notes were made on selfishness and cruelty growing in these returned souls. So many left the town and their dead behind, claiming it was better than corruption.

I was not allowed to report on these rumors. My boss said I was biased, having run the well a fair number of times already. Especially, he said, since one of those I saved was my son—"A mother could never doubt her son, and a son can't stand to let his mom know he's done wrong. That's how the world works." I tried to argue, but he made me leave the office so he could retreat for a nap. He was getting on in years and had already told the staff that when he croaked, he wanted to be left alone in the dirt. His words, not mine.

I didn't want to believe the rumors, but I caught myself questioning the others regardless. The girl I'd saved, we'd revealed the tragic nature of her murder, and she thanked me when I saw her—but I knew nothing of her home life. Sparky was a good dog, but whenever he chewed the furniture or tried to chase the mailman, I began to wonder.

Howard was an angel of a boy. Always perfect at social events, and among the top of his class in school. He'd been in the Little League for years and loved it. The boy was always smiling.

And yet, sometimes, his smile seemed too tight. Or he'd mutter, and change what he said when I asked him to repeat himself. I had no proof one way or another, and always told myself the paranoia was getting to me. My boss was wrong, a mother could doubt—but she'd try like hell not to believe it.

When I asked him about the rumors, both for the press and personally, Mr. Morgenstern gave no comment.

1990.

My hands clutched the steering wheel tighter. I leaned forward; I could barely see through all the fog. "Are you saying I shouldn't have brought you back? Don't you like living?"

Howard contemplated from the back seat. I caught him slouching in the rearview mirror and cleared my throat. He straightened. "I do. Just wondering though, if we bring Dad back, will he really be better? I mean, he might still be sick. We don't know."

"No one's reported dying of sickness and coming back still sick. The well cures all that."

Howard slouched again so he could press his head against the window. He wouldn't be able to see anything anyway, between the fog and the darkness of night. "Yeah, but most people kill themselves upon learning they're sick, before it takes hold, and let their loved ones just run 'em back. That's what Jenny's parents did."

"Well, we aren't Jenny's family. Your father will be fine." He had to be. The thought about killing him before the cancer could had crossed my mind, but I couldn't bring myself to do it. Neither could he.

We pulled into the driveway, the only ones there that night. I could barely make out the well in that weather. But as usual, Mr. Morgenstern came out to greet us, shoes clacking against the new walkway. He'd finally updated his jacket to one made of leather.

Before I could greet him, Howard asked, "Does this thing cure diseases? Like, serious ones?"

"A pleasure to see you too, Howard. It's been… seventeen years, hasn't it?" Mr. Morgenstern offered a hand. I shook it, as usual; Howie followed suit with reluctance. "My, how you've grown. And how is Sparky? Still around?"

"Somehow. Mutt refuses to die." Howard again answered before I could. "So, diseases. Does this well cure 'em, or just death?"

"Inquisitive. Just like you—runs in the family, I suppose." Mr. Morgenstern winked at me before answering. "It reverts the returned to whatever state they were in before their cause of death set in. A death stemming from illness means before the disease even entered the returned's body."

I tried to imagine how long ago that was. When we learned of the cancer two years ago, it was already in an advanced state. Would Kurtis return a few years younger than his death? I decided not to dwell on it—after all, I would find out in minutes, once I ran the well once more.

Howard asked, as I had so many years ago, "What's in it for you? You like being bothered by the dead all the time?"

"The dead do not burden me, no." Despite the fog, Mr. Morgenstern's eyes seemed to shine as he spoke. Those eyes never changed, not since our first meeting so long ago. "Helping others brings me joy, more than anything else on Earth. Is that so strange?"

"No," I said before Howard could pass another rude comment. "It is not. Now if you'll excuse me, I should start running. Unless, Howie, you'd like to try?"

He opened his mouth to speak, and I still don't know what I wanted his answer to be. But Mr. Morgenstern cut him off. "Those who have been brought back from the Orpheus Well are not allowed to take the trek themselves. Only you can, Catherine."

"Very well." Without looking back, I stepped to the edge of the field. The flowers were faint glows in the fog. My face already ran hot, remembering the creatures from last time—ones I'd dubbed hell-hounds for the fire that coated them. But ever since my husband fell sick, I'd trained for his return. I'd participated in marathons all year, each time pretending that burning fangs were right on my heels. I was ready, I told myself. I had to be.

I sprinted into the fog. My gaze darted in vain between the trees I could not see, ping-pong balls in an endless match. I had no idea how far I was from the well, or when the hellhounds would—

There. I heard the sizzle and crack of flames behind me. Already I could smell smoke; I pushed my body to move faster. A howl rang through the air, followed by yelps and barks too close to laughter. I was tempted to look. But that would slow me down, and if they caught up with me—

What would happen, if they caught up? What happened to everyone else who failed to reach the well? They didn't really keep running forever, did they? Then what—

No. No thinking about it. Just moving. Surviving. For myself and my husband. I charged headlong into the fog and ignored the growing heat behind me, the hellhounds growing ever nearer.

The earth quaked. A deep sound, not even a voice, bellowed. Something bigger joined the chase.

It felt like I ran for hours. The well never got closer, only the hellhounds did. And It, whatever It was. Maybe their master. It kept laughing like the ground was about to split and swallow me whole. It never faltered. The stitch in my side grew so strong, I thought I'd been bitten instead.

I collapsed onto the piled stone, muscles screaming in ways I myself could not. The sudden cold of night air struck me. The monsters vanished from the corner of my eyes. I blinked back tears. Gone, gone—but I'd seen something. Were my eyes deceiving me?

No time to question. I reached into the water for a hand that held back, strong as the day he placed a ring on my finger. Up Kurtis came, cleanest picture of health ever seen. But he didn't smile when his eyes met mine.

"You look like I should be pulling you out of here," he told me. "Do I look that bad?"

No, not him. But in the moment before the monsters disappeared, I'd seen their faces. Familiar ones. Faces like Sparky's and Howard's, baring their teeth from the bodies of burning hounds. And the quaking one—

No. I cannot. Do not ask me any more.

1993.

"You're mistaken. We're divorced now."

"So it's Ms. Florence again? My, what a pity. And after you brought him back, too."

We were in the cottage, Mr. Morgenstern and I. He made me tea. I didn't have a particular reason for visiting that day, other than loneliness. Howard left for college before his father left my house, and Sparky wasn't company enough to fill the resulting void.

"Honestly, I think it's because I brought him back." I took a long sip of my tea. It was sweet, unlike Mr. Morgenstern's cup that was black as sin. "Kurtis was younger and healthy again, so he just… you know how some people lose themselves in the world when they're given a second chance?"

"Miracles do change people." Mr. Morgenstern's voice hadn't changed over the years, still a comforting rumble like a familiar brook. In fact, I noticed that time had barely touched him, leaving only a few grooves worn around his features. I suppose, as the well's curator, its miracles were commonplace for him. He was just as constant. "What vice did he give his second chance to? Cars? Drugs? Another woman?"

"Fitness. Came to spend all his days at the gym, and weekends at marathons. I never saw him anymore." Another sip, then bashfully, "He did find another woman, though. Bicyclist. He was nice enough to break up with me before committing to her, at least. Always was a gentleman."

The cottage was silent. Outside the frost of the window, a man barely in his twenties ran the path. His gaze jumped more than his body—first time, I supposed. He had yet to really see things.

"What are they, Mr. Morgenstern?"

"Whatever do you mean?"

I gestured to the Orpheus Well, to the woods around it and the boy on his first trek. "The creatures that join the chase. There's more every consecutive run, aren't there? What are they?"

Mr. Morgenstern gazed into his tea, as if it held the answers. "Death is not a cheap thing. The lives it captures are precious coins caught in greedy fingers. The Orpheus Well can negate the expense, but not everyone finds this as joyous as I." He held his fine fingers over the steam, but did not drink. "Those beings you see? For those who incur a debt, bring too many back, the demons come to collect."

"Demons?" The word was lead on my tongue.

Mr. Morgenstern nodded, his bangs falling into his face. He smoothed them aside with practiced ease. "The closest word for them, at least."

"But they had my son's face. And Sparky's. And the woman I saved, and... and then there was—"

"Personalized terror tends to be the strongest. The scared are desperate, and the desperate make mistakes." He set the tea cup down, the liquid inside still undisturbed. "The well itself is a benevolent thing. That does not mean all around it are also such."

"So the rumors are false, then? About those who come back being... tainted somehow?"

I couldn't read what passed over Mr. Morgenstern's features, disrupting his passive smile. But the smile returned before I even realized it was gone, and my host was at his feet. "I really should check on our newest runner. See if his returned needs a coat. Ever notice how busy we get around the holidays?"

Left alone in the cottage, I could not finish my tea.

2000.

And now, this final time, I do not remember how I reached the Orpheus Well.

The last thing I recall, I was carried into an ambulance. Strapped to a stretcher. Something about a stroke, something about a flurry of doors and white hallways, something—

Then I wake up, standing, a battered corduroy jacket resting on my shoulders. My eyes adjust to a gray sky overhead, and fog obscures all but the path. For that's what's in front of me, the path to the Orpheus Well, still as green and fresh as the day I first ran.

"How did I get here?"

"I brought you here. I'm not surprised you don't remember—you had quite a harrowing night." Mr. Morgenstern steps out from behind me, those blue eyes shimmering. His hands are clasped behind his back. "But that doesn't matter now. Do you need time to prepare?"

"Prepare for what?"

"Your final run, of course." He tilts his head and smiles, but for the first time, the gesture is neither warm nor calming. "You died last night, Catherine. A stroke that led to a terrible fall, for one yet so young. That means it is time for you to walk the path, one last time."

I find it hard to believe his words. While my body feels old and worn, it is no different than it has been for the past few years. Age always left its mark early in my family, and I am no exception. Yet I realize that the world is quieter than it should be, and a moment's pause brings me to realize why. My heart is silent, hanging lifeless in my chest.

"So I'm running to bring myself back? I've never heard of that happening before."

Mr. Morgenstern's laugh rings hollow. "Not quite. You are a runner, after all. The rules are different for you. Though I must admit, you are the first to make it this far in a long, long time. Congratulations." He claps in time to the heartbeat I now lack. "No matter what happens, dear Catherine, you are to die. Not even I can change that. But if you reach the well, you get to move on from this, and your rescued ones can finish their natural lifespan."

I do not want to ask, but I do. "And if I fail?"

"Then it's the same as when anyone else fails. Your soul, and those of all you've saved, are mine. Your lives are forfeit. The game is done." Mr. Morgenstern slides off his leather jacket, then unbuttons his shirt and removes that too. The smell of smoke wafts through the air as his wings unfurl. I cannot look at them, it's too much like staring at the sun.

The pieces snap into place, and my legs threaten to buckle before the run has even begun.

Mr. Morgenstern strides to the starting line of the path. His hair parts to make way for twin horns. The flowers underneath are burned by hooves as he passes me by. His body continues to morph, but his eyes never change as he turns to me.

"This time, you know what you're fleeing from the start. You run against me, dearest Catherine Florence. Out of custom, you have a nine-second head start. We begin whenever you wish."

What can I say? I could accuse him of lying—but he never did, only avoided the truth. I could ask why this had to happen, but it was I who believed that a miracle like the well could have no cost. I had never thought to ask if there was a cost.

So I take a shaky breath for lungs that no longer need air, and I run—as we all must run, in vain, from the end.

The Orpheus Well has never seemed so near, and yet miles of running could not bring it a step closer. I realize this as soon as I begin. Even without the burden of living organs to weigh me down, I stumble. I am only human. Flowers crumble under my heels. I cannot flee in a straight line; the habit is too engrained now. I must look like Mrs. Mills did at the beginning. I am the woman who zig-zags like a field mouse.

Nine seconds are up. The rest of the time passes as slow as Mr. Morgenstern's hooves. I hear him right behind me, but he does not need to run. I imagine his body still morphing, that he is now so tall that a single step could bridge the gap and crush me. As if to show me this is true, his shadow grows past me, so long it touches the rim of the well.

Still I run.

It sounds like an earthquake behind me, and the wind grows hot.

The ground is unstable at my feet. I may run from Mr. Morgenstern, but it's not he who will catch me, but his home, not the white cottage but the circles of Hell below. I kick off my shoes for better traction. I feel the grass between my toes moments before the earth burns.

It looks like I could reach out one hand and touch the well, reach inside and grab the horns of Mr. Morgenstern's shadow. And out would come Sparky, and Howard, and every other smiling face I ever met in those depths, and they would thank me for saving them a second time. Yet I hear a thousand voices screaming behind me, and I know that thanks will never come.

"Falling isn't as hard as you'd think," Mr. Morgenstern says. His voice sounds like he's whispering in my ears. "I fell once too, you know. For hubris. I've taught the same lesson for eons now. Did you ever really think you had control over any life other than yours?"

As soon as the reluctant "yes" crosses my lips, that's when the earth finally lets me go. I fall in reverse, the sky growing farther and farther away. It's the same blue as it was in '68, the same blue as my guide's eyes. His voice drifts to me, from above, one last time.

"I do think it's time we move on. We've done enough damage here, don't you think?" A pause, like it's just another interview. "No, I have not forgotten. I'll grab her dog first."

CATHERINE FLORENCE, reporter for the *Valley Herald* since 1968, has compiled the most information, both personal and professional, on the last known appearance of an Orpheus Well. The diary containing these entries was found in her home while investigating the disappearance of her and her family; how she wrote the final entry is yet to be determined. The newest incarnation of an Orpheus Well, along with one Mr. Morgenstern, have yet to be found.

Having achieved a B.A. in English/Creative Writing from Mills College in 2014, **DORIAN GRAVES** retreated to the mountains of Oregon in order to hunt down new ideas to write about (and Sasquatch, but only because he keeps raiding the fruit orchard). When not writing short stories or an urban fantasy novel series, Dorian can be found traveling along the West Coast, designing increasingly ridiculous World of Darkness campaigns, or the "exciting" day job of selling shoes. Dorian's first novel, *Bones and Bourbon*, will be released by Ninestar Press on April 2nd, 2018.

ART BY **Luke Spooner**

LUKE SPOONER, a.k.a. 'Carrion House,' currently lives and works in the South of England. Having recently graduated from the University of Portsmouth with a first class degree, he is now a full time illustrator for just about any project that piques his interest. Despite regular forays into children's books and fairy tales, his true love lies in anything macabre, melancholy, or dark in nature and essence. He believes that the job of putting someone else's words into a visual form, to accompany and support their text, is a massive responsibility, as well as being something he truly treasures. You can visit his web site at www.carrionhouse.com

Кориолан
(KORIOLAN)

An account by Tamara Kohn,
AS PROVIDED BY ALEXANDER NACHAJ

System active.
Begin retrieval.
24 logs discovered. Filed under [BLANK].
Username: Kohn, Tamara.
Legal Clerk. Salvage Division. Terminus Station.
Terminus ID 02456.

Some things don't go according to plan.

I was supposed to be sipping a mojito in a window-side seat at La Rancha on Deck 22, watching the horizon slowly bend along the contours of our moon. Instead, I'm typing on a mechanical keyboard before a CRT-screen that's as stained as my shower wall.

Right after my shift ended, this guy Beck, the captain of some salvage vessel, contacted me. Literally knocked on my door. Said he needed a legal clerk ASAP to complete a five-man run out into the fringe. Derelict showed up on scans and they needed to know if it's an open bounty or listed for retrieval. I laughed. Almost slammed the door in his face. But then he pitched me the gig and promised time and a half with bonus if I signed on then and there, no questions asked.

How could I say no?

I suppose, if I had seen the ship beforehand, I might have reconsidered. Beck marched me right up to one those previous-century Bombardier AV "Space Hogs." No jump drive, a couple of pea-shooters that pass for a point-defence-system, and a single portside window caked-over with years of grime and neglect. Talk about an old clunker (named *La Damoiselle*, ironically). Apparently, I got called up by the only crew with a ship older than this bag of bones. (I'm 52, and I feel it. I'm allowed to gripe, okay?)

Onboard hasn't been much better. Half the panels on the ship are analogue. There's no entertainment devices patched in anywhere. The only consolation is that Manuel, the navigator, brought his Sony, and his taste in music isn't half bad. A little festive, but thank God it's not chamber music.

As much as I hate pushing tradition out of the way, that's the glorious life of hired-guns like me.

I'll have that mojito as soon as I'm back.

T.

Looks like our destination is that asteroid belt just past Corneo. Talk about desolate. Took us an hour of precision guidance just to make it through the debris field. Lots of rocks and other junk floating around out here. I have no idea how anyone at the agency got a clear reading of a derelict in this mess. It's total bedlam on the scanners, and

Beck even resorted to old-fashioned radar for a while there.

To kill the time, and keep my nerves in check, I chatted with the crew. French and Lambert are the same as everyone else in this corner of the system. Regular blue collar types. In it for the money, nothing else. I can't tell when either of them shaved or showered last, so I've been keeping my distance. Lambert even has that acrid smell of alcoholism about him. But Manuel, on the other hand, he's clean-shaven and I even caught him giving me a once-over with those gorgeous dark eyes of his. Maybe being the only piece of tail on a ship has its advantages—no matter how old you feel when you look in the mirror.

It's no surprise we ended up talking more. I asked about this job. He seemed just as miffed as me. Said the coordinates were forwarded their way by a clerk he knew at the agency. High priority, kind of hush-hush, but double pay. He let that second part slip unintentionally, I think. Guess my time-and-a-half wasn't such a big deal. Teach me to not ask any questions. But we'll see how it goes when my work starts. I might suddenly need a raise.

Anyway, we touched down a few minutes ago. Beck is a prodigious pilot, if nothing else. We're on a rock almost as large as Earth's moon. I got a decent view of the derelict using the viewfinder (more like a periscope if you ask me). Looks about a forty-minute walk from here. I think it's a freighter, but I can't tell the class. Not a lot of hull damage, but moderately decrepit. Half-buried in dust, too. Not a crash. Maybe abandoned?

One thing of note: it's got all this funny writing on its side. Big red letters. Whoever painted them was either drunk or half out of his mind, because some of them are backward and the rest look wrong. Either way, identifying her shouldn't be too tough. With any luck, I'll be able to sort out all the legal loops and claim this derelict in a matter of hours. Time to go figure out what we're dealing with on this godforsaken rock.

T.

Koriolan. That's the name of the derelict.

Turns out those big red letters weren't some madman's idea of giving their ship an unpronounceable name. They were part of an archaic writing system that belonged to a now-defunct Sol system conglomeration called FedRus. Ships like this one were in widespread use some two hundred years ago (seriously, that's not a typo... and I thought *La Damoiselle* was a relic). Oddly, this class of freighter was never designed for deep space travel. That wouldn't have been a big deal, except that this system hadn't technically been settled at that point.

What's more, most of these vessels were assigned for short-distance hauls between a planet's moons, off-world stations and that sort of thing (this one was stationed around Saturn, close to the conglom's HQ on Titan). To make it out here along the territorial fringes, much less out of its home system, well, it's not like they could fold space back in the day. It might theoretically have had enough time to drift out here, but the odds of hitting this exact rock and landing here more or less intact as it did? I don't know. My only guess is that it got dumped by a larger ship, maybe as scrap that they meant to reclaim later.

All in all, it's a bit of a mystery that's got everyone talking (and in the case of Lambert and French, spouting theories about wormholes and other nonsense). On the bright side, when something's this old, it makes applying the law of salvage a piece of cake. The conglom is long gone, and it's safe to say no one's expecting to find any crew when we board. Who knows, maybe we'll get a bonus from the agency or some museum to boot. This thing is practically ancient history.

T.

Christ, time flies. We just got back from the *Koriolan*. And, well—
The five of us set out in our environmentals. Beck led the way
with Manuel, while Lambert and French dragged their heels behind
us (and by that, I mean lugging their gear). When we reached the
derelict, there was a ray of sunlight, cracking through the debris field.
Shadows seemed to crawl all over it. It was oddly beautiful. Anyway,
just as the boys were powering up the torches, Manuel dusted off a
console, and to everyone's surprise, it still had some charge! What's
more, it was reading that the vessel was still pressurized.

Obviously, none of us thought that would be possible. Not after
years, or even decades. Still, Beck figured it was worth a shot. So we
cleared away from the hatch (in case anything blew out) and prepared
to open her the old-fashioned way.

After Manuel hit the disengage on the locks, it took a moment
for anything to happen. I heard some sounds from within, almost like
crunching or banging. Must have been some machinery resettling or
something. Then, a whole layer of dust suddenly snapped off like ice
on a windshield, and the airlock door slid open, wide and inviting.

Beck suggested Manuel and French stay outside with me until
we knew more, but I insisted on heading in. Daring, I know, but I'm a
darling for history if nothing else.

We pressurized in the darkness of the airlock, Beck, Lambert,
and I, our helmet lights our only company. Beck looked fairly stoic,
but I could see the greed and excitement in Lambert's eyes. For all he
knew, we were stumbling into a jackpot. He probably expected bars of
gold or something.

He was wrong.

When the inner hatch opened, it did so without any fanfare.
It simply slid open, and we found ourselves in the hold. And that's
where things got kinda weird.

My first thoughts were "What a mess." All the lights were out,
save for some emergency ones that must have snapped on when we

entered. Little red LEDs, low to the ground, giving everything a washed out and burned look. As we stepped inside, I nearly tripped over an industrial beam laying in the middle of the floor. Past that, dark steel girders from a collapsed shelfing unit criss-crossed and blocked our way. We had to crawl under them, brushing away dangling chains and support straps. All the while it was dead silent and kind of creepy in the stillness of the hull.

After we made it through, Beck spotted a console. Despite the language barrier, he pieced together that the generator was still intact. Gotta hand it to intuitive design. We could have turned the life support and other onboard systems back on if we wanted, but we settled on just the lighting system instead.

Talk about a difference. Even though a couple of panels were out, it was literally night to day in there. It was comforting to see one's surroundings, but also oddly disconcerting. Right away, we could tell things weren't as they should have been, not for a wreck or a crash or anything like that.

One of the shelves had collapsed, sure, but the others were still standing but emptied. Instead of seeing their cargo scattered all over the damn place, it was piled against one of the walls all neat and purposeful. It didn't make a lot of sense. What's more, we couldn't spot any doors or passages to the other sections of the ship. Beck pointed out that it was probably on the other side of Cargo Mountain.

So whoever was here last decided to make a block fort out of the ship's contents. And they couldn't have done it alone, or easily. Some of those containers could hold six or seven hundred kilograms, and there wasn't a rig or jack in sight.

We headed back outside (thankfully, no problems there) and talked things over. It was decided that we'd all come back to *La Damoiselle* for a quick break. We'll be heading back over there soon with some tools and rigs to start clearing out that cargo and get to the other compartments. I'm not sure what we'll find on the other side, but everyone's getting a little giddy. Lambert thinks maybe some smugglers planted a stash here and either forgot about it or got the burn.

As dumb as he is, he might be right. Something important has got to be on the other side; otherwise, why all the work keeping it sealed?

Plus, there's that other piece of circumstantial evidence.

It took me a bit before it struck me, but then I remembered that ships back then didn't use the same types of circuitry that we do now. By all measures, its old tri-lithium power core should've expired by now. Those things are supposed to have a hundred-year half-life at most, which means that someone must have replaced it before dumping it here.

To thicken the mystery, I dug up some more clues in the archives about FedRus shipping manifests. The *Koriolan* was never officially decommissioned. She was listed as missing. Missing! Well, safe to say we found her. Now I wonder what other secrets she's got in her hold.

T.

It's official. We're all calling it the "haunted house" now—colloquially, of course.

It took us about an hour to clear the cargo out of the way. Sure enough, we found not only the door, but also a whole mural of frantic writing. It was too messy to get a clear translation from my AR display, but it seemed to be more or less saying "closed." No shit. As if the crates weren't sign enough, whoever was here last welded the two panels shut. They must have really wanted to keep trespassers out.

Fortunately, we came prepared. Lambert and French fired up their torches and got ready to start cutting our way inside.

That's when we heard the banging.

It happened suddenly, like a dozen doors slammed in short succession. It seemed like it was coming from the other side, but the noise from the torches made it hard to tell. The moment the guys paused their work, things went silent.

It was almost the same as the noise we heard when we were first heading in. Manuel said it was probably some shelving units collapsing in another hold.

That or ghosts.

Everyone got a good laugh out of that. All the same, Beck went outside to check the area a second time, in case it was some debris hitting the hull, but he came back with a blank. No sign of any disturbance.

Maybe she is haunted after all. I wonder if that pays double on the salvage market.

French ventured a guess that maybe someone was on the other side, but we laughed that off too. It was possible that someone had been sealed off in there, but even if that were the case, the systems were shut down when we arrived. No one could have survived out here, not for long, and not even with some serious provisions. The cold alone would kill a woman, or man, in a matter of hours. Never mind their sanity after a week of being trapped in a place like this.

On the bright side, after we cleared the crates out of the way, I spotted an old tablet tucked away in a cargo sleeve. It still had a faint charge, but it also had an analogue jack. It got me intrigued enough that I came back to *La Damoiselle* with Manuel while the others stayed behind to get those doors open. With any luck, the tablet will have a manifest or some logs that could explain what the hell happened and how that ship got out here. If there's one thing for sure, this is turning into anything but the cakewalk I had expected it to be.

T.

It happened.

It's amazing what two people can get up to when they have the whole ship to themselves for an hour or two.

It began innocently enough. Manuel asked me what my plans were when we got back to the station. I told him I had a date with a mojito and a clear view of the moon at a certain restaurant. I fired off the name of the place. At that, his ears perked up. Turns out it's some distant cousin of his who runs the place. I asked him what he thought about it, and he said it was "honestly, crap." If I wanted some real Latin comfort, I'd have to go looking elsewhere.

"How far?" I asked.

"Not far," he replied, giving me a look that could only mean one thing. I put my hand on his leg, and he pulled me close.

I must say, he's sweeter than his tattooed blue-collar body lets off. He had protection with him and even had the courtesy to ask if he'd have to watch his back for my "ex" when we returned. I laughed at that. I couldn't help it. David won't be bothering anyone. Not unless they're afraid of ghosts.

He saw that it was a touchy subject, so he cracked a joke. "Only the ones on that ship."

Does it mean I've moved on? No, not quite, but it was sure as hell a move in the right direction.

Beck and the others should be done with the doors any moment now. Thank God for those little moments in between. Time to start working on that tablet. I'm sure they'll want to know what we turned up.

T.

Christ, I'm not even sure where to begin, but here goes nothing. After my little tryst with Manuel, we got to working on the tablet.

Had to splice together some cables and dig a few adapters out of his locker, but we patched into the tablet. I gave it a minute to charge, and then booted it up. Almost immediately, our system seemed to flicker, and almost like a long brown-out, but then it surged. I started to hear that banging sound, all around, like it was coming from every circuit board inside *La Damoiselle*. I was in the process of reaching over to unplug the bastard when everything stopped and we were back in business.

The OS was unlocked, and there were a couple of user profiles. Everything was in that odd language, but I could do a decent job translating through the UI if I kept my AR on over one eye. I found the admin account tagged under a user named Wlatislaw and started looking around. The last logs were dated some seventy-five years ago. Strangely, the database was accessed more recently than that. No additional entries or logs, just traces that someone signed in and looked things over. Though it would corroborate the "drag and drop" theory that the *Koriolan* was dumped out here more recently.

After skimming through, a few entries caught my eye during the final months of service. Turns out, shortly before the ship was listed as missing, the *Koriolan* was recommissioned as a science vessel under the command of some Dr. Kerensky. From the way Wlatislaw writes about him, Kerensky must have been some bigwig with the conglom. And not particularly well-liked either. About a dozen of the logs I skimmed through had a line or two ranting about diversions from protocol, the doctor's casual disregard for safety measures, and the like. Kerensky sounds like he was a real basket case.

Wlatislaw, on the other hand, seems to have been a meticulous crewman. He logged his entries daily, and even tagged them by category and priority. My kind of guy.

A lot of his flagged entries had to do with a project Kerensky had them working on, named something to the effect of "Dying Star." Something to do with mining in hazardous areas and maximizing machine output. Few details other than that the conglom was pumping plenty of cash into it. There was supposed to be a trial out near Pluto and results were expected roughly around the time the ship went missing.

However, they never made it that far. In one log, Wlatislaw referred to an accident. Two of the crewmen, Sergey and Pavel, were killed trying to contain some sort of power surge. Seems like some circuits got overloaded, and some out of control charge jumped from system to system, overloading everything. Wlatislaw was furious in his entry, almost to the point of being incomprehensible. It's clear he blamed Kerensky for the accident, saying the old "Theosophist" and "pagan" personally killed them.

Heavy stuff.

The last couple of entries after that were quite different. Lots of introspection, bits of poetry, a line or two from Dante for good measure (I guess some jobs really are hell). Wlatislaw mentioned a few fights breaking out, plenty of regrets, and then some odd stuff, almost like nightmares. He mentions seeing Sergey and Pavel standing by Kerensky's side. Then, for a time, that his body was not his own, that he was just a passenger, steered by a greater power.

Sounds like the stress was getting to him. I don't blame him.

I skipped ahead to the final entry. It contained a single line: "Dying Star isn't life. It's death. Keep it sealed."

That was enough for me. I wasn't about to let Beck and the others waltz into a science experiment that already got two people killed. I had the comm in my ear, but as soon as I dialled in, I heard Beck's voice calling me.

They got the doors open.

I was amazed, startled almost. Beck heard the worry in my voice. He laughed and said they were fine, all things considered.

As soon as they got the doors open, all the systems in the ship went haywire. The lights flickered, sparks shot out of the console, and

Lambert's torch backfired. If he hadn't tossed it when he did, he would have lost his hand. Beck was sure that they had somehow cut into one of the power conduits, one of the ship's major arteries, the way things were looking. He was in the process of getting everyone out when the systems suddenly went back to normal, without any fanfare.

He said it was the damnedest thing he ever experienced in a derelict. He even laughed.

I didn't echo the sentiment. I told them to get out of there, that there could be something dangerous in another section of the ship.

"Not to worry," he replied. They were already on their way back. Except, they weren't alone. They found a body, in an archaic atmospheric suit. The band on the arm, monitoring the person's vitals, glowed a faint green, the universal colour of life, and the name above the breast read "Kerensky."

I guess I signed off a little quickly there. That's so uncharacteristic for me. Then again, so's everything about this job.

Beck and the others made it back, but not before he and Manuel had a hell of a row over the intercom.

Manuel played it by the books, citing regulations and quarantine procedures. People don't just bring mysterious guests back on board. Beck said it was his ship, so he called the shots. Besides, if there was a survivor out here, they had an obligation to bring him on board. He seemed to be taking the moral high ground, but underneath his posturing, I could detect the truth.

He was as curious and surprised as the rest of us to find someone alive over there. If anything, it helped explain some of the weird stuff that was going on.

Or so we thought.

I was somewhere on Manuel's side. Not because he'd just recently become my squeeze, but reading those logs from Wlatislaw put me on edge. I couldn't believe it was Kerensky. No way that old lunatic survived out here for a couple of generations. It had to be someone else in his suit.

Lambert and French were less enthused about the whole thing, too. Finding a survivor would void whatever bounty they were hoping to get their hands on. They'd be paid for their hours, and that would be that.

In the end, Beck's word carried the day. They brought the survivor on board and rushed him into the corner of the ship that's being used for medical. When they set him down, I noticed his visor was all fogged over and our guest wasn't making any sounds. All we had to go by was the vitals monitor.

Beck bent over right away to attend to our guest, but Manuel grabbed his arm before he could. He advised him one last time about procedures.

Beck shook him off and snapped open the helmet.

A fetid, sour mist seeped from the crack between the suit and the visor. Most of us leapt back, but French got a good whiff of it. He keeled over and vomited right there on the spot. It was like the whole suit was filled with this terrible gas. It took its time to dissipate too, not going away before it filled the room and everyone's lungs got a taste of it. Real nasty stuff. After it cleared up, we got a good look at our "survivor."

It's not one of those things that's easy to describe. It's more like the kind of thing you need to have witnessed... not that I would wish that on anyone. Just thinking about it turns my stomach.

I've seen my fair share of burn victims, but this was something else. I'm no physician, but if I had to guess, it's almost like he combusted from the inside-out.

All of this, while still inside his atmospheric suit.

We put the helmet back on, just so we wouldn't have to deal with it any longer. It probably was Kerensky, after all. I guess a human body kind of goes bad like that, after spending decades rotting inside a sterile environment. Must be that the vitals monitor still had a charge, just like everything else on that damn ghost ship.

After our little catastrophe, I voted to jettison the body. It belonged back in the haunted house, not here with us. However, Beck shook his head. He figured there was no point taking it back. So that means we get to bunk with a corpse, but thankfully not for long. Beck had the sense at least to call it a wrap. He's getting us ready for take-off. We'll pick up the *Koriolan* with the mag-locks and then get the hell out of here. Not a moment too soon if you ask me.

We're still here. Christ.

We haven't even moved. Not one inch. We've been experiencing a power drain. We noticed it the moment Beck tried to warm up our engines. We were all strapped in and ready for take-off, listening to the drive kick in. First three checks cleared but then nothing. Turbines went silent and the alternators quieted down real quick afterward.

Beck sent Lambert and French outside to check if some debris got lodged in the thrusters and to de-dust things. When it was just the three of us, I brought up another theory. I guess I did a bad job at explaining things. Science was never my strong suit. Instead of catching his ear, all it did was get him furious. He had me immediately unplug the tablet, and even cited a few regulations from the agency about bringing in derelict tech. A little late for following the rules.

At that point, I guess I lost it too. I cursed him out and he cursed me back. Things got heated. I said some of the worst things I've ever said to a person. I'm a little amazed. I don't know where it came from. It wasn't the colourful sort I used to keep in reserve when I argued with David. This was dark and it was nasty. I think I even spooked Manuel.

Screw it. At least the tablet kept a bit of a charge. I have some reading to catch up on. There's gotta be some clue or something in here to explain what the hell is happening.

Lambert and French are back. They said there's nothing wrong with the engines as far as they can tell. I'm not too surprised. Manuel thinks it's the software. Everything we check seems clear, yet no engine power, and our reserves power is reading at under 15% and dropping fast. Beck gave me more shit for bringing the tablet on board. He thinks it infected our systems with a virus, but I've never heard of a rogue analogue program. He managed to get one hand on it, and nearly tossed it away before Manuel stood up. Things got nasty between them. If it had gone on any longer, I would have put money down on a fight breaking out between the two.

Now everyone's keeping to themselves, but at least I still have Wlatislaw's tablet. It's clear that whatever's going on with our ship has something to do with the *Koriolan* and Kerensky's project. Unfortunately, the more I read, the less I seem to understand. All I can say is that Dying Star was a hell of a lot weirder than I would have guessed.

Kerensky experimented on the two crewmen after they died. It was almost like he was trying to kick-start them back to life, the way you would with an old machine. Or at least, Wlatislaw certainly thought that was the case. At one point in his logs, he recorded a rant from Kerensky about how the human body is just another complex system, not much different from a ship or a space station. That we're all made of circuits. That energy can transfer from one to the other. He even spoke of souls carrying a charge. If they die out, all they need is a little juice, and they're back in action.

If I didn't know any better, I would have said Kerensky was reading a few too many books on the occult.

Whatever was going on, it's clear that Kerensky lost control of his project. Wlatislaw couldn't stop him, and they all paid for the price for it.

Though that got me thinking.

I was feeling loath to admit that the tablet might have caused our current drain. But ignoring all the hocus pocus, if Dying Star was about rebooting systems, then maybe there was something over there that could help get us back on track. I brought it up with Beck, but the bastard only ended up chastising me more about the tablet. He also forbade me from setting one foot off the ship. I told him to go to hell. Fortunately, that's as far as our spat went. He went back to the cockpit to brood, while I went down to our cargo hold.

Down there, I found Lambert tending to French. He'd been complaining about his chest this past hour. I guess that tour in the fuselage didn't help. It looked like he was running a fever. Anyway, he's not my problem.

Dammit, what's with me? Was I always this bitter? I suppose this is what cabin fever must feel like. Being locked up with a bunch of people you're starting to hate. Okay, not everyone, but still. I need to figure out a way to get something done or I've got this terrible feeling we're never gonna get out of here. It's not just because I'm sick of being on this rock, it's because we're so damn close to the *Koriolan*.

Their story didn't end so well.

Some progress.

Manuel finally got permission to send an official SOS to the station. That was a couple of hours ago. Still no response, but I'm sure we'll get something soon. Usually those boys at the agency are on the ball, especially with priority jobs like this.

Lambert is getting agitated. He's not just worried about French, either. I heard him talking to Beck, suggesting I'm the one messing with the systems. After all, I spend so much time alone, typing away on the computer. Fortunately, Beck didn't try revoking my privileges this time, but that didn't stop me from being under even more scrutiny and suspicions.

Manuel is saying we need to consider venturing back to the *Koriolan*. We could power up their life support systems and wait for rescue longer than we could here.

Our reserve power is at 8% and still dropping.

Manuel and Lambert just got back from the *Koriolan*. The systems over there check out a-okay. There's plenty of power and with so little hull damage, there's a fair chance the engines still work. I could see where he was going with this, but Beck was dismissive. He's got too much pride to abandon ship, even if that ship is an old box of junk like *La Damoiselle*. He wants us to wait until the last minute, which shouldn't be too long at this point.

French seems to have gotten worse. His fever is through the roof, and he's starting to ramble. Lambert thinks they brought back a virus from the other ship, or that maybe Kerensky was carrying it. Maybe it was that strange mist that came off his body and then disappeared. Maybe it got into everyone's system.

For a moment there, I was ready to believe him.

Christ, I read too many of those damn logs. Now I think I'm losing my mind, too.

At least Beck consented to toss Kerensky out of the hatch. Bastard is probably lying there in the dust not ten feet from the bay doors. He's part of the scenery now.

So be it.

I must have dozed off, but then the sounds woke me. I heard banging on the walls. It was almost as if it was coming from inside my own head. I woke Manuel, but he didn't hear anything. I wanted to go and check on Kerensky, but he told me to stay calm and relax. Power reserves are almost out, but life support is stable. He set an alarm to wake us up in a few hours. He stroked my hair, and let me rest my head against his knees. He fell asleep shortly after that, but I'm still awake.

I'm tempted to go over to the *Koriolan*. I might try it when I'm sure everyone's asleep. Lambert is still up and French too, but he's half out of his mind at this point. I just need to stay awake a little bit longer and make my move.

I couldn't do it. I fell asleep and had the worst dreams.

I dreamt that I was back in the *Koriolan*. That I was moving through its corridors. I was alone and it was dark. Somehow, I made my way to the science deck. It was easy to find, it was almost like I knew the way. When I walked in, the emergency lights flickered to life. There was a console, and some switches. I hit the most prominent ones. A feed started playing. It was only visible through my AR. Everything was written in that language. But I understood it without the translation.

This was Dying Star.

There was so much power here. Power beyond understanding. Whatever it was they were working on, they had tapped into something incredible. I could see it all so clearly now. Kerensky hadn't failed. He had done exactly what he set out to do. That crazy bastard.

And then, I realized I wasn't alone.

I turned, quickly. In the passage behind me, I saw one of those archaic spacesuits. It was just standing there like it was the most natural thing in the world. I called out, but there was no answer.

Instead, it started to walk toward me.

It moved with a broken, shuffling gait. When it got close, the lights came on around the visor. Inside was dark, misty-like, but it cleared as it got closer. It got so close our helmets almost pressed against one another. That's when I saw the face.

It was David's face, hidden behind the visor.

His eyes were closed, like he was sleeping. I tried to look away, but I couldn't. His lips moved, and I heard my name. I didn't want to answer, but I did. Then those eyes opened, grey and empty.

I knew it wasn't him. Even though it had all the features, even the scar on the cheek beneath the eye he got hurt in that bar fight. But it wasn't him. It was someone else pretending to be him.

So I did the only thing that was natural.

I started to laugh. And he laughed with me.

Things are bad. Power is down to 3%. Beck and Manuel tried a full manual reboot, including a visual check of every circuit they could get their hands on. Everything looks fine. No damage, no shorts, nothing wrong as far as we can tell. And yet, still no power in the engines and life support is on emergency reserves. It's as if everything is exactly as it should be, but all the energy is just seeping out of it, going somewhere that's not here.

Beck's finally talking about moving everyone over to the *Koriolan* and riding their systems for as long as we can.

French fell into a coma.

The last thing he said before he passed out was that he saw me and someone walk across the planetoid's surface, off toward the *Koriolan*. He was either full of shit or it was the fever. No way he could make anything out through that caked-over port-side window.

Either way, Lambert went bat shit at the revelation.

He started rambling, screaming at everyone, calling us traitors and liars. He asked Manuel how much the agency was paying him to let us all rot out here. Did he think he could get away with the bounty all on his own? The two of them traded blows. Beck tried to split them up, but Manuel landed a mean one on Lambert. Right in the jaw. Man knows how to throw a punch. Knocked Lambert back, hard. He hit his head against the console. He'll need stitches, that's for damn sure. But now he's out, too.

I don't know how we'll manage to move them in time, but at least there's some silence.

Beck's gone out to try and find a clearing, some place far from here and these hills, where the sky is open and there's less debris in the way. He brought one of our portable transmitters with him. He's determined to reach the agency. If he can get a signal, there's still time for them to send a rescue op before the generators die. I can't believe he's still holding on to his ship.

If the power miraculously comes back on, Manuel and I are both talking about leaving him out here. It's a shitty thing, but he'd still be able to walk back to the *Koriolan* for shelter. Otherwise, what are our options? Wait for the oxygen to run out? I can see that Manuel is worried about Lambert and French. Me? I don't know.

I really don't know.

I haven't found a way to tell anyone that Lambert is dead. Died in his sleep. I think French is gonna go soon, too.

It's tough to explain, but all I know is that whatever was over there, got over here. It's in our systems and in our minds. We're all just a bunch of giant circuits waited to be tampered with.

It's funny knowing that I was right. Someone did dump that goddamn derelict out here, far from everything.

And now it's ours for the taking.

Listen, I know what this is. No point in lying to myself. Writing all the time. Keeping it casual, but regular. It's a sort of therapy, self-medication even.

After your accident on Corneo I thought that… I don't know what I thought. Only that maybe it would make things more real, while still giving me time to adjust, to let it sink in, to get all this pain off my chest. I guess I was wrong.

A couple of years goes by faster than you know.

I guess I've never been the same, and maybe never will.

I guess I've been using you as a crutch. Living with my ghosts this whole time.

I'm sorry, David.

T.

Manuel and I couldn't wait for Beck any longer. We went over to the *Koriolan*. He checked the bridge while I made my way to the lab.

It was easy enough. Apparently, I knew the way already.

But then, that's where everything went wrong. I knew what I was looking for, but I just sort of lost my way. Like I was somewhere else, watching. That's when Kerensky, when he—

At least, I think that's who it was. It all happened so fast. If I had known, I would have slowed down. I didn't mean it. I don't even know where I found the wrench, only that it was so heavy and the sound it made when it hit his helmet.

I can't tell if it was your face, or Manuel's, or Kerensky's. Maybe it was only an empty suit, all along. I don't know anymore.

All I know is I don't believe in ghosts.

I don't believe in ghosts.

I don't believe in ghosts.

It was somewhere after morning, when I found myself halfway between the *Koriolan* and *La Damoiselle*. I felt it, over my whole body. It was as if a shadow passed over the surface of the rock, like the whole galaxy, every constellation, went dark for a full heartbeat. Imagine how different that would be. When you look out into the stars, you expect them to be there.

I found myself asking, what if the night sky went dark, forever? It was the most awful, empty feeling, and yet also somehow the most liberating thing I've ever experienced. The knowing part, that is.

I think I know what Kerensky was talking about.

We're all dying stars.

I'm sure Beck saw me laughing. But he couldn't hear it. He can't hear anything anymore.

It's me. It really is me. I think.

The life support systems have run out, but there's plenty of juice left in my suit.

I don't have many options.

If I take the escape pod, who knows where I'll end up. Stuck somewhere or lost in the debris. Maybe I'll end up drifting and find myself in some other asteroid belt, becoming some other *Koriolan*.

All I know is I can't go back to Terminus. Maybe I'll take it some place far away. I can't let anyone else find this. It'll keep a charge, keep a goddamn charge forever, if there's more life out there. He won't stop waiting. He's in everything already.

The *Koriolan* is death, and Kerensky is its face.

This is my last message. I want to say how much I love you, but all I can think of is the dark and how much it's pulling me.

T.

End retrieval.

Panwar's journal. 03/02/2303.

The *Yamuna* has finished her intercept of the derelict. I've finished reviewing the ship's records. The last log was dated ten years ago, almost to this day. No sign of the crew or the other vessel they mentioned.

Preliminary analysis: it was still flight-capable. The survivors abandoned *La Damoiselle* for the *Koriolan*. After departing, they failed to return to Terminus. Cause, unknown. Just a hypothesis.

We did retrieve a tablet. It doesn't seem to use a standard interface language, and I don't have the patience to translate it. Nevertheless, I'm bringing it back to Terminus for analysis. We'll be home in a matter of hours. The boys in the science lab should have a field day over this.

I'll post more this evening.

End entry.

TAMARA KOHN was a Class II legal clerk. She completed her qualifying certificate and compulsory degree at the New Maritime Law Organization in 2282. Her husband, David Tanner, died four years later, shortly after their joint transfer to Terminus Station.

ALEXANDER NACHAJ lives in Montreal, Canada. He lectures part-time at Concordia University, where he is in the process of completing his Ph.D. and spends too much time reading and writing. His work has appeared in *Grievous Angel*, *Shotgun Honey*, and *Right Hand Pointing*, among other places. You can keep a tab on him over at his blog: www.anachaj.ca.

a pocket guide for
MISTRESS HORNE'S
home for weary travelers

A brochure by Mistress Madison Horne,
AS PROVIDED BY GWENDOLYN KISTE

Greetings, prospective traveler! I'm so thrilled you've found our brand-new pocket guide. (I certainly hope the eager corvid who dropped it from the sky didn't frighten you too much!)

If you're reading this, then you're probably in search of the perfect place for a getaway (and really, who isn't?). As the purveyor of Mistress Horne's Home for Weary Travelers, I'm pleased to offer the finest in accommodations, and I would love for you to choose my establishment for your journey.

Are you still unconvinced—and a little shaken—thanks to the corvid? (You don't have to keep looking up, you know; he's already returned home to me.) Then please settle back for a moment and allow me to share with you some of our very best features!

Historic Home

You might be wondering at what kind of place you'll be staying. My home was built in the 1920s by my namesake, Miss Madison Horne, who established it after some nebulous yet dastardly Manhattan scandal ended with her broken engagement and abrupt retirement from society life. A few old-timers claim that I look just like her—"an uncanny resemblance," they whisper—and since she was apparently quite a beauty of her era, all I can say is *Thank You!*

The original Miss Horne's unlikely seclusion here is most certainly your gain, since her exquisite taste furnished the house in a delightful Art Deco style that resonates with guests from all eras. High metal ceilings and jagged edges and wallpaper with silver designs that seem to ripple like water whenever you touch them (but that's just a trick of the eye, mind you).

And the best part of your visit to my home is that you won't require directions! If you need us, we'll be there. You might be stumbling through a thorny forest during a storm as gray and hopeless as heartbreak. You might feel in that moment so misplaced, as though you don't belong anywhere, but you'd be wrong. In a clearing, there will be a light, burning clear and yellow on a porch. You'll walk to it and find us there, my crow waiting for you at the door.

Or perhaps you'll be lost in an unfamiliar city, abandoned and scorned and armed with only a folded white handkerchief and a pocket full of hope. The hope won't be for nothing. We'll be there, the only townhouse with a light on. No locale is too far-flung: wherever you need us, you'll find us.

Affordable Rates

No two guests at my home are ever the same. You might be running. Or you might have grown too tired to run. Regardless of circumstance, I'm happy to welcome you. Even if you don't boast a penny to your name, so long as you want to be here, I will have a room waiting. Check your luggage and regrets at the door, and I'll take care of everything else.

Spacious Estate

While we're more than happy to pick you up anywhere, our permanent location is in the wilds of New England (we prefer not to divulge the address, even though every generation of snooping locals discovers us anyhow, cloaked façade and sleight of hand be damned).

But don't pay the locals too much mind—we have plenty on the grounds to keep you busy. On the porch, lazy windchimes jingle in the afternoon breeze as you recline with a book and a spot of tea on the porch swing. In the parlor, the Victrola plays a thousand tunes without a hand ever dropping a needle. Around dusk, you might hear the babbling and giggles of an infant coming from what used to be the nursery, but I assure you it's only an echo of the wind.

These features, lovely as they are, might offer little comfort to you at first. You'll likely spend your first few days sequestered in your melancholy. While this is not recommended—huckleberry scones and card games in the parlor are far more preferable—I understand that it's a normal part of my guests' early itinerary. Take whatever time you need; there will always be a tray of high tea delicacies, still warm from the oven, waiting on the sideboard whenever you're ready.

In the evenings, the crow sings an elegy, and the sweet rain whispers secrets on the copper roof. Curled up in your bed, you can lie back and listen, or if you'd like, you can share secrets of your own. You can unfurl all those heavy truths weighing down your heart. Perhaps you'll whisper to the walls about the promises someone shattered like stained glass, or the bruises that speckled your body inside and out while nobody cared enough to notice. Or maybe you'll murmur about your family and their expectations that bound you up as tight as barbed wire. You can share it all, what made you want to run or disappear or never exist at all. Or you can say nothing. The truths are yours to do with as you please.

But remember: once you're my guest, you're safe. Those things won't find you here. Or if they do, they'll wish they hadn't. I'll make sure of it.

Guest Privacy

While you can find us whenever you need, that unfortunately means others might discover us too. Rest assured that I do not take kindly to trespassers. (And if you're wondering how I identify them as trespassers and not valued guests, the sneers on their faces and torches in their hands are usually the first giveaway.)

The families and lovers who drove you off might arrive to reclaim you. It's strange how much they want you back once you leave on your own. In the dark and the cold, they'll descend on the house. (Why do they always come under veil of midnight? Too embarrassed after what they've done to show their faces in daylight, perhaps?)

At the sound of their voices at the door, your hands might shake, and your skin might turn blotchy, but don't worry. You retire to your room with a mug of warm milk, and as your esteemed hostess, I'll do the rest. These invaders might fancy themselves strong, but their heavy footfalls won't get past the foyer. With a crow on my shoulder, I'll hold them back. They might try to persuade me, of course, to tell them where you are. They might try to outright coerce me, to wring the truth out of me, their calloused hands wrapped around my wrists, my waist, my throat as pale as fresh cream in the moonlight. Believe me, they won't be the first. Many have tried—bless their rage-filled hearts—and they'll need a good blessing if they want to make it out the front door after that. (Don't be alarmed if my crow flashes you a red smile in the morning.)

But perhaps they won't be filled with such impotent fury. They might arrive after the remorse settles in their bones, so deep even forceps and a scalpel can't excise it. They'll creep toward the estate in the night and toss rocks at all the windows until they find yours, and they'll sob and beg for forgiveness. But this time, you won't listen. You'll turn away and close the velvet curtains tight, and you'll smile to yourself because sometimes, tears and apologies come too late.

Flexible Checkout

Here at my home, there's no formal checkout time. You might sleep in forever, or you might be an early riser who needs only one night to rest on your travels. Either way, I won't keep you. If after a day or a week or a season, you awaken one morning and find yourself healed and ready, then simply come to the front desk and bid me farewell. I'll want to see you off, and the crow will want to give you his benediction. And we'll both remind you how you can always come back any time you need.

Of course, some of my guests like it here so much that they never check out at all. And since I have ample room, I'm more than happy to accommodate them. If you'd like, I can accommodate you, too.

Thank you for taking the time to read this brief guide about Mistress Horne's Home for Weary Travelers. I hope I've answered all your questions about my lovely establishment. Naturally, if the wind changes its course and you find your own path, you might not require that getaway after all. But please remember: if you ever need us, we'll be waiting for you.

I'll always be waiting.

MISTRESS MADISON HORNE resides in an undisclosed location in New England. She welcomes you to rest your lonely soul at her home, any day or night, whoever you are and wherever you roam.

GWENDOLYN KISTE is a speculative fiction author based in Pennsylvania. Her stories have appeared in *Shimmer, Interzone, Daily Science Fiction, Black Static, Nightmare,* and *Three-Lobed Burning Eye,* among other outlets. Her debut fiction collection, *And Her Smile Will Untether the Universe,* is available now from JournalStone. You can find her online at gwendolynkiste.com.

can't be
LOCKED DOWN

An account by Vicky Sheppard,
AS PROVIDED BY ALANNA MCFALL

Wanderlust can settle into your bones. I spent years after I finished school traveling across the country: slinging my backpack over my shoulder, hopping on my bike, and taking off for somewhere new. Indigo, my mountain bike with its scuffed but vibrant purple paint, was my only consistent traveling companion in those days, and the two of us saw, felt, and tasted more of America than most people can hope for.

Eventually I developed an ache in my back and a shakiness in my knees that demanded longer stretches in one place, but as soon as I felt steady again, I was always back on the road. I envied Indigo the ease with which she could trade out new parts for broken ones, but the frame of her, her bones, were always there with me. She felt every traveled mile as surely as I did, even if her frame did not give out as easily as mine.

Because she had stuck with me so faithfully over my more

adventurous years, I made sure to incorporate Indigo into my settled city life as well. Her bulky frame and thick wheels were not designed for a commuter's life, hopping on and off buses and trains, but she worked well enough (and in one memorable incident, survived a showdown with a car quite admirably). The only real issue became where to put her when I went places that she could not follow.

Colton, Iowa, was not really a bicyclist's city, despite how much I tried to make it one. A smaller bike could have likely been ignored while chained to a signpost or bench leg for several hours, but Indigo stood out, and I soon racked up more talking-tos and passive-aggressive notes than I knew what to do with, not to mention outright tickets. I needed real bike racks to go about my day with Indigo in tow, and I soon had a mental list of where they were scattered across the city. Even places that I had no intention of stopping at, stores that I had no interest in, and paths I had no reason to stop along, would be flagged in my mind if they had their own bike rack. And I quickly developed my favorites.

The one that stood out in the course of my day was the rack half a block from my job. More than a bare metal loop sticking out of the pavement, it was a tiny construct for all of the hippies who worked in the strip mall with its health food store and artist boutiques. The sticker for the women's art gallery that I slapped on Indigo's wide frame made her right at home in the little half-shed.

A thick piece of steel with a dense layer of green paint snaked up and down a couple feet across the pavement, offering purchase to lock bikes of all different heights. The small wooden roof was held up by four more green painted poles, so a determined group could fit eight bikes underneath it, out of the rain and shaded enough to not leave bike seats burning hot in the sun. That was a pain I knew more than anyone needed to. It was the smallest thing, in the grand scheme of the city and of my life, a tiny convenience that made my day ever so slightly easier, but I appreciated it. And I liked to think that Indigo did too.

I worked at that art gallery for over three years, but even that stretch of time was interrupted by me taking trips, taking off for a week in between exhibitions to ride Indigo as far as I could take her. I rarely had the time or funds to fly somewhere scenic, like I once had, but just being out on the road and somewhere different was enough. I pointed my wheel in as many different directions of the compass as I could, seeing where a three days' journey would get me and what I could do there. In the Midwest, the answer was most often "look at corn fields" (with an occasional shake up of "look at soybean fields"), but it was the journey that counted. I would come back to my apartment at the end of the week and wash the road's dust off myself and Indigo, but there was a place deep inside that it collected, turning into beautiful memories like a pearl in my chest. All that wanderlust, the satisfaction and relief from satisfying it, and the beginnings of it growing again, would be with me when I rode to work on my first day back, and when I locked my bike to that rack. It was a small structure, barely a fraction of a building, but it was something built to facilitate travel and therefore found affection in my traveler's heart.

And it must have found favor with other people in Colton as well, because after I had been in town for about a year, I started noticing similar bike racks popping up. More and more when I was riding around town I would see a little wooden roof here, a strip of painted green metal there. It certainly made my days easier, knowing I was more likely to be able to find a place to lock Indigo while I got groceries or went out for drinks with a friend. It seemed like anywhere I wanted to go, there was a green metal bike rack with a scrubby wooden roof, waiting for me.

But no good things can last, as they say. In January of the beginning of my third year in Colton, I decided to take a few weeks after the gallery's Christmas show closed and point Indigo south. My only real goal was to keep riding until I escaped the snow, and enjoy the feeling of traveling in and out of seasons, rather than having them change around me. I rode a snaking path down through Missouri and eventually wandered myself to a friend's place in Arkansas, someone who I had met on the road during a previous trip. The two of us (three if you included Indigo, four if you included his bicycle Mattie) took a handful of smaller trips around the state using his home as the spoke in the center of our wheel. At the end of it all, I climbed back on my bike and took the long, meandering trip home to the regular rhythms of my adult… well, more-adult life. So you can see how after such a nice, satisfying trip, it was a disappointment to return to my routines and find my favorite bike rack gone.

I commuted from my small apartment to the gallery on my first day back, as I always did; when you travel as often as I do, you learn how to jump back into your routine easily. But I pulled up to where I usually parked Indigo and had my heavy U-lock most of the way out of my bag before I looked up and noticed the bare patch of pavement where the structure had once been.

Nothing looked broken or damaged, rather that the entire construct had been lifted and carried away without so much as a scratch on the sidewalk around the blank patch. Neat holes were left where the bars had met with the ground, and if it had not been for those empty post pits, it would have been like the bike rack was never there.

It was done so neatly that I assumed the managers of the strip mall had paid to have it removed. There had been occasions when bikes had been left there for several days at a time (not by me; I could never be separated from Indigo for that long), and they must have gotten sick of the clutter on their sidewalk. I grumbled and resolved to tuck Indigo into the gallery's basement for a few days until I found another good rack, but there was nothing to be done.

My boss Mara was confused when I wheeled Indigo in through the back door, but I could only shrug and promise her that it would not be a permanent situation.

"Can't you lock it on the bike rack on the sidewalk?" she asked.

"That green one with the awning thing?"

"No, they took that one down while I was gone. I'll find another good one in walking distance, don't worry."

My boss looked confused while I nestled Indigo back by the thermostat and tried to keep her out of the way. I heard Mara walking through the gallery and the tinkling of the front door being opened, then closed a moment later. Footsteps coming back through the gallery, then Mara's face poked back into the office space. "I could have sworn that thing was there yesterday."

I shrugged. "I guess someone else in the strip thought it was an eyesore?" The rack had been getting a smattering of graffiti lately, and more than a few band stickers had found their way plastered to it over the years.

"You'd think the landlords would have sent out a notice," Mara said with a frown. "Let's hope they set up a replacement, even if it is smaller. Half of the hippies who come by the gallery ride bikes, and we can't afford to not be hospitable."

That was the last I heard of the bike rack issue for a few days, and I did manage to find a nearby rack to store Indigo at, that was out of the way, if lacking a bit of the character of the other. One day, Mara came in with her mouth twisted in a scowl and told me that the leasing office had no idea where the rack had gone, that they had not been the ones to get rid of it.

"Someone just picked it up and stole it!" she said, with her hands flapping in the air, exasperated that things were happening around her gallery that she did not know about. "Plucked it right out of the ground when no one was looking! There aren't even any scrapes or damage. Someone put a lot of thought into stealing this one bike rack."

"Mara, I had no idea you cared so much about the bicyclists of Colton," I said with a laugh as I poured myself some more coffee in the breakroom.

"It's the principle of the thing," she insisted. "Would you steal a

whole parking lot? An airport? A dock? No? Then why would you
steal a bike rack?"

There was not much to do past shrug when Mara got onto a topic,
so I sat back and let her outrage pass over me. Maybe it was a side
effect of all the travel, but I found it a lot more difficult to get worked
up about small things in those days. I certainly could not claim such
peace of mind all the time, but in an ideal situation, I could carry the
small good things with me when I traveled, and ride away from the
bad ones. This would make my life slightly less convenient, but such
is life. I tried to keep the same reaction in mind when I stopped seeing the green bike racks anywhere in town, as if the whole of Colton
decided they were no longer good enough.

I, in turn, decided that Colton was not a good match for me. It
had been a nice enough place to call home for a while, but that wanderlust was in my bones, and I needed to let it loose at least some of
the time. I rented a small storage locker for some of my things, packed
any essentials into my backpack and saddle bags, and took off down
the road, looking for that next adventure.

First, I decided to head east and stay with some friends of mine
in Ohio. It was just getting into the warmth of spring, so the day-
long rides with Indigo were pleasant and smooth as I made my way
through miles and miles of corn fields and farmlands. I spent some
nights camping with friends or friends of friends that I had made
over the years, the occasional night in a roadside motel, and the rare
night here and there sleeping under the night sky (with Indigo's chain-
lock wrapped loosely around my ankle and my knife tucked into my
pocket; a woman traveling alone can never be too careful). It was a
lovely calm night in Indiana when I made my home for the night in a
motel and rode Indigo farther into town to grab a bite to eat. I found
a sweet local diner off the main street and was about to start searching
for a signpost to chain Indigo to when I saw it.

The rack was perched right at the corner of an intersection, a spot that seemed a little too in the way for most people to park their bicycles. The green paint on the snaking metal pipe was scratched and chipped in places, and a dense layer of dust covered the pipes that held it to the ground. The town of Oakfield did not seem that dusty, but it had clearly gotten all over that bike rack.

Now metal bike racks, even in that particular shade of forest green, are by no means rare, and I could see the coincidence of them having the exact same shape in a scattering of different towns. But the small section of weathered wood boards stretched over the pipes like a fragment of a roof was far less common. There was little about Colton that ever made me nostalgic, as it had only ever been a waystation on the map of my life, but seeing this bike rack made me smile. I crossed the road to lock Indigo to it while I ate.

I stayed for almost two hours, after getting caught in a flirtation with a waitress and being persuaded to stick around for a leisurely dessert. The sky was dark gray, almost black, but warm and comfortable, and I was looking forward to a slow ride back to the motel. But the calm night and apple pie coma were jarred away with what I saw when I looked across the road.

Thank god Indigo was still there, or I would have been very mad indeed. But my bicycle was right where I had left it, with the U-lock around her middle and the chain lock snaking through the front and back wheels. No, it was the rack itself that was missing, leaving Indigo alone on the street corner.

I crossed the street in a state of pure confusion. The closer I got, the stranger the whole scene looked. Neither of the locks were broken or jimmied open; they did not even seem to be scratched. The pavement was unmarked, and as far as I could tell there were no holes where the bike rack's poles would have gone in the first place. Had it not been grounded in any way when I locked Indigo there?

A woman walked past me on the sidewalk, heading for the convenience store farther down the block; I stopped to ask her if she knew where the bike rack on the corner had gone. She looked at me like I was crazy, said she had lived a couple blocks away for five years and never seen a bike rack here. I wondered if maybe I was going crazy, or if Oakfield, Indiana, had some very dedicated pranksters. I rode back to my motel and kept Indigo in the room with me. In the morning, I was mostly able to brush it off, too busy sending a text to the waitress to see if she wanted to get lunch before I left town. It was a bike rack; there was not too long that it could stay in my mind.

I left town the next day and made my way farther east, visiting friends new and old along the way. I stayed with a cousin in Pennsylvania for a few weeks, doing odd jobs and contracts with their small theatre while I planned my next move. I come from a family of travelers and wanderers, so I was nicely at home camping out in the RV where my cousin Joel lived with his wife. I mused a bit then that perhaps the wanderlust was something genetic that had been with me since day one. That may be true, but the events of the next months certainly taught me that it could be developed as well.

Speaking with my cousin and poring over maps, I realized that I had never made a proper cross-country trip, starting at one end of America and biking until I reached the other. Joel's theatre troupe was going to be starting a tour soon, snaking their way from the East Coast to the West and back, and he pointed out that if I travelled at a consistent pace, I could meet them at a handful of stops along the way. It would be an ambitious endeavor, a longer trip than I had ever taken in one go before, but I felt like I was ready. Who knew, maybe I would even be able to settle down for a longer stretch after knowing I had seen the country from end to end.

I had an old flame in New York to see before I started on my way (and I think a stubborn part of me wanted to start the trek right on the coast). I spent a week dodging angry taxis and having people try to saw through Indigo's locks, but it was a pleasant time overall. It was nice to be in a city that was made for pedestrians and bicyclists, even if I could not stand being that cooped up in the long run. There were bike racks and posts to lock things to on most blocks in Manhattan, but none stood out as suspicious (or green and strangely roofed).

I started on the trip in the beginning of April and pointed my front wheel west, with a fully stocked backpack and a phone full of downloaded maps. Some trails were full to the brim with people stretching out after a long winter, but most of the time I was riding alone, just me and Indigo. Those were the times that I most often saw the racks.

Sometimes it was in a place that a bike rack would normally be, in little alcoves and corners of city streets. Sometimes it was at the beginning of hiking trails or near train stations, which seemed like a perfectly logical place for a bike rack, even if it often clashed with the local architecture. Sometimes it was not even pretending to blend in. I saw a green bike rack with a wooden roof dead in the middle of an industrial park in Ohio, surrounded by cars and dumpsters. I saw a green bike rack in the center of a community plaza in Illinois, on top of a pagoda only accessible by stairs. I saw a green bike rack in a cornfield in Iowa, not too far from where it had all started in Colton, yards and yards away from the road and with no clear paths through the plants to reach it. I never locked Indigo at these racks, but that time I almost traipsed through the corn out of sheer spite. I was being stalked by a bike rack, and that was putting me in just a bit of a weird frame of mind.

At first, I wrote it off as a coincidence. Then I wondered if I was seeing things, if perhaps the isolation of the road was getting to my head in a way it never had in the past. Was there some deep-seated memory or trauma associated with bike racks in my mind? I could not dredge up anything, so if it was there it was buried deep; my bicycling experiences were on the whole very positive. So if I wasn't crazy, was it a new architectural trend? Some long-distance art installment? A strange and subtle meme? I had no idea.

It finally came to a head in Nebraska. I was biking through a more wooded area and broke out the tiny lightweight pop-up tent from my pack in the evenings. When I went to sleep, I was in a small clearing in a forest, at least two miles from any road, and Indigo was chained to a tree right outside my tent. When I woke up, nothing around me had changed, save for the green bike rack outside my front tent lap, with its little roof blocking some of the morning glare from my eyes.

"Alright, that's enough, what is going on?!" I shouted into the early morning calm. A few birds startled and flew away above me, but no voices answered. The bike rack was blocking my way directly forward, so I kicked the flaps aside to get out and stand by Indigo. She, at least, seemed fine.

I tramped through the woods in a wide loop around my campsite for the better part of an hour, having fished my knife out of my bag and ready for a fight, or at least some kind of confrontation. None found me. The trees and bushes were dense and I had been aware enough while making camp that I could tell no one else had been through. Damp mud from a rainstorm the previous day had preserved my, and only my, footsteps. So finally, I had to turn to the only tangible thing I did have here.

I planted my hands on my hips and glared at the bike rack. "What are you doing? Why are you following me?" I felt ridiculous, but I was mad, and it was not like there was anyone to witness but birds and a few squirrels. "Did I do something to you? Did I wrap my chain too tight around you or scuff your paint once? Have I somehow offended you and need to make amends?!" My voice was rising with my temper, echoing slightly in the clearing. I spread my arms wide in a defiant plea. "I was literally only using you for your express purpose! You are a bike rack! I locked my bike to you while I was at work! I didn't paint graffiti on you or stick gum to your pipe, and I know other people did. Go haunt them! The kid who worked at the bodega on the corner practically turned you pink the week he tried to quit smoking; doesn't he deserve a cross-country haunting more than me?"

There was no answer. I am not sure if I was expecting one, but stranger things had happened. The bike rack just stood there. I was completely done with its shenanigans and started to pack my campsite up as quickly as I could, cramming delicate tent poles into my backpack with far less care than they deserved. After ten minutes, I unchained Indigo, wrapped the chain around my waist and hopped on to ride away from the strangest haunting I had ever heard of.

When I reached the main hiking trail, the bike rack was there.

I kept riding.

When I reached the edge of the woods where the trails merged with the road, the bike rack was there.

I kept riding.

It was there in the parking lot of a hotel I stopped at for the night. It was in a different spot at the other edge when I peeked out the curtains in the morning. I was scared to take a shower lest I open the curtain and find it in the bathroom, though I had not seen it go indoors yet. I got back on Indigo and kept riding, putting up with its increasingly frequent appearances and trying my best to ignore it. This lasted a little over a week.

It might have gone on for a lot longer if it weren't for a bumpy trail in Colorado. I probably should not have been riding Indigo along it, it was so slippery from recent rainfall, but I wanted to make it to a meetup with Joel by nightfall. I was sore and soggy and not looking for any sort of nonsense when I saw that stupid haunted bike rack again. On its side. In the mud. Like an idiot.

I almost crashed into a tree from laughing so hard. It looked like one of its corners had been half on the trail, half on a rock, and it had overbalanced. It was just so undignified for some sort of supernatural entity that had driven me half mad over the last several weeks. How scary could this thing be if it could not even stay upright? Had I been wrong to think it creepy in the first place?

It looked so sad and absurd with its roof part sticking into the mud, so I leaned Indigo against a tree and went to help it. I had started thinking of it as a thinking being recently, as a thing out to torment (or at least annoy) me, so I saw no harm in trying to talk to it while I hauled at its poles to pull it up. No one else was around to see if I was just crazy.

"Okay, so this is kind of ridiculous now," I told the bike rack while leaning back with my hands wrapped around the poles holding its roof in place. "What could you possibly be getting out of this? Are you trying to scare me, or are you just bored? Was Colton not interesting enough for you? Because that's a pretty fair reaction to Iowa in general." My boots slipped on the wet rock, and I grunted as I tried to maintain my grip. "I guess I can see how you would want to do some traveling of your own."

With a great deal of angling and shifting, and only slipping in the mud myself once, I managed to haul it upright. I brushed some globs of mud off of the green snaking pipe and paused to look at the band stickers scattered across it. Some were clearly newer, and one had a logo I recognized. My cousin had rambled at length about the band World's Biggest Hipster Mustache in Portland. I had never seen them, as they were not yet popular enough to tour. It had been years since I found myself in Portland.

"You haven't been following me—" I said slowly, one hand on the bike rack's pole. "You've just been… traveling? All over the place?" There was no response, though I will admit that by this point I was half-expecting one. "But even if you've been all over the place, running into me this often can't—it cannot just be a coincidence."

I shifted and settled the rack until it sat on more even ground, then stepped back and put my hands on my hips. "So you like to travel, but you get lonely, maybe? I don't want to be so presumptuous as to think you only like me."

But then again, I had been the one who used this bike rack the most back in Colton. How many hours had Indigo spent chained to this thing over the years I lived there? I had always been sentimental and believed that Indigo was shaped by all the traveling I did, that it worked its way into her being as it had into mine.

Who was I to say that that couldn't be passed on?

"Okay, you and I are going to come to a deal," I said. I knelt down in the mud so that I was more at a level with its green pipe, which seemed as much like the main part of its body as anything. "You can't keep popping up in so many places. It is seriously creeping me out, and not useful if you might disappear when I have Indigo locked to you." I paused to let the words sink in; it was metal, so maybe they had a long way to sink. "But I would be interested in seeing you sometimes. So how about this," I went on, with an idea popping into my head. "I know I'm going to be in Salt Lake City next month. I don't know if you really understand calendars or... you know, I'll worry about that later. If you think this sounds like a good idea, find me in Salt Lake City on the fifteenth, but not at all before that. If that works, we can figure out more of a plan from there. Agreed?... I am going to hope you agree."

With no more sign of a response coming, I gripped one of the poles and moved my hand slightly, hoping it read as a handshake and not some strange grope. "So I hope to see you in a month. Um... have a good one." I gave it a little wave, resettled my backpack, hopped back on Indigo, and took off down the bumpy trail. I glanced back once and the bike rack was still there.

I looked again a few seconds later, and it was gone. I could only hope it was going somewhere fun.

I continued my trip, and did not see a single glimpse of a green bike rack with a roof while I was on the road. I rode, camped, rode some more, stayed in hotels, rode. I met new people, chatting with strangers and talking with friends in almost every town I stopped in. But the majority of the time, it was just me, my thoughts, and Indigo together on the wavering lines between civilization and wilderness. No strange haunted bike racks to be seen.

I made it to Salt Lake City by the fourteenth and settled in for a long visit with my cousin and some other friends, resting and restocking for the rest of the trek through the desert (I was taking buses for some stretches of badland; I was a traveler, not suicidal). I did not notice any extra or unusual bike racks anywhere, but I was a day early, and it had always managed to find me before. As strange as it sounded, I had started to miss the thing.

I did not see it on the fifteenth either. Or the sixteenth. I started to get worried that it would think I had been rude. But when I went on an errand run on the seventeenth… well, let's just say I had a very familiar place to lock Indigo while I bought groceries.

"Alright, so you're not good with calendars," I said to the bike rack, keeping my voice down to not look too insane to passersby. "But it is nice to see you. Now let's talk schedules. I need privacy sometimes, but I think there are some things you should see. You're going to love Burning Man."

Wanderlust can settle into your bones. I have always believed that and likely always will.

It can apparently settle into pipes as well.

VICKY SHEPPARD is a born and bred traveler from a family of like-minded nomads. She has been walking, riding, and driving her way around America since her early teens and shows no signs of stopping as she gets older. Her memoirs of her time on the road and her interactions with paranormal phenomenon, titled *My Bike, The Open Road, Some Ghosts, and Me* is expected in bookstores next year.

ALANNA MCFALL is an actor and science-fiction writer based out of the Bay Area in California. She has published pieces on *Mad Scientist Journal, Escape Pod, Alliteration Ink,* and many more, across a range of mediums. You can follow her work on her website at https://alannamcfall.wordpress.com or on Twitter at @AlannaMcFall.

thump HOUSE

An account by Mari Guerrero,
AS PROVIDED BY M. LOPES DA SILVA

We never thought that Addy would get the seizures. Mom always made sure to buy bottled water, and never let us drink from the tap. It was expensive to buy all our water that way, and sometimes we really couldn't afford it, but Mom called it a necessity. People in town had been getting seizures for decades, and everyone had a theory, but Mom had already worked it out; the primary source of income for Woodward was the paper mill, and the mill was right off the river. It stood to reason that they were dumping too many chemicals in the water, and we were drinking them right up.

The paper mill flatly denied responsibility for the seizures, and scientists were brought in every once in a while to take samples of the water, but there was never an a-ha moment where we felt like someone had figured it all out. The scientists got a lot of "inconclusive" results. The paper mill donated a lot of money to the Woodward Hospital, just in case. People needed to work. We grumbled on.

Sometimes I cheated and drank water from the fountains at school, but Addy never did. I knew she didn't. She was the good kid— the one who did her homework every night and never got detention or stern lectures. I wanted to hate her for that, but I just couldn't. Addy was a *genuinely* good kid; she liked when people were happy, and always tried to make me laugh or smile when I griped. I tried to explain to people that she was like a pet dog or a cat, full of this blank, joyful energy that made me want to scoop her up and put her on my shoulders while she prattled on about penguins or bacteria or whatever had caught her attention that day. I was the bad example, the older sister who couldn't get her shit together, but Addy wasn't like that at all.

But now we were all in the emergency room at Woodward Hospital, ringing my sister's bed with a curtain drawn around us. The curtain felt heavy on my back, and it was weird to be in that cramped space, like being stuck in a play held on the smallest stage possible. Addy had been sedated, and the doctor was giving us a hopeful spiel. "No need to get worried yet—it might be epilepsy—"

"We're *hoping* for epilepsy?" I asked, and my voice was loud.

The doctor glanced at me funny; the skin on her face looked tired, but her eyes were wide awake. Mom put her hand on my arm, but I moved my arm away.

"The alternative, of course, is that she might have… the local affliction," the doctor replied.

Of course she meant the seizures. I suddenly hated the doctor for dancing around it, for mincing her words. Woodward seizures didn't end; they lasted for every waking second of your life, and only heavy sedation stopped them. The people in Woodward who had "the local affliction" lived mostly in their dreams, like victims of a Sleeping Beauty spell, their families left behind to take care of the sleepers.

Mom was crying now, quietly. I felt hot and a little dizzy. I gripped the metal handrail of my sister's bed, but I didn't feel any steadier.

I drove us back to the house, which was rare, because Mom hated the way I drove, but she didn't say anything about my speed or the stoplight I blew off because there wasn't anybody else on the road, anyway. Instead, she was muttering vaguely about the paper mill and contacting Gary. Gary Caruso was the lawyer who'd taken care of Mom's divorce a few years ago. I said out loud that I didn't think Gary would be able to handle this sort of thing. Mom looked up at me, her eyes narrowed.

"Of course Gary wouldn't, but he'll know someone who can help."

That pissed me off, but I couldn't say exactly why. So I just drove her to the house, sitting on my anger.

Woodward sometimes gets written up in articles on websites that post a lot of weird crap, and we'll get tourists every once in a while, waving their phones around and trying to figure out what the hell is wrong with our town. It's not just the seizures—sometimes locals "catch the wind in their ear"—or get a loud roaring, like a strong wind, stuck in their heads that no one else can hear. When I was in middle school, I watched a bunch of people shooting a T.V. special about Woodward. They were standing in front of the elementary school, talking about Tommy Fowler, a kindergartener who woke up from nap time seizing. An Asian woman with pink hair and a clipboard came up to me.

"Hey, did you know Tommy?" she asked.

"I like your hair," I said. I'd known Tommy; I'd even been in his class, back then, but I didn't want to be on camera. What the hell was there to tell, anyway? We woke up from our naps, hazy and warm, and Tommy was thrashing on the floor, his little fists beating the carpet while his back arched—Christ.

She laughed. "I like yours, too!" I'd had my hair up in big, goth pigtails then, with plastic skulls in the center of the bows.

We kept talking, and she eventually asked me if I'd ever known someone who'd caught the wind in their ear. I told her that it had happened to me, once, but I didn't want to be in their show. She'd gotten really excited, then, and given me her business card. Her name was C. Park, and she said the C stood for Cora. She'd wanted me to get permission from my mom to visit our house and talk more.

I hadn't called her.

It had been at least three years since Cora had given me her card. I took it out of my wallet; the card was soft at the edges. Cora lived in Los Angeles, and had probably forgotten about the show she'd worked on in Woodward three years ago.

But maybe she hadn't.

I dug my mom's smartphone out of her purse. After a bustle of useless activity, she'd sort of worn herself out, and I'd told her to go to bed. I could hear her faintly snoring now through the door. An icon of the Virgin hung there, in the middle of the cheap plywood.

I called the number.

She picked up on the second ring. "Hello?"

"Hey, this is Mari Guerrero—I don't know if you remember me? We met in Woodward a few years ago." I was speaking a little too quickly.

"Hey, hey—" Cora interjected. I fell silent. "Wait a second, Mari, did you say? Wow! Right, on that Woodward special. I don't even work for that company anymore."

My lips felt dry; I started picking at them. "Yeah, I was the girl who caught the wind in her ear. I'm sorry I never called you. And this is going to sound weird, but I was wondering if you could help me out."

"Really?"

"Yeah, my little sister—" I had to stop, swallow; my mouth was so dry. "My little sister, she's started having the seizures."

"Oh my god, I'm so sorry," Cora exclaimed. "That's awful. I just, I don't know how I can help you."

I licked my lips. "So, tell me, how old is the paper mill, anyway?"

"Uhhh, I don't know if I remember that offhand. Wait, I have a file with a bunch of notes from the shoot in it. There's some historical stuff in there. What if I send it to you?"

"That would be great." I gave her my email address.

"So Mari," Cora said after a while, "would you mind telling me about what happened to you? About the wind in your ear? If you don't want to talk about it, I'd understand, but you've got me on the hook here."

That again. I hadn't discussed it in a while. It wasn't something I wanted to think about, really.

"You know, Mari, there's other places in the world that have unexplained phenomena—have you heard of the Hum?"

"What? No," I said.

"In certain parts of the world—England, Scotland, even New Mexico—a small percentage of the population will start to hear this constant, awful sound that others can't. It's driven people mad. It's a thing."

"They call it 'the Hum'?" I asked.

"Yeah."

"It wasn't like a hum," I said, and then I could hear it; my memory playing it back in high-def horror. The constant scream of the wind, blotting everything else out, melting everything into a pain that made you want to plunge your fingers into your ears and tear the damn thing out, no matter what else you damaged along the way. Smothering and inescapable, trapped within your own meat.

"I was in second grade." I looked ahead and stared at the painted face of the Virgin, trying not to let the fear grab me. "I was upset—some kids at school had been making fun of me, and I felt like it wouldn't end, no matter what I did, so I was going to run away. I stuffed my backpack full of cookies and crap and went into the woods. It got dark, and I got lost, and that's when I realized that I was close to Thump House."

"Thump House?" Cora sounded strangely excited.

"Yeah, it's this really old building that looks almost like a hill, it's all covered in grass and vines and stuff. It's a place that kids dare each other to go into—really creepy. At night it was sort of pretty, though; the light made all the leaves look, mm, like metal, you know? Like pieces of silver." I swallowed again.

"Why do the kids dare each other to go in?"

Wedging the phone under my ear, I went to the fridge and pulled out a bottle of water. "Because it's haunted."

"What? Why didn't we hear about this?"

"Well, why would it matter?" I asked.

"What do you mean?"

"People get the seizures anywhere—in their own homes, usually. It's not like they went to Thump House first."

There was a pause. "So you know for a fact that your sister never went to Thump House?"

That irritated me. "I know my own sister, yeah."

"Sorry, I didn't mean—"

"It's O.K.," I continued, "but I know that some people catch the wind, and never get seizures, and some get both, and some go and get neither, so there's nothing to hook them up together, right?"

Cora was silent. I could hear paper or something rattling around on her end of the line.

"O.K., tell me the rest," she said.

I was only in the second grade; I'd been stamping through the dirt all day and I was tired. All I could see were the leaves, the branches of trees nearby, and the doorway. There wasn't any door, and it was dark inside, so I couldn't see anything from where I was standing—it was just darkness. A hole. I'd heard a little bit about Thump

House—people see ghosts there—but I also knew that the older kids would screw around and smoke weed there sometimes. If the older kids could handle it, I thought I could, so I went in.

And, you know, I was a huge fan of ghosts, back then. I loved Halloween. I thought maybe that I could reason with a ghost if I came across one.

So I went inside. I stopped just inside the doorway to wait for my eyes to adjust, it was so dark. And first all I could see were these walls, covered with markings. A lot of the markings were graffiti—the usual boring crap kids think up. The walls were old, and cracking, too. Pieces of them had crumbled over the years.

But as my eyes kept adjusting, I kept seeing more things. Words and symbols I didn't know, that made me squint and gave me a headache when I tried to look at them for too long. And a couple times—it might have been a trick of my eyes, but it *seemed* like some of the lines might be moving.

I was starting to get really creeped out; you know that feeling? When your eyes feel like they're getting larger and larger but there's nothing they can see to stop that awful prickle in your neck and arms, and you're just waiting for something, but you don't know what, and in that long moment everything gets really quiet even though you're screaming inside. That's what it felt like. And I was having trouble breathing, but I took another step inside, then another.

There was nobody there.

I sat down, against a wall that had the least amount of scribbles on it, and I was holding my knees just sort of rocking myself, trying to feel brave. So I decided to sing a little. I don't remember what I was singing—something I'd heard on the radio, I think. But it was sad, this lone little girl's voice in this strange, dark place, and I stopped after a bit.

I turned my head to the right—just naturally, like a reflex—and inches away from me there was this woman, crouched down on the

floor, staring at me. My whole body just, whoosh—electric! All my
muscles twitched at once, and I was screaming, but in the middle of
screaming I suddenly couldn't hear my own voice.

Because everything was replaced with the... wind.

I don't know if you can understand how terrifying this was—it's
just this, loud, screaming awful thing—it drowns out everything. The
woman was gone, but the sound was stuck in my head. And I ran,
right out of Thump House, into the woods. I tore up my jeans that
day; Mom was really angry about that. But I couldn't hear her yell at
me, or anything, I was just grabbing my head, banging it sometimes
against walls, trying to do anything to get that awful noise out of me.
I think she called a doctor or something. I had to have shots to put
me to sleep, and in the day they had to tie me down so I wouldn't tear
at my ears or bang my head. That lasted for three days. Then, just as
suddenly, in the middle of the third day, it stopped.

It turned out that Cora was making a documentary—she called
it a "personal project"—about haunted houses. She'd shot over 6,000
hours of footage so far, but she'd been hoping to find more "obscure"
haunts. Thump House was everything she was looking for, and she
had enough money set aside to travel to Woodward for a while. She
wanted my help, but I started to get angry.

"Look," I said finally, "I appreciate that you want to make this
movie, or whatever, but I'm trying to figure out what's going on with
my sister."

"Mari," Cora replied, "there's a lot of strange stuff going on in
your town, don't you think it might be connected?"

She had a point, but it still seemed awfully thin to me.

Cora said she'd be there on Monday.

I asked Mom if I could use her laptop. She'd been on the phone all morning, and looked like hell. She stared at me for a few minutes before she nodded. I pulled the ancient grey monster out of her messenger bag. Mom would have to go back to work tomorrow—she couldn't afford to take any time off. Her job at the paper mill involved a desk, but it wasn't cushy, and it didn't pay well. I could only imagine what it was like for her—clocking in at a place that might have turned her daughter into a permanent vegetable. I made a fist and punched the back of the couch, out of Mom's sight. She probably heard the springs squeak, though.

Cora had come through and emailed me her production notes. They were all written out in her handwriting, which was luckily tidy and easy to read. I started poring over the notes, looking for anything that might be useful.

I saw written down: Woodward Paper Mill, 1930. Next to it was: First recorded seizures ~~1850???~~ ~~Millicent Henforth~~ 1933 Roger Carter. I hit the print screen button.

A lot of the notes were pretty straightforward—stuff I'd heard about or seen before. Names that were vaguely familiar. Then there was a list with a huge "X" through it. Cora had written:

Burned-Over District
Spiritualists
table thumpers
late 1830s (?)

I print screened that part, too.

The rest of the notes didn't seem too promising. I hit the print screen button on a couple more pages, then went to hunt down the image files I'd made. I renamed and saved them on a cheap flash drive I had for school. Then I started inputting words in a search engine. First up, "Woodward Paper Mill 1930." A few clicks later revealed that 1930 was indeed the date when the Woodward Paper Mill finished construction and opened for business. Then I typed in "1850 Millicent Henforth".

The first link to pop up was typed all in caps: MILLICENT HENFORTH, AMERICAN SPIRITUALIST. I clicked on it.

There was a black and white picture of a very unhappy-looking woman in a stern black dress. She looked uncomfortable, and her eyes had the sort of long stare that makes you start walking faster, especially at night; but they were not the eyes of the woman I'd seen in Thump House. There was an article, and I read it after faithfully print screening it and adding it to my collection.

Millicent Henforth (1802-1853) is one of the lesser-known Spiritualists of the American Spiritualist movement. Professing that the living can communicate with the spirits of the deceased, Millicent became a compelling force within the Woodward community, and held many "table thumping" séances, similar to those performed by the notorious Fox sisters.

Unlike the Fox sisters, her table thumping sessions were never discredited or revealed as hoaxes, though this may in part be due to the fact that she became afflicted with debilitating seizures that ended her career. Within three years of contracting these seizures, Miss Henforth passed away, likely due to the extreme stress on her health.

Millicent Henforth is best known for organizing the creation and construction of the Astral Palace, known colloquially as "Thump House" by Woodward residents. Claiming that the idea came to her in a dream, Miss Henforth commissioned several artisans and construction workers to build a place "perfectly attuned to the preferences and predilections of spirits." Five years of construction resulted in "a marvel of artistic weirdness" that is preserved today only by one daguerreotype, taken hours before Thump House caught fire and burned to the ground.

Then there was the picture.

It was a strange, crawly thing to look at. Thump House looked more like a sculpture than a building, mounded into weird plaster blobs and towering horns. It was covered with symbols and text that wrapped around every curve and orifice of the thing, like tattoos on skin.

The rest of the article didn't have much to provide—apparently nobody found out who, if anybody, set fire to Thump House. I spent more of my time chasing terms down the search engine rabbit hole, then pushed the whole thing aside. I was hungry. I made myself a sandwich, and then went out and took the bus to the hospital.

Cora Park had traded her pink hair for a rainbow array. I liked it, and told her so.

"Thanks!" she laughed. "I'm lucky my last boss thought so, too."

I hadn't had my hair done in a while—it was just long and shapeless—now I thought about maybe saving up some money for it.

Cora opened her arms up for a hug, so I hugged her. It was a little awkward, but nice.

"How's your sister doing?" she asked.

"Not good," I said. "The same. The doctors are ruling out epilepsy."

"Shit. I'm so sorry." Cora squeezed me again. "I really hope she pulls through."

"People in Woodward don't 'pull through,'" I said, stepping back.

"Sorry," she repeated.

I looked at the ground. Cora was wearing black boots with tiny hot pink stars all over them.

"You know, I appreciate your help, but aren't you supposed to be in school?"

"I'm taking the week off," I said. Mom would be angry when she found out, but I could handle that later.

She nodded. "So, I need to talk to your mom first—"

"If we bring Mom into this, we're done," I said.

"I'm going to have to get her permission—"

I turned around and started walking away.

"Hey!" I paused; Cora sounded mad. I turned to look at her, and I was right—she was pissed. "If you want to find out what's happening to your sister, you need to work with me, Mari."

There was something to what she said. "We'll involve Mom when we need to. Not right now. I don't need her telling me not to do this," I replied.

She tapped the corner of a notebook she was holding with a long fingernail, thinking, then said, "As long as you promise me that we will talk to her, and soon."

"I promise," I said, annoyed. I sounded like a little kid.

We were walking to Thump House. Cora had a messenger bag with her, and pulled out her phone from a side pocket, asking me if it was O.K. to record our conversation. I said "sure," and we started talking. Old leaves from last fall sloshed under our feet. The light was grey, but reassuringly bright. I had an old, ratty sweater on to cut the chill.

"Why did you cross that part out, about Millicent Henforth?" I asked after a while. I showed her the image I was talking about, which I'd printed out at the library along with the others and stuffed into my pocket in a fat, quartered paper square.

"Oh, that—the director said that her seizures didn't count, because a doctor who treated her at the time said that they were 'likely epilepsy.' It just confused things too much, so we cut her out."

"Was she the only case of seizures you found that happened before the paper mill was built?" I wondered.

"There were a couple more cases, but they were similar—more 'maybes' instead of 'definites'—so they didn't work for the director back then. But let's include these cases, for our purposes. I have more notes on them saved on my laptop. So what does that change, having three more seizure cases between 1850 and 1930?"

"It means that the paper mill probably isn't the cause," I said.

"Right." She nodded. "In that article you sent me, it didn't mention when Thump House was constructed, so I looked it up. It was built, and destroyed, in 1849."

I thought about that. "Well, it's before the seizures started."

"Right. O.K., so we have a building made, and destroyed, in 1849. And seizures start happening a year later. And 'catching the wind in your ear' isn't recorded until even later—I think the early 1940s. But let's put that fact aside for one second. Did you know that there's nothing online about ghost sightings at Thump House?"

"I know." I frowned. "I checked too. But people around here have been seeing them for forever."

"How long's 'forever'?"

"Uhhh—" I stalled, thinking. More leaves broke beneath my feet. "I heard that Jeremy Aldo's great-grandfather saw one—his grandpa's maybe in his nineties now?"

She laughed. "You're going to make me bust out a calculator now, huh?"

"Hey, I'm failing math," I said.

"Really?" Cora asked, glancing at me. "You seem like a smart cookie."

"I read a lot."

"Hmm, I never got to ask you—big question time! What do you think you want to do eventually?"

"Leave Woodward."

"Ha-ha." She spoke the syllables out loud. "You know what I mean. It's O.K. if there isn't anything, too."

"I'm serious," I said. "I know it sounds like a joke, but I mean it. I hate it here. It's a small town, and some people are nice, but most people aren't. My mom gets hit on by creepy white guys all the time, and it happens to me, too, if I don't do anything about it."

"How do you 'do anything about it'?" she asked; I snuck a glance at her, and she seemed genuinely interested.

I mangled a smile. "I wear shitty clothes and get into fights with everybody all the time. If I'm a crazy troublemaker, I'm sort of untouchable, you know?"

She was quiet for so long that I looked up at her. Her eyes were a little too shiny. She suddenly pounced on me with another one of her embarrassing hugs.

"Why were you running away that day?"

Cora asked this after we'd been walking for a while, her voice quiet.

I grimaced. "Because I like girls, and the other kids were giving me a shit time about it."

"I'm so sorry, Mari. I promise things will get better."

"I know. Because I'm leaving Woodward."

We went quiet again for a bit. I was mad at myself; I always made things awkward. But when I looked up at Cora she smiled at me, and I felt a little better.

"I'm going to say one thing, Mari, and then I'm going to lay off you, but the harder you study, the farther away you can go. Something to think about."

As lectures go, it wasn't the worst that I'd heard. "Then I'll think about it."

She smiled again; she smiled more than anyone else in Woodward. I wondered if it was a Los Angeles thing. After a while, her smile faded.

"Mari, there's something you need to hear. I wasn't going to tell you this, because it'll screw the hell out of my documentary, but I think it might be important. And I'm not so great at objectivity in my work, anyway. I was digging around, and I found this quote about Thump House—it's the only one I could find that's exactly like it."

Cora read aloud from the screen of her cell phone. "Mary Trench, a self-proclaimed medium and vocal critic of Millicent Henforth, later claimed that Miss Henforth had built a 'psychic fly trap.'"

"What does that mean?" I asked.

"It doesn't say." She turned the screen of the phone toward me so that I could see it.

"So—" I mulled it over. "Do you think that Thump House somehow catches ghosts?"

"I think that Millicent wanted to make a place that attracted ghosts, but no, I don't think Thump House catches them."

"Why not?" I was curious.

"Because it doesn't explain the seizures, or catching the wind."

"The sound could be from ghosts," I ventured, my skin prickling a little.

"Maybe, but why the seizures? It didn't fit for me. So I looked up Mary Trench. She wasn't even alive when Millicent Henforth was— Mary was big in the sixties. Do you know what she was famous for writing about?"

"Nope."

"Astral projection."

I stopped walking. Cora walked forward a few more steps then stopped, looking at me. "What?"

I nodded with my chin. "We're here."

We both stared at the dark doorway, surrounded by branches and leaves and tall, wispy grass. The leaves held the grey light so that even now, they looked almost metallic. It was quiet. My legs were sore. I hadn't walked this far in a long time. I didn't want to go inside. I stared at the doorway while Cora softly explained astral projection to me.

"Have you ever had a dream where you're flying, but it feels hyper-realistic? Like you might really be leaving your body and flying around? Some people believe that your soul, or your 'astral body,' is actually leaving your physical body and traveling."

I was staring at the doorway. The shadows hid most of the words and symbols scrawled inside, but there were pits and marks on the edges of the plaster, peeking through the silvery leaves.

"Addy," I said suddenly, and my voice rasped on my sister's name, "she had dreams like that sometimes. She told me about them."

Cora spoke excitedly. "So what if this place traps astral projections instead of ghosts? And what if the 'ghosts' that people see are actually astral projections?"

My mouth felt very dry. "My sister's in there?"

Cora shook her head. "I don't know—this is just a theory, Mari."

I thought about my sister trapped in that dark place, her sunshine caught in those weird plaster walls, and I shoved my fear aside and started walking up to the doorway.

"Wait! Mari!" Cora was stumbling after me.

At the doorway, I stopped and let her catch up.

A strange coldness waited there, in the air. Already my arms and neck were prickling. I stared at the darkness, willing my eyes to adjust. But then Cora took out a flashlight from her bag and began moving the artificial circle of light across the walls inside. We slowly walked forward together. The circle revealed more symbols, more words. Pinned beneath the light, none of the marks moved, not one inch. It was when the light moved on, and your eyes were still dazzled, that the markings seemed alive.

"Addy?" I called out, feeling stupid.

Nothing but our own breathing, our own footsteps.

We pushed farther in. The space grew narrow, as if we were in a hallway, but there were no other doors or doorways to enter, just one long, snakish path. The markings on the wall grew larger in size. They were suggestive of a lot of things, but too abstract to pin down. Occasionally Cora stopped to take still images of the walls, in addition to the video she recorded on her phone. We walked for half an hour more, then the hallway ended. A pile of dirt and rocks and tree roots blocked our way. Worms and white insects winced away from the flashlight.

"Addy?" I called out again; nothing.

"Let's head back to the entrance and eat something," Cora suggested. We turned around and headed back. Sometimes I called out my sister's name when I thought I heard something, but mostly I didn't.

We ate lunch a few yards away from the entrance of Thump House. Cora had picked up some junk at a gas station on the way into town, and we ate cold sandwiches and drank lukewarm sodas. Cora had bought a small salad for herself that she was having second thoughts about. I had one bite of the sandwich and set it aside; I couldn't eat much.

She was trying to distract me. Cora talked about other haunted houses she'd documented in the past. Places with creaking stairs and cold spots and levitating glassware. I asked if she'd ever seen a ghost. She shook her head.

"No, but when I was about three years old, there was a window in my house that would always open up on its own when it was shut. My dad said that it was just bad carpentry, but my mom said it was a Gwisin—a spirit with unfinished business—and would leave little offerings out."

"So what happened?" I asked. I was barely paying attention to her.

"Either the Gwisin finished its business, or liked my mom's cooking, or the carpentry fixed itself; the window stopped opening when I left for college."

"Maybe it was trying to get your attention, and gave up after that," I said.

She shrugged. "Maybe."

I went quiet again. I thought about the cold, long hallway we'd just wandered down, and those plaster walls inside Thump House, covered with lines. Lines like the bars of a prison; my sister stuck behind them. My "best friend" didn't cover it; Addy was the only friend I'd ever had.

I was facing the entrance of Thump House, staring at the darkness, when I thought I saw a flicker of movement in the shadows. I sat up straight, my eyes wide.

"Did you see that?"

Cora looked at me. "No. What did you see?"

"Something," I said. I stared at the darkness, waiting. "Addy?" I called out.

More nothing—just the entrance surrounded by leaves. Even though I couldn't see anything, I could suddenly feel that electric strangeness flooding me, making my heart flutter and my skin crawl. My eyes grew wider, and I stared down the hole, every inch of me just looking, waiting.

I saw it again—a dim movement, a flicker of light.

"Addy!" I shouted again.

I glanced down at the remains of our lunch. There were black plastic utensils there, a knife unused, still on a paper napkin.

I grabbed the knife and ran inside Thump House. Cora was calling my name, but her voice sounded far away.

I was in the dark, running. I stumbled over rocks and roots and filth that oozed beneath my feet as I crushed it. I called out my sister's name, my hands against the walls so that I wouldn't fall. My left hand hurt with a sudden, sharp pain—I had brushed against something that cut me—I could feel my own blood greasing my fingers.

I looked toward my hand in the dark out of habit, not expecting to see anything, when I saw a pale hand on top of my own.

I screamed. The hand covering mine was small, clearly touching me, but I felt nothing. As soon as I screamed, the hand vanished, pitching everything into darkness again. Behind my eyes, I could still see it; small fingernails, creases along the knuckles. Had it been Addy's hand?

I could hear Cora calling me from a long way off. I decided it was Addy's hand, and kept my bloody palm pressed against the wall, then brought my plastic knife up. I was going to break those bars; I was going to set her free if I had to tear every damn wall down to do it.

I slammed the plastic knife into the wall, just where my fingers were, and that's when I caught the wind in my ear again.

My guts winced, my limbs shook, but still I plunged the plastic knife into the old plaster, gouging out the marks, smearing my blood into the awful damp muck that I couldn't see. The sound was inside me again, shutting out all sounds, vibrating in my bones and blood. I couldn't hear Cora anymore. I kept stabbing and scraping at the walls. The plastic knife shattered, but I kept going with the handle.

When Cora eventually caught up to me, I could see more of the wall, and dragged the handle through the markings that I'd missed. The handle fell. I kept going, digging my fingers into the disgusting plaster, tearing out everything I touched. I could feel Cora's hands on my wrists, sense her trying to pull me away, but I kept kicking and stabbing at the walls for as long as I could, my blood crusting over part of Cora's rainbow.

The wind hasn't left me.

I hear it constantly—screaming, wailing, pushing me down. It's stuck there, inside me.

But I got to see Addy wake up. I was at the hospital, a few rooms down, and I left my room one night to go see her. I was sitting by her bed when her eyes opened, and she looked at me, and held my hand and cried.

She doesn't talk anymore. That's what I understand, anyway. People write things out for me. That's O.K.—Addy knows who I am. Most days she just likes to sit next to me, holding my hand.

Cora let me know that a lot of people have woken up from their seizures. All of them are quiet now; nobody says a thing. The doctors say it's a form of shock.

I think I have all their screams trapped inside me.

MARI GUERRERO has relocated from Woodward to an undisclosed location in northern California, along with her mother and sister. The Guerrero siblings are currently receiving care for the trauma that they sustained while living in Woodward. She is featured in the 2015 documentary *Another America* by Cora Park.

M. LOPES DA SILVA is an artist and author from Los Angeles who has crafted comics, illos, and articles for *Blumhouse, The California Literary Review, Queen Mob's Teahouse,* and *FEM Magazine.* Her short story "The Carving" was published in *Threads: A Neoverse Anthology.* Her work frequently explores themes of obsession and anatomy, and boldly celebrates the fantastic and strange. You can read her collection of eerie short stories, *The Dog Next Door and Other Disturbances,* as an ebook on Amazon.

stand not between
A CAT AND HIS PREY

An account by Ankhu,
AS PROVIDED BY CHRISTINE LUCAS

One of these days, I swear I'll write down an account of all the weird places my cat has run off to.

I envy the scribe you'll employ for such a task, Lord Embalmer Ankhu, comes the answer. It's delivered in a deep, masculine voice with growls lingering beneath the finely articulated words. *Or should I pity them, for all the horrors you'll introduce into their dreams for every night thereafter?*

Trust Nedjem, my soft-pawed rascal, to lead me to a place where the gods' voices reach mortal ears so effortlessly—so *shamelessly*.

"My Lord Anubis," I say between gasps. "Thank you so very much for your support."

Rest. I need rest. I've walked too far under this heat, and my old bones insist I should find a nice shadow by the Nile to catch my breath. There. These palm trees seem secluded enough. The frogs and the crickets can gossip all they want. They won't laugh at the old man trudging through the banks of the Nile to find a wayward cat. They won't mock his stained linen and disheveled appearance, the old robe more befitting a farmer than the High Priest of Anubis. They know. They were there—they, or their kin, forefathers and foremothers—when I fished my first cat—my first Nedjem—lifeless from the river many years ago. By all the gods of mourning, never such a day will dawn again. Not if I can help it.

Then you should have chosen a more obedient cat, Ankhu.

"My Lord Anubis, *he-who-is-upon-his-mountain*, is that our Lady Bast who snickers in my ear? When did obedience creep into feline hearts? Has Apophis, the Great Serpent of Chaos conquered the Cosmos and had everything spun on their heads? Will Ra's Solar Barge sail from west to east from now on?"

A growl answers my insolence. But mirth lingers beneath it. There's indeed snickering at the edge of my consciousness. That is never good. But, for now, those damned horseflies have found my skin a suitable breeding ground. A palm leaf shoos them away, at least for a while, before they start to sting.

Another set of wings flits by my head. No buzzing with its passing, only a chilled path against my cheek. The fingers of someone—or something—dead.

Come here, child. My eyes half-close as I tilt my head sideways to see. Not my first time to use the Sight to catch a glimpse of the Unseen, and certainly not the last. And every time my heart flutters, resisting the glimpse of what's not meant for mortal eyes.

There. Not a man's essence, but a bird's. A pigeon's. It flits above the tree line, still confused. It doesn't understand why the heat no longer bothers it, why it feels no thirst or hunger, no need to go peck on grain and crumbs. It doesn't even know why it feels like there's a hole in its gut, its entrails missing.

A chuckle at the edge of my hearing. "Thank you, my Lord Anubis, for this unique connection with my cat's supper." It has to be Nedjem's supper, otherwise the connection wouldn't be as strong. *Where?* The question scares the spirit, and its flight becomes frantic. *Where*, I repeat as softly as possible—but how to comfort my cat's latest in a long line of feathered victims?

The flight regains a steady, even carefree glide, and the ghostly bird turns in mid-air and heads north. It flies lower over the treetops now, until it approaches a clearing. There's a feel of terror tingling each and every feather. It nears the place of its death. Before its terror shatters our link, I catch a glimpse of a structure between the trees. No, not a building—a big boulder, in the center of a barren circle of yellow star-sand.

My head burns, my wits thrown back into my own body, the sudden pull of gravity shoving the air out of my chest. Of course Nedjem would go there. Couldn't he have gone south? There's a similar stone, roughly resembling a statue, south of Thebes. A stone foreign to these parts. Star-stone, the old folk say, carved into Sekhmet's liking when time was still young, all likeness now gnawed away by relentless winds. A shrine to the lion goddess, some folks still say. And it even has a priestess and a colony of cats—Nedjem's kin, may Bast bless his fruitful loins.

I know better. That ancient statue, be it of Sekhmet or gods-know-what, is not a shrine. It's a watchtower, and the priestess its guard against Egypt's foes from every realm in the Unseen. But this other statue? I have never seen or heard about it.

Where are you leading me this time, Nedjem?

My gut rumbles as I'm nearing the statue of my vision—I've already missed my lunch, my wine, and my honeyed dates. The figs I plucked on my way here are stiff and bitter, and my water skin is almost empty. The slow waters of the Nile taunt my thirst. But Sobek's children may be sunning their hides in the shallows. I'd rather not be crocodile supper today. Or ever.

With every step now the foliage thins, the trees around me yellowish and sickly. The crickets and the frogs have fallen silent; even the ever-swarming horseflies keep their distance. Now I tread on dried brown leaves as the rich mud gives way to brittle soil. In turn this becomes star-sand: sand scorched by star-fire, by heat so great it turned it to glass. How have the locals not looted this spot already? This yellow and cream-colored glass is greatly favored amongst Thebes' jewelers and can bring a hefty price. Such stones have adorned regalia and pharaonic funerary masks.

What do the locals know, that they leave this place alone?

So today is the day that the Lord Embalmer of Thebes will prove himself reckless and less prudent than illiterate farmers.

One more day in a long line of such days, comes the mocking growl inside my head, as I set foot into the clearing.

"My gratitude, my Lord Scale-Holder Anubis, for your confidence in your servant. May I be so bold to inquire if you have anything useful to add? As in what's this place, and where my rascal of a cat ran off to—*this* time?"

There's your cat. Why don't you ask him?

And indeed he is. I can see his hind legs, his upper body hidden behind the statue that at this distance resembles more Ptah, the Creator God, than Sekhmet. Nedjem growls.

I tiptoe closer, but my steps are not as noiseless as I'd like with the crunch of thick, glassy sand beneath my feet. The shards prick the soles of my sandals—my new sandals of fine leather that bear no mark yet of Nedjem's teeth. The cat bristles and jumps up, his eyes dark and unblinking. He's gawking at me as though he doesn't know me. Worse yet as if I'm an intruder, like he eyes the cook when he catches him with his paw in the barrel of salted fish.

My guts take a dive to my feet. What has happened to my cat?

Has some evil spirit possessed him and turned him against family and kin? Has—

All dark thoughts dissolve in the slow breeze that now carries Nedjem's purr. He greets me with little trills of mewing that warm my heart, but he won't come. Now he growls again. No, not at me, at something hidden behind the statue. I circle around the base of the large stone to the bloodied thing marring the golden sparkle of the star-sand. That poor pigeon wasn't Nedjem's only prey today.

But what is that thing? A malformed crab that crawled out of the shallows of the Nile? No, its carapace is too dark, like coagulated blood, too thick and probably shelters wings. Can it be a monstrous scarab, out of some sinkhole leading to the Underworld? But scarabs have no teeth gleaming ivory and sharp. It doesn't appear to be any of Duat's creatures—not that I've seen them all or measured their shadows. But I have seen evil magic before, the merging of different beasts to mock the handiwork of the gods. One step closer, and I inhale brimstone and fire and I hear the rumbling of distant thunder even beneath Ra's merciless midday light.

Whatever the gutted thing is, it is not of Egypt. And neither is that other beast, a few paces away from the corpse: a six-legged creature, slightly bigger than my cat, with leathery scales instead of fur. It too tries to pry the kill away, and does so with a massive beak that could easily snap a man's backbone. A bird's head, folded leathery wings, six legs—*what* is that beast?

Trust Nedjem to try and steal an otherworldy monster's kill.

Thank you, my Lady Bast, for this cat, this prank—I mean, this *gift* that keeps on giving.

Silence at the edge of my hearing, but I'm sure there's divine snickering somewhere above my consciousness. Because if there's not, if the gods themselves keep their silence and their distance, I might have crossed a border I shouldn't have.

It's Nedjem's fault. *Again.*

"Nedjem!" I snap my fingers. "Leave that disgusting thing alone and let's go home!"

Nedjem glances at me—a shocked, indignant glance at my snapping of fingers in the presence of a rival. Of course he doesn't move. He turns his amber eyes back to his beaked opponent and its two clawed forepaws now claiming the kill. He growls again—a half-hearted growl, but the beast replies with a screech that makes the back of my neck burst with goosebumps. That awful sound drills into my head. If I hadn't had every hair on my body removed like any self-respecting priest, I'd be as bristled as my cat.

"Nedjem!"

Now there's a tentative pace backward, as if acknowledging defeat. But he still won't come. The rascal expects me to move in, scoop him up and carry him away, so it will be my fault he forfeits the prey. *Again.* My shoulders slump.

When I first donned the priestly garb, so many decades ago, I assumed the title of *hem-nedjer*: servant to the gods. I've faced many a foe, evil spirits and entities from elsewhere, I even stood against Apophis, the Serpent God of Chaos himself. But, my Lady Bast, no scribe has ever listed in a High Priest's duties carrying pet cats away from the presence of monsters.

But perhaps that's a duty that comes with being human. So I move in. One step closer, and my gut misses my lotus-scented cloth. I hold my breath at the creature's stench, so I won't expel those pitiful figs I had on my way here. Another step closer and my rascal retreats again, slightly arching his back so I can pick him up. One more step under the yellow eyes of the beaked monster, and the air behind it ripples. A gateway.

My Lord Creator Ptah, when you dreamed this world into being, did you dream it hole-ridden, like the sponges from the sea up north?

No answer, and I suspect I'll soon pay for my insolence. But now bigger problems gather ahead. Images float behind air thick as a waterfall. A memory of a dream forgotten at dawn pricks my heart, and it oozes yearning. Once, at another time and place, chasing after the same cat stealing from another monster, I caught glimpse of a quaint little town somewhere beyond. A cat-riddled town, set on a pocket of time and space between sleep and waking, its cobblestone streets made of the dreams of a thousand cats. But no, it's not that Ulthar-place that appears beyond the waterfall of star-sand and breeze.

Another desert stretches beyond, not golden like the sands around the Nile, but crimson and purple and black. A mountain taller than the pyramids spews ash in the distance—far in the distance, I hope, for the ripples in the air make it hard to estimate. Strange trees grow just behind the portal, trees uncomfortably similar to oversized mushrooms. They cast shadows on shrubs with too many thorns and—Anubis help me—little mouths? A shadow approaches, a shadow in the shape of a man, roughly two heads shorter than myself, and much thinner. Yellow, lidless eyes like the beaked creature's eyes shine upon a grey, oval-shaped head, over a non-existent nose and too thin lips. It—he?—wears an ankle-length grey robe and holds a staff—a walking stick? Or a weapon?

"Nedjem." Not a request. "Come. *Now.*"

In the same heartbeat the words leave my throat and Nedjem scuttles behind my ankles to perceived safety, the voice of that grey individual echoes clear and feminine in my head. Her lips never move.

Nibbler? There you are. Come here this instant!

A moment of awkward silence, of measuring each other from head to toe, then a long sigh of understanding.

Nedjem, comes her voice, softer—even playful now. *You named your rascal "Sweet One?"*

So she knows my tongue. And she speaks in thoughts. There's a moment of ambivalence, between possible threat and camaraderie. Then I shrug. I have traveled too many hidden roads and met too many unique sentient creatures to let such a detail unsettle me.

"He can be sweet. Occasionally. When he's well-fed." I smirk. "And, 'Nibbler'? With that beak? What does he nibble on?"

Wyrms, comes the reply. *Wyrm-lice, to be specific.*

"Wyrms?" No. I've definitely not met those.

The thought has barely formed in my mind when she shows me those wyrms. Serpentine bodies, great leathery wings that can span the width of the Nile, and crocodile-sharp teeth that even Sobek himself would envy. The image comes void of any emotion, any alignment. I cannot tell if those creatures side with Order or Chaos. Perhaps they're both. Perhaps they're neither. Perhaps such finite concepts, like Order and Chaos, do not exist in this world beyond.

The image shifts and one of those wyrms flies closer, so close that I can number the scales on its underbelly—and its lice. Little disgusting pests, they look like a cross between scorpions and centipedes, and the size of goats. An eager chirp from Nibbler—so those are her favorite catch. Perhaps they're juicy and ripe beneath that black carapace—

Anubis help me, what am I thinking?

I blink to restore my vision to my here and now. Once my eyes regain their focus, they center on Nedjem—wide-eyed, perked-eared, whiskers-licking Nedjem.

"No. I'm not getting you one of those. And no, you can't catch one yourself. Unless you grow wings and a beak like Nibbler, I don't see how you can."

If he wants—

"No," I cut her off. "Don't give him any ideas. Please," I add in a softer tone.

She smiles, a smile of still lips and lidless eyes, but she smiles all the same, with little creases all over the grey face. A true smile, more honest than the grimaces that noblemen and court officials have flashed at me in the past. Now she nods, and waves with her three-fingered hand to her own beaked embodiment of mischief.

Come. Time to go home.

Where is home, I want to ask. Can I come too, to study the wonders and the wyrms of your land? But I keep the voice inside my throat, the burden of my office heavy on my wandering heart.

Nibbler squeaks her protest but makes her way toward the portal. Her middle leg grapples the corpse on her way and drags it along.

No! Leave that where you found it!

I blink. "She didn't find it here. Nothing like that lives along the Nile."

I'd know. Nedjem would have brought me one already. I'd have buried its half-eaten corpse alongside the birds and frogs and mice, and everything else he's brought me, in the great tomb of feline slaughter that has become my back yard.

She glances back at me.

It's not from here either.

Now does dread creep up my toes, up my calves, and worms its way into my spine. Where did that thing come from? Was it brought here? Or sent?

I shift my weight to calm the tremor of my legs—no, it's not my legs that tremble, but the ground beneath. Something is coming. We lingered too long.

Or, perhaps, we lingered enough. To stop it.

The clearing around me shifts in a whirlwind of once and now and tomorrow and elsewhere and neverwhere and beyond, in a quake of space and time. We now stand not in a clearing alongside the Nile, but in a tunnel. The boulder and the trees are still around, their roots and branches caught in between and betwixt. This strip of land by the Nile is now part of a long, grand corridor between the realms, with sturdy but translucent doors every ten paces. It resembles the pathway of the dead too much for comfort, the pathway the dead must tread to reach the Hall of Judgment. Only the doors alongside that path have guardians—*Neba, Set-qesu, Uamenti, Neheb-ka,* and so many others—demons with wings and fangs and the heads of lions and hawks and creatures of the hidden realms. No guardians here, but this Grey Lady and myself. A hiss by my feet completes the picture with two more guardians: Nedjem and Nibbler.

Will we be enough?

A portal within a portal bursts open, and other creatures like the slain one swarm through, a horde of malformed scarabs scurrying along impossible angles to squeeze through. Nibbler squeaks and charges. Her beak tears though carapace and flesh, gutting monster after monster.

Nedjem's gaze darts from me to the advancing horde and right back to me, and there's a quiver in my heart. It's not like him to ask permission. Is he scared? Why? What does he know?

"Yes," I tell him, for this battle is greater than the both of us.

A low howl leaves his throat, a howl unlike his usual vocalisms. It's neither the ear-drilling yowl of mating nor the ever-pestering meowls for food. This one echoes on more levels than one and suddenly it's clear: a call to arms. Cats appear from everywhere: atop the branches, from under bushes, from the realms of dream and waking. Along with the cats of Egypt, their spectral kin have answered the calling: the dead, the lost, the unborn, the reborn, they await the walls of reality to fall and allow them in.

Nedjem doesn't wait. Alongside his wives and siblings and cousins and children, he charges at the creatures.

Far be it for the High Priest to remain idle while his cat fights. I speak the incantation and let the ghostly cats pass through, amongst the living, and join the fight.

How valiant, comes the mocking voice inside my head. *Call upon the Royal Scribe and have your title changed to Herder of Felines Past and Present, Oh Lord Embalmer Ankhu.*

What a surprise.

"How kind of you, my Lord Anubis, to offer your counsel at this perilous hour. Where in Sobek's scaly ass have you been till now? Do you, perchance, have something actually helpful to add?"

My child, do not speak ill of my crocodile brother's posterior, for a comely posterior it is.

"I will atone later, oh Lord." I kick a bloodied creature away, and something snaps: my new, expensive sandal, along with the creature's neck. A group of cats jumps on it, feasting as if Egypt's mice and pigeons have been extinct for months. "But for now, could you please help?"

A long divine sigh at the edge of my hearing. *Fine.*

My body tingles as if touched by the Nile's lightning eels. The power starts caged in my chest, building up with every heartbeat, as if my old heart pumps out divine grace mingled with blood. Rarely have I called upon the aid of the gods, for they are fickle with their grace. But this torrent of unspeakable creatures swarming upon Egypt is unlike any other foe I have encountered. My incantations and spells can slingshot the dead, the undead, and everything in between back where they belong, but these? These are merely beasts, as far as I know, and those I've never learned to fight.

The tingling reaches my tongue and my fingertips, and I raise my arms. When I speak the words of warding, they echo the power of the Eternal.

"Get thee back, thou enemy of Ra! Thy head shall be cut off, and the slaughter of thee shall be carried out. Stand still, stand still, and retreat by this spell!"

Merciless light bursts out and blinds the horde. They screech, and their cries drill their way into my head. Many fall belly-up on the ground, convulsing, their guts exposed. No cat in Egypt will sleep hungry tonight. They'll curl up, their claws finally blunt and their whiskers bloodied, and they'll doze off licking their fur clean of gore.

Good.

At the other side of the veil, the Grey Lady holds her own. Her expression hasn't changed, her posture still dignified and composed, but she now holds her staff with both hands. She commands no army of Nibbler's kin, but her staff emits circles over circles over circles of bright light. Every circle is a sicklesword of power that cuts with effortless finesse. The bodies of countless slain creatures pile around her in neatly cut pieces that would shame the most skilled of butchers.

Ah, such dignity can put the High Priest himself to shame; I now stand in ruined sandals and stained linen, in the center of a ferocious bloodbath, with heads and limbs and entrails hoisted upon every branch to be eaten later.

Another incantation, another wave of creatures slain, and the invasion stops. Is it over?

You should know better than to ask such things, comes the reply.

"Thank you for another lesson in humility, my Lord Anubis." My voice comes out short-breathed and raspy. Every incantation scrapes my throat as if dragging hooks along my throat. I'm getting old, too old to hold back wave after wave of invaders. "I do not suppose you—"

The rumbling thunder beneath the veil drowns out all sound. Any words I meant to say slip from tongue and memory. Is this what an approaching cataclysm sounds like? Rarely have I heard thunder and seen lightning in all my years, but I have listened to travelers' tales of lands with never-lifting fog and month-long rainfall.

But neither rain nor fog nears the veil. A monstrous claw, bigger than a grown man, hooks at the edge of the portal.

The cats scatter, and now every bush and branch and cluster of trees has yellow, unblinking eyes watching the enemy at the gates. The Grey Lady's circles of light barely scrape the claw. I tilt my head sideways. And in the same breath, I wish I didn't.

No, you fool!

Anubis' bark comes too late. I have already seen the entity lurking behind the veil, struggling with fang and claw and horns to tear the gate open and squeeze through. No, it will not squeeze through.

It shall *march* through and trample down sphinxes and pyramids and hyposthele halls until only dust and ash remains, and the Nile runs black with poison. The fool that I am, I seek to know more. Where does this creature stand? Not with Order; it cannot be Order. But is it Chaos? Is it another of Apophis' minions?

The fierce roar knocks me back, and I lose all sight betwixt and between and beyond. I lie on bits of gore and blood-soaked star-sand, breathless and bereft of any grace. The vision of that creature that fancies itself a god and the realm that spawned him singe the caverns of my heart.

No Order. No Chaos. Only hunger for what it was once promised by long-dead disciples and long-silenced priests. For innumerable eons, it slouched through black silt and brittle soil in its desolate home, devouring starlight, spawning malformed spies to track down a crack in the veil between the worlds. Until one succeeded.

A rough lick on my cheek and an urgent half-growl, half-mew. *Nedjem.* I wet my cracked lips, but no voice leaves my parched throat. Another lick, then Nedjem bites my shoulder and bleeds me back to reality. I push myself up and, for a moment, I wish I hadn't. The entity has crossed the veil and stands in the narrow strip of netherland between Egypt and the Grey Lady's domain.

Words—no, even *thoughts* fail me at the sight of this monstrous being from beyond. Like a blind man trying to grasp the enormity of an elephant by touch alone, my wits fail to grasp... *that.* It's higher than the pyramids—no, it's taller that all the pyramids I've ever seen stacked on top of each other. It has wings and claws and horns and too many heads, too many mouths. Some mouths flash rows upon rows of ivory fangs, others pout with forked tongues lashing in and out. Great wings stretch out, casting a deadly shadow in more realms than one.

The timid hope that it will choose the Grey Lady's realm dares to peek its ugly head, but I push it out of my thoughts. No. The High Priest will not wish ill to allies against evil. And we need those allies.

We need more than her; if any fight requires divine intervention, this is it.

There's a distant murmur at the edge of my hearing now. Muffled deliberations I'm not privy to, divine councils I was not invited to—never mind that I am the one standing in gore against the enemy at the gates. Will they help?

Another image follows: the possibility of gods disinclined to get involved. Bast and Sekhmet are too busy purring and grooming each other's fur. Anubis chases his own tail, and Ra has gone fishing upon his Solar Barge. Isis makes another mold—a new, *bigger* mold for her husband Osiris' cut-off penis, and I don't have time for all of your excuses.

And still, divine silence. Is it fear? Or have they grown bored with this world and to Duat with it, let the entity devour it all?

But we humans—and their cats—are still here. What in Apophis' name can we do against that?

Please do not speak my name in vain, comes the hiss inside my head.

This sussuration is all too familiar; I have stood against the Great Serpent of Chaos before, but all the things he hissed at me were never as articulate. Curses and slurs and promises of eternal suffering as he takes his time digesting me, yes. But not such a calm, even—Anubis help me—*cultured* voice.

Your new friend across the worlds has called on reinforcements. Will you remain idle, Lord Embalmer Ankhu?

The Grey Lady! I look beyond the gateways, beyond the folds of monstrosity, and see my grey friend surrounded by winged beasts. Are those the wyrms of her world? They have to be, with their scales and wings and fire-breathing snouts. I count at least five, the biggest amongst them a red matriarch. It has to be a female; her lidless eyes glow with fierce protectiveness, reflecting the fierceness in Egypt's female cats twofold. The Grey Lady speaks in a low, guttural tongue:

wyrmtongue, its sound familiar but long forgotten, like a dream I should remember but do not.

And the wyrms charge at the God of Empty Worlds.

If only Egypt had a champion of similar stature—

I want to roll my eyes. Thankfully, I compose myself before I do, and pray to all the gods I know that I won't choke on the next words that leave my throat.

"My Lord Apophis, Oh Great Serpent of Chaos, will you, perchance, *get your scaly tail down here to help?*"

A spine-tingling sound, a cross between a hiss and a chuckle answers me.

And what will I get for my trouble, after my mutt of a brother awoke me to assist you?

I glance ahead, at the flock of wyrms pushing the fiend back, closer to Egypt. And I'm here, useless, negotiating with fickle gods. Damn and damn again.

"What could I possibly give you?"

Ma'at, comes the answer. *Harmony and Balance,* and there's no jest, no ridicule in the hiss, only a sliver of truth that slips through my fingers like Nile's water.

"If it falls within my power, I will."

Oh, it is. Now, call your mangy cats back so they will not slow my advance.

"Fine." I stifle the chuckle that would only infuriate him. He loathes cats, for Ra assumed the form of a great tomcat to slay him in the past. So I glance down at Nedjem by my feet. "Stay." I glance around, at the others, as if in any life I could stare down Bast's children. "Stay." Nedjem blinks.

I swear I hear Bast and Sekhmet and all their feline brethren snicker. But the cats do stay when the enormous serpent rises from the Nile.

A rainbow of scales, the smallest among them the size of a

soldier's great shield, shines as the serpentine body unfolds upward, higher than the Great Pyramid. And still the entity from beyond towers over him, a god that walks among distant stars. Rarely have Apophis' fangs gleamed in sunlight, for he enamors darkness and all the creatures that lurk in it. But not today. Today he rises from the sacred Nile, and a crown of light shines atop his head. No, it's not a crown: it is the *benu*-bird. The phoenix, Ra's own soul, its tail firestorm and its wingspan the crack of lightning. It has come to fight alongside his eternal adversary.

You cannot have this land, hisses Apophis. *It is mine to devour whenever I desire so.*

A cacophony of howls answers him, the dying screams of countless empty worlds. I cannot look up; the light of the *benu*-bird's tail blinds me. The wyrmfire threatens to singe my skin, and Apophis's forked tongue drips venom. But down here, far beneath the warring gods overhead, I spot what the many legs and tentacles of the abomination are scheming. They stretch the opening wider, crack by crack, cubit by cubit, to let hordes of malformed minions in.

I cry to the Grey Lady—can she hear me over the thunderous heavens above? Her face remains emotionless through the ash and smoke. Her grip is now white-knuckled around her staff. She hears. She nods. Can she manage? I do not know. But I must hold my end. *We* must hold our ends.

I clasp my hands on my chest and speak the ancient words to call forth an army to fight alongside the cats of Egypt.

"Lord of the Underworld, Gatekeeper of the Eternal Bars, now open quickly, Key-holder, Guardian, Anubis, and send up to me the spirits, send the dead forthwith for service in this late hour."

Word by word, the incantation tears away pieces of my own soul. Around me, a maelstrom of broken bones and dried sinew rises from the sands: the dead return to defend their homeland. Soldiers, farmers, fishermen, even thieves and murderers. They all come to my side, their bodies swirling sand and bleached fragments. And behold, the mugger stands abreast with the constable, and the laundress at the right of the noble and the merchant. They wield ancient blades and pickaxes and branches and rocks and the bones of those who couldn't gather enough substance to answer the call. Others line up behind me: the priests and priestesses from now to the dawn of time, when the Great Sphinx was but a kitten in the Creator God Ptah's bosom. My parched throat is grateful, for they will add their voices to my own when the horde crosses the threshold.

But… but what if they don't?

The thought hits me like the granite forepaw of the Great Sphinx.

Took you long enough, my child, comes the growl inside my head. A playful growl, and again the image of a puppy chasing his tail flashes in my thoughts. *Had you thought this earlier, Apophis would be still in slumber.*

"I don't remember any meaningful counsel from you, my Lord Anubis." I blink. I don't need puppy images in my head now. I need doors, and spells to shut them for good.

Is this so? Well, here's some insight: in all your years as hem-ned-jer, *have you never encountered a series of barred doors?*

My shoulders slump, and it requires effort to keep me from banging my head—my thick, *thick* head—against the ancient boulder that might be a statue. I knew that. How did it slip my mind? The road through Duat to the Hall of Judgment is lined with doors, each with its own guardian. Only two doors here, and each does have a guardian, one leading undead, the other commanding wyrms. And cats, Nedjem's rub against my calves reminds me. But all my studies, all the spells and incantations in my memory open those doors. Would shutting them be much different?

Nedjem mews. He wants to charge again, and I see another deity lingering behind those eyes. Bast has come to stand with her children. Good.

"No, boy. Enough bloodshed for one day," I tell him, and I swear he pouts. There's enough bloodshed in the heavens as it is. Apophis and the wyrms burn and cut and lash at an impossible foe who sprouts new tentacles from every torn limb, new fangs from every poisoned mouth. And down here, a hand falls heavy on my shoulder. Not just one hand, no, but many, the hands of my brethren. At this late hour, despair breeds clarity and I know. I know the words I need to speak, and may Thoth, the Scribe God, fly them upon his ibis wings to their target.

"*You shall not be! Your grasp shall not be! Your plan shall not come to fruition! Your power shall not be! You shall not approach Egypt!*"

My hieratic staff is back home, my regalia forsaken atop my bed. I kick off my ruined sandals and stained linen. Barefoot in my loincloth I shall cast this spell of spells—barefoot like the day I shall walk into the Hall of Judgment to have my deeds and days numbered. My throat strains, my voice comes out too weak, too little. I clench my fists and utter another line from the incantation from before time, when other gods warred in the heavens.

"*You shall die in the circle of foreign lands! You shall not penetrate to the two banks of the Nile!*"

And now my words do not fly alone. There's a soft murmur that lightens the granite of my voice: the magic of paw and fur. The cats, blessed be the little souls, have sat up. Like miniature statues of Bast herself, they employ their own secret tongue and speak the incantation with me. And I know that Bast herself chants with me.

"*Loathing of Ra, disgust of every great god!*"

One more line and others join me. The dead whisper alongside the cats, their voices the breeze over the Nile, and the buzz of mosquitoes and horseflies. But that breeze waxes to the west wind, and the buzz gives way to swarms of locusts. There's power now building up beneath my feet, and the statue beside me tremors. Across the veil, the Grey Lady adds her voice to my own, her lips moving for the first time since I met her. Not in whispers, not in cries, but all that and more: thoughts, hopes, fears, she delivers the spell in more ways than one. And when the wyrms add their ever-burning songs to the rest, Apophis recoils. He will not speak—this I know, for the same words have been used against him before. He casts a yellow glare at me, then breathes divine essence into the boulder that tremors.

A burst of ancient light explodes. The Cosmos gasps and all portals shut down. The backdraft kicks me like a herd of angry mules, and I fall hard on my back. The fall punches the air from my chest and I just lay there, breathless and bereft. Everyone's gone: the dead returned to their rest or torment, most of the cats have scattered.

No sign of the Grey Lady, her Nibbler, or the wyrms. My friend! My friend... I didn't say goodbye. Will I see them again? A hidden part of my heart believes I will. I hope it's right.

Silence. At last. I center heart and thoughts to a lone acacia leaf spiraling its way down onto my head. It's over. It has to be.

As I lay there under the hot sun, Nedjem climbs atop my chest and licks my face. Other cats follow his lead, and I find myself clad in purring fur. I close my eyes and breathe in this moment of stillness. Alas, this too is cut short when something bigger than the boulder hides the sunlight.

Taking a nap, Oh High Priest Ankhu?

Of course Apophis wouldn't leave me alone. The choir of feline growls holds the monstrous head back—or so I hope.

Control your pests, he hisses. *I come to claim my reward.*

I pop one eye open. I'm too tired for formalities and titles. "What do you want?"

Ma'at. Harmony and Balance.

"You've told me that already. Care to explain?"

An impatient snort of his nostrils, and a cloud of poisonous breath. I gag, but remain still. I doubt I could move anyway.

I fail to see why my mangy mutt of a brother favors you so. You are so... thick-headed. The next time he speaks, his words are slow, as if explaining the use of a spintop to a toddler. *There is a statue of the Lioness south of Thebes. There's another one here—of what or whom, this is hidden from me. I wish it to be mine. Order has its shrine already. Shouldn't Chaos have one as well?*

His words lift the fog from my mind. Can he be right? This arrangement could enhance balance and prohibit similar incidents in the future. So I nod.

"I swear on my seal ring that I shall do as you ask."

An indignant snort. *Swear not on trinkets blessed by my brethren! Instead*—his snarl grows wider—*swear on the life of your mangy fleabag!*

Nedjem hisses, but I nod. I will do this, because I know it must be done. The Serpent of Chaos departs, and I seek some much-needed solace from fur and purr. Calm now, Nedjem assumes his favorite spot atop my head.

My cat-headed sister insisted I should bring you fresh robes and sandals, comes the low growl in my head. *But I see you are appropriately clad already. And a fitting headdress, if I've ever seen one.*

My eyes snap open the minute a folded robe and a pair of sandals land on my chest. The cats scatter, and I pick myself up. Clad in thankfully clean clothes, I start my way back. Behind me, Nedjem drags the slain creature that started everything back home, for a late supper with his kin.

Leave that down, I want to scold him, but my words find no voice—only a warning: isn't this how all the trouble started?

ANKHU is the High Priest of Anubis in Thebes, the capital of Egypt during the early New Kingdom era. Low-born and an albino, he found sanctuary in the Temple from a very young age. Rumor amongst the townsfolk has it that he can communicate with and command the dead, the undead, and everything in between. In Thebes, no one crosses the High Priest. Moreover, no one messes with the High Priest's cat, Nedjem, lest they find themselves with ghost-infested houses—or worse. You can find more here: https://werecat99.wordpress.com/man-and-mau/

CHRISTINE LUCAS lives in Greece with her husband and a horde of spoiled animals. A retired Air Force officer and mostly self-taught in English, she has had her work appear in several print and online magazines, including the *Other Half of the Sky* anthology, *Daily Science Fiction*, and *Space and Time Magazine*. She is currently working on her first novel. Visit her at: http://werecat99.wordpress.com/

OUTLIER

An account by Mary Williams,
AS PROVIDED BY JULIAN DEXTER

This town is suffocating.

It's not just the unbearable, unending heat. The people, too. Every day is the same routine and the same conversations, blurring together in a haze of boredom. I'm drowning in stagnation.

There's only one day of my childhood that truly stands out to me as unique: the day when a stranger came to town. We don't get strangers. Usually, the only new arrival is through birth, so a fresh face in the peak of adolescence got the town talking. They stared at the hill at the edge of town and then huddled together to produce harsh whispers. His very presence offended their monotony.

But that's what drew me to him. He was a long-sought breath of fresh air that I hadn't even known I'd needed. I followed the trail of whispers and disapproving gazes, and once I found him, I watched him from a distance as he lay there on that hill, peering down at the town below. There was something exciting about seeing a new face that didn't belong to a baby, and my eyes drank him in with a thirst, as if he was an oasis in this miserable desert.

Although his face was shielded by a wide hat, I could still see that he had handsome blue eyes and a strong jaw. I was just twelve or so. I guess I was a good five or six years younger than him. His striking appearance intimidated me, so I decided to turn around and head back, but he spotted me.

"Hello."

I froze and looked back at him. He had sat up and was staring in my direction. Fear raced through me for a moment, and I considered running. However, the reason curiosity can kill a cat is because it's more potent than fear, so I turned to face him. "Hello," I replied. My hands were folded behind my back, and I shifted from one foot to the other.

I wasn't sure what else to say, and it seemed that he had the same problem. Eventually, he silently patted the grass beside him to invite me to join him. I was cautious in my approach, but I hoped not to the extent where he'd notice. And so I plopped to the ground about a foot away from him, the dry grass scraping roughly against my exposed ankles and poking at me through the fabric of my skirt.

He leaned back so his arms supported him, and I'm sure the grass cut at his palms. Still, he was silent. I figured that I would need to be the one to talk if there was going to be a conversation, so my mind raced for a topic. Finally, I settled on the most obvious question. "You used to live here?"

He looked over at me and used one thumb to push back the brim of his hat. "Kinda," he said.

I waited for him to expand on his answer. When he didn't, I went on to the next obvious question. "You moving in, then?"

"No," he said. "Not yet. Moving out."

I stared at him, trying to puzzle out his cryptic answer. He was terse and direct, yet his answers had just put more questions in my head. He waited for me to ask another question, but then turned his attention back to the sun setting over the town. My focus was still on his profile as I struggled to come up with something to ask him that he wouldn't see as stupid, but I soon turned to stare instead at the colorful sky as well and quickly found I enjoyed his company more while just listening to the bugs buzz their heat song.

As the final splashes of color faded from the sky, I heard him shift as he pulled himself to his feet, and I looked up at him.

"Well, I should be off now," he said, before I could ask him what he was doing.

"Will you come visit again?" I asked.

He stopped in his tracks and seemed to ponder his answer. Eventually, he shrugged one shoulder, back still toward me. "I might."

And with that, he turned and headed up and over the hill and out of sight.

I climbed to my feet to watch as he vanished. Darkness had begun to crawl across the hill, and it brought with it the promise of the cold of night. I knew I should return home, but there was more I wanted to know.

I made up my mind and raced to the top of the hill, desperate for a glimpse of him off in the distance, heading to new lands. I reached the top and kept running down the other side, my eyes scanning for some sign of him. However, all I saw were the empty, unending plains of dead patches of grass specked across eggshell-cracked earth stretching out as far as the eye could see. The only clue of him ever passing this way I noticed right as it became too late for me to stop my desperate charge: strange indentations in the grass as though something large had been resting there recently. Then I smacked right into the barrier like a bird hitting glass and blacked out.

When I came to, I was crumpled, cold, and sore on the side of the hill that faced the town. This place hates it when anyone tries to leave, and so feeling my punishment in aching muscles and bruised limbs, I hobbled home.

But the stranger changed my life. I was struck with a sense of curiosity and hope. Books were a rare commodity, but I collected as many as I could and spent hours each day poring over tomes that told of times beyond this one repeating Wednesday in the midst of June I'd experienced my entire life. The books gave me ideas, and I snuck out to behind the hill, just before the edge of the barrier, and brought my ideas to life in the form of a machine. My theory was, if I couldn't leave the "where," I'd find myself a "when" that would let me out instead. After all, this curse had to have a beginning, even if it didn't have an end.

My device worked.

My theory was wrong.

I explored the edges of the curse as an ant trapped under a glass feels for an exit but just loops about its prison in an endless eternity. The curse had warped time into a strange Mobius strip, and no matter how far I went forward or back, I could find neither beginning nor end. My hopes crushed, I accepted that the only way out of this place was through death and returned home what seemed to be mere moments after I'd left. My machine, I left behind the hill for the elements to deal with, abandoning it as a mocking monument to my pitiful attempts to escape.

The stranger never came back. Not that I'd expected him to. But with each day that passed, I fell more and more into despair and found myself yielding to the dreariness of my fate.

I soon married, and with that came children. Each one brought something resembling joy back into my life, even as I regretted bringing another creature into this forsaken land. I tried to ignore the weight that returned to my heart as I watched each grow up and succumb to the humdrum. Even my own offspring blurred together into a monotony so that it was difficult to differentiate them in my mind. Yet of all my children, there was one who stood out.

Ben was a bright young boy who reminded me of myself when I was younger. He had a spark of hope about him. My heart ached as I watched him read over my old books. I could see him getting ideas, and I soon regretted telling him stories of my younger days, of the stranger and my attempt to escape.

And as he grew up, I saw that he had my blue eyes, and his father's strong jaw. My blood ran cold as I recognized him properly for the first time. There's a strange feeling in watching your son grow into someone you've seen before, and whose fate is painfully ambiguous.

And then, he was gone.

I tell people I don't know what happened to him, but that's a lie.

The moment I realized he had vanished, I ran out of the house and up over the hill. However, all that remained were the marks where my machine had rested, crushing the long-dead grass into the dirt for all those years.

He never came back.

This story is but an excerpt of the writings of **MARY WILLIAMS**. All that's known about her and the unusual town she supposedly lives in is contained within a notebook that was found abandoned out in a field at the base of a hill. Although the landscape surrounding where the book was discovered matched details noted in its pages, an investigation yielded no evidence of the town ever existing.

JULIAN DEXTER is a writer and English tutor who comes from a long line of teachers, avid readers, and English nerds. He lives in Washington with his cat and spends his free time pretending to be other people in various role-playing games.

ART BY **Ray McCaughey**

RAY MCCAUGHEY writes, draws, doesn't talk much, and sometimes is a good friend. He studied at Carnegie Mellon University and lives now in Pittsburgh, Pennsylvania.

kingsport
ASYLUM

An account by Krista Bolmer,
AS PROVIDED BY DIANA HAUER

"I thought you were the gates of hell, once. You gave me such nightmares." I shook my head, allowing my gaze to travel over the metal and stone creation before me.

Despite the rust, the cast-iron gates of the Kingsport Asylum were still beautiful. Elegant lines and the stylized "K" in the center gracefully disguised the bars designed to keep patients from leaving. I rubbed my thumb on the edge of my Nikon D800's smooth, black edge, stroking the camera like a talisman.

"But you're dead now," I whispered. "I helped kill you." Self-consciously, I tucked a strand of gray-streaked brown hair behind my ear and shook my head. "I'm anthropomorphizing a gate and a building. Better knock it off. People might think I'm crazy." I forced myself to laugh at my own awful joke, because no one else was there to hear it.

The gate wasn't locked. I kicked it open and walked through. I shook off the chill that seized my bones and strode down the cracked, weed-infested driveway. Thick trunks of elderly trees lined the way. Some might be as old as the institution, which was founded in the mid-1800s. I waded through drifts of autumn leaves to lay a palm against a gnarled oak with a trunk half as wide as I was tall. Scars on the bark commemorated young love, but while the heart enclosing the initials was still visible, the letters had blurred with time. There was probably a metaphor in there, somewhere, but I wasn't here for love.

I was here to face my demons.

Kingsport had once been a beautiful place. I read somewhere that the Victorian-era asylums all seemed to follow the same pattern. They opened with the best of intentions, degenerated into abusive houses of horror, and then were closed and forgotten. The buildings were left as a creepy monument to the dead hopes and past suffering of the people who walked through, or were dragged through, the gates. Kingsport Asylum was no exception.

I turned and looked back at the gate, swinging slowly shut. My camera was a comforting weight in my hands as I lifted it up to my face. The scene through the viewfinder was comfortably distant. It gave me another level of separation, of objectivity, beyond that which time granted. The gate was stripped of the emotion I had laid over it, and I saw it through the dispassionate lens as a collection of shapes, lines, and shadows. I pressed the button. With a click, I captured the image. It was mine, now.

For a moment, I just stared down at the digital screen on the back of the camera and examined my feelings. I was so lost in introspection that I jumped when my phone rang. My heart raced, and I gasped as I tried to collect myself before answering. On the fourth ring, I tapped the answer button. "Hello, Dr. Wu."

"So formal, Krista. I thought I would call and see how you are doing. Are you all right?"

Even though she couldn't see it, I smiled. "Sorry, Gail. It's this place. Asylum rules."

"What do you mean?" asked Dr. Gail Wu. She had been my psychiatrist for almost five years, though we had known each other much longer. I joked that by now, she must know my mind as well as she knew her own. She responded that no one could truly know what lay in the depths of another person's mind. Most people cannot fathom what lay in their own depths, let alone someone else's.

"They punished us if we addressed the doctors or staff informally," I said. I could hear the flat tone in my voice that crept in whenever I talked about that time. "Ten swats with the paddle, or a slap in the face if they were feeling lazy."

Gail was silent a moment. We had trod this ground before.

"I know you won't punish me," I said, forcing life back into my voice. "It's just an old pattern. Old habits, hard dying, you know how it is."

"I'm glad that you can recognize that, now," said Gail. When I had first sought her out, I was in crisis. It took a long time and a lot of work before I could even see or name the problems I was facing. "You understand that you don't have to do this alone, right? I can be in the car and with you in fifteen minutes. Just say the word."

I sighed. "I'm thirty-eight years old, Gail. This place has been closed for twenty years. It's important for me to face this. And yes, I want to do it alone. It just feels right. I'm not sure why."

"You're familiar with the lone hero archetype."

"Going alone into the cave to face the monster?" I mused. "Maybe, but it feels more like the underworld journey. Go into the depths, find wisdom, face your fears, and then come back transformed." Even though Gail couldn't see me, I nodded as I looked down at the blank camera screen; it dimmed if I left it idle. "Yes, that sounds right. Though I'm not sure where the photography fits into that mythos."

"We can talk about it at our next session. I'll have the phone near me. You can call or text any time," she said.

"Thanks, Dr. Wu. Gail, I mean." I squeezed my camera again.

Blocky, solid, real—it reassured me. Phone in one hand, camera in the other, bracketed by technology while surrounded by the past. "I'll call you later."

"Will you be at the seminar this weekend?"

"Of course. I'm eager to get Krav Maga's take on women's self-defense. Later, Gail." I ended the call.

For a moment, I stared at the phone. Twenty years ago, I would have killed for a lifeline like this. I could have called for help. When they didn't believe me, I could send them proof. Pictures, videos, or audio recordings would prove I wasn't lying or delusional. Maybe I wouldn't have needed to testify.

"Daydreaming, Krista," I muttered as I turned the phone to silent mode and shoved it in my pocket. "It happened. You survived. Can't change the past, so let's go back in and face what remains of it."

I continued up the drive to the remains of the main asylum building. It was as big as I remembered. Columns bracketed the ornate front door, still standing closed after two decades. Red brick walls, decorated with lighter bricks around the windows, stretched in both directions as far as I could see. Four stories, three wings, and at least five outbuildings. Kingsport Asylum once housed thousands of patients and staff. Even dead and lifeless, with some windows boarded over and others broken, it had a nostalgic Victorian beauty to it. It reminded me of the fragile ladies of days long past, with their white faces and sunken eyes, the glamour of the dying or almost dead, fragile flowers fading in the light.

Today's gray sky and skeletal trees fit my mood. If I was going to design a haunted house for adults, this would be my starting point. I took a few pictures of the door, then turned and surveyed the overgrown landscape, taking it all in before I took more pictures. "The view as people came in," I looked at the door, "and the view as they left," I looked back at the garden. "I wonder how many saw the door going in but never had a chance to see it on the way out." No one knew for sure, but it was in the thousands. The asylum had its own graveyard, at the back of the property. They had stopped burying people in it years before I walked through the doors, but the numbered grave markers remained as a mute testament to the dead. Some of the dead, anyway. Patients whispered that there were many more graves, unmarked, around the property. A few said that the corpses of inconvenient patients were ground up and put in our food, but I'm pretty sure they were delusional. I hoped so, anyway. Those burgers were one of the few tasty meals they gave us.

With my back pressed to the door, I took pictures of the way out. I had stalled as long as I could. Slowly, I turned back around. The door was solid wood with decorations carved in the surface, dark with age, but still handsome. I stepped back and took another picture. Then I took a deep breath and turned the handle. It wasn't even locked. In a weird way, that made sense. Who would be crazy enough to break into an abandoned loony bin?

The door was stubborn. I had to put my shoulder against it and push until it opened enough for me to squeeze through, if I sucked in my not-too-ample gut. Photographers do a lot of walking, so I'm in decent shape.

Inside, pale rectangles on the floor showed where desks and furniture once sat. I didn't remember what the lobby looked like. I had only seen it twice: once when I was committed and again when I left. Both times, I cried, though for different reasons.

I tried to imagine the hysterical fourteen-year-old girl I had been. She was dragged in by her parents, then quickly collected by the orderlies who shuffled her off for processing. That girl had screamed and sobbed and begged and pleaded as the two burly men took her through the double doors and down the hall. I took a few pictures in the lobby and then slowly followed the path that I imagined I had unwillingly walked over two decades ago.

"This is different," I said to the room. The only answer was my slow footfalls echoing in the empty space. "Today I walk in willingly, on my own terms." My voice sounded strong and steady despite the remembered terror of a frightened girl beating against the inside of my chest. "I'm not a helpless child anymore."

I took a picture of the frame where the double doors had hung and then walked through into a hallway. The first few rooms must have been offices. They held little interest for me. Maybe my parents had spoken to a doctor or administrator in one of those cozy, welcoming rooms. Or perhaps they had arranged everything over the phone, which seemed more in character for them.

My breath caught when I got to the next room. It was still paneled in the remains of white tile. Bins and boxes were piled in the corner. The water fixtures and hoses were long gone. The drain was rusted through to leave a dark, gaping hole in the middle of the room.

I closed my eyes and tried to resurrect memories blurred by grief, fear, and time. The orderlies dragged me in here. No, they brought me to the doorway, shoved me in, and slammed the door behind me. Four hard-eyed nurses then took custody of me. They took my clothes, my shoes, even my hair tie; then they washed me and performed a cavity search. I was still a virgin. They weren't gentle. Afterward, they hosed me off with cold water to "calm me down" and gave me the clothes that would be my uniform for the next three years.

Still half in the memory, I walked through the room and took pictures. Some of them might show viewers the bleakness and sorrow of the people who passed through here. Others, I was sure, would have meaning only to me. With every image captured, I gained a little bit more distance. By the time I walked a full circuit of the room, I was trembling. I kicked over a sturdy-looking bin and sat down to rest and allow my knees to stop shaking.

I tapped the menu on my camera to look through the pictures I had taken. A few of the images from the driveway were blurry or uninteresting, so I deleted them. The images from the doorway made my breath catch in my throat. Yes, those were keepers. I would have to reflect on the lobby images for a while.

There was something wrong with the picture of the double doors. I squinted and tilted the camera, hoping it was a trick of the light. No change. The white-yellow blobs in the doorway were definitely pixels on the view screen, not reflections on the screen surface. I zoomed in on the spot and cycled through some of the filters, hoping to figure out what caused the flaw in my image.

My heart dropped when I realized what it was. Or rather, what they were. Two large figures dragged a smaller through the space where the double doors used to be. The figures were ill-defined, so I couldn't make out actual faces, but I had impressions. Anger and malevolence radiated from the larger ones, probably orderlies, who dragged an emaciated, ragged figure by the ankles. I couldn't tell if the patient was male or female, but I could make out wide, sunken eyes and outstretched hands clawing at the tile floor.

For a moment, I pictured myself in her (or his) place, hopelessly trying to resist an implacable force dragging you into unknown torment from which you know there is no escape. Despair, but you keep fighting anyway, because to stop means you have given up any hope of a life outside.

"Breathe," I whispered, forcing air in and out of my lungs. I tore my gaze from the image and looked toward the light shining sullenly through the windows. "I'm not there. I got out. That isn't me. I don't know what it is, but that isn't me. It wasn't me. I survived. I am free." Except I wasn't really free, was I? One strange picture and I was right back there. The memories held me down with even less mercy than the staff had shown.

I continued looking through the images. There was nothing strange until I got to the rear of the tiled intake room. A spray of light like water filled the image. My chest was filled with ice as I once again played with the filter and zoom settings to decipher the mysterious image. A face grimaced at me, eyes squeezed tightly shut. The rest of the body was obscured by a stream of water. Was someone being hosed down? My traitorous imagination pulled me into the image, and for a moment, I felt the icy jet of water pressing my body against the cold, hard wall. I fought to keep my arms by my sides, because if I tried to protect my face, then they would spray me there instead. People drowned that way.

"Where the hell did that come from?" I whispered, covering my eyes with my hand.

I didn't expect an answer, but I got one.

"Where the hell did you come from, and what are you doing here?"

I jumped up and clutched the camera to my chest. "Sorry, I didn't know anyone was here," I stammered, trying not to stare. The speaker was a stocky, blond person, perhaps four feet tall. Sturdy boots with steel toes tapped a rhythm on the floor as dark eyes glared up at me, hands on hips. Short-cropped hair and work clothes disguised any hints of gender.

"Well, I am and you shouldn't be," the little person growled. "I'm the groundskeeper, and I'll thank you to keep any jokes about garden gnomes or dwarves to yourself."

"I hadn't even thought them," I said. "I'm just here to take pictures."

"Why?"

Why indeed? I looked down at my camera and stroked it thoughtfully. "A project, I guess. I'm a photographer. This is a personal project of mine."

The hard face softened slightly. "Connecting with your past, are you?"

I winced and nodded, gaze still fixed on the screen.

"We get that here, sometimes. I'm sympathetic, but this is not a safe place to be wandering about."

"Have other people been here to take pictures?" I asked.

The groundskeeper raised an eyebrow. "Some, but most just want to look around. Why?"

"Did any of them mention strange light artifacts in their pictures?"

"Show me."

I knelt and turned the screen to show the stranger, surreptitiously glancing at his or her face, trying to get a read on gender.

"I'm neither," snapped the little person. "That's what you're trying to figure out, right? If I'm a man or a woman?"

I blushed. "Sorry. That was probably rude."

"Not as rude as some, believe you me. I'm non-binary. I don't identify as a man or a woman. My name is Dakota, and my preferred pronoun is 'they,' in case it comes up. As in, 'I was trespassing and the nice non-binary person didn't call the police, even though they probably should have.' Get it? Now show me the picture with the weirdness. Oh, crap." Their hands gripped the camera and held it tightly as their wide eyes examined the image. "How did you get this?"

"Same as usual. Point, focus, press the button. I'm Krista, by the way."

Dakota shoved the camera back at me and pulled out what was either a large smartphone or a small tablet and tapped the screen several times with the stylus. After a few moments, their eyes widened and they looked from the screen to me. "What did you do in here?"

I stood up and stepped away, bothered by their intensity. "I walked in and took some pictures. I swear, I didn't break anything. All I did was turn the bin on the side to sit, and I was planning on putting it right back when I left."

"All right, all right." Dakota closed their eyes and rubbed their temple with two fingers. "But taking pictures wouldn't account for these readings. The wear in this room was twenty points higher when I took readings last week. Now—" They clapped a hand over their mouth and squeezed their eyes tighter shut.

The doorway was only a few feet away. I could probably outrun them if I made a break for it. Slowly, I took one step toward the exit, then another, moving as quietly as I could.

After a moment, perhaps counting to ten, Dakota shook themself, put on a professional demeanor, and turned to me. "I would be happy to escort you through the building to take any further pictures that you like, but I must insist on reviewing all the images before you leave."

"No, that's all right. I think I'll just go." I took another step toward the door, not bothering to be quiet, and not willing to turn my back on the strange little person.

"Wait, please!" Dakota reached a hand out to me. "I'm sorry I scared you. Really, I want you to keep taking pictures. I just want to observe."

I narrowed my eyes at them. "Why? And what did you mean about 'the wear was higher' before? What are you taking readings of?"

Dakota's mouth tightened. "You might want to sit down again. I'll explain, but it's a doozie."

Dakota dragged a decrepit stool over, brushed it off, and sat down. "You've heard of haunted houses and ghost stories, right? Of course you have. Bad things happen in a place, ghosts stick around because of unfinished business or they don't know they're dead or whatever. Except the ghosts aren't souls, they're memories. With me so far?"

"Not really," I said, sinking slowly onto my seat. "But keep going."

"Let's say someone is horribly murdered in a cabin in the woods. Every night, that memory replays. It's like a stain. The more times the mess falls, the worse the stain gets. I'm on a fabric metaphor here, so bear with me.

"There are things you can do to make the stain better. The spiritual equivalent of stain remover or bleach, or just water to dilute it. Either way, it's one drop of bad stain, every night or every full moon or whatever cycle it is on. It can get ugly, but you can hide or avoid the stained area."

I nodded. "Okay, I do laundry, I'm with you. You're not really a groundskeeper, are you?"

Dakota grinned. "Not in the traditional sense, no."

"Okay, so if one horrible murder makes a small, ugly stain, what kind of stain does a place like this make?" I asked, waving my hand vaguely at the room.

Dakota tapped the side of their nose. "You catch on fast. The Kingsport Asylum was founded in 1854. These walls have witnessed lobotomies, murders, torture, madness, and abuse of the worst kind." If Dakota noted me cringe at "abuse," they didn't mention it. "When a lot of stains drip-drop onto fabric over a long period of time, it weakens the fabric. And when the fabric gets thin, then the things that are supposed to stay out start getting the idea they can get in. They want in, so they make sure that people like me don't make any progress in trying to clean or dilute the stain or fix the damage."

"In this metaphor, what exactly does the fabric represent?" I asked.

"The walls of reality. And this," they turned their tablet to show me an incomprehensible collection of line graphs, "is a reading of the levels of energy leaking from outside into here. My employers hired me to monitor this site and try to keep the situation from getting worse until they can figure out how to reverse the damage."

My head was spinning. "So, what does this have to do with me walking around and taking pictures?"

"First off," Dakota ticked points off on their fingers, "the readings in the rooms you have been in are lower than the last time I came through. Second, the improved areas seem to correlate roughly with the altered pictures on your camera. Third, we have taken a lot of pictures here. Some of them showed lights or the hint of a figure that shouldn't be there. None of them had the clarity or definition of the images in your pictures. I need more data so that I can understand what's different about you or your pictures."

"Were any of your previous photographers residents at the asylum?" My voice was softer than I wanted, like my younger self was asking the question rather than me.

Dakota thought about it. "No, I don't think so. Maybe that's the key. I'm sorry, but I have to ask." They chose their words carefully. "Would you say that you suffered here?"

I curled around my camera and nodded, fighting to keep the moisture from leaving my eyes. I hate how sometimes the simplest questions can bring me to tears.

"You don't have to tell me anything more if you don't want to," said Dakota. "Not my business, and I won't pry. Please just keep doing what you were doing. I'll follow a little ways behind. You can pretend I'm not even here."

For about a minute, I sat silently and breathed. Dakota waited, patient as an Easter Island stone head. I hadn't planned to have company on this trip. I wasn't sure that I wanted a witness, but I knew in my gut that if I left now, then I would never come back. That settled it. This place had hurt me before, but it hadn't beaten me. I wouldn't let it beat me now.

I stood up and put my camera back in picture-taking mode. For a moment, Dakota and I stared into each others' eyes. I didn't know what to say, so I just nodded and walked slowly out into the hallway. The lobby and the exit were to my right. I turned left.

I walked down the gray hallway, lit by sunlight that filtered through the gray clouds. Decorative bars on the windows made interesting patterns of light and dark against the faded wallpaper. I paused now and then to take pictures. A discarded toy overlaid with the striped shadows. The view out the window, an overgrown orchard framed by brick on one side and cast iron on the other. The building was in remarkably good repair, considering its age. Back then, they built things to last.

The security doors and gates in the hallway were long gone, but I took pictures of the scars that remained. Plaster bled through the wounds in the wallpaper. When I realized I was stalling, I turned and forced myself to stand up straight and stride down the hall. I couldn't help but remember the gray-clad child that I was, shuffling along in her slip-on shoes, shrinking in on herself. Back then, I tried to be quiet and unnoticeable. Bad things happened if they noticed you. Today, I didn't care who noticed. I didn't sneak, I marched.

It was hard. Dr. Gail's encouraging words chanted in my ear like a mantra. "You're not a victim, you're a survivor. They tried to break you. You survived. In the end, you broke them. You're strong. You can do this."

The hallway opened into the children's day room. They considered children less of a security risk than adults, so most of our facilities were on the first floor. Doctor offices were on the second floor, adults on the third floor, violent patients and treatment rooms on the fourth floor. They had mostly stopped using electroshock when I got there, and totally quit using lobotomies sometime in the 1980s. The rooms had been kept intact, though. Maybe it was for the history, more likely as a reminder that they could still do that to us if they wanted to.

Remnants of cheerful cartoon animals peered back at me from the walls. They were more sad than creepy. Most of the staff tried to make our time here happy. Most of the staff were kind-hearted and compassionate people, but we never forgot that they were our jailers. The wrong word to any of them would find us answering pointed questions from a psychiatrist at best, shot up with drugs and put in isolation at worst.

On the chalkboard, someone had written "I'm scared." I walked over and looked closer. There was no chalk. In the dust, I wrote, "Me too." Then I took a picture of it. I took lots of pictures in the day room. Dakota followed me at a discrete distance, staring down at their tablet and making notes. They asked to see the pictures before we left the room and moved on to the next area. Only one place showed abnormality: a figure huddled under a ruined table. I looked away before I could be drawn in. Dakota peered at it and made lots of notes.

"Could you go on to the next? I would rather not touch your camera. It looks expensive."

"It is," I said, absently flicking to the next picture. I had taken several that included the table, from different angles. The figure was still there in the next image. "It's a business expense, so I can justify it. Tax deductions, you know." I advanced to the next image. Different angle, but the figure was still there, still recognizable, but in a slightly different position.

Next image, it was still there, but lighter.

In the next two images, it was lighter still.

In the final image I took that included the table, it was almost gone.

Dakota asked, "Would you take one more picture of that table? I want to see something."

I glanced down the next hallway and shuddered, torn between wanting to put it off and wanting to get it over with.

"Please?"

I sighed and turned to take one more cursory picture of the table. When we checked it, the figure that had been huddled beneath it was gone. "What does it mean?" I asked.

"I'm not sure," said Dakota. "But the readings got progressively lower the more pictures you took. Are you okay to keep going?" They tried, and failed, to keep excitement from their voice. If they hadn't sounded so guilty, I would have been angry. They knew what they were asking.

Lucky for Dakota, I planned on going forward anyway. "The dormitories are next," I said. "I lived here for three years."

Dakota nodded.

"It's likely to be . . . hard. But I have to do this. I *want* to do this. If I need your help, I'll ask."

"Otherwise, back off and keep my yap shut?" asked Dakota with a wry smile. They mimed zipping their lips and throwing away the key.

I smiled wanly and nodded. Then I squared my shoulders, stiffened my spine, and retraced the familiar path from the day room into the girls' dorm.

I remembered this hallway being larger. Or maybe that was because I always shrank in on myself whenever I left the day room and the relative safety of witnesses.

Doorways lined the hall. Some of the doors were missing or broken. I paused to photograph a few of them. One had a large white square in the back corner when I reviewed the picture. Curious, I tapped it to zoom in for a closer look.

Cold cloth pinned me down. Ice was piled on top of the wet sheet. My teeth chattered. A nurse in an old-fashioned uniform looked down at me like I was some sort of a bug. "This is what happens when you act up, John. We need to calm you down. This is for your own good. So be a good little imbecile and stay quiet, or I'll have to get the gag."

I choked and stumbled back, leaning heavily against the wall. Long habit kept my grip on the camera iron-strong. "That's messed up," I said when I could breathe again. "Dakota, I can taste rubber in my mouth. That wasn't my memory. They never gagged me in that room. What's going on?"

Dakota shook their head. "I don't know. I've seen psychics who connect so deeply with places that they can see what happened, and mediums who talk to the ghosts and hear what happened there, but I have never heard of someone actually being drawn into the ghostly memory of a place." They bit their lip. "Are you sure you want to keep going? I'm not sure this is good for you. Or safe."

"I have to keep going. My room is two doors down. I'm almost there." With an effort, I forced my legs under me and my spine straight again. My knees wanted to tremble. I flexed my legs and started walking slowly down the hall. This time, I didn't stop to take pictures. Nothing existed except for me and the door to my old room.

Once upon a time, it had been white. Now, the white paint peeled away to show green underneath. Under the green was brown or rust—I wasn't sure which and I didn't care. The number plate was gone, but I could find this room again anywhere. I paused long enough to take a picture, then I gripped the door knob. One more deep breath and I pulled it open.

I caught a glimpse of a rusty bed frame, a smashed dresser, and peeling paint in a filthy room. Then it was gone.

The room was pristine. A small twin bed with a thin mattress and once-white sheets under a gray comforter squatted in the corner. The only lights were the window and the overhead light, inset and protected so that patients couldn't get to it and hurt themselves. The dresser was light blue, the only spot of actual color in the white-gray room. I looked down and saw gray patient clothes hanging as loose on my thirty-eight-year-old body as they had on my fourteen-year-old body.

Then it was dark and I was in bed, huddled under the sheets in the dark. I prayed the door would stay closed, that they would pass me by. Heavy footfalls came closer, passing all the other doors until they got to mine. If I hadn't felt the rush of cooler air, I wouldn't have known the door had opened. More footfalls, and then a heavy weight settled on the foot of the bed. "Get up quietly, Krista. It's time for your shower."

Strong hands gripped the back of my coat and pulled me out of the room. I stumbled and landed on my butt, curling protectively around the camera and its delicate lens. The hands were still on me, touching me. Frantically, I slapped them away until I recognized the voice talking to me.

"Krista, are you all right? Ow, dammit! Quit hitting me, it's Dakota. Open your eyes, Krista."

I forced my eyes open and looked up into theirs. Dakota's arm was around my shoulders, propping me up so that I wasn't laying completely in the dirt. "What happened?" they asked.

"It," I licked my lips and swallowed hard. My mouth was very dry. "It was a memory."

Dakota nodded. "Oh. Yours?"

"Yes."

"Bad?"

I couldn't force the word out, so I just nodded.

"I'm sorry."

I shook my head and climbed unsteadily to my feet with Dakota's help. "Don't be. I survived," I said. My stomach rolled. I leaned over and dry heaved, but nothing came out. "I'm all right."

"Are you sure you want to keep going? You don't have to do this," Dakota said.

"Actually, I do." I straightened up. It was getting easier to do that. Every time this place made me want to curl up into a little ball and hide, I stood back up and walked on. Story of my life, really. "This place has haunted my dreams. It colored every moment of my life and the way I see and interact with the world and people from the moment that I walked in until now." I looked down at Dakota. "I came back here to face it, because I need some damn closure. I want to walk these halls on my own terms. If I leave now, if I flee," I stifled an angry sob. "It will be so much worse if I can't make it to the end. Because that means that it won. I'm not going to let my past win."

I walked stiff-legged back to the door of my room. A few steps away, I paused and took a picture of the door ajar. I took a few more standing in the doorway, then I closed my eyes and stepped into the room.

Nothing happened.

Slowly I opened one eye, then the other. It was a dingy, dilapidated old room, like any other on this floor. Standing inside it still made me want to throw up, but I forced my gullet back down as I turned around in a slow circle to take it all in. With the patience and detail of a forensic photographer, I documented the room.

"What's taking so long?" asked Dakota. They were still staring at their tablet.

"I'm not planning on coming back here," I said. "So I want to have a complete picture of this place as it is now to remind myself that this room isn't the one burned into my memories." I looked over at Dakota. "Does that make sense?"

Dakota nodded. "While you've been doing that, I sent some queries about your experience. Closest thing I found was a medium who was working with a psychic exorcist at another asylum. The psychic started experiencing the memory rather than just catching glimpses of it. He said it was like some thing, some power, filled the ghosts or the memories and pulled them in. 'It was like a human sticking their hand in a sock puppet and then smashing a fly' according to the report."

"Why were they attacked?" I asked.

"Near as I can tell, because they were making progress. Their readings are similar to the ones I've been getting here, but to a lesser degree. Leakage has decreased on all spectra and wear has decreased to almost nothing," Dakota said.

I raised an eyebrow. "That made no sense to me. Can you go back to the fabric metaphor?"

"Basically, you reversed the rubbing that was wearing a hole in the fabric and made the stain drip less frequently and less badly."

"Or maybe I put a patch on it," I mused, looking down at my camera thoughtfully. "Is it possible that I'm capturing the badness with my photographs?"

Dakota shrugged. "Lots of people have taken pictures here over the years, including ghost hunters that would give their left nut or ovary to grab the images you got without even trying. There are too many factors at play here for me to advance a solid theory. But Krista, if the beings who want to get in can weaponize your memories, this could get really bad for you." They bit their lip and shuffled their feet a little. "I might not be able to pull you out of it next time. You could be trapped in your past."

"It wasn't exactly the past. I had my adult body in the memory." I looked down at my hand and clenched my fist so hard that it shook. "Oh wow, I was in the past with my adult body and memories. I have fantasized about this for years."

With a feral grin, I turned and strode quickly down the hallway. Memories of past friends peeked out at me and beckoned from the doorways, but I had eyes only for my goal. Dakota ran after me, short legs pumping to keep up with my long strides.

I turned abruptly into a tiled hallway that led into darkness. There were no windows here, but I had come prepared. I pulled a headlamp out of my pocket and stuck it on my head, then walked into the shower room.

Darkness surrounded me. Whispers filled the air. The voices were familiar, but there was a strange undercurrent to them. Something darker, more sinister, thrummed through.

"*Open your mouth. There's a good girl.*"

"*Go ahead and cry. No one who hears you will care.*"

"*If you don't cooperate, we'll kill you and grind up your body for tomorrow's lunch.*"

I pressed my hands to my ears and stumbled deeper in. "Where are you, you bastards? Show yourselves! Face me!"

Darkness dissolved into light.

Instead of a camera, I clutched a threadbare towel and a washrag to my chest. One of the orderlies, Stan I think, guided me with a meaty hand on my shoulder. It occasionally trended downward to caress my back, or lower. I walked faster to try and escape it.

I caught a glimpse of myself in the mirror. My 17-year-old face stared back at me. I stopped in my tracks, ignoring Stan. I knew which memory this was. The technicians had pimped me out to a couple of their friends. They figured I was old enough to take it. It had been the last straw for me. I looked down at my familiar body, the curves of a woman rather than the rail-thin frame of a teenager, and smiled.

"*Come on you little slut,*" *sneered Stan. He grabbed my collar to drag me inside.* "*You know you want it.*"

"*You're right, I have thought about this day a lot,*" *I said quietly.* "*I fantasized about it."*

This wasn't in the script. Stan turned to me, alien confusion swimming in his eyes.

I grinned at him. If I stood up straight, I was as tall as him. "Every damn self-defense class I took, I replayed this night in my head. Because I wished I had known then what I know now." *I hauled back and buried my fist in his gut, then grabbed his head and bounced it off my knee. He fell, and I kept punching and kicking him until he stopped moving.*

If this were real life, the men waiting inside would have come out to see what the commotion was. But in the past, they had not, so they didn't now. I had time to catch my breath. When I was ready, I ducked into the supply closet and pulled the wooden handle out of a toilet plunger. Weapon in hand, I walked into the shower to face my demons.

Their eyes weren't quite human, and their screams were more like howls, but I didn't care. In the past, my screams had echoed off the walls until they left me bloody and broken on the tile floor. One had turned on the showers as he left to wash the blood and evidence away. This time, I was the one to turn on the showers as I left.

When I turned for one last look, the room was empty. My nightmares were gone.

Light dazzled me as I left the shower room. I paused to get my bearings. "How long was I in there?" I asked.

"About five minutes," said Dakota. "Did you know that you were laughing almost the whole time? It was creepy as hell."

I shrugged. "What can I say? I was fulfilling an old fantasy. Would you mind holding a light while I take some pictures? A flashlight isn't ideal for this, but between it, the flash, and my headlamp, it will get the job done."

As I had in my old room, I took a lot of pictures, thoroughly documenting the room. It was different, though. A weight that had lain on my shoulders for a long time was gone. I felt no urgency. I knew in my bones that I would never need to look at these pictures again.

"What happened in here?" Dakota asked, then looked quickly away. "I'm sorry. I shouldn't have asked."

"It's all right," I said. "I was sexually assaulted here as a young woman. Multiple times. For years, I hated myself for being so weak. I kept thinking that I should have fought back. I wanted to go back in time and hurt them, save my younger self the pain and humiliation she suffered." I flexed my hand. Why were my knuckles sore if I hadn't really punched anything? "I didn't time travel, but this was still therapeutic as hell."

"Oh," Dakota stared at me, wide-eyed. I wished for a mirror so I could see the look on my face. It probably wasn't a nice one. "Are we done here?" they asked.

"I have one more place to visit," I said. "Upstairs."

"Is there someone else's ass you need to kick?" Dakota asked.

"No," I said. "I already fought and won the battle that mattered most."

The stairs were in shockingly good condition. Dakota admitted that their employers, which the groundskeeper still refused to name, performed enough upkeep to maintain the stairs and roof. We made it to the second floor with no trouble. I walked all the way to the end, past the prestigious offices with windows and nice views of the garden. The appointment rooms and doctors' offices were all up here. My target was the smallest, at the very end.

Its door was missing, but the checkerboard throw rug remained. All other furniture and decorations were gone. I stopped and took a picture.

"You're smiling," said Dakota.

I nodded and closed my eyes.

"You can trust me, Krista," said Gail Wu. She was studying for her doctorate in psychiatry. Interning at the institution was one of the final hurdles she had to clear in order to earn her degree. "I promise you, whatever you say is just between you and me."

I eyed her suspiciously. Three years of threats made me wary of such promises. I confided in a doctor once before. He'd accused me of lying and had me drugged up and sent to solitary. Solitary was even worse than the shower room. Fewer potential witnesses.

Something about her earnestness reached me. This was our third session. She hadn't pushed, but somehow, she coaxed me out of my shell. Now she wanted me to trust her. I knew for a fact that she didn't know what she was asking of me. Maybe she suspected something, but she couldn't really know how bad it was in here. Every survival instinct screamed at me not to say anything to her.

But I did. Slowly, haltingly, I told my story. She asked me if I would be willing to let her record it. "Danger, danger!" screamed my internal survivor. Out loud, I said, "Yes."

"We brought Kingsport to its knees," I said. "This is where I found the courage to finally blow the whistle on this place, and a new doc doing her psych internship had the guts and integrity to do the right thing with it. I ended up telling my story three times: once to Dr. Wu, once to investigators, and once in court."

Dakota stared at me. "You're the patient whose testimony closed Kingsport for good. I saw the articles, but your name was never printed because you were a minor."

"It wasn't only my testimony. A lot of other patients spoke up once they realized someone was willing to listen. I just got the ball rolling." I stepped into the room and took a few more pictures. These were bleak, but I hoped that some of the brighter emotions would show through. Not everything that happened in this place was awful.

Sometimes people were healed.

"What's next for you?" asked Dakota.

"I go home and process images," I said. "And figure out what to do with them."

"I contacted my employers, and they want to speak with you about those pictures."

I raised an eyebrow. "Am I going to get sued?"

"No, but you might get offered a bunch of money and possibly a job," said Dakota. "They want to understand how you did what you did and if it can be replicated elsewhere. I'll understand if you say no. This is some weird, scary stuff. Most people can't deal."

"Who are your employers?"

Dakota's mouth quirked. "Would you believe I work for the National Park Service?"

"You're kidding me."

"A small group of concerned citizens provide funding and coordinate with the NPS to help monitor certain buildings on the National Register of Historic Places. There's a think tank that correlates the data provided by us and similar teams worldwide. The eventual goal is to reverse the damage and keep reality from being invaded by the things you encountered today."

I blinked a couple of times and then cocked my head to regard Dakota. "What got you into it?" I asked.

"I love the science and solving mysteries," they said. "The work is interesting, pay is great, and benefits package is awesome."

"What's the catch?"

"For you? Maybe doing this on a regular basis." Dakota hesitated, then blurted, "You relived some awful stuff today, and there is worse out there. Are you sure you want to do this?"

I stood up a little straighter and smiled down at them. "I'm a survivor. After today, I think I can face down anything."

KRISTA BOLMER is a freelance photographer who lives in Albany, New York. She shares a farmhouse with two cats and a horse. Her work has been featured in galleries and magazines throughout the United States. She volunteers for SIA (Survivors of Institutional Abuse), a nonprofit organization dedicated to empowering and supporting the healing of adults who have been subjected to emotional, physical, or sexual abuse in private or government institutions, detention centers, or foster care. Visit www.sia-now.org for more information.

DIANA HAUER is a writer of words, both technical and fantastical, who lives in Beaverton, Oregon, with a dog and a husband. When she is not writing, she enjoys gardening, hiking, and studying martial arts.

OSHIMA

An account by Ani Toomanian,
AS PROVIDED BY NYRI BAKKALIAN

Twelve years on, I can never forget it. The tsunami took a lot away, but the little shrine on Oshima Island survived. Maybe I should be surprised, but I'm not. After all, *she* has a way of making miracles happen.

It was an Inari shrine of the senior-most court rank. The old weather-beaten sign proclaimed its name as *Oshima Shinju Inari Daimyōjin.* It was just a few minutes' walk from the train station in central Matsushima. Beyond the town, the pine-clad islets of Matsushima Bay look stately in the seaside sun. Little boats float by. Tourists noisily amble along the coastal sidewalk. But around the bend and through the trees, over the little bridge and onto Oshima, you find quiet serenity, and the little shrine.

Pebbles and pine needles crunched and rasped underfoot. Rough-hewn holes punctuated shady rock faces, and mossy, time-scarred Buddhist statuary seemed to peer out from the shadows. I remembered something one of my teachers casually mentioned, before we came here, and felt my steps slow.

People still ask to have their ashes scattered here.

Well, I thought, *if it's a graveyard, then it's probably one of the most beautiful graveyards I've ever seen.*

The sun set behind me. To the east, the sky was awash in dim reds and oranges. My heart was full: I'd crossed the little bridge intending to let go of mental and emotional baggage. After half a year on the road, after family drama and political violence and trauma I'm still unpacking half a lifetime later, I was desperate. The bridge's name was Enkiribashi, the Bridge of Tie-Cutting, so it seemed fitting to cross.

I stood beside the little shrine, unsure if it'd happened yet. Didn't the gods send signs anymore?

Around the bend, my teacher chatted with his other students. The shorebirds called a greeting to the reddening sky. I leaned against a tree and tried to slow down, to take it all in. After gorgeous vista upon gorgeous vista, my heart was so full it seemed like it could burst.

It seemed almost painfully beautiful. In the near foreground, a few boats floated at anchor. In the distance was the big island, Fuku-urajima, where the stories had it that the goddess Benzaiten dwells.

For a moment, I glanced over my shoulder at the little shrine. That's when I saw the woman who'd paused beside me.

There was an odd radiance about her. Had she been in the tour group I'd arrived with, or was she a local? And why was my vision suddenly such a blur?

"Miss, forgive my intrusion," she said in Japanese that sounded old for someone who seemed so young. "Why are you crying?"

Hands met cheek met wet, warm tears. Dammit. I *was.*

Words failed me. I shook my head and managed a hint of a shrug.

"You're lost, aren't you?"

"It hurts," I rasped, and pointed to my chest. After all I'd seen, all I'd endured, I didn't know how else to describe it. "It *hurts.*"

"I saw your arrival with the others. You seem to carry a great weight." As she came closer, I could make out her features a bit more clearly. *Is that hair tie red brocade?*

"Hear me. It will not be easy, but you will weather the storm. You are stronger and wiser than you know." She paused, and glanced to the east. "In time, the sun will shine."

Who are *you?* I wanted to ask.

The woman simply laughed. Then, suddenly, I was alone.

On the way home to Sendai, I pondered the shrine, the sunset, and the woman who'd come to comfort me.

Sleep was elusive that night. How many people had seen what I'd seen? How could I be sure I wasn't crazy?

Years passed. Not long ago, I learned that local folktales tell of the deities around Matsushima appearing to people when they are most in need.

I thought of the woman by the shrine that still sits beneath the pine trees' shadow.

Sleep was again elusive that night. But in the morning, I remember awakening to a glorious dawn over the distant mountains. I could hear her words echoing in my memory.

In time, the sun will shine.

ANI TOOMANIAN recently earned her Ph.D. for research on folk religion in northeastern Japan. Despite frequently being on the road, she has yet to return to Oshima.

NYRI A. BAKKALIAN is a queer Armenian-American and adopted Pittsburgher. A military historian by training, she's an artist and writer whose work has appeared on *Inatri*, *Metropolis Japan*, *Gutsy Broads*, and *Queer PGH*. She has a soft spot for local history and unknown stories, preferably uncovered during road trips. When not hunting for unknown history, Nyri can most often be found sketching while enjoying a good cup of Turkish coffee. Check out her blog at sparrowdreams.com, and come say hello on Twitter at @riversidewings.

the
SAFE HOUSE

An account by Jean Fontaine,
AS PROVIDED BY GEORGIE HINOJOSA

I'm not crazy, so you know. Just because I was suicidal, it doesn't
mean I was crazy.

I still remember what my therapist, Kathy Swan, said that day
when she first told me about the Safe House. She looked me right in
the eyes and said that we were stuck. That there was no getting better
for me until I could confront what happened to me so long ago. I
couldn't, though. We'd get close, and I'd see flashes of things: I'd smell
incense, I'd see a dark purple. But my mind would shut it off before it
went further, and I'd be unable to focus on it any longer.

So with her dour eyes set in her aged face, Kathy said, "Jean, the
only thing we can do here is drastic. You must go to this location for
the weekend, and whatever happens, you cannot leave. It's a cabin
called the Safe House, and you must stay the whole time. I *mean* it.
You will be alone, but do not worry, for I will leave you food, drinks,
and everything else you need there."

I'm not young anymore, mind you. At 42, most of my best years were behind me, or so I thought. I had been with my therapist for years, and I was desperate for something better. Life was an endless cycle of disappointment, and suicide had been something we both knew was weighing heavily on my mind.

A few days later, I drove to the first coordinates she gave me, which turned out to be for a large sign with an arrow painted on it. I scoffed at how strange it was for her to send me on a treasure hunt like this, but admitted to myself sadly that I really had nothing better to do with all my time. On the drive, my gaze kept going back to the revolver that was poking out of my bag in the passenger's seat. I had left that part out with her, but what can I say? There's something poetic about killing yourself in a cabin in the middle of the woods, alone. Just the nature of the struggle, I guess.

I finally pulled up to it after some more driving. It was very remote, which is why it was so hard to find. I took my bag with me after parking and went up to the front. It looked normal enough on the outside—wooden exterior, with some short stairs leading to the door, and a window in the front. I went up to the door and looked under the welcome mat, just like she told me to. There was a key hidden. I unlocked the door and went inside.

Everything that happened next, I'm able to tell you with certain clarity because it was all burned into my brain so I'd never forget a thing. I don't think the house would ever let me forget what happened that weekend.

As soon as I walked in, it struck me just how normal everything looked. The floors were dark hardwood, and the walls had a few lights, but not many. There was a large red sofa facing an old CRT television screen, and there was a nightstand next to it. I dropped my bag onto the small table and went to explore my new, and perhaps final, place.

I kept walking straight and came into the kitchen/dining space, which had appliances that looked like they were from an older time.

There was a fridge, oven, and sinks, and they were all spotless. Opening the fridge, I appraised the food available and was not disappointed; clearly, my therapist had stocked it with my favorite items. I briefly wondered whether that was an abuse of our relationship to get me such things. There was also a single door in the dining area, near the table, which seemed off colored compared to the other parts of the house. I needed to use the restroom by then, and told myself to check it out later.

The restroom itself had a tub, toilet, and mirror. I looked at the reflection of who I'd become. I was 42, but looked so much older, I thought. There were wrinkles all over my face—laugh lines, crow's feet, more—and I just looked so tired. I closed my eyes, taking a breath, and looked again. I was shocked. For a split second, I was looking at my younger face, with my optimistic, beaming eyes, my smooth skin, and longer blonde hair falling to my shoulders. It was me from my college years. I blinked quickly, mind racing as I tried to make sense of it, but in the mirror, it was just my older, more tired, sad self looking back. I thought that so strange, but if only I had known what was to come.

The last room was the one I would be sleeping in. It was extremely simple, possessing only a small bed with covers and pillow, a table and chair, and an old mechanical typewriter on the table, with a sheaf of paper next to it. Finally getting over the shock from earlier as some figment of my tired imagination, I looked at the typewriter with a touch of bemusement, a grimace on my lips. She had always wanted me to journal my feelings, I suppose.

I went back to the front room of the cabin and tried to find my bag, but couldn't. Instead, there was only one picture resting on the nightstand, a picture that I always carried with me every day in my bag, but one I showed and told no one of, not even Kathy. It was of my ex-husband, David.

David and I had been together for twenty years when we

separated sixteen months prior, and we'd been officially divorced for four of those months. He was an artist, with hands soft from plying wet clay to fit any shape he desired. When we had first met, I had been a star-struck groupie in awe of his talent and what he *could* be. Then last year, he told me that, after all this time, he couldn't be with me anymore. He wanted to go out too much, and with my chronic pain I couldn't follow; he wanted to be creative and constantly positive, and though I tried my best, I couldn't muster the strength to keep up. So he left me.

He had this smile in the picture, one of his signature grins that would have looked stupid on anyone else. His eyes held a twinkle that shined like diamonds, and he just looked so damned confident. Tears started to burn down my cheeks as the memories flooded in.

The day we took that picture he had given me the camera, wanting me to be the artist for once. I took so many shaky pictures that day, so many worthless ones. But this picture was the gem. It captured him as I saw him. I had done that, and I had been so proud.

That feeling of loss that had been waning in me the last few months roared back with a vengeance. All my yoga, poetry writing, picture taking—all of it to build a cage around these emotions failed. The pain crawled within me, its thousands of serrated claws piercing into my flesh and bones as it sprinted toward my heart to consume it.

I screamed into the quietness of the cabin. I kicked the sofa, and in doing so, I struck my foot against the wood of it. I cried out again, my sorrow giving way to a wrath I hadn't verbalized in years. I kicked the sofa again, and this time it gave. I grabbed the nightstand and threw it across the room, where it broke against the front door. I picked up the TV and slammed it to the ground, the glass shattering and flying around. Then I turned and made my way to the bedroom.

My gaze caught the typewriter. It looked so heavy, sturdy, and big. My once weakened, gaunt hands clasped onto it, feeling the cold metal in them. I pulled it up off the table and heaved it with effort, and

I threw it out the door of the room, a satisfying crunch of noises as it clanged into the wooden floorboards with a large thud.

As I look back over that first day in the cabin, I think how lucky it was I couldn't find my bag, how I couldn't find my gun. I know things would've ended so much quicker if I had. Instead, my energy spent, I fell onto the bed and pounded the mattress with my fists, sobbing into the pillows for what felt like an eternity. Then, eventually, I fell fast asleep.

I woke up a few hours later, moonlight streaming through the window in the bedroom. My body felt transformed from the sleep—not tired and sore, like I had imagined it would, but vibrant and bursting with energy. Pangs of hunger throbbed in my stomach, though, and my thoughts turned to the delicious food I saw earlier in the kitchen.

That was, until I looked at the table near the bed. Because sitting atop it, in its own majesty and weight, was the large, mechanical typewriter. It looked exactly like the one I had seen when I first entered the room, and I just knew it had been the one I had thrown earlier. I inspected it, running my fingers over its cold form. There were no dents in it, no parts where the metal gave in. It was pristine.

I left the room and looked around the hallway. There were no marks in the floorboards whatsoever. I was walking quickly now, my head in a flurry of trying to remember. There was no way it had been a dream. It had been too real.

In the front room sat the nightstand and the TV was where it had been, in perfect condition. There was no broken wood, no glass strewn across the floor. I couldn't find the picture, now, and still no bag, but other than that, everything was in its place.

It was all too much, I thought, and I went to the front door and opened it quickly. I stepped back, my mouth drawn wide in shock, because it didn't open to the car I had parked earlier in the front. Instead, as the door slowly pulled back, I saw myself at the end of a hallway standing in front of an opening door, but from the side view. I stared in disbelief, then slowly raised my left arm and waved. The woman with my features and my clothes did the same exact motion. Panicked, I checked behind me and to the sides. There were no other doors in my line of sight for this to be remotely possible. Yet I saw myself all the same. Not thinking clearly, I did the only thing I could figure at that time. I stepped forward through the door, and fell through darkness immediately.

A little scream escaped me as I tossed around, but I didn't slam into anything, or even fall for very long. I landed atop soft sheets, with a pillow near me. I looked and saw I was back in bed.

When I looked around the room, I saw the typewriter, which I knew for certain I had thrown. I got up, went back to the front, and there was my bag atop the nightstand, and there was the unbroken TV. I went to the front door and pulled it open with force. Outside, there was my little sedan, the green of grass in morning dew, and cold wind that licked my face. I hovered before the barrier, looked outside, thought about leaving. Then the hunger pangs came back, stronger than ever, and I promised myself I would leave after I ate. I closed the door and went to the kitchen.

Searching through the pantry and fridge, I found the ingredients to make chocolate chip pancakes, as well as sides of bacon and sausage. It was my favorite breakfast, and I was astounded that I had the energy to make all of it as well as I used to so many years ago. David had complained in the later years of our relationship that I had given up on making him food, but he had been wrong. I hadn't. My body had. It was in near constant pain from the fibromyalgia, and he didn't see those hours I spent when he wasn't there trying to recreate the meals I used to make for him. I would knock flour over, drop pans and spoons, and I'd have to use what little energy I had left that day to clean up the failures by the time he got back home. I felt so mortified he'd walk in on me cleaning up all of these cooking messes that I eventually just stopped trying altogether and would drink my nutrition shakes alone.

But today, here, there was no wavering in my palms, no weakness in my arms. I lifted the pans and threw ingredients in them easily, cooking the different items together. It reminded me so much of younger me, before I became so sick and weak. I lost myself in my cooking and set the food down at the table, a feast for one. I was so proud of myself. I scarfed it down like a hungry dog who found its way into a food storage; it tasted incredible and was the best meal I'd had in so long.

After I almost licked the plates clean, I gave them a quick wash and put them in the dishwasher to run later. I looked over the kitchen and dining room, and my gaze fell upon the off colored door again. It was purple, while the walls were wood paneled like the floors. My stomach full and interest piqued, I walked over to it and opened it, a small shock as I somewhat expected to see myself at the end of a hallway again.

Instead, it was shelving stocked full with crafting supplies. Yarn, glue, copper wire, glitter. All the things I used to pour my heart and soul into decades ago when I had worked for a local crafting store, selling my works to an eager public. I saw their happy faces again, smiles because of my angel cups that they looked so in love with having bought. I crafted so much before I was sick.

A spurt of energy arose in me, and I started to grab all the craft supplies my hands could carry. I dropped them onto the dining room table. Sunbeams bathed over the yarn and glue from the dining room window, and after collecting my things, I set to work immediately. I started to bend the copper into wings, and knit the yarn into little angel bodies where their little yarn heads would sit. I glued buttons onto those heads to give them eyes, and fashioned a tiny smile on each with a bit of black yarn. Then I put their bodies over the bottom of a cup, so they all had stable bases to stand upon.

It had been years since I could make just one yarn angel. But there, at the table, I quickly started my third, then fourth, all in succession with no break between. I made little bugs and animals out of copper wire, placing colored marbles in between the parallel frames to fill out their bodies. It was a small happy village I was creating. Then I found a little unpainted house in the back of the closet and brought it out. I added snow to it and colored the house and the trees. Hours must have passed through all this, but I couldn't tell. The sunbeams still came in and bathed the table, and I felt no less energy from all the crafting.

Finally, I had my little village on the table, the angels dancing with the animals. There were dozens of creations in my small scene, and I stopped and just admired it. My thoughts, usually so fast and hard to keep up with, were silent. All of me was in awe of what I did. I raised my hands, skin so thin as to be translucent and lined with veins as they were, the hands I had cursed so much for shaking and being unable to do the simplest of things anymore, and I smiled. In this moment, they seemed so beautiful. I brought them close to my face and kissed each hand, a tear rolling down my cheek as I did so.

I wanted to preserve the display, so I went to my bag to grab my camera. I had brought it in hopes of snapping pictures of wildlife while I was out here, and the camera had become my savior over the last few months as I tried so desperately to get over David. I held it aloft and found my village through the viewfinder, and with no need of a tripod this time—for there was no shake in my hands—I snapped a few pictures of the gorgeous display I created.

Putting the camera down, I saw that the sunlight coming through the windows was waning. I had lost myself so much in crafting that the day was already passing! I moved all my creations to different spots in the house, so they could watch over me. Maybe I'd leave them here for my therapist as a thank you for the food. I went back into the kitchen, and with no feeling of fatigue within me, I got the things out

I needed to make a five-star dinner. Just as before, I cooked with gusto and ease, and just as before, the food was delicious to the last bite.

After filling myself up for the night, I had the idea to see if anything was playing on the TV. I went over to it and pressed the on button and sat looking at my own reflection in the darkened glass for a couple of seconds. I couldn't quite make it out, but I swore there seemed to be some change in my features. Before I got too deep into it, though, the television flashed to life. Looking at what it was showing, a paralysis hit me, and my breathing sharpened to where it felt like each inhale was tearing into my lungs. I reached into the VCR slot, but there was nothing inside. I couldn't take my eyes off the images and so I just sat there, dumbstruck, on the floor.

There was David, looking so unbelievably handsome in his tuxedo the day of our wedding. His smile touched his eyes, and there was the spark there that he had only for me that the film caught perfectly. We kissed, and I could almost taste him upon my lips like I had that day. I was crying, and he was crying, and watching the video, the tears flowed again. Next, it was us at the reception afterward, his deft artist's hands cutting into the cake and serving it to our guests. He shook the hands of every one of them, and he looked so damned proud to be married to me. Oh, how that would change so much. In the video, I was beaming at him, my eyes never leaving his wondrous features.

The next scene it was him and me outdoors on a hike. He loved to see nature so much, and he looked so rugged in his jean shorts and sleeveless tank top, his muscles bulging from the effort. His skin was tanned and his hair cut short, how he always liked it. I followed dutifully behind him, catching him in the camera. That was one of the best days I remember with him, because I could keep up with him in his element, and again he was so proud.

The scenes passed faster, a montage of seemingly every happy moment that kept me up at night. All the times we smiled, and laughed, and were happy together. It was those memories that would interrupt me every day when I was trying to move on, those memories that stabbed through my heart and forced me to confront how much I had failed him. Things would trigger them to come up and flood me, my taste, my sight, my hearing. Everything would give way to these beautiful mental scars I had.

After a time, though, the scenes started to change. Gone were the times he showed off his pride of me to others, gone were the days out in the sun. Instead, it started to show videos of things I remembered clearly, but there was no way anyone could have videotaped them.

We were in his studio late one night, and he had already thrown a few sculptures against the wall, shattering them. He hadn't been accepted into an art gallery he had tried hard for, and our bills were piling up. So, he got angry and destroyed the pieces he had worked so hard to make. He destroyed what he thought wasn't good enough. As if he read my mind—as I feared about my own place in his life—he turned on me and started yelling.

"I wouldn't have to apply to these third-rate hacks if you could get promoted at that damned crafts store! I'm the only one working for us, Jean! While you just make stupid little yarn ornaments, I'm pouring everything I have into making enough money to keep us afloat! Grow up, dammit!"

There was so much anger in his eyes, and that night had been the first one I saw clearly that there was no longer any spark there for me. I had shuddered in front of him and broken under his wrath, and I fell and sobbed. He stood over me and yelled more, the veins in his neck throbbing, his spit flying. He cursed me for being so weak, and he yelled about how he regretted the choice he made with me. He shut himself up almost immediately, but I looked up at him, stunned into silence. He quickly apologized and knelt to hold me. I let him, and I felt so slimy now to see that. He told me he'd never say something so untrue again, and he was right, in a way. In the coming years, he'd repeat all those words, but they'd always be true from that point on.

In the next scene, I was following him, again, at the summit of a hike. But I had already been struck sick for months, and he knew that. It was his birthday, and I prepared all week to follow him, to give this to him as his gift. My body wouldn't let me, though, and before we even started the incline, I told him I couldn't go. The pain was ravaging my body, my nerves were firing signals like crazy, and it just wasn't possible. I thought he'd yell at me again, like he had done so many times before, but he didn't. He simply looked me over coldly and said, "Then go sit down, old lady. You're not going to ruin my birthday." Tears fell again, of course—they always did by then. Most of my life was crying, by then. Crying at how weak I was, crying at how I disappointed him, crying at how I couldn't do anything to be of some value to someone. And I did feel old, sitting there for hours, waiting for him. I didn't eat when my body demanded it, I didn't drink though my throat quickly felt bone dry. I punished myself that day to show him, in some way I hoped he'd understand, that I was sorry. That it wasn't me, it was my body. But deeper down, I knew that was a lie. I had always been weak mentally, and it had just started to show itself physically, too.

More scenes flashed, montages. David yelling at me for not cooking anymore and throwing the pots and pans around. David with his hands around my neck, pressing me against a wall because I tried to talk back to him. He left bruises, but I hardly went out, so who would see them anyway? David throwing away my crafts because I wasn't using them. He sneered that they belonged to "another woman I wouldn't know." David getting drunk after a particularly bad gallery night where they called his works blasé and derivative. He hit me in the mouth, sent teeth flying. The dental bill was in the thousands. He never got drunk around me again, thank God. A quiet home, where David avoided me and didn't talk to me, so we ate in silence and I stayed in my room.

The last scene was something I couldn't quite place. It wasn't in our house, and I didn't see David. It was a bedroom with posters all around the walls of mandalas and other psychedelic images. There were small sticks of incense burning in the background. And there was something purple, but I couldn't make it out. It was bobbing…

The TV shut off, and I was faced with my reflection in the black screen. But that wasn't the only reflection there. Behind me.

No.

I turned and looked up. There he was, the tanned skin, the short hair.

David was here. How? Why?

I wanted to cry out in joy, I wanted to hug him, but I did neither. I didn't even move.

Because David was angry.

"Didn't I tell you that these stupid angels were worthless?" he barked. He had one in his hand, and he was squeezing it, the wings crushed under his force.

"They—they aren't worthless!" I retorted.

"They are! Just like you." He made his way toward me, his solid build moving in a terrifying quickness, just like the nights he would—

"You run to this house to kill yourself, and you can't even do that right!" The veins in his neck bulged, and his face turned a dark red. He nearly screamed the words now. "Do you even know where the gun is? The one I bought for you to protect yourself with?" He spat out the last few words. "What is there even worth protecting?"

My paralysis finally broke, and he was right, I still didn't know where the gun was. It was nowhere in sight. I scrambled to my feet, feeling a youthful agility I had thought lost long ago. He was in front of me and advancing, blocking the hallway, so I looked at other options. My gaze caught the front door, and I knew anywhere was better than here. He lunged past the sofa to grab at me, and I ducked out of the way to the side, then went for the handle. It turned easily and opened, revealing my car, the grass, and a night sky full of stars. I took a step out, preparing to sprint to the sedan, when I fell through. Good enough.

I landed in the soft covers of the bed once more and sprang up. Looking down the hallway, I saw him getting up from where he had lunged at me, brow furrowed in confusion. He looked around, saw me in the bedroom, and started running toward me. I reached for the door and slammed it, fingers fumbling with the lock in just enough time to close it off. I backed away as his mass thudded against the door, but it held.

My gaze scanned the room, but there was still no gun. All that was in there was the typewriter. He was banging on the door viciously with his fist, and I didn't know how much longer it would hold. I put my hands around the typewriter's frame, readying to heave it, when my finger slipped in my panic and struck a key, hammering ink to paper. The thudding on the door stopped for a split second. Oh, I thought. Ok.

I sat down and considered for a second if this was crazy, and decided it was. I searched in my head for what to write, but it came immediately from inside up to my fingers, and they clicked away at the keys without my brain telling them too much. I started to pour all my feelings onto the page, all the times David had hurt me or belittled me, all the times he wasn't perfect like I had made him out to be, or even that good of a person in general. I complained about his shoddy art and skill, complained about his lack of empathy and cooking acumen. Like a torrent of water, the words burst forth from the dam I had held them behind for so long. Each new word reduced the pounding on the door, and it got weaker and quieter until I couldn't hear it at all. Yet still I typed. Decades of thoughts I was too afraid to express to others colored the pages in their black ink. All the thoughts I had turned against myself, I now turned against him.

Throughout the hours I spent at the typewriter, the cogs in my head ran, and I finally pieced it together. This house *was* odd and different. It was forcing me to confront my past, to help me get over David and reconnect with the things I used to love. It didn't go by the rules of the world outside; it was only doing what was necessary to help me. To its rejoicing, I'm sure, I gave in. It felt alive, like it knew what it was doing, guiding me. I wrote and did crafts every day and cooked for my own fun. I found an antique radio that knew all my favorite songs, and I sang and danced to them, looking as foolish as I wanted. I would find his picture around the house in odd places, and I would cry through the night and feel the pain violently moving through me. I'd yell and scream and trash the house, and it would be fixed in the morning. Eventually, after what felt like months of all this new schedule, I could look at his picture and remember the good times and bad, but I hated myself for none of it. The house had worked. I was ready.

Or so I thought. As I was whistling along to a song and cooking up the pancakes, bacon, and sausages, pain shot up my wrists into my hands. My eyes widened as the pan fell from my grip, too heavy now, and slammed onto the floor, spilling the food everywhere.

Pain started to surge to the rest of my body. The numerous aches and joint weakness returned in force. The house had protected me from them, allowed me to know what life was like without living with a withered and frail form. Then it took that feeling away, and I was back to my husk.

I fell to my knees, crying. I sobbed more than I had for David, because while I could escape him, I couldn't escape this body.

"Why did you do this to me?" I shrieked into the empty house.

It had been so blissful to live without the pain. Everything had been perfect. But even through those months, I knew this all had been a vacation, not a future. It had been like every other thing I tried to make my life better: good for a while, but there was no cure for me.

Well, actually, there was still one.

"I won't live like this! I can't!" I screamed. I got up, shakily, to my feet. My knees were sore and bruised from falling to them to cry. Putting my hands on the counter, I walked toward the front room. There was the gun, finally, on the nightstand. Maybe the house did still have mercy. I hobbled over to it, hand bracing against the sofa. As I got close, though, the sofa fell away. So did the front door, and the other furniture. It was just me, the gun on the nightstand, and wooden walls around us. I was in a hallway now, somehow. As I moved toward the gun, trying desperately to get a hand on it, the hallway began to stretch out away from me, taking the nightstand with it.

"No!" I yelled, weakly. I hated how I sounded, and I hated more how I felt.

I chased after it as it extended farther, my scrawny arms pumping at my sides and my chest heaving.

"Give me my gun!" The words struggled to exit my mouth, scratching my throat as they went up.

It shot away into the distance, and looked to be going faster now.

Damn my body for being so weak, I thought. Damn me for never being enough. I can't even kill myself, if that's what I want.

"Give me. My gun!" I screeched, and a fire lit within me. It was the fire of hate, of every raw piece of anger I felt toward my body and my mind for all the weakness I had over the years. For still being weak.

"This isn't how it was supposed to turn out!" I roared into the hallway, and it flew farther from my grasp. "I wasn't. Supposed. To turn. Out. Like this!"

My muscles burned and I knew I couldn't move much farther. With all the effort I could muster, I gave it one final shot.

"Give. Me. My. Gun!" I screamed at the top of my lungs at the house, the entirety of my fury charging through my gnarled and scrawny body.

Then, immediately, the dot on the horizon stopped, then rocketed toward me, the walls of the hallway collapsing into one another. What stopped a foot away from me was no longer my gun on the night stand, but instead it was a door with a sticker of the logo for Guns' N Roses on it. The door creaked open slowly, revealing a room with mandalas and other psychedelic posters on the wall. I felt déjà vu as I looked over the space. The scent of incense wafted into my nose, and I could hear two voices intermingling as they came over to the bed. I finally remembered what the room was, what the event was. It was the night I had said no.

It was my younger self, back when I was 20 and new to college, and I was in the dorm of my boyfriend at the time, Scott. He had been a rocker, with tattoos, piercings, and a demeanor that bucked what society thought—or so my naïve self bought into at the time. He was my first love, and he was horny. We had both done a little pot and drank, and he was trying to get me to take off my clothes. I remembered that part of the night. At first I had felt aroused too, but then there was something about him that was off. He was too grabby, too pushy. Something inside me felt wrong, and so I told him no.

Before my very eyes, his face changed. Gone was the guy I had fallen in love with and been with for months, and instead anger fell over his features. He stopped asking me to take off my clothes, and instead he grabbed me and shoved me onto the bed.

"I know you want it", he said, "stop acting like you don't."

I had been paralyzed in fear back then too, and when he pressed himself on top of me, his hands ripping at my shirt, only then did something light within me. I started to thrash, to try and yell. One of his hands went over my mouth, stifling me, while he pushed down harder. I tried to push him away, and his other hand held my wrist down. My left arm flailed, desperately searching for something. Yet here I stood, the older version, and the house was forcing me to watch and relive it all over again. I felt sick to my stomach and I was shaking, my tears burning down my face. Thoughts flashed in my head, and I couldn't stop them.

Before that night, I had been a straight A student. I had been so happy and fearless and just damn strong. I had wanted to conquer the world. Then that night broke something inside me. It showed me just how weak and vulnerable I really was. It made me feel like glass in a world of stone.

I couldn't blink or shut my eyes as I watched him on top of my younger self. It was here, this part, that I couldn't breach in therapy. Something happened next. I'd flail, and then something would happen, but there would always be interruptions in my thoughts that would keep me from figuring out what. Instead, my thoughts jumped ahead.

There I was, after that night, staying in my dorm the night my friends went out to the parties, scared to death that any of the men there could be just like Scott.

There I was, in my thirties, staying with David, because though he scared me, he could protect me. Because he was right about me being weak, and I needed someone, something to prove I wasn't, even if it was just miserably trying to be homemaker.

There I was, in my forties, my body weaker than it's ever been, my thoughts going fuzzy more often. I had always been so weak, mentally and physically, I thought.

Before the thoughts could flow in further, they were shunted away, and my full attention went back to the memory. My hand flailed desperately as his lips pressed down against my neck, as his body felt heavy on mine. Finally, after what felt agonizingly like an eternity, my fingers grasped something and I swung it with all my might.

It had been his purple lava lamp, and it slammed into the right side of his face. The purple lava spilled out over him and onto the bed, and red started to pour out of the glass that was embedded in his raw face. I shoved him off of me and ran for his door, leaving.

In the present, I was awestruck. This whole time, I had blocked out what had happened the rest of the night. For the last twenty-two years, I had thought that he had overtaken me, that I had been too weak, but in reality—

I was still watching my younger self leave. She bolted out of the door and ran down the street, going to my house. Then she stopped and turned around. Her eyes looked straight into mine, and she walked toward me. She didn't say anything, but instead held her hand out when she reached me and handed me a shard of the glass from the lava lamp. She gave a small smile as I looked down into it, and I saw my reflection. I saw the bags under my eyes, the wrinkles settled into my face, and the gauntness of my skin. She stood in front of me, inches away, and she spoke with her soft voice.

"I see strength, and courage, for making it this far. I don't see a weak person, at all. I simply see someone who did the best she could in the situations she was given, the only way she knew how. And that will always be enough."

Finally, deep down inside me, something clicked.

Images flooded my head again, but they were different. I saw the empty space in Calculus where Scott used to sit. He was gone because *I* had hurt him, defeated him. I saw myself in the rest of college, getting straight As and pouring my heart and soul into getting my degree. I saw the anger on David's face, not because I was worthless, but because I wouldn't let him truly break me and he knew it. I saw myself at the crafts store, excelling in my art and making the lives of others brighter because of it. I saw all the times in my life I had always thought were signs of my weakness or failure. But now when I looked, I saw instead all the amazing things I could accomplish as I dealt with trauma, abuse, and even chronic illness for the rest of my life.

Then, I was back in the front room of the cabin, and I looked around. The scenes and memories had all fallen away. Looking down, there was no longer a shard of glass in my hand, but the gun. I knew that this was it, the last test. The house had done all it could, but it was giving me the final say in whether I die now or not.

I cracked the cylinder and looked at the single bullet waiting in the chamber. I closed it again, admiring the finish on the barrel and the grip. I cocked the hammer.

One shot meant no more pain in my body. No more sleepless nights, no more foggy memories. No future where it was going to get worse. No more depression and crying for hours and hopelessness. Even after all this, there were some things the house couldn't fix, it could only try to have me accept. I stared hard down at the barrel. Then I started to walk.

Going toward the entrance, I opened the door and gazed out. There was my car, all the grass, and some trees again. I pointed the gun down at the grass itself, and I pulled the trigger, the single bullet going down into the grass and knocking up dirt.

Relief flooded me, but in a way, I think it also flooded the house. I turned to look back at it, and I smiled. It was just as cozy as I had hoped it would be. It still had my crafts out around the house, and I hoped they could add help to whoever came here after me. I closed the door until I heard a satisfying and final click, then checked my phone. The clock started to work again, and it showed that it was Sunday, two days after when I had arrived, though in the cabin it felt like nearly a year had passed. I didn't feel much older, besides the chronic pain that was there. Still, I was happy, and I couldn't help but smile. The Safe House had earned its name and saved my life. How many lives had it saved, I wondered? Kathy's?

I hadn't told another soul besides Kathy about what had happened until now. I figured, finally, that if it could help someone else like it had for me, it would be worth it.

So if you need help, look for the signs, ok? Far out there, in the middle of nowhere, maybe where you never imagined. But look hard enough, and you'll find it.

The Safe House.

Let it help you.

Because it will keep you safe from the most dangerous enemy you could ever have—

It will keep you safe from yourself.

JEAN FONTAINE is a 44-year-old woman from Illinois. She has two fur babies, Chico and Taquita, whom she loves dearly. She makes her living by selling crafts both in her local stores and flea markets, and worldwide on Etsy. She also runs a group online for fibromyalgia survivors to come together and share their stories.

She's happily single.

GEORGIE HINOJOSA is a 25-year-old content creator in Orlando. A lover of science fiction, horror, and fantasy, he especially likes technology and things that play with perception. He also has a fondness for corporate and mainstream popular culture, which balances out his geeky tendencies. He's written numerous short stories, a non-fiction book, and a novel, but this is his first published work.

the language
OF THE MUD

An account by Janis Keegan,
AS PROVIDED BY BETTY ROCKSTEADY

I missed him, yeah, and that was awful, but somehow the worst part was trying to find it again, those eight or ten inches of earth that stole my father. I knew if I found it, everything would make sense.

I needed to hear what he had been about to say. "I really—" what? I really fucked it up this time? I really miss her? I really miss *you*?

I just wanted to know the end of that sentence.

I just wanted to find the spot again.

I pored over the dirt and the mud and the grass over and over, nose to the ground, trying to find a hint—a wavering of motion, an echo of his voice, a whiff of that sweet-rot scent.

Was it here, or an inch to the left? Was his right foot right here, right where mine is, or was it tilted toward the trees?

I was seventeen. My dad was staying at some shitty hotel outside of town, and my mom was refusing to take his calls. I dunno why he was driving around that morning, but he caught me skipping school and drove me home, an excuse to talk to her, or maybe an excuse to talk to me. Well, I wasn't saying much. He followed me into the backyard and watched as I lit a cigarette. He frowned but kept his silence because, hey, I wasn't the one with substance abuse issues, was I?

I wish I had been nicer to him that day. Every day.

We sat on the picnic table. The wind bit through my sweater. I was puffing away, watching him sweat. I wasn't even really mad. Mom was the one who was mad.

"Do you think she's ready to talk?" he asked, and I shrugged and said something, said whatever, said I dunno, why don't you ask her? He got up from the picnic table, stretched, took two steps into the backyard, shuffled his feet, said "I really—" and then he just fucking disappeared.

He didn't sneak away. He didn't leave. My eyes were on him the whole time.

Two steps. Shuffle. Gone. The grass rippled, and that was all.

How did I react? I don't know. I really don't. A few minutes there just kinda escape me. I think I screamed. I probably screamed. I didn't black out. I didn't block out some traumatic event. I didn't lose any time *before* he disappeared. I remember *that* perfectly. My dad, tall and broad shouldered and smelling only just a little bit like stale beer, stretching, walking, shifting his weight, "I really—"

And then just grass.

Mom got home a few minutes later, and I was still staring at the lawn. I would have thought I was on drugs too, if I were her.

Life went on. Can you believe it? Boring old life went on. But days passed, and there was no call and no money and eventually yeah, even mom started getting worried. Their fights never went on this long.

She thought I was covering up for him. She thought I knew exactly where he was and just wouldn't tell her.

I *didn't* know exactly where he was. I didn't even know exactly

THE LANGUAGE OF THE MUD

where I saw him last. I almost knew though. Within a few inches. And whenever I could escape her notice, I was in the backyard. Trying to figure it out.

The ground was solid beneath my hands. Shouldn't it be softer somehow? Shouldn't it be changed?

Should I have been afraid? I wasn't afraid. It wasn't like it was quicksand or something. I didn't think I would fall down there after him. I just wanted to know.

I kept looking and looking until his voice came on the wind. "The last time the grocery store was so busy." Just a fragment. The words floated by, and I wasn't even sure I heard them.

I wanted to tell Mom, but she was on the phone with Aunt Susan, bitching about Dad, and was "not in the mood for your bullshit today."

They loved each other, you know? Even with all that fighting, even with all the times he left and came back and left and came back, they loved each other. She counted on him. She counted on the fighting and the apologies. It was part of their routine. She didn't understand why he didn't come back this time.

I sat out back smoking all spring, waiting for something to happen. I heard him every now and then. "The consistency is off." "Down here in the muck and slime." "Arcs of vision passed by." Nonsense phrases. Bits of things. I wrote them down, tried to piece them together. The worst thing was, the more I read over them, the more familiar they seemed, until I wasn't sure if it was something I heard him say once or if I had actually heard it there, and if I did hear it, was it because I was standing in the right place at the right time? Was it right here? Was it exactly right here, or was it a step to the left?

He was just gone.

I started waking up at night, snapping abruptly out of dreams, and when I woke up, I didn't go outside, even though I wanted to. I would wake Mom up if I walked past her room. But I looked out the window, and I looked at the spot, or near the spot, and I just kept playing those moments through my head.

"I really—"

I really wished he would come home.

So it was one of those nights, and our neighbor's fucking dog got off his leash again, and he was bounding through our yard, and he was circling the spot, and my heart was in my throat because what if, what if—but our neighbor came up behind him and grabbed his leash and pulled, but then the leash went loose and the dog was spinning and barking and alone.

Mom didn't believe me, of course she didn't, not even when the dog got hit by a truck and the newspapers started piling up next door.

I was glad the dog got hit. He ruined everything.

I couldn't hear Dad anymore. Well, I could, but it was all twisted up with the neighbor's voice now, and the words were even more mixed up, and I didn't know which ones were his and which ones were hers.

How had she found it so easily, without even trying? I couldn't find it, no matter how many hours I spent out there, inches from the ground, dirtying up my jeans.

Sometimes I skipped school to sit out there. Sometimes I couldn't help it. I shuffled into the backyard after math class once, and a man was there. He looked familiar, like a neighbor maybe, but not a close one. He was dressed in a suit, carrying a briefcase, like he was on his way to work, but instead he was in *my* backyard, circling *my* spot, a wrinkle of concentration on his forehead.

I was pissed. I didn't want more people here. I didn't want them to fuck up the voice more.

I didn't want someone else to find it.

"What the hell are you doing?"

He just looked at the ground, then at me, then back at the ground, his eyes big and round and wet. He shuffled his feet, stepped forward and back.

"Get the fuck out of here." All my teenage bravado. And he was reluctant, but he did step away, brushed past me, and I stumbled over to the spot and listened.

"Get the dog inside and wash behind your ears." Her words, his voice, someone else's cadence. I was furious.

I stopped going to school. Mom was never home to get the calls from the principal. I just erased the messages from the phone. I camped out in the backyard all day, and when people showed up with their wet eyes and desperate faces, I could tell them to fuck off before they even got started. Before they even had the chance to ruin things.

"Lots of feathers here this time of year."

But I couldn't keep them away all the time. I had to eat, at least when Mom was watching. I had to sleep, at least when I could. I didn't catch anyone else disappearing, but I knew when they had, because the words changed again. Dad's voice got farther away, everything got all mixed together.

I didn't want to spend all that time out there, but I couldn't help myself. A bad habit, worse than smoking, and I just couldn't shake it. I would shower, get dressed, make my lunch, tell myself I was going to school, and then all of a sudden it would be hours later, and I would be sifting dirt between my fingers, rubbing my face against the grass, watching ants crawl by and wondering if they would disappear too, listening for the voice that rarely came now, and when it did, it was all wrong.

Mom and Aunt Susan caught me one afternoon. I didn't even realize I was there until I heard Mom's tired voice. "Get out of the mud." She didn't sound mad, just tired. I stood up, brushed the dirt off my knees.

"What are you doing out here?" Aunt Susan laughed. "Aren't you a little old to be playing in the dirt?" I muttered something, but my gaze kept drifting back to the ground.

"What are you looking at?" There was something off in her voice, and she stepped toward me, and the spot I was looking at was way off, because she was still a few feet in front of me and then she was gone.

The sound that came out of Mom's throat was awful. And it's even more awful that my first instinct was pleasure. I *told* her. I was right. But the look on her face made me feel small and ashamed. Her hands fluttered by her sides.

"What did you do?" Tears were coming from her eyes. She never cried in front of me, and didn't seem to realize she was doing it now.

And then the voice, unsteady. "Get out of the—I wouldn't." My dad's voice, but all mixed together with Aunt Susan's and the neighbor's and everyone and all jumbled up and I felt dizzy.

Then Mom was down on her hands and knees, digging with her bare hands, and her nice skirt was getting all dirty, but the dizziness passed and a jolt of energy burst through me, because I knew, I just *knew* that she had it. She had the exact spot. I don't know how she got it so quickly but she did, and I had to help.

The grass was sticky like moss and peeled back smooth from the earth. The dirt beneath was black and wet and pungent. Mud smeared our hands like oil. We dug.

It takes a long time to dig, you know. It wasn't easy, but we didn't stop. My nails broke and my back ached and I didn't stop. Mom's skirt was filthy and she didn't stop. Dusk came and we didn't stop. We barely made progress—the dirt kept coming and we had only our hands, and they dove deep into the organs of the earth, and we were so determined, and we couldn't stop because we had the right spot.

I started to get tired. Mom's hands slowed down. Time slowed down.

I was suddenly very conscious of each handful of dirt, very conscious of the voices swirling around us with their nonsense phrases.

It accepted us, finally.

The muck slid away from our fingers, and the hole tunnelled down and let us in. Just a few feet down, but it was enough.

Broken, rotted scraps of wood lined the sides of the hole, spreading it open, and the digging got easier. My blood pounded through me, felt too thick.

And then my broken nails hit something, sent vibrations reverberating through my hands. Mom reached in, and together we reached deep inside and the voices whisper-shouted and something burst.

A torrent of brackish water erupted from the hole, covering our filthy shirts. It stung. I backed away, yanking Mom's sleeve, pulling her back with me. The sickly-sweet smell hit and my eyes blurred with tears. I blinked past them, stared into that pool of water, my gut empty with despair.

My reflection gazed back at me with vacant eyes.

The stench of rot grew stronger, and my throat filled with bile. A sickening yellow mist blurred my vision. I started coughing, and mom started coughing, and voices all around us started coughing. I couldn't stop. I couldn't breathe. I couldn't breathe. I couldn't breathe. The air was too thick, too heavy, too wet. My mother wheezed and clutched my hand and for one merciful moment, the hole left my mind, replaced by the all-consuming need for air, and we stepped away, we pulled each other inside.

Dad was sitting on the sofa, smiling.

"I'm so happy to see you guys." His voice was not his own. Not at all. He stood up. I felt the blood drain from my face, but Mom surged forward and embraced him.

He smiled at me, and I couldn't breathe. I still can't breathe, not like I used to.

The muck covered the yard for a few days, sludgy, impassable. Slowly the ground sucked it all back up, and all that was left was dirt and grass. I could never find the spot again.

I kept digging. I dig and dig and dig, and I can't find it. I can't even hear the voices anymore, but my dad is back, and Aunt Susan is back, and my neighbor is back.

None of their voices sound right. None of their clothes fit right. Not even their skin fits right.

I'm not the only one looking now. There's always someone else. Sometimes there are dozens of us, shuffling our feet, looking at the ground, sweating and pacing and running our fingers through the earth.

I wish I could find the spot.

I wish I knew what he had been about to say.

JANIS KEEGAN is a Canadian high school student, although she doesn't spend much time at school lately. She's been awfully busy outside. She misses her father.

BETTY ROCKSTEADY is the author of a variety of weird horror fiction, including her novellas *Arachnophile* and *Like Jagged Teeth*. Her short fiction has appeared in *DOA III, Eternal Frankenstein*, and all three issues of *Turn To Ash*. Betty also does pen and ink illustration. Find out more at www.bettyrocksteady.com or connect via Facebook or Twitter @bettyrocksteady.

the girl who
GIVES ME SUNSETS

An account by Harry Grahame,
AS PROVIDED BY ALI ABBAS

The apartment is seventies drab. It has the dry, stale chill of being unoccupied for years, but someone has kept the surfaces dusted and the spiders at bay. The kitchen is orange and the bathroom olive green. The linoleum cracks and curls at the edges. The only sign of refurbishment is a new gas boiler, a gleaming incongruence on the kitchen wall.

I don't plan to be here long. My contract is only for a month, filming a promo to attract investors to a proposed development. I thought I'd left Portsmouth behind, but I can't resist the lure of being headhunted. Besides, I need the money.

The wallpaper on three sides is beige and brown, an eyewatering interlocking pattern that matches the rest of the apartment. The fourth is blank canvas cream with a single oil painting providing a splash of colour: a glorious sunset with cacti in silhouette. It only serves to highlight the narrow alley outside the single window. I try to move the painting, to raise it to a better height, but the fittings are hidden and it won't budge.

There is no signature. No label. The deep shadows around the bottom of the painting merge in the muted light of the room. I like it. I find myself warming to the place just because the painting is here. I squash down that swelling emotion. I left this town because leaving is all it ever warranted. I'm going to stick to the plan, make my money, and not get attached.

The apartment's owner is an Emily Grey. I know her name from the paperwork. Her listed address is a PO box in Frinton, a three-hour drive away. My client recommended the letting agent, and he had something ready for me to rent. Over the phone, it seemed like a good option that would save me from finding a place to live. The letting agent handed me the keys and a copy of the documents on the street outside. His suit was creased at the back, as though he had driven a long way and hadn't hung the jacket up.

"You're here to work?" he asked.

"Yeah. They wanted someone with local roots." I played it down. Film work isn't proper work around here. "I guess I fit that description."

"Lucky they found you. If you don't like it, just pop the keys in the post, but I'd give it a week." He shifted uncomfortably, unwilling to look me in the eye, raising my suspicions about what I was walking into.

I was underwhelmed when I first walked in, but it's cheap and clean, and that painting keeps drawing my eye. I mail the papers to the box in Frinton, and a direct debit mandate to my bank.

The landlady's reply is waiting for me the next day. The envelope is smudged, as though posted in the rain, and there is no stamp on it. The note inside is handwritten. "Mr. Harry Grahame, I hope you enjoy your stay. Please let me know if you need anything."

It is signed with a flourish. There's no email address, no mobile number. Even the paper is old, yellowed with a faint watermark. I try to put it away in the small table in the hall. The drawer is stuck fast.

The café downstairs gives me the password to their Wi-Fi every morning with my flat white and pastry. It closes at seven, and the Wi-Fi with it. There is nothing to do in the evenings except listen to music on my laptop and stare at the painting. It drags me in, easing my mind into a reflective calm.

My bank calls a few days after I have moved in. The direct debit has not gone through. I try the agent. He doesn't pick up. This is a pain I don't need; there are no creatives on the project, no researchers or runners, the agency has me doing everything. It gives me another reason to hate small town work, to hate this small town.

I find the agent's office while scouting locations for establishing shots. The windows are whitewashed from the inside. The shadow of "Portsmouth Properties" is just visible in the blistered wooden sign above the glass. Layers of posters and graffiti show it has been shut for years.

I ask the grocer next door about it. He opened his store three years ago, and the office was long closed by then. I head back, out of time for the day.

I write a note to Emily Grey that evening, explaining that I have every intention of paying the rent, when I have the right details. I don't have a stamp. I'll have to make time for the post office. I don't understand how she can run her business by snail mail alone.

The next evening, there is another letter waiting. I recognise her handwriting. This one has been hand delivered. She can't be shuttling back and forth from Frinton, she must be lodging locally.

"Don't worry about the rent, Harry. I'm sure you're an honest man. I've fixed a few things. The drawer has been unjammed. I hope you like the new painting."

I open the drawer. It's filled with bric-a-brac. Scissors, a comb with teeth missing, paper clips. There's a CD: The Spice Girls. It makes me smile. I haven't thought of them in a long while. I take it with me to inspect the picture.

Another painting, this time of a sunset over the ocean. I try to move it, but it's as immobile as its partner.

I pull out my laptop to play the CD, and my unsent note about the rent drops out. I didn't get time to go to the post office. It takes me a minute to realise what has happened. She has pre-empted my excuses because the deposit payment didn't go into her account. She can't have known the bank details are wrong. Besides, had I posted the letter, it would not have arrived in time for her to reply. I put it all down to her being polite but cautious, the little improvements and the note together saying: I'm willing to trust you, but you had better hold up your end.

I fall asleep in the armchair, looking at the painting and remembering someone humming "Viva Forever," sometime in a foggy past.

On Saturday, I start by Googling Emily Grey. The page fills with results, but the name is too common to find out who she is. I try to narrow the search, but nothing relevant surfaces. I try the letting agent next, but there is only an old advert on Yelp. I steam open the envelope with my first note and write her a new one, promising to sort things out, and thanking her for her patience.

I spend half an hour queuing in the post office before trying to find out more about the letting agent. There's a run-down hardware store across the street, shelves stacked high with cardboard trays of screws. The old man behind the scarred wooden counter brightens with hope when he sees me. It dies when he realises all I need is information.

"Geoff," he says, "That was the chap. Closed down the business years ago, moved away. Some trouble. I don't know what. Keep myself to myself." He suggests the library. From an ancient ledger, he pulls out an invoice for the emulsion on the windows of the letting agency. He gives me the date, says he hasn't seen Geoff since then. No other customers come in while I am there. I pick up some hooks and a small claw hammer because I think I should buy something. His smile when I pay makes it worthwhile.

The library closes early on a Saturday, and does not open at all on Sundays. If there are answers there, I must wait. I'm restless and uneasy, nothing here fits right. Perhaps my client was doing Geoff a favour, making him the middleman to rent out an apartment. Small towns breed debts and obligations between the local businessmen, and they'll pay a premium to trade with their own. I had thought that was why they picked me out of London's crowded media scene, a prodigal son making a film about how his small town is catching up with modernity. Instead, I get the feeling there are walls being thrown up. In a week, they have not yet taken me to the development site I am supposed to film, and yet all around there are signs of gentrification.

I pace the apartment, wall to wall, fingers trailing on the worn frames of the sunsets. The room is too small. I saw a tiger once in London Zoo, prowling and half mad in its enclosure. I'm starting to regret coming back, no matter how much they plan on paying me. I throw myself into the chair and the paintings calm me, the still forms of the cacti whisper that there is more to life than this. Over the ocean, a storm is rising, sending scudding clouds in pink and purple across the evening sky.

"I like them both," I whisper to myself. Online, I look up pictures of other sunsets to see if I can identify the artist. It is a subject populated by hacks. There are too many. I snap the laptop shut and head down to the café. I'm in no mood to be alone.

I put my restless mood down to Portsmouth, as I sip a large chai latte. I grew up surrounded by its grinding poverty, relieved only when the navy ships came in and sailors spent their hoarded pay.

Foster care is the work of saints, but sometimes even the kindest people just don't fit as parents. I suspect that most of us in the system harboured dreams of a real family, a real place in the world. We just never spoke of it, wary of the sign of weakness, shy of holding on to a hope. It's worse when siblings can't stay together. I had an older sister once, an entire world of family in one freckled face. I remember now—she used to love the Spice Girls, and would hum that tune to me, before the system split us up for the trouble she was in. By the time I was sixteen and free, I had given up hope of finding her. If I'm honest, it still hurts that she never looked for me. That cold never warmed, and left all my memories of Portsmouth frigid and unwelcome.

When I'm the only customer left, I ask the manager about the apartment. She doesn't know much, just that it's been empty for years. She thinks the whole building is owned by one guy, but the café chain deals with that side of things. There is an offer in her eyes, but the chai sits uncomfortably in my queasy stomach. I stumble out, trying to make sense of what she has said. I pause on every other step when I head upstairs, processing.

The hammer and the hooks have moved. There's a third painting on the wall. A winter sun dips over the bare branches of a forest. There is no note.

I stamp on my rising panic with cold practicality. Every room, every cupboard, every shadow is examined and discounted. I am alone. I lean my suitcase against the front door, not trusting the locks.

Only then do I succumb to the tremors, down on my haunches, back pressed into the wall, until I can summon up the courage to crawl to bed. Sleep does not come until the small hours.

I lie in on Sunday morning, listening to the café come alive. Fathers bring their toddlers for a babyccino and to discuss yesterday's football. They're not local. They drive in from the smart outlying villages, leaving the shopping to their wives. The real locals probably hate them, but still accept their cash.

I'm one of the outsiders now. I got myself some skills and I got out. I don't belong anymore. The truth is that I never did. Without my sister, there was nothing holding me here.

The suitcase hasn't moved. I pull open the curtains. Muted light lifts the room. I write another note to Emily Grey, asking her to let me know before she visits, and to ask again for her bank details so I can resubmit the direct debit mandate. If she really is lodging close by, I may just pin it to the door instead of posting it.

An emergency locksmith charges me well over the odds for deadbolts and a new chain. He checks the window as well. I'm still restless, switching on the kettle for him, taking the few strides down the hall to examine my new locks, pacing. He offers to sweep the place for bugs. He seems earnest and full of genuine sympathy, his tone reassuring and willing to believe.

"The stalkers are more sophisticated these days. We have to be too," he explains.

I hadn't thought of her that way. His words darken the room again, but at least I don't feel vulnerable anymore.

A night of security restores my perspective. I've met my share of unreliable agents over the years, and protective building owners, suspicious of their tenants. Miss Grey was probably just trying to be discreet about Geoff's failings, and checking up on me at the same time.

I'm sipping a coffee in front of the paintings, winding myself up to go to work, when my client at the ad agency calls, cancelling the contract. His client, the one proposing the development, has died suddenly. There's nothing he can do; *force majeure*, he says and hangs up. I don't have a job now, and soon Emily Grey is going to want the rent.

At least I'm free to go to the library. Old copies of the weekly local paper are held in boxes. I start at my target date and go backwards. Geoff Clement is on the front page two months before his office closed. The years since have been hard on him, in the picture he is trim and sharp.

He faced charges for negligence. The tenant in his apartment died from gas fumes, leaking from the boiler. He tried to blame it on her drug taking, to write her off as a bohemian artist whose life was in some way precarious by definition. The police found an addict's paraphernalia, but it was carbon monoxide that killed her.

I'm living in that apartment. The victim was Emily Grey.

I have to read it several times over before the words sink in. Emily Grey was a tenant. Have I signed an old tenancy agreement with her name still on it? Did I misread that elaborate signature? The article is perfectly clear: Geoff Clement was the owner of the whole building, renting out the apartments and the shop space through his own real estate agency.

My fingertips are pressed into the desk. I need to sit, but my limbs refuse to obey. My trembling hand moves of its own volition. I burn precious mobile data to check his name. His local paper has a newsfeed. He died yesterday, in his garage, in Frinton. Suicide, a hose from the exhaust into the back window. He has no family.

Everything in the apartment is old except for the gas boiler. That is his admission. His negligence did kill Emily. My jaws clench, teeth trying to grind through each other. With one act of contrition, after all these years, he has made his escape.

Dread freezes my anger. Who has been writing me notes, and who has been giving me sunsets?

The melamine surface of the desk swims under my eyes, blurring in a wash of vertigo. I leave the newspapers and stumble away, knocking the archive box to the floor. The librarian glares and bustles over. I shove him aside and head to the door.

I run. My car is parked around the corner, but I have to run. I stumble up the stairs and fumble for the new keys. The locks are stiff. The door catches on a thick envelope on the mat, and swings back at me. I snatch it from under the door and blunder inside.

A fourth painting hangs on the wall. The armchair sags under my weight. Another sunset, over a beach. Two children run along the water line. The girl is older. She is not shown in any detail, but there are pigtails and the flare of a dress. The other child toddles behind. They're skipping, holding hands.

I've lost control of my lower lip. It twitches and spasms like the prelude to a storm of tears. I know the girl in the painting. A shudder starts in my belly and ricochets through my mouth.

"Emsy."

There is a note on the floor.

"You don't need to write me letters, Harry."

The memory in the painting enfolds me. I stare at it, trying to focus as the little boy sings his sister's name "Emsy, Emsy." The marks in the corner are not a broken groyne, but initials: EG. Now I know what to look for, I lurch to the other paintings. EG, hidden in the corners. Two lumps amid the cacti are two children sitting shoulder to shoulder. There is a boat amid the dark swells of the ocean, by the torchlight of my phone I see a shading hinting at two small passengers. And they sit in a tree watching the snow fall.

I need to see more. I punch another hook into the wall. A second, not caring where. If I give her the hooks perhaps she'll give me more sunsets. My heart thuds harder than the hammer, the hooks slip and shudder against the painted wall. I miss. The hammer bursts through, revealing a space where there should be none. I turn the hammer and rip away plaster with the claw end. Thick lumps drop on the faded carpet.

The space is only a foot deep. There are paintings lining the hidden wall, I can see the frames and only a splash of colour from the hole I have made. I don't need to see them, they are all sunsets. Glorious sunsets that have refused to leave this drab apartment, that will not come off the walls once placed.

I drop heavily into the chair and find the forgotten envelope. The postmark is from Frinton. Inside are deeds, in my name. The whole building signed over to me from Geoff Clement. There is also a note on thick, pure white paper. The job was a lie, one last step towards his atonement.

Grey, Grahame. She must have changed her name when she left the foster system. Did she ever look for me, or did the trouble that took her away, when I was still too young to say her name properly, keep her in its grip? I lean my head against the rough surface of the oil paints. In some lucid moments between the bonds of her addiction, she painted her own escape, and every time she took her baby brother with her. She didn't forget me. I have an anchor to this town. Sometimes siblings can't stay together. Sometimes they find their own way back.

HARRY GRAHAME is a freelance film maker who escaped his small-town upbringing as a foster child at the first opportunity. He is single and lives in whatever rented accommodation his latest project allows him to afford.

ALI ABBAS is a writer, carpenter, and photographer born and bred in London. He is the author of *Like Clockwork*, a steampunk mystery published by Transmundane Press; *Image and Other Stories*, a collection of seven short stories that examine themes of love, loss, and the haunting nature of bad decisions; and *Hajj—My Pilgrimage*, a light-hearted and secular look at the pilgrimage to Mecca that is at the heart of the Islamic faith. His short story/love letter to London "An Absolute Amount of Sadness" was published by *Mad Scientist Journal* in their *Fitting In* anthology. You can find out what he is up to through his blog at www.aliabbasali.com.

HUM

An account by Doris Thompson,
AS PROVIDED BY AUDREY MACK

I see the town beneath the water. Just below my boat, the tip of a steeple juts close enough to touch. It was white once, I think, but now the rotting wood is mottled green and grey with spreading algae. If I touched it, would it crumble? There are no fish that I can see, and the only thing that disturbs the smooth surface of the water are the ripples from my oars as I row. The lake is deep, and I cannot see the bottom, but I know that just out of sight lies the rest of the town. My imagination makes houses, schools, and shops out of the shadows.

There is not another soul here. It's hard to believe there ever was. The lake sits in the center of a valley, tucked between hills covered in trees of rust and amber, and the only sound is the whisper of their dying leaves as the wind rifles through them. My fishing pole lies at my feet, forgotten. I've lost sight of the stream that brought me here; when I turn around, the opening is gone, hidden by the drooping branches of a willow. Or was it over there, behind that outcropping of slate?

Instead of turning and finding my way back, I row farther out onto the lake. Curiosity overwhelms my unease. Sometimes I think I see a blur of movement behind me, but when I turn my head to look, it is only the shadow of my oar, or the wake of my boat. The air is cold, cold, cold. My fingers are numb, so I pull them into my sleeves and let the boat bob in the center of the lake. The wind dies down, and there is silence.

What is this place? The man I rented the boat from did not mention it, nor the woman at the bait store. There were no signs. Perhaps to those who live nearby, a flooded town is nothing more than a piece of history.

A deep humming disturbs the silence, almost a throb, so low that it is felt more than heard. I shift in my seat and scan the shoreline, searching for the source of the sound. There is nothing to see but the trees and the pebbly strip of land that encircles the lake. Where is it coming from? Who is it coming from, man, or machine, or animal? It is mournful, like a whale song, and I have the unsettling realization it is coming from below me, in the water. I have the sudden desire to be away from here. With clumsy hands, I take up the oars and start to paddle back the way I came.

The sound grows louder with every stroke, until my ears are ringing and I want to throw down my oars and clap my hands over them. Instead I push on, driving the boat through the water with all the speed I can manage. Sweat slides down my spine. It takes only minutes to reach the willow tree, I am sure, but it feels like hours, and my muscles shake from exhaustion and adrenaline as I slow the boat. I close my eyes to push through the curtain of branches. They slide over my shoulders like fingers and catch in my hair, and I bat them away frantically, feeling foolish when I open my eyes again and there is nothing there but leaves and sticks. Nothing. There is nothing there. No stream to lead me back, just the tree and the forest stretching behind it.

If only the humming would stop, I could think. But it doesn't, it drones on relentlessly, and the sweat cools, and my fingers ache, and I curse the lake and myself. Then I turn the boat around and row along the edge of the water, looking for the stream I know is there. I find inlets and coves and trees, endless trees, but nothing else. I am just about to turn back to the willow tree when I see something on the farthest shore that gives me hope. A person. I wave my hands above my head and bellow, and I think they turn to look at me. Relief, so powerful it drowns out the incessant sound, floods me, and I row with renewed vigor across the lake.

The clouds creep across the sun, and though I am getting closer, all I can see of the person is that they are tall and slim and grey. All at once my panic seems absurd. I pause at the center of the lake, not wanting to seem a lunatic, and peer down into the water, letting my heartbeat steady and slow. Without the bright sun overhead, the town under the water is clearer. There are paths between the buildings, a row of houses. A swing set sways in the underwater current. My imagination places a child there, kicking her legs to make the swing go higher, hair streaming behind her. The boat tilts, my face is inches from the water. I tumble backward, rocking the boat violently the other way. It is a long time before my stomach drops from my throat. When I look toward the shore, the stranger is gone.

No, no, no. I grab the oars and row toward the spot I last saw them. Even if they are gone, there must be a path I can follow out, and I hold on to that hope as the wind picks up again. No longer is it a gentle breeze through the trees; it is a gale, trying to drive me back. My hair whips against my cheeks, but I press onward and the boat creeps toward land.

Fifty feet from the shore, I realize I am humming. I cannot place the tune, but when I stop, the other sound grows louder and louder until I begin again just to drown it out. At last, the bottom of my boat scrapes land. My shoes fill with water, and I slip and stumble on the tiny pebbles, legs like water, dragging the boat behind me until it is safely beached. The shore is nothing more than ten feet of rocks before the line of trees begins. Though I call, cupping my hands around my mouth until my voice echoes back at me, the stranger does not reappear. There are no footprints to follow.

Hope flees as swiftly as it came. If I could only get the sound to stop, I would be able to think clearly. I sink down onto the shore and sit, elbows on my knees and head in my hands. I do not know how long I sit there. Dusk has come up around me, but there are no crickets, no owls, only the humming. There is a music to it now, a grandmother's lullaby heard through the fog of sleep, and I hum along to it as I get to my feet. When I find the source of it, I know I will find my way out.

Something moves in the corner of my eye. I turn and the stranger is there, standing on a cobblestone road. A linen white steeple pierces the sky behind them. I blink, and they are gone, and the road is gone, and the steeple is gone, but something bobs in the water, dark and sleek like a seal. I call to it. It gets closer, swaying, until it bumps against the shore and I realize it is nothing more than a piece of wood smoothed by the water. A hallucination. I have spent too long on the water, beneath the sun, and it has addled my mind. Still, I cannot resist turning to look for the stranger again, and the town I saw behind them.

I do not find the stranger, but I do find the cobblestone road. It is half-buried by dead leaves. I kick them aside as I follow it to the forest's edge and pause there beneath an oak tree, but one step into the woods and the humming turns to a screeching wail. I back away, squeezing my temples, until the gentle lullaby returns. Following the road back leads to the water's edge. I do not know how I missed it before. Crouching at the shore, I can see the path sloping down along the lakebed. It goes on endlessly, as far as I can see. Here, the song is so sweet. It fills me with a longing for home. I dip my hand into the lake and it is warm, so warm, it chases the chill from my bones.

There is no harm in it. I shed my clothes and step into the water.

A swim will clear my mind. The moon is an engorged pearl hanging overhead, and it bathes the water in a silver glow that is better than any flashlight. I wade in deeper, and the water embraces me like a lover. What had seemed an illusion before is as real as my own body; the town is there and whole, and the stranger waits for me, hand outstretched. They are beautiful.

Why had I ever tried to leave? The stranger's song is a promise. The road beneath my feet pulls me forward like a current and I cannot refuse, I do not want to. The town beneath the water waits for me, and the song beckons me home.

DORIS THOMPSON has three grandchildren, an overgrown garden, and fingernails stained black from her years as a mechanic. She recently retired and sold off her auto shop in order to spend more time exploring the world and breathing in something fresher than diesel fumes. Her favorite adventures end with a large piece of pie.

AUDREY MACK is a proofreader, book reviewer, and reader of all things fictional, with a special interest in the odd and unexplainable. She lives in New England on a quiet, little farm and spends much of her time in the woods, dreaming of the monsters dwelling just out of sight.

REMNANTS

An account by Tek-Kuan Chin,
AS PROVIDED BY TIMOTHY NAKAYAMA

My third eye is closed. But I don't need to use it to know that there's something not quite right about the abandoned orphanage at the end of the lane.

From my vantage point in the middle of the street, I take in the orphanage in its entirety. There's not a single picture of it online, but thanks to Google Earth's Street View, I was able to get a good look at the building before driving all the way here.

The building itself is unremarkable. A two-story brick and stone affair, plain red-tiled roofing, wooden railings on the balconies of the top floor. The small plot of land it sits on is enclosed by rusty wrought-iron fencing, the spear-tipped pickets standing like flimsy, spindly black sentinels who long ago lost their battle with the encroaching thicket of trees that hem the orphanage in on all three sides save for the entrance side leading out onto the street.

I've never been to an orphanage before, but the Fairfield Girls Home looks exactly how I imagine a decommissioned orphanage built in the early 1900s would look.

But it isn't the building's architectural charms, or lack thereof, that has led me to the conclusion that there's something weird going on with this orphanage.

No.

It's because of two phone calls I made to my cousin a week ago.

It began when I received his message.

Just finished meeting with client. Need your help. Cleaning up property. Call me when free.

I knew what sort of "cleaning" he was after.

"Hey, where's the property?"

"What property?" he asked.

"The one you messaged me about."

"What message?"

This was only an hour after I'd received his message.

After checking his message history, he laughed and apologized, telling me about the rough day he'd been having and how he must have completely forgotten about it.

That should have been my first clue that something strange was going on. But at that point, I was merely skeptical, wondering whether he was hiding something from me. Chee Kong doesn't do rough days at work; he doesn't do forgetful either. He's the anal-retentive, workaholic, Type-A cousin who hired some hotshot interior designer guy to work on his house and office space in the CBD to make them "maximumly efficient." Chee Kong is a fish that swims in the great ocean of stress.

But I kept my silence as he told me about Fairfield Girls Home, how the Fairfield City Council had been meaning to tear it down for years but never got around to it, and how they've now hired his company to do it so that the council can reclaim the land for the construction of a local college.

Then came the interesting bit. In the file the council had given him access to, Chee Kong discovered that all five of the contractors who had previously been awarded the project dropped it soon thereafter, declaring the project unfeasible. The reason Chee Kong got in touch with me: one of those five contractors had also noted that several of his workers refused to set foot inside the building—they claimed that the place was cursed.

"Sounds exactly like your kind of gig, Kuan," he said.

I told him I'd think about it.

It wasn't long before my intuition started kicking into overdrive. Playing a hunch, I called Chee Kong again, two hours later.

"What are you talking about? What orphanage?"

That confirmed it: something seriously weird is going on at the Fairfield Girls Home.

I embrace the quiet, study my surroundings.

A thick swath of trees lines the edge of the cul-de-sac, wild and ornery things packed so tightly together that it's hard to see beyond them.

The progression of houses on the orphanage's side of the street stopped three-quarters of the way in from the main road, giving way to fields of overgrown grass and thickets of trees. The houses on the other side, however, continue all the way to the end.

Catching movement out of the corner of my eye, I turn around in search of its source, and find myself looking at the house directly across from the orphanage.

Like all the other houses along the lane, it's decades old, the exterior paintwork peeling off in patches, the roof sagging in most parts, the lawn the size of a postcard.

The movement came from the people gathered behind the front

window. At this distance, I can't see enough to make out their faces, but the three of them are standing in a way that makes it obvious that all three are looking at me. They probably know all their neighbors, so I imagine they're wondering what I'm doing here, in the middle of nowhere, looking at a…

I frown. Something's wrong. Feels wrong. I'm on the proverbial train of thoughts, heading *somewhere* because trains are supposed to take people somewhere, but I can't remember which stop I'm supposed to get off at. I know I'd been thinking about *something* just a moment ago, but when I try to recall my thoughts, I get nothing. It's like someone placed a huge black blot over the last few minutes of my memory. It's a black hole in my mind, and I cannot peer through.

Without knowing why, I let my gaze fall upon the house before me. I see the three figures crowding behind the window; they're too far away for me to get a good look at them but I know they're observing me. Wondering what I'm doing here. But… the way they're standing, they're also looking at something directly behind me.

Curious, I turn around—and see the orphanage.

What happens next is surreal and disorienting. The black hole is whipped away, and all my thoughts and memories are exactly where I left them a moment ago. I remember why I'm here and what brought me here.

What just happened?

In only a matter of seconds, I completely forgot about the orphanage. As if I'd never known about it. It was only because I intuitively grasped that the people behind the window in the house were not just looking at me but also at something behind me that I had the presence of mind to turn around.

Something strange and unnatural is at work here. I think I'm one step closer to understanding Chee Kong and his memory lapse. The Fairfield City Council, why they've been taking forever to tear this place down. The contractors who were awarded the job but abandoned the project before they even started.

There's an immediate itch to take my eyes off the orphanage again, to test out my semi-solid theory, but I know if I do that, there's a risk I might walk away from here without ever knowing why I came. I keep my gaze steady, and begin walking.

My first few steps are slow, unsteady, but my ravenous curiosity lends vitality to my body and soon I stand before the orphanage's black gate.

It's chained and padlocked. Not a problem for me. But there's an easier way in. A little to the left of the gate, two of the pickets in the fence have broken off due to rust.

An exercise in flexibility and balance and I'm through.

The seed heads of the waist-high grass blow gently in the breeze, a slow, dancing cloud of yellow and red. I use my hands to part the grass and make my way onto the stone path that begins just past the gate and leads to the orphanage's front door.

As I walk, I wonder whether the people who live in the house across from the orphanage are calling the police. After all, I'm trespassing on what is very likely government land. I'm not bothered by that though. I've got Chee Kong and his buddies on the council on my side.

What worries me infinitely more are the secrets hidden within Fairfield Girls Home.

A person with my set of skills *and* any measure of self-preservation would have rejected Chee Kong's offer. But what I've discovered over the years is that, for people who have my skillset, self-preservation doesn't come into the picture.

Sure, we take precautions; it would be extremely foolish otherwise. But for those of us with the sight, it's as if there's an invisible thread fastened around us, and no matter how far we drift away, that thread will eventually draw taut, catch us, swing us back in an arc so that once again, we come face to face with the other world only we can see. We see the ebbs and flows. We see things in this world most people can't. Most of these beings are benign, a rare few even all right to be around. But some hate us and refuse to co-exist peacefully. That's when you need the precautions. And a great big helping of common sense.

It's been awhile since I've utilized my eclectic skillset. I left that part of my life back in Malaysia. Chee Kong knows that about me. I've been here in Sydney for two years now, working a mundane 9 to 5 office job, an underwriter at a small, family-run insurance agency in Circular Quay.

He thinks that offering me a cut will entice me, get me to make use of my talents again. Well, the money's great. It'll whittle down the loan on my new two-bedroom in Balmain.

But the money's just an added incentive. The hunger to discover the truth, that invisible thread tugging me closer, these two are a lot stronger than whatever money Chee Kong is throwing on the table.

I reach the steps that lead up to the front double doors. Whoever the current owner of the orphanage is, they didn't bother with chains and padlocks for the doors. The only security to prevent unlawful entry is the doors' deadbolt lock.

The windows on either side are too high up for me to see anything more than the beige walls inside.

For a building that's been abandoned for more than two decades, it looks to be in very good shape. Which is surely part of the mystery. After all, if I got through the missing pickets in the fence with little difficulty, what's stopping anyone else from doing the same? Even if they couldn't pick the lock, they could just bash the door down or smash the windows to get inside. From what I'd read online, that's exactly what happened to a decommissioned orphanage in Goulburn. People just ransacking the place, hoping to find anything of value. Squatters making the place their own. Graffiti all over the walls.

Arsonists setting the furniture alight. Even ghost tours organized for thrill-seekers.

So why hasn't anything of the sort even remotely touched Fairfield Girls Home? Why is there just a grand total of three mentions of Fairfield Girls Home online?

I move on to the backyard, making sure I keep the orphanage in view the entire time; this building is not going to get the better of me.

On one side of the backyard are two wooden posts that once served as a clothesline, on the other a tiny toolshed. There's a back gate built into the fencing on the farthest side, chained and padlocked like its front counterpart.

The back door is my next stop. Simple deadbolt like the front door. I take my lock-picks out and it takes all of ten seconds, but when I try to open the door, it doesn't budge. Could be one of two things: something heavy stacked up against the door on the inside, or the door has swollen badly over the years.

I make my way back to the front of the building. As I consider the double doors before me, I begin pondering why my third eye has remained shut. There's a definite conflux here. It's weak, but strong enough that even those without my talents could pick it up if they're sensitive enough and know what to look for. Like those workers who thought this place cursed.

I've been expecting my third eye to show me something, anything, that would offer a clue to the orphanage's mystery. If there are non-human beings in the vicinity, whether benign or malicious, it should open.

The fact that it hasn't worries me. I wonder what it means.

I take the steps up to the doors. When I'm done picking the locks, I gently push both doors back; they swing open to reveal an entrance hall, and a narrower staircase hall beyond it.

The smell isn't as bad as I expected. But just because I'm helpless to resist the pull of whatever forces are at play inside the orphanage doesn't mean I've given up on common sense. From my jacket, I whip out my P2 respirator and strap it onto my face.

And then I enter.

The floor is tiled, the ceiling made of stamped steel. On the right of the hall is a small room with two baroque-style sofas and nothing else. A reception room.

Two more steps and I pass under a molded archway that leads into the longer, narrower staircase hall. I don't go up the staircase for now.

I continue down the hall. There are two smaller rooms, which, judging by the size and the furniture in them, could have been sitting rooms. Another room is longer and has a chalkboard—a class or study room. A room that's much bigger has two trestle tables, each paired with two benches of the same length. A refectory. There's a laundry room, although the two machines inside look more like creepy alien spaceships than laundry machines. Farther down the hall is a short flight of steps that leads down to a steel door. Storage probably. Another staircase at the end of the hall. This one is made of stone and girded by brick walls.

Finally, I reach the back of the house, where the kitchen is. There are shelves, tables and chairs, an ancient stove, and a small space that must have served as a pantry.

I try the back door again. It won't budge. Swollen door it is then.

Considering everything I've seen so far, this orphanage looks perfectly ordinary, perfectly mundane. Nothing I've seen so far suggests that there are entities here or that the building is rooted to anywhere but the physical world.

Maybe I'll find what I'm looking for upstairs.

I head back to the stone staircase with the brick walls around it. I realize now that this must be fire-proof stairs, an alternative escape route in case a fire broke out.

I'm halfway up the stairs when my third eye finally opens. Only not in the way I expect. It bursts open so suddenly and forcefully that

I stumble backward, almost losing my footing.

My insides are roiling with a fear so cold it burns. It's never happened before—my third eye going from completely shut to wide open instantaneously. I don't know what it means.

The only thing I know is this: I must get out of here right now.

Acting on fear and instinct alone, I throw myself off the stairs. My heels thump heavily down onto the tiled floor but I don't feel the impact. I propel myself forward with each pump of my legs. There is nothing else in the world but me, the double doors, and a world of life and safety waiting for me on the other side.

My fear gives way to recklessness. I push myself off the floor and sail wildly forward into the air, hands desperately scrabbling for the world outside.

Eternity is passing me by as I hang in the air. Graceless and lumbering, I fly past the doorframe. The small part of my mind that has yet to sink below the ocean of panic engulfing me recognizes the possibility of tumbling down the steps and injuring myself. But another part of me, a more primitive part whose skills have been honed by dozens of encounters with beings not of this world, knows that there are some situations where pain, even death, are preferable options.

I don't land so much as crumple into a heap on the ground. I stretch out my hands before me to soften my fall, cry out in pain when my palms and knees slam into the ground.

Cursing, I get up to my feet—then stiffen.

No.

I am in the same entrance hall I just jumped out of. In front of me is the same staircase hall I sprinted through. To my right is the exact same small reception room, with the exact same sofas.

I swivel on my heels, but I already know what I'll see.

Through the doors I just jumped past is the mirror image of the entrance hall I'm standing in now. It's like I'm peering into a mirror. The only difference is that there isn't a me standing on that side.

The effect is so disorienting that I fall to my knees. My breathing comes in ragged heaves, and I smell sour fear sweat on me. Gripping the edge of the door, I pull myself up and take slow, deep breaths to calm myself as I try to come to grips with what I'm seeing.

When I've beaten the panic back with the iron fist of calm, I try walking out the front doors a few times. It's no use. I just end up walking into the other side's entrance hall. The effect is so eerie that I soon forget which one is the original entrance, the one I leapt out of, and which one the mirror image.

I look out the windows on either side of the doors. There's no grass, or stone path, or any sign of the outside world—the only thing I look out on is the mirror image of the entrance hall. Going through the windows works exactly like going through the doors—I just end up in the same place.

My first guess is that I've inhaled some sort of airborne spore or toxin that might have spread throughout the inside of the orphanage over the years and I'm now suffering from the subsequent mental hallucinations. But I quickly dismiss this possibility. I'm wearing a P2 respirator *and* spores wouldn't account for my third eye opening so forcefully. I take out my phone—there's no connectivity.

Whatever's causing this is beyond the realm of science; I'm firmly in otherworld territory here.

My mind returns to the moment on the stone staircase. This is the first time my third eye has opened so widely, so quickly. In the past, it's always opened a fraction upon entering premises where a spirit resides, and continues opening the closer I get to the spirit. The more powerful and malevolent the spirit, the faster and wider it opens.

But never as wide as it is now. Not even when I came face to face with that penanggalan in Sumatra. It's as if this place is forcing it to go beyond its limits. My limits.

That means I'm in uncharted territory. It detected nothing at first, then somehow picks up the emperor of spirits? Is there something lurking here that can somehow *mask* its presence? A spirit that can change my perception of space? Is that even possible?

If the answer to that is yes, I am seriously out of my depth here.

It almost feels like a trap of some sort, like I took the bait, entered this place, and now I'm stuck in the trap's slavering jaws.

I take slow, deep breaths, chant several mantras to sharpen my focus. The tension in my muscles dissipate, my mind beats the waves of panic back. I'm resolved to finding a way out. I'm not about to give up and die.

If the front doors and windows don't work, perhaps those in the kitchen might.

As I pass the two sitting rooms, something at the edge of my peripheral vision draws my attention.

It takes me a moment to realize what had caught my eye. It's the room itself, everything in it. The furniture is several shades lighter. The mold growing on the wall is gone. The blanket of dust on everything is nowhere to be seen.

"What are you doing here?" says a husky voice from behind me.

I recoil in horror, my heart jackhammering in my chest. I spin around to stare into the face of an elderly woman covered head to toe in the black and white of a nun's habit. Her face is set in a scowl, her almond eyes shining with naked irritation.

"Sorry, Sister Mary," say two voices in unison behind me.

I turn around with trepidation and see two young girls standing together, both dressed in navy blue tunics over white short-sleeved blouses, cinched at the waist with white crochet belts. They are skinny little girls, maybe six or seven; both are dark, their features clearly that of Aboriginal people. From their lowered eyes and look of guilt on their faces, it appears that they're the recipients of the nun's ire.

"Get going to class now," Sister Mary says.

"Yes, Sister Mary," the girls mumble. As they flee down the hall, their outlines blur and they fade away into nothingness.

The nun harrumphs and ambles off in the opposite direction, disappearing in the same way. I'm standing alone in the hall once more. I peer into the sitting room; age and dust cover everything, as they had before.

Thoughts race through my mind, coming to me fast and furious.

The state of the room before and after, the way the girls and nun spoke and dressed, it's obvious that I've just seen a vision of the past, a moment in time before the orphanage was decommissioned.

But it's the nature of the vision that puzzles me. The girls and the nun are not spirits. Whether benign or malicious, all spirits have an aura about them, the aura's color depending on the spirit's nature and intent. My third eye picked up no such aura about them. They're not specters of the past, doomed to replay the events of their lives repeatedly. But then, what are they?

I have always trusted my third eye's observations without reservations. But right now, I'm at a loss to interpret its observations. It makes no sense to me.

And why am I seeing visions of the past? I know, from Master Yu's teachings, that there are certain places and conditions that will produce visions visible to those with the sight, but I've never actually experienced that.

Something happened here, something that made this place more than just an orphanage.

I continue walking down the hall.

Before I can take more than a few steps, I hear a woman's voice.

"New South Wales was founded in 1788."

It's coming from the study room. The room has two doors, one on either end. Warily, I step up to the door closest to me, and peer in.

A nun, younger than the first, stands in front of the class of girls, gesturing at an unfurled map of Australia hanging on the blackboard.

The girls in the front appear to be doing their best to sit upright and pay attention. Those at the back are doing a good job of hiding their restlessness. Two blonde-haired girls in the back row wait until the nun has her back to the class, before they grin and make faces at each other across the empty desk between them.

Nun and girls dissipate into nothingness, and I am left staring at a blackboard that hasn't seen chalk in twenty years.

My ears suddenly pick up the soft susurrus of many young girls talking at once. I make my way toward the refectory, where I see the girls sitting at the trestle tables, eating and chattering, all under the watchful eyes of two nuns seated at a small table in the corner.

The girls have split into two very distinct groups, each group claiming a table for their own. The larger group of girls are white; theirs is the louder, more gregarious group. The Aboriginal girls number only five; theirs is the much quieter table. The five of them exchange nervous glances as they eat.

One of the girls from the larger group says something and suddenly the chatter at their table dies down. All of them stare at the Aboriginal girls, eyes and faces set in quietly menacing masks. The Aboriginal girls huddle closer together.

A heavy sadness starts descending on me. These Aboriginal girls must be part of the Stolen Generation—Aboriginal children who were taken from their families, to be assimilated into white Australian society, on the premise that it was for their own good. It is an indelible strand of history that, to this day, threads its way through the very fabric of this country.

One of the white girls says something too soft for me to pick up, upon which her whole table laughs. The Aboriginal girls say nothing but hold each other's hands in solidarity. The nuns watch on, but do and say nothing.

The moment in time fades away.

I walk on, past the stone staircase, stepping into the kitchen at the back of the orphanage.

Sister Mary and one of the nuns from the refectory are preparing food. They wash, chop, slice, cook, and move about the kitchen briskly, effortlessly, without getting in each other's way.

"But why'd they refuse?" says the shorter, stockier nun. "They must know we're full up here."

Sister Mary harrumphs. "They only care about what's just under their noses, Agnes."

"But we're all the same, aren't we?" Sister Agnes protests. "We're just trying to do right by these girls. Give 'em a better life."

"They don't care if we're chockers," Sister Mary says. "Getting them to take in one of our girls is like pulling teeth. Always looking down on us. Oh, Parramatta Girls Home is so great, not like Fairfield Girls Home. Pure bunkum. Just because they get the state's money!"

Sister Agnes shakes her head. "If they've got all that money, they'd be able to do wonders with our troublemakers!"

"Troublemakers, hey? Girls got under your skin this morning? The usual lot?"

Sister Agnes nods. "Always the same." A frown breaks out on her face. "Sometimes I feel—"

The good Sister Agnes never completes her sentence because she and Sister Mary fade from view.

I try the backdoor again; it still won't budge. Moving to the only window in the kitchen, one that faces the backyard, I peer out and see yet another strange sight. Instead of the green of grass and the clothesline and toolshed, I see only thick, billowing clouds of gray, through which I can see nothing. I try to open the window, but no matter how hard I push, the panel, like the door, refuses to budge.

I check all the other windows on this floor. They're all tiny hopper windows, barely large enough for a cat to pass through. Gray clouds, all of them. Yet somehow, the orphanage is lit by sunlight coming in from the same windows.

This feels more like a trap every passing second.

I climb the stone stairs. It takes me to the balcony I saw from outside, with a wooden railing that comes up to my torso.

I should be looking out at grass, the street outside the gate, the house on the other side, the sky, the trees beyond the cul-de-sac—but all I see are clouds of gray.

I slowly walk to the edge of the balcony, grasp the rough surface of the railing, and try to pierce the billowing grayness with my third eye.

I see... nothing. Not the absence of anything, but a complete, total void. Over the wooden railing, there is only non-existence. The orphanage is bounded on all sides by void, by nothing.

Vertigo overcomes me. My knees start buckling; I grab hold of the wooden railing to steady myself.

After a while, I regain my sense of gravity. I let go of the railing and look out once more at the grayness. There will be no escape for me here.

I inspect the long landing that is the balcony. There are doors on both ends of the balcony. Next to both these doors are the two flights of stairs that lead back down below. Between them are two more doors.

I go for the door at the end of the balcony that's closest to me.

Inside is a long and narrow room that runs to the back of the building. Two rows of bunkbeds line up along opposite sides of the room.

Suddenly, the beds are no longer grimy and dusty. There's a girl for every bunk in the room. Away from the prying eyes of the nuns, the girls are carefree, unguarded. They are also all white. For a moment, an inexplicable feeling of envy washes over me—the wish to belong to a large group of friends and family, to be part of something greater. But before I can put a name to this feeling, it is gone. And so too are the girls.

I walk out onto the balcony and am about to open the second door, when a girl, one of the two blonde-haired girls I'd seen making faces at each other in the classroom below, appears before me, looking pointedly at the door.

"Your stories are horrible!" she says. "Baby-killing giants! What sort of rubbish is that! We don't want your jungle stories here!"

The girl is about to say something more but fades away before she can.

I open the door and peer into another dormitory, this one barely larger than a broom closet, with three bunk beds, one for each side of the room. I see the five Aboriginal girls, huddling together on one of the bunks. They speak softly, in a language I don't understand. It sounds like they're comforting one another.

The vision fades. I move on to the next room. A shower room. I wait for a bit, but I see no vision here, so I make my way to the final door on the other side of the balcony.

It opens into a small anteroom with four doors. Each door leads to a bedroom that holds a bed and mattress, a desk, and a private bathroom. These must be the nuns' bedrooms. One of the rooms is larger than the rest and has a metallic five-drawer filing cabinet in the corner. There are many folders inside. I peruse a few. Admin stuff. Invoices and expenses, student records, records one can now easily store on a hard drive. This room must be the head nun's room, serving as both bedroom and records room.

I pace around a bit, but there is no vision here for me.

As I step out onto the landing, I freeze. A dark shape is hurtling toward me, cutting the distance between us in fractions of a second. I try to fall back into the anteroom but the creature's movements are unlike anything I've ever seen. I've barely taken half a step back into the room when it leaps up into the air and slams into me, causing me to lose my balance and fall.

The only thing I register before my world turns black is that, once again, my third eye confirms that this is no spirit.

The tiles of the floor feel icy cold against my cheek.

I'm still alive. But strangely, there's no pain.

I open my eyes, all three of them. I get up, dusting myself off. How long was I out for?

Bigger question: what was that thing?

I check all four private rooms again. Nothing. Shower room and the girls' dormitories. Nothing. No sign of it.

If it's not a spirit, what is it? It can't be a vision, can it? Visions don't slam people into the ground and knock them out cold. But now that I'm free of the fear that had paralyzed me, I begin to wonder. Did it knock me over? Or had I been so terrified of a vision that I stumbled, fell, and hit my head?

I don't know.

If it's a vision, like the nuns and girls, does that mean that this thing too is a moment in time? Is everything strange about the orphanage linked to it? Did this shadow creature prowl the halls and rooms of the orphanage all those years ago?

Suddenly, a new possibility presents itself. The trap becomes a puzzle. If the visions are of what happened here in the orphanage in the past, there must be a reason why I'm seeing them. Perhaps the key in my escaping this trap is to figure out what happened here all those years ago.

I should scour the orphanage for clues. There may be more that I've yet to discover.

Time is the one thing I have a lot of.

The next vision plays out in the refectory.

There are no people in this one, only a completely devastated dining hall. The trestle tables and benches are black and in pieces. Broken plates and glass litter a floor so black I can barely make out the individual tiles. The scorch marks go all the way up the brick wall like shadowy fingers reaching for the ceiling.

I see what might be a clue on one wall. Three long black slashes, too well-defined to be scorch marks.

The vision fades and the refectory is at it was before, with the only black in the room being the spots of mold on the walls.

What was that scene about? A fire or explosion of some sort? But if what I'm seeing are visions of the past, why is the refectory and everything in it in one piece right now, with no scorch marks anywhere to be seen?

The three black slashes against the wall. My mind immediately goes back to that shadowy *thing* that I encountered on the upper floor.

Is this creature the orphanage's mystery? Is it the reason why I find myself trapped here, doomed to view visions of the past until I finally die of thirst and starvation? Well, I'm not going to lie down and call it quits. I may not be as powerful as Master Yu, but I'm no lightweight either.

I head over to the kitchen. Physical weapons do about as much damage to supernatural creatures as bullets do against a tank. But I feel naked without one. My third eye can see many things, but it is not a weapon. I have chants, mantras, symbols, and my will, but those require focus and time, things I might not have when some shadow creature comes barreling at me at the speed of sound.

A rusty chef's knife is the only thing I can find. My fingers glide over the edge of the blade, my lips whisper a chant. When the final syllable has been uttered, I tuck the knife under my belt. The knife's better than useless now. A *little* better.

Before I can trudge off in search of more clues, another moment from the past plays out before me.

"What are they doing out there?" says one of the two nuns standing by the window that looks out into the backyard. Their backs are to me.

I sidle up to them. It's Sister Agnes and the younger nun, the one I saw teaching in the classroom.

"I don't know," says Younger Nun. "They don't really play with the other girls."

"They are different," says Sister Agnes. "Their kind were here in an earlier age. They know things the latecomers do not. They know things we know."

I didn't notice it at first, but now that I'm standing beside them, it becomes apparent: there's something different about their voices. Deeper, coarser, raspier. There's the other thing as well: wispy jet black strands, moving sinuously within the confines of their eyes.

"Where's the other one?" Younger Nun says.

Sister Agnes looks back toward the staircase hall. "I saw her a moment ago."

"She's the troublemaker."

Sister Agnes nods. "I—" The nun cocks her head. "There's something—"

"What is it?"

"I don't know. I think—" Sister Agnes stops mid-sentence, turns around, and looks straight at me.

"What manner of creature are you?" she says, her eyes trained on mine.

I stumble back before Sister Agnes' steely gaze, flinching as if I'd been hit. She's speaking to *me*.

Younger Nun walks over. "What is it, Agnes?"

"There's something here."

Her hand shoots out and clamps onto my wrist. Her grip is bone breaking.

Thin lips curve into a hideous grin. "Got you."

My other hand shoots straight for the knife at my belt, but before I can draw, the nuns dissipate into thin air and I am standing alone in the kitchen, my heart racing wildly.

A vision isn't supposed to be able to leave its imprint on the material world, but the dull ache in my wrist tells a different story. I consider the myriad of possibilities until I settle on the only one that makes sense: the longer I remain trapped here, the more I become part of the orphanage's past. That's how Sister Agnes, or whatever's possessed her, could grab me—the past and the present are somehow overlapping each other.

And I'm trapped between both.

The next vision is that of Sister Mary in the laundry room. I don't know how, but Sister Mary seems to tower over me, her hairy palm brandished upward and outward like a sledgehammer about to mete out punishment to the wicked.

"How dare you raise your voice!" she roars. "Don't you dare talk to me that way, girl!"

Sister Mary's hand descends from the heavens, righteous fury lending power to her ferocious swing. The sound of a furious smack reverberates down the hall. I spin round to see which girl she's slapped, but I see no one. Sister Mary and her fury are gone.

That's when I hear it. A girl singing. I don't understand the words, but I don't need to speak the language to know a sad song when I hear one. The words aren't the most important thing about the song. It's the rhythm, the pace. It starts off languid and slow, a musical lament to the beginning of all things. It continues with several variations, before the tempo speeds up and the words drive home the song's theme in a fierce counterpoint, reaching a high-pitched wail, before coming down again, dying off with a somber finality that crushes hope, joy, and life. And then the song begins all over again.

It's coming from the stairs that lead down to the room that I haven't been to yet. Funny, I've been all over the rest of this building, but I didn't think to go down there. The steel door is unlocked. I step into what appears to be a store room. Ladder, brooms, mops, buckets, and broken chairs.

I wait for a moment from the past, but there is nothing. Only the ghostly singing. Where is it coming from? I check all the dark spaces of the room where a spirit might hide. But my third eye finds nothing.

My two normal eyes however, are drawn to a spot in one corner of the room.

I walk over and get down on my knees. About a foot from the floor, someone's drawn something on the wall with black paint. The art is rudimentary at best, but more important than the drawing's artistry is the story it tells.

There are two groups of stick figures. In the larger group, six figures stand in a row, holding hands. Under one stick figure is the word "Me". The five others are named: Bimbeen, Jippa, Nardoo, Toora, Wyuna.

The stick figures in the second group are bigger than the first. The four of them have names as well: Mary, Agnes, Stella, Jane. All four are enclosed by the tail of what appears to be a half-lizard, half-human creature, and they have what appear to be flames or a fire burning above their heads. The creature's tail and body weaves around the four, but the creature's head comes to an inch above the "Me" stick figure's head.

All the pieces of the puzzle begin falling into place. It doesn't take long for me to fully understand the significance of the drawing.

The drawing is not a vision. It's a drawing made by a girl decades ago, a girl who must have sat in this exact spot, lonely and scared.

It's the mystery behind Fairfield Girls Home.

Only once I fully grasp the girl's story do I realize the singing has stopped.

I get up, stamp my feet to get the blood circulating again. I glance down at the pitiful knife under my belt and I smile ruefully.

What a fool I've been.

I'm not here to kill a monster.

I'm here to guide a soul.

There's a decent organizing system in place in the metallic filing cabinet, so it only takes me a few minutes to find what I'm looking for.

As I expected, the Sisters had two files to help them keep track of the students—one for the Aboriginal girls, another for everyone else.

I open the file I'm interested in and go through the papers inside.

But why'd they refuse. They must know we're full up here.

I should have paid closer attention to Sister Agnes' words. In the dormitory reserved for the white girls, there was a girl for each bunk. But in the much smaller dormitory, I saw only five girls, even though there had been six bunks.

I shudder as I come to the list of names.

Jippa. Wyuna. Toora. Nardoo. Bimbeen.

There's another one. A sixth name.

The one who's in none of the visions because they're all from her point of view.

From the inner pocket of my jacket, I take out two important tools of the trade: joss sticks and a lighter. I take three joss sticks and light them up. A few seconds later, I blow to extinguish the flames, leaving the ends smoldering. The wisps of fragrant smoke curl and dance through the air, rising toward the store room's ceiling and out through the air vents that lead to outside the orphanage.

Eucalyptus leaves would be more fitting for the smoking ceremony, but dry eucalyptus leaves are notoriously hard to store inside one's jacket.

Once the smoke grows thick and strong, I begin the ceremony.

"Whoever is here," I say, "I want you to know that it's safe to come out." I blow on the joss sticks to create more smoke, and to guide it toward the air vents.

"I bring safety. I know the way." I look up into the smoky tendrils wafting upward, my words directed to the air. "Follow the smoke, Apanie. Follow it. It will set you free."

I repeat those words three more times, always careful to blow the smoke in the right direction.

After a while, I don't need to look behind me to know that I'm not the only one in the room.

She isn't a vision.

"Ngaluunggirr?"

I only know a few words from the various Aboriginal languages, but this was one of the first I learned. I turn around, get down to her level so that we stand as equals.

She is apprehensive, confused. To my third eye, she shimmers brighter than the stars.

"No, I'm no Cleverman." I smile. "But I'm here to show you the way, Apanie."

"You know my name."

"Yes. I know what you've done. You've been lost. Caught between here and there."

She nods.

"I bring safety," I say. "I'm here to show you the way."

"I'm scared. I jump among the soft spots, but I can't see the land."

"I understand your fears. I understand what happened here, Apanie."

"I was scared," she says. "I couldn't control it. It was too much for me."

I nod. "What happened here is not your fault."

"I was sad," she says. "I was sad because they took me away."

"From your family."

"Yes. From my family, from my life. Lonely. Sad. So sad."

"I understand. What they did to you was bad."

"I didn't want it to happen. I didn't want the Malingee to come."

"You were scared," I say. "You couldn't control your powers. It came from the Dreaming. It came here, grew stronger because of the hate and the fear that was here."

"I just wanted it to stop. To stop hurting everyone."

Even though it was hurting the people who hurt you.

"What you did was very brave," I say. "You stopped it from leaving the orphanage. You took it away from here. Banished it back into the Dreaming."

Glistening tears flow down her cheeks. "But it killed everyone."

I choose my next words carefully. "You stopped it from harming anyone else. It was the right thing to do. The only thing you could do."

She looks at me with those big round eyes of hers, eyes that now hold hope within them. "I can stop standing on both sides?"

"Yes. Travel on into the Dreaming. There's no need to linger here."

She thinks about this for a moment, then smiles shyly. "Thank you."

"Goodbye, Apanie," I say. She's already gone by the time I say my last words. "Your family is waiting for you."

I look up, peer through the smoke with all three eyes.

Reality unravels around me, the fabric of my universe rips and I am lost to everything and nothing.

"He is not of the people. Who *is* he?"

I open my eyes and look up into the faces of three people hovering above me. Three people who had been watching me from a window. I see the sun, the clouds, the sky. I smell the wind. I feel the hardness of the asphalt needling into my back.

The old woman answers the younger man. "Yes. He is not of the people. But he has the way about him."

They talk like I'm not there.

The younger man snorts. "Everybody's got the way nowadays!"

"Don't be rude," says the older man. "He guided Apanie back to the Dreaming."

"We had to wait so long!" the young man cries out.

"What is written cannot be willed along or hastened," says the elder woman. "You should know that by now, Birin."

The young man, Birin, shrugs, and says nothing more.

The elder woman looks at me, and says, "Thank you, stranger." She smiles, but I know it's more than a smile because an immense wave of peace washes over me.

I blink, and they are gone.

I stay like that, lying on the street, watching the clouds go by, basking in the warmth of the sun.

After a while, I reluctantly turn my head, just enough to sneak a peek.

Fairfield Girls Home stands where it's always stood.

I turn my head the other way.

The house across from the orphanage looks the worse for wear. It's as if no one has stayed there for years.

I close my eyes. Minutes pass. The orphanage is still in my mind.

I lift a hand, reach for my jacket's inside pocket, and take out my phone. A few swipes and I'm making the call.

"Oi, Kuan," says the voice on the other end. "You calling about the orphanage again? How many times, man! You settled it yet?"

I smile, but I don't say anything. I end the call, let the phone slip from carefree fingers.

I don't bother getting up.

It's too comfortable.

TEK-KUAN CHIN is a disciple of the legendary Master Yu Jang, Founder of the Order of the Seven Paths. Although he was considered a late bloomer, having only awakened his third eye at the relatively late age of sixteen, Tek-Kuan soon gained mastery over three of the Seven Paths, surpassing many who had begun their training at a much earlier age. Upon attaining the rank of senior disciple, Tek-Kuan started his new career as a spirit-hunter for hire. When an encounter with a penanggalan almost left him dead, Tek-Kuan decided to try his hand at a 9-to-5 job instead.

TIMOTHY NAKAYAMA was born and raised in Malaysia and currently resides in Seattle. His short stories have been featured in various anthologies such as *Fish, Lost in Putrajaya, KL Noir: Yellow, PJ Confidential,* and *Little Basket 2016: New Malaysian Writing.* He has also written short stories in comic form, many of them featured in anthologies published by GrayHaven Comics.

CAUTION

An account by [CENSORED],

AS PROVIDED BY LYNDSIE MANUSOS

LOCATE

We're here because of wonderment. Every day, every project, every cleanup, is a moment of awe. I use caution. I abide by the manual. I atone for beholding.

Kelvin and I step out of the car. Trees line both sides of the street in thick, green-black walls. The sunrise hovers far away, the horizon gone, covered by the clot of trees. The humidity blankets us. I unbutton the top of my collar and inhale. Despite the heat, though, the air feels good. Smells good. Thick with sap and the smell of hot leaves and flowers. A roasted, sweet smell.

Kelvin wipes her forehead. "Christ," she says. She turns and knocks her knuckles on the car window. The car speeds away. I watch until it becomes an inky dot at the end of the road.

"Onward?" I ask.

Kelvin sighs again, fanning herself. "I guess."

The end of a single CAUTION ribbon edges out from the trees—a breadcrumb trail. We follow it, knowing this is how it goes. Each day begins with a caution ribbon, and we follow the word until we reach its source. I check my back pocket and feel the tiny palm-sized manual. I received the manual on my first day, years ago. My copy is now worn and flexible like soft leather. The words in the manual are as bold as the CAUTION snaking through the forest. I can recite the entire manual word for word. During these walks, I start from the beginning, praying the words.

CAUTION: *The enclosed material is strictly limited to those possessing CLEARANCE LEVELS. Examination or use by unauthorized personnel is forbidden and punishable by federal law.*

We walk for half an hour in a purple gloom. It's cooler in the forest. Sometimes Kelvin leans down and picks up a rock, smells it, rubs it with her thumb, then either throws it off or pockets it. Kelvin is fond of rocks. She's able to bring a rock or two from each location home, despite rigorous security quarantines. It's her way of keeping track without keeping track; she says she does not mark them or label them. Occasionally she licks them. I don't know if she lines them up on her bedside table, or if there's some glass case with a lock and key where she hides them. All I know is she likes finding it—the right rock.

"They're my rosary, in a way," Kelvin said the first time I asked about it. "My way of holding on to things I know to be true."

A beautiful sentiment. Kelvin talks about our sworn duty as if it's poetry, sad and circular as a song.

I hear voices ahead. We come to a clearing in the forest and stand there, taking in the day's work. The view is never the same.

A chronic shock. Kelvin groans. She grips a stone from our walk through the forest. It's unremarkable, save for a little red spot on the edge. Quartz maybe. I glance at the spot and wonder if it's some sort of spore or stain. She sees me eyeing it and pockets it. Ah. The right rock.

The cleanup zone is a goddamn mess, but it's a beautiful goddamn mess. Our job is to clean up the beautiful goddamn mess.

There are tree trunks stacked in a Lincoln-log fashion in the middle of the clearing. Trees of the ages. Giant evergreens pulled by the roots like weeds and laid end-to-end, alternating to create a giant wall. Pock-marked holes dot the area, old graves where trees used to rest. Construction lamps blanket the site and photographers run about like ants to document the scene. I enjoy the bustling of the photographers. "The Purple Picture People," Kelvin says. The purple nametags signify their level of clearance.

The rising sun casts a slow blue shadow from the giant wall. I can't help but shudder, then I giggle, and finally feel sick. I put my hands on my knees and stare at the ground. A familiar swimming sensation, as if I've breathed in vapors from a bleach spray. No, I will never get used to such phenomena.

Kelvin leans into me. She says nothing. Only stares. Her face is not unkind. She nods to her right. They've created a small path that circles the perimeter of the structure. I breathe in deep and exhale, letting the awe leave my chest. It feels a little better.

Aside from watching me react, Kelvin always seems to take each location with the same tired expression. She said she started the day I did when we were partnered up and sent to our first site, but she swallows these sites instead of reacting to them. She soaks them in.

We edge around the structure. The clearing is about the size of a football field. As we circle it, we realize it's not just one wall of branches but two. They angle to make a three-dimensional arrow pointing toward the rising sun.

The roots at the end of the trees look like messes of old hair. Even from a distance, the insects and worms are still thriving on them, only now realizing they're above the ground. The movement of the trees must've been soft, precise.

"Like Stonehenge," I say aloud.

"I'll never understand," Kelvin says. "Why can *this* be destroyed but not other wonders of the world?"

"Above our pay grade," I say.

I grin. Kelvin does not laugh.

"I guess," she says.

The operational manual is published for the information and guidance of all concerned. It contains information on determination, documentation, collection, decontamination, and disposal of debris, devices, structures, craft, and any perceived occupants.

It is tragic to witness the wonderment and then bury it, burn it, or replace it with something mundane.

It is critical that the disposal be discreet and complete, the manual says. *Refer to the concept of true crime suspects: Make it look like it never happened.*

I cringed the first time I read those words, but then again, the manual has a point. We are murderers, in a way. We obliterate life. We clean up the star-stuff as if it were dust.

"You know, maybe that is the point," I say as we walk farther around the structure. "Maybe it's supposed to be ephemeral."

Kelvin nods and wipes sweat from her forehead with her shirt sleeve.

She and I have this conversation often, changing opinions and points of view each time. Our chats have veered on religious on some occasions and dry theory. We've employed the science and the spiritual. The ghostly and the real. It seems right, even righteous, each time. I enjoy this back-and-forth. I hope it comforts Kelvin as much as it comforts me.

"Like performance art," Kelvin says.

My chest feels warm and soup-like, and it's not the humidity. I make a mental note when I'm able to make Kelvin smile in an unhidden, lopsided way. When it appears, it shows the chipped canine she got when she was five and fell face-first on a concrete step. It was the first story she whispered to me about her past, leaning in and tickling my ear with her voice. She regretted telling as much. She had grimaced, asked me to not report it. Of course I didn't. I hold onto it. Her smile—showing that imperfectly perfect tooth—is when I feel less alone.

All personnel and equipment involved in recovery, documentation, and cleanup will undergo thorough decontamination procedures immediately after operations have been completed.
Each person at the beautiful goddamn mess site has a purpose. Kelvin and I clean up the wonderment using a special liquid tailored for each site. We are forbidden to know the exact components of the liquid, although from my experience, I can detect trace amounts of ammonia and—oddly enough—citrus. It reminds me of Cara Cara oranges, sweet and cherry-like. My mother used to make juice out of the oranges before breakfast.

The liquid not only cleanses but *scorches*. They dubbed it "Scorched Earth" due to its effects. It melts. The liquids cause any sites to look burnt without using fire. Fire calls too much attention. Fire creates smoke. Smoke creates signals. Curiosity. The manual states curiosity is unacceptable. Better to use Scorched Earth.

Within an hour of arriving at the site, we're given a fold-out table, a white tent, and two clipboards with the necessary forms. The liquid is delivered separately via a food-delivery service van. It's a different vehicle each time with a different driver. The driver looks dazed and unreasonably euphoric. His eyes glaze over.

"Howdy, pals," he says, tipping an oversized trucker cap that says "I Walk the Line" in block letters.

Kelvin and I glance at each other. We know the look. The unreasonably polite and chipper nature. The driver is one of many we encounter, a man who will go to work tomorrow exasperated because it's Wednesday and not Tuesday.

He'll ask himself, *What happened to Tuesday? Where did it go?*

The driver walks back and forth, carrying black jugs under his arms, until they're stacked in a small pyramid where Kelvin and I set up. The driver also brings two Scorched Earth Suits. Jumpsuits that feel like raincoats.

"Have a good night now," the driver says. He tips his hat and walks back to the truck.

"Texas," Kelvin murmurs. She zips up her suit to her neck.

"No way," I say. "Louisiana. He sounded like my great-aunt."

Kelvin shakes her head and walks over to a jug and unscrews the cap. I smell the ammonia and Cara Cara oranges. It's a strong scent, funneling up my nose and into the back of my throat. We need water bottles. SE causes rapid dehydration, and, Christ, it is hot.

"You had a great-aunt from Louisiana?" Kelvin says.

She smiles. It's a door. I want to tell her more. I want to tell her my great-aunt used to send homemade beignets and over-spiced gumbo. I only knew her by those packages and the occasional "happy birthday" phone call, because she never came to family gatherings.

I arrive at these moments with eagerness. But then a photographer in a purple tag walks by, snaps a picture of the jugs, and continues on. I blink from the flash.

"I had," I begin.

Kelvin holds up her hand and nods to something behind me. I turn to see Marines filing out of a flock of military Humvees. Men and women, stone-faced and alert. I see a few miss a beat as they get out of the vehicle and catch sight of the structure. A single beat. A needle-like hesitation with stars in their eyes. That's how I separate the veterans from the rookies. They are here to inspect, as they always do, for danger.

"It's okay," Kelvin whispers. "Never mind."

"But I did," I say. "Her name was…"

"I said *never mind*," she says. "It's my bad. I brought it up."

Caution and comprehensiveness are paramount to a successful cleanup.

We carry jugs to one of the ends of the wall. We start at the base and work our way up. Another team will come after eight hours and relieve us. We're lucky this time to be one of the first teams on site. We get to see it as it was when it was made, either by design or by accident.

During the cleanup, Kelvin and I work in silence. Handling the liquid takes up most of our attention, but the act of destruction is something—at least for me—to be silent about. An act of humility. I use this quiet to think about memories that bring me comfort.

My life has always been a kind of cleansing. As a child, I used to go with my mother on trips to clean the summer lake houses. My mother enjoyed cleaning. It calmed her. She frequently had panic attacks, and cleaning staved it off for a while. My father encouraged her to search out another way to find peace, but she said she liked cleaning spaces. She liked the transformation, the way a house will be in one shape when she enters and an entirely different shape when she leaves. She used these transformations to focus on broad strokes, circling motions, and sweeping in zig-zag patterns with a broom.

Such structure brought my mother peace during the day, but her attacks caught up with her at night. I remember waking up to her sweeping the kitchen downstairs or mopping the bathroom in a cold sweat. Her hair hung in greasy strings over her face and her nose shined red from crying.

"Leave her be," my father said. "She needs an outlet."

When I got older, I wondered, *an outlet from what?* And then I wondered, *an outlet from whom?*

Kelvin goes back for another jug while I splay the rest of mine along the base of structure. The grass and soil shrivel to flameless ash. One end of the arrow starts to sag. The insects and worms from the roots scurry away. I hear their retreat. Little clicks and hisses.

After an hour of cleaning, Dr. Morikawa arrives to check in. She's the only last name I know with this job, and the only other constant at these sites for me other than Kelvin. Everyone else seems to change or have no face. Or maybe they're the same but I never remember.

Morikawa is a kind woman who wears a different shade of pastel hair every time we see her. This time it's a subtle pink, but with the wet-hot air, it's darker and clumped on the side of her face. The pink matches the large plump scar she has over her left eyebrow. She never talks about the scar, or even mentions it. Kelvin once whispered that despite her petite stature, Morikawa could kick our asses.

"She's seen worse," Kelvin said. "She's seen war."

"Why do you say that?" I asked.

"Because of the scar," she said. "And because she's the only one I see who's not in uniform but wears army grade boots."

"That doesn't prove anything," I said. "We wear steel-toed boots." I tried to be funny, to get another smile out of her, but Kelvin shook her head.

"I know a fighter when I see one," Kelvin said.

Dr. Morikawa waves us over.

"You know the drill," she says. "Arms out and mouths open."

She takes our blood pressure and temperature.

"Some team members are experiencing side effects today," she says. "We've had to quarantine two. Could be the humidity here—fuck Midwest summers, am I right? In any case, it's nothing serious yet, but I want to take the necessary precautions."

She takes out a clipboard from her messenger bag.

"Are either of you experiencing any abnormal symptoms?" she asks. "Itchiness, blurriness, or shortness of breath?"

Kelvin says no. I shake my head.

"I need verbal confirmation," Morikawa says.

"No," I say.

"Any sudden anxiety or paranoia?"

"No."

"No."

Morikawa writes more on her clipboard then shoves it back in her bag. She takes a bottle of pills out of her pocket.

"Take one of these if either of you start to feel different," she says, handing the bottle to Kelvin.

Kelvin rolls it around in her palm and frowns.

"It may cause some dizziness so I'd sit down after taking one," Morikawa says. "Keep drinking water. I'll check in with you two again at 1300."

Morikawa throws her bag over her shoulder. She points at me. "You still having a hard time sleeping?"

"Occasionally," I say. "The prescription helps me sleep, but I have nightmares."

Obscure, ominous nightmares. Dreams about dark, windowless rooms where I can't find my way out and all I hear is the sound of someone gulping. Dreams about cobwebbed dining rooms with hooved chairs that move each time I turn around and high, keening, yipping sounds, as if the chairs are injured dogs. Indescribable dreams. Lonely dreams.

Similar dreams kept me up as a child. I feared sleep so much or awoke from nightmares with such disorienting horror that I jumped out of bed and paced my room. Sometimes, when my room was too claustrophobic, I snuck downstairs. That's when I often found my mother sweeping the kitchen or cleaning the sinks. Occasionally, my mother noticed me watching her from the staircase and handed me a mop.

"You too, baby?" she asked.

She never pried.

I wondered if she and I had similar dreams. Or maybe even the same one. Maybe she was in another room, just as dark, just as lonely, listening.

We cleaned together then, fighting off our demons in silence.

Nowadays, the nightmares are products of the sites I clean. The larger-than-life structures I destroy. Nightmares about ash and mountains of black jugs.

I dream the structures resurrect. I dream they return with a vengeance.

"Yeah, that's an unfortunate side effect," Morikawa says. "If they get too traumatic, let me know and I can prescribe something else."

She nods to Kelvin and walks away.

"You should've told her," Kelvin says. "Last week you said the nightmares were getting worse."

"Yeah, but it's nothing that unusual," I say. "You mentioned you've had a nightmare or two lately, right? How can anyone not have a bad dream or two after stuff like this?"

I wave my hand toward the stacked trees.

"And besides, I hate using drugs to sleep," I say. "I feel like it's fake sleep."

Kelvin sighs.

I stick my tongue out at her to catch her off guard. She scowls, then smiles. It's the lopsided smile.

I'm two for three.

CLEAN

This section details the responsibilities of persons or units making the initial contact.

It takes a few hours to make a noticeable dent. We gulp water and splash it in our faces. The heat rises as the day goes on. We create ash from what was once godly. It dissolves.

I want to finish the story about my aunt. It's as if Kelvin clipped the edge of my tongue, and I'm still reeling. Once in a while, we catch each other's eyes, holding a jug and sweating profusely in our suits. She smiles politely but not in her imperfectly perfect (or perfectly imperfect) way, and I try to return it, equally polite and acknowledging. Is this what it's like to fight with a spouse or sibling? I had always wanted a younger brother or sister. I asked my parents about it until I was in junior high, when my father sat me down—alone and without my mother—one of the many times he lectured down on me, and said it wouldn't be healthy for my mother to "do it all over again."

"Once was enough," he said. "We love you. But once is enough. More than enough. Can that be enough for you, too?"

Any unplanned encounters with entities or biological organisms are to be reported immediately to ranking officials (see Appendix A for lists by unit) and the onsite medic. It is important contact be limited to military personnel to preserve both site and national security.

I reach a rhythm with Scorched Earth. I wait for this rhythm to arrive at every site. It's a blur of time when I no longer feel tired carrying the jugs. I'm confident pouring the liquid onto the structure. I step out of the way when the ash crumbles. The day becomes routine, normal almost, to the point where I can look at Kelvin and the purple photographers and anyone else at the site and think, "We're at work. We're working."

Nearly half of one side of the arrow has disappeared. The ash blankets the ground behind us as Kelvin and I move toward its point. Ash covers our suits. We look like firefighters.

At one point, Kelvin puts down her jug. The mid-day heat is overwhelming. She puts her hands on her knees and spits into the ash.

"It's so hot," she says. "I feel like I'm going to throw up."

"You should take a few minutes," I say. "Go get some more water."

"Aren't you melting, too?" Kelvin asks. "I feel like we're melting. We even look like we're melting."

I set down my own jug.

"Do you need one of the pills?"

Kelvin scoffs and stands up straight. She looks toward the sky, and I follow her gaze. There's not a cloud in the sky. Not a single wisp. No sign of coming shade, not unless we retreat into the forest. I look at the edge of the clearing. The forest seems to beckon, devilish. *Come away, come away to forest. Come away to the shade.*

"I'm fine," Kelvin says. "Although I doubt anyone feels 100% in this heat."

"It's okay if you need a few minutes," I say. "Go and grab some water."

Kelvin's black hair is bundled with sweat. She takes off her gloves and re-ties her hair in a ponytail. She blows a stray strand out of her eyes.

"You sure?"

"I'm sure," I say. "I'm in a good rhythm. I'll cover this area, and then you can cover for me later."

Kelvin exhales as if she's been waiting for it, the affirmation. I would go with her, so I could talk to her more, maybe whisper a story about my aunt. But I feel good using the Scorched Earth right now. In this moment, it feels like it needs to be used. It's a sprite on my shoulder, urging me on.

Kelvin smiles.

"Don't work too hard," she says. "You might pass out, and I need you to help me finish. I'll bring you a full water bottle in a few."

That was another smile. Three today. Three is such a true number. A fairytale number. Three means a beginning, middle, and end, and with half the day to go, I can have a whole new story of smiles by the time we clock out.

I pour more Scorched Earth. There's something about the way ash forms from the bark and branches of the trees. This is the closest to viewing "magic." A wondrous alchemy of one part of nature changing into something else instantaneously, without a normal catalyst.

The last time I saw such a change was after my mother left. I was in high school. We don't know where she went. I still don't know if she's alive.

For a time, my father felt the need to find her. It was a mix of guilt and early stages of Alzheimer's. He felt that, despite her anxiety, she was a rock he clung to. She was so structured and clean it brought him structure and shine. Without her, the structure crumbled, the shine dimmed, and I couldn't rebuild either on my own.

I remember how he used to stick post-its on the fridge. Hundreds of them. With little notes and memories of her. He called the post-its an "investigation."

- She swept counter-clockwise, not clockwise
- Bronze hair
- She hates the ocean because it's too deep
- She prefers lemon vinegar to Windex

While in college, I came home on weekends and cleaned off the fridge. A cruel ritual. I knew it. I thought it would make her absence sink in better, that she was gone, would forever be gone.

"She's not coming back," I yelled against his cries.

"They're mine! They're mine! They're mine!"

I tore them off the fridge, throwing them out by the handful. I ripped a few in half, the ones that seemed too real, too accurate. Memories that erupted in my own mind, rose from deep within my throat to build a bulbous glob of bile.

"These are not yours," I said. I tied the trash bags and took them to the dumpster.

He cried like I had cried when he wouldn't allow me to sleep in their beds after a nightmare, when he took the mop from my hands and yelled at Mom for encouraging me. I was glad he cried. It felt right to see it. The tears, real and flowing. He seemed the most human then, however lost.

Each weekend I came home, and the investigation had returned. Hundreds more post-its, stuck to the fridge in the same patterns and shapes. Memories I could've sworn were re-written with exacting precision, word-for-word from the ones I had thrown out. I took the trash bags with me back to college. I burned them in the fire pit in the backyard. I cancelled his online subscriptions so he couldn't order more. I shredded them in my dorm room.

My father barely remembered that I had thrown out the last

bunch, because there they were again. The investigation ongoing. At some point, I gave up. Soon the cabinets pulsed with them. The drawers. The toaster. The flower vases with wilting, dead flowers. They all had post-its of her.

I was an orphan by the time I graduated. I cleaned out the house before selling it. It took dozens of trash bags to clear out the post-its. I burned them all. Bag after bag. The neighbors would have usually complained about all the smoke, from dusk till dawn, as they did when my father started fires and forgot about them when he went to bed. They used to call me about it. But when I burned all the bags of post-its, there was only silence. The lights stayed off next door. I imagined they were watching me burn it, the bright paper curling inward. I guess they decided to leave me in peace with it until there wasn't a single note left.

At the goddamn mess site, I reach a part of the structure that's too awkward to pour the Scorched Earth on unless I remove some stray branches and leaves. The manual says this can be accomplished if it means a safer, more efficient way of cleaning. I put down the jug and take off my gloves. It's an odd place for such a pile of sticks and leaves to lean against the wall, as if a lean-to was built. I could crawl under the branches and push them out. It's the best option, to get it out of the way quickly. I go on my hands and knees and crawl in.

The shade, however brief, is wonderful. Just a sliver of a drop in temperature feels like a cool breeze. I want to laugh with relief. I should call Kelvin. She'd like the smell of the dirt and leaves along with the shade. It would be a beautiful respite.

I turn around to call out to her, but then I feel it. A breeze. A brush of air that raises my hair and dots my neck with goose bumps. I shiver. The smell of leaves seems to increase, becoming this all-encompassing green smell. Mowed grass and sweet pine and hot maple leaves from the sun and sap all mixed together. I look around the tiny crevice. A little farther under the lean-to, bathed in shadow, is a little clump of dirt that looks piled over, like a rushed attempt at a sand castle. The dirt begins to shake, and I feel and smell the breeze again, cool and delicious.

Out of the dirt stretches what looks like a petal, and then another, then another. Five petals reach out of the dirt. Five, greenish purple petals, translucent-like, extending from a center that looks like the pollen in a sunflower. It even floats a little like a sunflower, but it's too low to the ground, too colorful. The petals stretch as if sleepy, and I inhale the green scent. It rocks me. My nostrils sting, and my head stretches with the petals.

"Kelvin!"

I try to call out. The flower continues to shiver, to brush off the dirt to expose thick stems and leaf-like tendrils that shovel away the dirt. Tiny dustpans push the soil away.

"I'm just here to clean," I whisper and begin to back out on my hands and knees. "I'm here to clean."

The flower stretches again, and I fall face first into the dirt, my head lurching and pulsing from the smell. It's not that it hurts. It doesn't. It doesn't hurt at all. In fact, I want to crawl closer to it. My brain orders me. Tells me to take a big whiff and let the fuzz clear away. But the manual has alerted me to these types of interactions before.

"*Kelvin!*"

Save me. I need her to save me, yet I cannot yell it. It's hard enough to bring Kelvin's name out of my lips, and yet again the flower seems to listen and stretches, unfurling farther and farther. I claw at the dirt. Why am I not out of the lean-to? How do I not feel the heat of the sun?

CAUTION: Any unknown organisms should be treated with extreme care. When in doubt, destroy it, however extraordinary.

Remember, national security and public safety is priority number one. I look over my shoulder. My Scorched Earth. The liquid of ashes. It's out of reach; I can't see where I left it. I have not been cautious enough. I have not been careful.

The flower doesn't quite look like a flower anymore but rather a gossamer butterfly, complete with a shock of baby blue along its wings. The five petals have become three, no four, and they flap steadily; the slight breeze emanating from the wings moves the rest of the dirt away. It's perfect, it really is. Whatever it is, it is an essence of perfection. If I could just hold it to my nose like a teddy bear or a softly-lit candle. And the way it smells, oh God, if it could be bottled and shared. A cleaning solution for dirty houses and dirty people. A cleanser. Unnaturally natural. Something my mother would have so appreciated in all its freshness and glory.

SCORCH

The night before my mother left, she wrote a dozen letters and tucked each of them in a wad under my pillow. They began with tips and tricks of how to clean things. How to clean a toilet. How to clean a hardwood floor. How to get stains out of bed sheets. How to clean mirrors. She spent the first few pages of each letter expressly describing the process. How to make the dirt seem like it never existed. She left a list of her favorite cleaning solutions and how to mix some of them. The rest of the letters consisted of what she loved most. The way they transitioned from cleaning to love was spotless. I reread them over and over again, not sure how she did it. One sentence was about the way vinegar water was the best way to clean spots off a glass shower door and the next was about how she loved the way I cartwheeled as a child, the way my butt stuck up more than my legs, as if I was "sitting on the sky."

I kept the letters for years until I landed the job cleaning up classified sites. Sites like this. With impossible structures. Part of the background check process involved reading everything there was about me. Everything. From social media posts and former job performance reviews to private journals and old grocery lists left on my own fridge. The letters were the last thing I wanted to turn in. If I hid the letters and didn't turn them in, they would've been discovered, and I knew I wouldn't get the job. I desperately wanted the job. To experience the wonderment. To lose myself in a community of workers who likewise wanted to lose themselves.

So I burned them like the post-it notes. I dropped them in a metal trashcan and lit them with a candle lighter. They billowed up and around the bucket, the smell of smoke rising into my bedroom. I opened the window to let the smoke out and watched the paper shrivel and burn until there was nothing left but smeared ash. Then I poured water in it and dumped it on the nearest grass. They probably knew I burnt them. I expected them to ask why. They never did. I assumed it meant the letters posed no outward threat to security. They were not a clue to my mental stability or instability. They had half a dozen doctors and psychiatrists assess me in such a way that I felt a product of the project itself. Was I the explorer or the explored?

The butterfly flower continues to pump the green breeze outward, and all I can think of is Kelvin and those letters. Kelvin's smile and my mother's preparedness. My mother left with specific instructions on how to remain clean. I hope the reason she never returned, never came back to me, was because she trusted me. She trusted me, at the time at least, to continue her work. What would she think of me now? What would she think of Scorched Earth?

Kelvin grabs my ankles and pulls. The flower's wings flap as if in a fit, and I nearly black out from the smell.

"Shit," she says, peering into the lean-to. "What the hell is that?"

"I called you," I say.

I put my hands over my face. There's the sunlight, blinding and white-hot.

"I heard you scream," she says.

"I didn't scream, I called you," I say. "I called your name."

"Quiet," she says and raises her hand.

"Give me a smile, Kelvin."

"Stop," Kelvin says.

Kelvin scrunches her face. Her nose and forehead wrinkle. I've never seen so many wrinkles on her before. How many are there? Four. Four solid wrinkles on her forehead. One for each wing on the butterfly.

"Hey, we need Morikawa, please! Send her over."

I hear a whistle. Movement.

I feel so goddamn hot. The total opposite of the lean-to. A raging fever-like pulse. Like a curling iron on my back, or the heat erupting from a toaster oven. It's in my lungs. I want to go back into the lean-to. I want to see the butterfly.

They bring a stretcher, and I'm rolled onto it. Morikawa stands beside me and starts poking around my nose and mouth.

"Did you ingest anything? Swallow anything?"

"No," I say. "It was cool. It felt so nice."

Morikawa turns to Kelvin. "Where's the last SE jug he was using?"

"I can't find it. I could've sworn—I can't find it."

"That's going to be an issue. Do you have yours?"

"Yes."

"Go and finish it."

Wait. Wait.

"No wait," I say, holding up my hand.

Morikawa grabs my wrist and lays it back by my side.

"Quiet," she says. "Standard protocol."

"It's *alive*. It's not supposed to burn."

Morikawa sighs. She puts the back of her hand on my forehead and takes out a small flashlight. She shines it in my eyes and asks me to follow the light.

"Please don't let her, Doctor."

"It's not in my authority to stop her," Morikawa says. "I'm following orders. Same as you."

She puts the flashlight away. She brings out her clipboard and writes something down. I can hear the pen grinding along. She's pressing down hard. I wonder if she's ripping the paper. It sounds annoyed, almost angry. What did I do that could have been avoided? I followed the manual. It led me to the butterfly.

"You know what the manual requires," Morikawa says, as if she heard me. Maybe I said it aloud.

Then I hear the screaming.

Morikawa covers her ears. It's glass-shattering. A black hole of a scream, endless. It's not Kelvin. I close my eyes and imagine the flower, the butterfly. I imagine the wings flapping, fearing the black jug that Kelvin holds over it. Knowing. I imagine the wrinkles on Kelvin's forehead and nose and how scrunched they must be now. She pours the liquid and the butterfly screams. Weeping. Melting. Burning. Crying. Charring. Ash.

It was so loud and then so quiet. Morikawa looks past me, and I turn my head to follow her gaze. Kelvin holds an empty jug, her face ashen and pale. She wipes a sheen of sweat from her face. Then she drops to her hands and knees and vomits.

"Shit," Morikawa says. "Somebody get me another damn stretcher."

They lay her next to me. I think to myself: aren't we a wondrous bunch. They bring IVs and call off all teams onsite. I hear voices. Something about the current operation no longer being efficient. They'll have to use real fire now. It will burn some of the forest. It will engulf animals and insects and flowers. It is not as contained as they had initially reported. I forget what the manual states about these kinds of missteps. I turn to Kelvin, and she's staring at the sky. Her hand is in her pocket. The one with the rock she found. Her unremarkable rock. The manual would require me to report it now, but I will not. It's not like they won't find it later; let her have this peace. Let her feel the breeze on her face.

All personnel and equipment involved in cleaning operations will undergo decontamination procedures after those operations have been completed. If operations cannot be completed per manual regulations, project leaders and ranking officers will have the authority to contain the site by any means necessary. This includes operations and methods not expressly listed in the manual. Some examples may be found in Appendix 2.a.

"Kelvin," I whisper.

She turns her head. Her eyes are glazed like the trucker's, and I wish I could finish my story. I wish I could tell her about the letters.

She frowns. It's a perfectly imperfect or imperfectly perfect frown. We know our employers do not take kindly to such failure. I am afraid to close my eyes now, my body open and prostrate on the stretcher. I am afraid to lose Kelvin. I am afraid I will wake up tomorrow and wonder, *What happened to Tuesday? Where did it go?*

[CENSORED] grew up in a lake town in the Midwest and now works for an organization that specializes in the recovery, documentation, and cleanup of vulnerable or at-risk locations. [CENSORED] believes caution and comprehensiveness are paramount to a successful cleanup. [CENSORED] was last seen at a forest cleanup site in an unspecified region of the United States.

LYNDSIE MANUSOS has published fiction in *PANK*, *Apex Magazine*, *Midwestern Gothic*, and *The Masters Review* blog, among other publications. She holds an MFA from the School of the Art Institute of Chicago. You can follow her on Twitter @lmanusos or visit her website at https://lyndsiekay.wordpress.com/. She lives in Chicago.

visitor's guide to the waterfalls of
FROSKUR NATIONAL PARK

A guide by Harriet Strange,
AS PROVIDED BY KATHRYN YELINEK

F orget snow-capped peaks, burbling streams, and meadows of alpine wildflowers. You're traveling to Froskur National Park for its waterfalls. Good choice. Froskur boasts 283 named waterfalls, more than any other national park. And yes, they can kill you.

So heed the advice of a park ranger before you go.

If you have little ones in tow or just want a quiet picnic spot, look no farther than Lambkin Falls, located off the central loop road at mile marker 17. The widest of the park's stationary falls, Lambkin pours a modest 10 feet into a large, shallow pool perfect for wading. Should you or your offspring venture too close to the falls, carnivorous torrent fish will chase you back to the shallows. Picnic benches under buttonbark trees make a convenient place to apply antiseptic and bandages. Rest assured that no one yet has died at Lambkin. After a successful visit, leave a grape, orange slice, or other piece of fruit as an offering to the falls.

The more adventurous traveler should ride over 150-foot stationary Blackeye Falls, one of the tallest in Froskur, found off dirt access road 6 in the northwestern corner of the park. Park Service staff rent bubbles made of the transparent skin of local Froskur deer, perfect for viewing your trip over the falls. We keep trained medical staff on standby, mostly for broken bones and concussions—improved bubble padding has reduced mortality rates to a mere 4%—and grief counselors patrol the viewing platform, should family or friends witness your final journey. I recommend reserving a bubble at least two days in advance during the summer, and be sure to throw in your offering of sticks and stones *before* venturing over the falls.

Of course, you should not come to Froskur without visiting at least one of its twelve known migrating waterfalls. Unexplained by geology, hydrology, or magic, these peripatetic wonders exist nowhere else in the world.

Weeping Woman Falls, the most popular, lies just north of mile marker 112 on the loop road. Here water drops 32 feet from either the left or right of a prominent granite boulder at the lip of Weeping Woman Creek. The flow switches from left to right and back again several times per hour. Some rangers insist that whistling triggers the flow to migrate. I insist that Weeping Woman, like all migrators, is simply temperamental. Thousands of visitors a day whistling at her probably doesn't help. The dappled pool below the falls makes a refreshing place to soak your feet on a hot afternoon, although pregnant women, children under six, and those with certain chromosomal abnormalities should not touch the water. Local brides used to bathe in the pool on their wedding nights in the belief that the flow determines their firstborn—left of the boulder for a girl, right for a boy. Modern science remains skeptical, but don't chance it—and throw in a single grain of rice as an offering.

If you visit Froskur in March or September, consider planning your visit for the migration of Persephone Falls (visible from the loop road at mile marker 66 in spring and 72 in fall). More water drains over Persephone per minute than any other falls in Froskur, which leads to fast-flowing rapids at her base. Each spring and fall, within a week of the equinox, the falls and 10 miles of river migrate over the floor of Whimpering Valley. Nothing surpasses watching the falls and river churn over the landscape at up to 15 miles per hour. Equally thrilling is watching the daredevils who camp along the inner shore of the river in hopes of beating Persephone in the Semiannual Persephone Dash. Runners camp light and sleep in their shoes, waiting for the moment when Persephone stirs. Then it's every runner for themselves. Anyone who reaches Persephone's other home before she does wins bragging rights and a free pint at the Rumbling Tap Inn. Should you witness a successful dash, be sure to join in the post-run festivities, pour locally brewed Running Dog Pale Ale as a libation, and leave us park personnel in peace to collect the remains of those who didn't outrun Persephone.

If you listen to no other advice, listen to this: under no circumstances should you approach Old Scratch Falls. The 12 square miles in the park's remote southwestern corner where he usually lives, we fence off and patrol with dogs trained to bite the kneecaps off trespassers. Check the boards in the visitor centers for Old Scratch's daily location, since he roams at will in the park's 3,000 square miles and even, on occasion, outside of it. Know, too, that if you attempt suicide-by-falls, we will not rescue you if you change your mind. No one knows what triggers Old Scratch. Candidates include breathing too loudly, wearing plaid, and disrespecting other falls. Just remember the Ph.D. student last summer who left a candy wrapper instead of rice at Weeping Woman Falls. The next morning, Old Scratch thundered over where his cabin had been, and I found pieces of the cabin 5 miles downstream. We never found the student.

So when you come to Froskur National Park, enjoy the scenery, respect the falls, and above all else, pick up your trash.

HARRIET STRANGE has over twenty years of experience as a park ranger, twelve of them at Froskur National Park. She's hiked every trail in Froskur twice and has completed the Persephone Dash five times. In her spare time, she enjoys brewing kombucha and growing sundews.

KATHRYN YELINEK lives in Pennsylvania, where she works as a librarian. She is a graduate of the Odyssey Writing Workshop. Her fiction has appeared in *Daily Science Fiction*, *NewMyths.com*, *Metaphorosis*, and *Deep Magic*, among others. Visit her online at kathrynyelinek.com.

sector
5

An account by Liu Shin Hung,
AS TRANSLATED BY E. R. ZHANG

[*Translator's notes*]

[*Officer Liu was a member of the TS* Monologue *who perished in the Vaila Incident. Most of the electronics were destroyed by the electromagnetic field, rendering the majority of digital records unusable. However, Officer Liu kept a written journal, which was pulled from the wreckage by the retrieval drones. Originally written in a lesser known dialect, the journal suffered some damage in the blast. The following is only the closest approximation of what Officer Liu may have attempted to convey.*]

We've arrived in Sector 5. MY [*Officer Chang Mei Yang*] was occupied with the December Project and did not heed my warnings. I repeatedly told Migraine [*appears to be a nickname for Commander Mya Grace Lain*] that I didn't want to enter Sector 5. Although some of the crew shared my misgivings, we were overruled. The stray aster-oid damaged one of our main engines, and the strain it took on our remaining ones ate up a lot of fuel. We need to touch down and fix the engine, as well as refuel, if we want to make it to Sector 1.

I still feel we could have at least reached Karam if we dropped to normal speed instead of pushing for SOL travel. It's more populated than Vaila, in any case. I dislike the idea of landing on a planet that its own inhabitants abandoned. Tyrone thinks I'm being paranoid. I think I have good cause. I mean, it's been abandoned! Probably for good reason! What if the Auto-Miners haven't extracted any more ore or fuel? We won't even be able to launch.

Migraine says we can at least dock and relax while we hail for help. After all, their on-world hailing system is much more powerful than ours.

I guess the majority wins, but for the record, I'm protesting.

The place is as abandoned as an abandoned place can be. The only things left are the AIs who were used to launch the last ships. They greeted us as if nothing was wrong, but this place gives me the chills.

Everything is spick and span, testament to the Thelordicans' programming and scientific minds. Their AIs and self-cleaning machines have functioned pretty well even after so long. Apparently, the whole facility is an efficient solar-powered machine. During the winter, when Vaila's path is farthest from their sun, the machines power down. Then, during their spring and summer, they power up and continue cleaning like nothing ever happened. The Auto-Miners have been working on and off for the better part of a century. A few of them have broken down, but that's to be expected. All in all, it looks so much better than I would have thought.

I'm not too keen on staying for long, but needs must. Since we've landed, there's no choice for it. I will head out with the away team to gather some perishables. According to my research, the local fauna and flora are actually edible, although we have to steer clear of the Jardi plants because Shan is allergic [*Shan most likely refers to Officer Ashanqwe of the Qwa race, who blister upon contact with Jardi sap*].

Kononnya*, [*unclear what this means*] the fabrication units were making strange sounds. I checked and double checked and triple checked, but I couldn't find anything wrong with them. I nearly decked Officer Parker [*or possibly Officer Petrus, both are non-engineering crew on the* TS Monologue] for suggesting a good oiling was the only way. He thinks that oil solves all problems! No! Squeaking or groaning of the machines may indicate problems in the connections that need oiling, but knocking sounds are probably due to loose parts!

MY and myself have gone over everything so many times I think I'm going cross eyed. I would prefer to sleep on the ship as usual, but Migraine asked us to sleep on the planet-side station instead, just in case anything happens to the ship. Some people are using it as an excuse to get some personal space, or get into each other's personal space.

Tyrone likes the planet-side rooms because they're bigger and well, more limbs need more space, but I feel that it's so unlived-in and impersonal [*actual text mentions a lack of aura*].

Someone's been prowling around outside in the middle of the night. I heard footsteps thunking around. I wonder who? Everyone looks well-rested, and my room is a little out of the way, so I wonder who came down to my section. Or maybe they got lost? I guess the base is strange enough for some of us to get lost. I mean, I myself got turned around yesterday while looking for the sun deck.

Everyone swears that they shut down the fabricator last night. It overheated and died this morning, so obviously someone didn't do it right. Tika [*Officer Atika Izad Ahmad*] is repairing it as we speak, but it's gonna take two or three days to make sure everything is running fine. Three days too many, I'm telling you!

SOMEONE KEEPS KNOCKING ON MY DOOR AT MIDNIGHT. EVERY TIME I GO TO OPEN THE DOOR, THERE'S NO ONE THERE. WHEN I FIND OUT WHO IT IS, I'M GOING TO KICK THEIR BUTTERY [*seems to be a toned-down epithet*] ASSES BACK TO TERRA FOR MISUSE OF TRANSPORTER TECHNOLOGY.

Ryno [*Officer Karyno Lopez*] and MY said that they heard the knocking as well. No one admits to the prank. I have no idea how they could have pulled it off, cause there's no one caught on the cameras.

I'm starting to think there's someone else here.

I think Vaila's rotation is messing up my circadian cycle. I keep falling asleep midway through doing things. MMO [*nickname for*

Officer Msaoqw-Mqovbelzu-Ocuesn] poured me some of the herbal tea they made to help me focus, but I've been drifting. I fell asleep trying to hail any passing ships yesterday. The days here are just so long. Even with the adjustments we made to the artificial lights in the station, the daylight just drags on and on and on, and the nights just last forever! I'll be glad for Terra's short cycles.

In any case, the interference from the passing asteroids is making it hard to get the signal out. It's really terrifying when all I hear is silence. There's no answering call, not even a passing ship that we can ask to help send a message.

At least the fabricator is up and running. We just need a few more panels before we can start repairing the engine and get out of here.

[*pages have been torn out*]

MY is in the medical ward.
Someone pushed her off the sun deck.
I know our crew.
No one would do such a thing.
And she definitely didn't fall.
There's someone else here.

I woke up in medical. I only remember going to breakfast with Ryno. Witnesses say that MMO just stood up and backhanded me across the room. It took everyone to subdue and sedate MMO. Migraine shoved MMO in the holding cell under heavy sedation.

God, my head hurts. MMO's like a gentle giant [*actual text reads green mountain*]; why the hell would they hit me? I mean I get it if Ty up and punched me in the face, cause I tease him all the time, but MMO?

What is going on?

We had to quarantine Shan on the ship in the intensive care unit. Someone rubbed Jardi over their bed. I'm not sure they'll make it. I had to peel off so many layers of skin. I donated some of mine to the pool so that they can at least start to heal.

No one has been out of the station, and I know for a fact that the Jardi plants are nowhere close enough that someone could sneak out, pick that many, and then come back in time to stuff them into Shan's bed.

If we were all in the station, who the hell did this?

It's not who.

It's "what."

Tyrone woke with gouges across his chest, and Ryno's hair had been cut. This thing went through locked doors to fuck with us. I checked all the security footage. There's some white spotting [*unclear what this means*] and static, but nothing else. The AIs have not noticed anything. Or if they did, they are keeping silent.

Whatever this thing is, it's not physically present. At least, I don't think so. Either that, or it has some serious cloaking abilities that can get past AIs and intense security protocols [*some words have been stained black*].

Something is attacking us. We need to get off this planet as fast as possible, but we don't have enough materials.

I mean, the panels are done, and Tika is working round the clock with the rest of the engineers to fix the damn ship, but we don't have enough fuel to clear orbit. The Auto-Miners need at least another two weeks to get enough fuel. I keep saying that we should plan an away team to find abandoned ships or vehicles. We could drain their fuel at least. It would be easier than waiting around for this thing to screw with us. Migraine says there's safety in numbers. There's no guarantee that the away team would even come back.

The interference has lifted. I put out a signal. I don't think anyone will hear us, but I hope to GOD that someone does. It's not just knocking anymore. I hear the sound of children crying, talking in the lisping sounds of the Thelordican language. I hear them laughing and playing outside. Migraine is reluctant to let us all back on the ship with MMO still in holding, cause they keep having violent outbursts. I'm so scared that I don't dare to sleep, but I keep nodding off. My dreams are filled with violent endings for the whole crew every time I doze off. What's going to happen if I close my eyes for the whole night?

Migraine had to rescue one of the engineers from the generator. One moment, she was tapping away on the panels, and the next thing we knew, the engine powered on and nearly sucked her in! Fortunately, Migraine was close enough to yank her out of the way. I don't think this thing wants us to leave. It's playing with us.

MMO's dead.

Migraine delivered breakfast, and MMO was just stiff on the ground. I just [*blacked out words*] can't have gotten past all that [*unintelligible*] and then MMO is so hard to kill!

It's insane. This thing is having fun toying with us. They keep laughing outside the room. It's not just me. More and more people hear the laughing too. It thinks that MMO's death is funny. It's laughing at us.

Funeral is tomorrow. We're going to stasis MMO [*the cryopreservation method used to keep the bodies of crew members intact until burial*] until we can get the body back to Sector 1.

No no no no no no I want to leave I want to leave I want to leave I want to leave let me leave let me leave leave me alone leave me alone leave me alone please stop please stop leave me alone LEAVE ME ALONE

If it won't let us leave? Fine! We won't! I've rigged the generators to each other and keyed the access to my communicator. I will blow this place up if it comes to it. MY thinks I'm crazy. She keeps saying it's just a stroke of bad luck, but this isn't bad luck. MMO is dead! MY nearly died! Shan is in intensive care! Accidents left and right. People getting hurt all over the place. I don't want this to be how it ends, but if I need to, I will. If we die, we're taking it with us.

Ryno found the arm of one of the junior officers. Just an arm left. There's nothing else. We only know it was Walter because of the tattoo he had on the arm.

There's NOTHING on the security footage, just him walking down the corridor one minute, then nothing. Then an arm.

Then when the junior officers went to get the fuel from the Auto-Miners, they found the rest of him stuck in the cogs of the miner, completely drained of blood.

It took us twelve hours to get him down and the Auto-Miner is now broken.

Migraine says we need to stay calm. I AM CALM. I'm SO FREAKED OUT THAT I AM CALM. The way I see it, we're all going to die before we can refuel. Either we die attempting the launch because we don't have enough fuel to escape Vaila's gravity, or we die one by one, slowly picked off by this thing. It's just a matter of time.

It's got Migraine. It's got Migraine I know it. Migraine don't look the same there's the crazy look. MY doesn't believe me. nOboDY believes me when I tell them that Migraine doesn't look the same or act the same they tell me I'm paranoid but I'm not I'm not I'm not we need to mutiny or something remove Migraine and get out of here as soon as possible because we're going to die we're going to die I don't wanna die please let me leave let us leave please

hel -

it's me

i t i s m e

[*The above was the final entry in Officer Liu's journal. The next page was covered in indecipherable glyphs and the page after it had only a bloody handprint. It is unsure if Officer Liu met with an accident or perished in the explosion that destroyed the base and everything on it. Initially, the* TS Chrome *intercepted the signal that Officer Liu had dispatched, which only read "DO NOT COME TO VAILA. LEAVE." It was unusual behaviour from the* TS Monologue, *which prompted the deployment of the* TRS Titan. *Upon reaching Vaila of Sector 5, the team discovered that it was impossible to land, due to the destruction of the base and all landing docks. The retrieval drones were dispatched to the surface to examine the blast site. Some of the crew's bodies were recovered from farther away, most probably having been thrown clear by the force of the explosion. The bodies that were recovered showed signs of having been in a fight. The forensics team speculated that the crew fought amongst themselves before the explosion occurred. Officer Liu's journal suggested the presence of a malicious entity that was targeting the crew members one by one. Without further evidence, it is not possible to conclude whether Officer Liu was right or wrong. Regardless, the* TRS Titan *has been cautioned regarding this issue and has been forbidden from sending any crew to the surface to prevent this from reoccurring. The Thelordicans could not be reached for comment.*]

OFFICER LIU joined the Terran Space Exploration Project at the age of 24. After completing basic training, they were assigned to the *TS Monologue* as an engineer slash communications officer, where they served until the Vaila incident. Officer Liu loved old and obscure languages, as evidenced by their personal journal, and worked hard to create dictionaries of dying languages.

ZHANG does not work for the TSEP as a translator, but rather a microbiologist. It just so happened that they were the closest available person who had a rudimentary knowledge of the journal's language. Their current project involves the transcriptomics of the bananapocalypse.

ART BY Kristen Nyht

KRISTEN NYHT is an architect and urban planner with Quinn Evans Architects. From the beginning of her career, she has loved the process of sketching as a means of conveying ideas and feelings associated with places. Kristen rarely travels without a sketchbook and draws whatever buildings strike her as interesting, whether by world-renowned architects or untrained men and women. Kristen has worked on a variety of building types, everything from small churches to a major renovation of the National Air & Space Museum in Washington, D.C. Her passion is for more sustainable living at all scales, from tiny houses to whole neighborhoods. Kristen has lived in diverse places on both coasts and abroad, finally settling in Ann Arbor, Michigan, where she lives with her husband and two sons.

the high cost of ANSWERS

An account by Nat MacDonald,
AS PROVIDED BY MICHAEL M. JONES

I needed good answers, so I was on my way to see a very bad man. People were vanishing in the Gaslight District, and while I strongly doubted my next appointment had anything to do with it, he was the most likely place to start for information. I just wondered what it would cost.

The Gaslight District has always taken its tithe of visitors; it's subtly alive, with an oft-capricious hunger. It ensnares unwary visitors, unwise travelers, and unlucky residents with its changing streets and array of tricks, like a fairy tale witch's gingerbread house. It devours, misleads, and transforms according to an ancient fey logic. But it's never greedy, and rarely cruel. People who live outside the Gaslight take little notice; their memories of the missing fade quickly. Longtime residents like myself know better than to poke a sleeping giant, lest it take interest in us instead. It's the dark heart of Puxhill, far older and weirder than it has any right to be.

That's what made this latest rash of disappearances confusing and all the more worrisome: folks of all sorts were going missing, at an unprecedented rate, including many who were traditionally considered "safe." Poof, into thin air.

Desperate, a collection of the interested and affected had hired me to get to the heart of the matter. I'd have taken the case anyway—missing people are a staple of the private investigator's life—but Polly herself, owner of the Theatre of Dreams and the closest thing the Gaslight had to a visible community leader, had sweetened the deal by doubling my usual fees up front without even batting an eye, just to make this a top priority.

My name is Nat MacDonald. I deal in mysteries and secrets, and the Gaslight District is my area of expertise. Though I grew up in Puxhill proper, where things are a lot more normal, I was conceived here; I followed the Gaslight's siren call home once I came of age. When things get a little too weird or out of hand, when boundaries are crossed and rules broken, I ferret out the perpetrator and see justice satisfied.

I paused in front of a small nondescript door set in between a European-style bakery and a vintage clothing store. A small brass plaque simply read, "Willoughby: Recoveries and Disposal." When I twisted the doorknob, the door swung open easily. I swallowed hard and entered.

A single fixture hung from the ceiling, casting a dim light. Set to swinging by the breeze of the door's opening, it threw unsettling shadows across the few furnishings, which mainly consisted of several battered filing cabinets and a large oak desk with two chairs—a comfy leather one behind, a rickety wooden one in front. The air smelled of blood and faint foulness, as though something awful had happened here and the memory still lingered. The room's sole occupant leaned back in his chair, feet propped up on the desk, nonchalantly eating broken glass from an old ashtray.

Jay Willoughby and I were just about polar opposites. He was a short, solidly-built fireplug of a man, with corpse-white skin and a shock of hair the color of dried blood. I was tall, thin, and dark-skinned, with close-cropped black hair. The only thing we had in common was our love of good suits—his rendered in a stark black and white, mine a classic dark blue, tailored to play down what curves I had and grant me a more androgynous look. I secretly feared we'd run into each other at the tailor someday.

"Jay," I greeted. A few strides brought me to his desk.

"Nat," he responded. He didn't offer his hand, I didn't offer mine.

"I've come because—"

"Yeah, missing people," he interrupted with a dismissive wave. "I know. Have a seat."

I remained standing. That chair looked really uncomfortable. "So what can you tell me?"

"What *can* I tell you? A lot. Most of it would shatter your faith in humanity, keep you up at nights, and drive you to drink. Wrong question. What will I tell you that's relevant to your case? Just enough to get you started." His words held no rancor, just a world-weary statement of the facts, chilling for its simple honesty. "You know there's a price for my information."

"What sort of price?" I'd never actually haggled with Jay Willoughby before, but I'd heard stories. He rarely dealt in actual money, preferring services, goods, even secrets. Dealing with him was like playing with a scorpion: sooner or later, you'd get stung and it would be your own damn fault.

"Depends. Normally, I'd ask for a favor to be repaid later, but the way I see it, this benefits us both. So for this piece of news, I'll let you off cheap. I want crème eggs."

"You want *what*?"

"Those foil-wrapped crème eggs. A shitload of them. See, I got a fondness for them, but I'm too busy to get them myself and they're out of season at the moment. So get me a couple dozen cartons. Crème, not caramel."

"I… okay, fine. I can do that." I studied him for any signs of a joke, but he seemed dead serious.

Jay smirked. "Good girl. Okay. Here you go. The Grey Quarter has set up shop somewhere in the Gaslight."

"Who?"

"No reason why you shoulda heard of them, I guess. They haven't come around these parts in decades." He shrugged, and leaned forward, taking his feet off the desk. "The Grey Quarter are what you might call 'acquisition specialists.'" He made mocking finger quotes, derision clear in his voice. "Only they specialize in stealing people, by whatever means necessary." He leveled his gaze on me, and I knew exactly what he meant. Drugged drinks. Dates under false pretenses. Kidnapping. If they didn't steal you through subtle means, they'd drag you off the street.

"What do they want with their victims?" I asked.

"Depends," he said. "They serve a very special range of clients. Cults who want people they can brainwash and condition. Faded gods demanding specific sacrifices. Unspeakable beings with unnatural appetites. And sometimes, powerful people who want their enemies to vanish in horrible ways. The Grey Quarter makes these things happen. Ugly people for an ugly business."

My stomach clenched in revulsion. "Dear Lord."

"If there is such a guy, He's turned his back on this batch. No one seems to know just who they are, or where they're hiding. They're extremely good at staying under the radar." Jay's sudden smile was wicked and toothy, like a shark that's just gotten the punchline. "But you and I both know they made a mistake when they came here."

"How's that?"

"Because they're poaching in my territory, and I can't stand that. These guys are good, but greedy. They'll call down the wrong sort of attention with their shenanigans, and move on once it gets too hot to operate, leaving people like me to suffer the backlash."

Given what I knew of Jay Willoughby, this didn't seem a bad thing. I almost said so, when he held up a hand. There was crusted blood under the fingernails. "Zip it, Nat. You can't say anything I haven't heard before. You white hats are all alike, when it comes to tolerating necessary evils. Trust me, I serve a purpose. I got an ecological niche. The Gaslight needs me just like it needs you. You want to argue, find me when this is over, and we can scream at each other over drinks."

I doubted that, but I slowly exhaled while counting to ten. He was right. I needed his information, and as selfish as his reasons were, he was still better than nothing. "Okay. Now what?"

Jay shrugged. "Go find the Grey Quarter, wherever they may be hiding." He reached into a desk drawer, and brought out a small wooden icon, which he laid down between us on the desk. It was shaped like a raven, and stained the color of his hair. "When you track them down, break this. It'll summon my people to... deal with the problem."

I didn't take it, not yet. "Your people?"

"You're not a fighter, or a killer. You don't have the instinct, and you'll almost certainly be outnumbered. This is part of the deal. You take my help. With your particular skills, you're the best hope for finding the bastards, but once you do, we can move in and eliminate them."

Our gazes met in a contest of wills, mine narrowed, his intense. I knew he wouldn't back down. Reluctantly, I took the blood-stained raven. "I'm not using this."

"You will. Now scram. And don't forget my crème eggs when this is over."

I left without another word, slamming the door behind me on the last of Jay Willoughby's hungry laugh.

Back in the well-lit, comfortable surroundings of my own office, I caught Rebecca up on the latest developments. She frowned as I spoke, hands twisting with unconscious worry. "I really don't like the sound of this."

Rebecca Rice was my office manager and girlfriend. She was also dead. She'd been one of the Gaslight's casualties, only she came back as a ghost. We met when she hired me to solve her murder. As her case unfolded, we developed a connection. As a result, her ties to the living world fluctuate on a daily basis, depending on the strength of our relationship. Someday, we'll have to address this issue, but so far we've both been studiously ignoring the problem, for fear we'll hate the solution. Instead, we try to pretend we're as normal as any other couple.

"I know. What galls me is that he's right. I probably will need his help again before it's all over." I plunked the blood-stained raven down on my desk, eying it distastefully. "This thing reeks of old, bad magic."

Rebecca drifted over to look at it, and the color drained from her. Literally. Normally a pretty blue-eyed blonde wearing a sky-blue sundress over black leggings and flats—the outfit she'd died in—she became little more than a translucent suggestion of herself. "Nat," she gasped.

"What?" I took her hand. Our bond allowed me to touch her, and I willed life and reality back into her, restoring some of her vitality. "What's wrong?"

"You don't recognize that symbol?" Her voice was faint and horrified. With her free hand, she etched a design around the raven, leaving a trail of ghostly frost on the desktop. Before she'd even finished, I realized what had horrified her so.

"The emblem of the Corbie Boys," I said with disgust. The

Gaslight's resident gang. The dark flock. Men of ill fortune who left misery in their wake. The ones who had killed Rebecca as a sacrifice to an ancient, nameless goddess. We routed them in our last encounter, and our paths hadn't crossed since. "Those are Jay's people? I should have known." Come to think of it, why hadn't I known? I mentally kicked myself for letting it slide.

"Nat, you can't ally yourself with *them*," Rebecca said firmly, the color slowly returning to her form.

"You're right," I agreed. "Though if I have to choose between evils... I'd rather have them as allies than enemies." I avoided Rebecca's gaze as I wrapped the raven in a handkerchief and tucked it in a pocket. I knew I couldn't take her disapproval... or worse, disappointment. It felt like I was betraying her, but what could I do? Some whispered instinct told me I'd need the blood-stained raven before this blew over. I'd learned the hard way to follow my intuition, even when it made no damned sense at the time.

"Fine," she whispered. Ghostly fingers touched my chin; I followed their subtle urging, turning my head to meet her eyes. They were a deep, dark, stormy blue, the realest part of her. "I hate the idea with every fiber of my being, but I trust you." Her lips met mine in a soft kiss, startlingly warm given her condition. For several long moments, we stood there, wrapped in each other's arms, finding shelter from the outside world.

And then it was time to go to work.

It took me a good long while to find the secret lair of the Grey Quarter, but I had a secret advantage: the Gaslight District itself saw them as unwelcome intruders, and it wanted them gone. I could feel its irritation, like a kid poking at a loose tooth. It guided me, through signs and portents, as I walked its winding paths and spoke to one person after another. I uttered the name of the Grey Quarter time and again and followed a trail of breadcrumbs made up of rumors and whispers. This is why Polly had hired me, why Jay had made his dark bargain with me: we all wanted rid of the Grey Quarter, but only I could follow the Gaslight's hints and subtleties to the root of the problem. As always, it worked through me, and I served its interests.

Slowly, I traveled deeper into the twisting heart of the Gaslight, where streets have no names and storekeepers speak obscure dialects of forgotten tongues, where miracles can be bought and sold, where the barriers between worlds grow hazy. I almost never came this far in; only my certainty that I was supposed to be here gave me the confidence to continue. This was something left over from a time when the world was young and strange, protected by the rest of the Gaslight and the city of Puxhill outside like a butterfly in a chrysalis.

And then I found them. The Grey Quarter. They'd set up shop in a temple raised to a long-dead deity, turning a place of worship into a place of anguish. I peeked through a window and saw at least a dozen men and women bustling around. Their features were sharp and cruel, their clothes a uniform dull grey, their movements purposeful and practiced. They attended to dozens of prisoners, separating them by some unknown logic. Some had been bound hand and foot, others stuffed into cages, or chained in a line. Some still wore the clothes they'd had when abducted, some were naked and shivering. As the Grey Quarter organized their victims, consulting checklists and consulting with one another, I realized that they'd been divided according to their clients' needs. My gut told me they were being prepared for transport. The Grey Quarter had fulfilled its quota, and now it was time to deliver. To sleeping gods and hungry beings and ambitious cults. I couldn't let that happen.

But what should I do? I'd done my job and discovered where our missing people had gone. Now was the time to backtrack and tell Polly, let her summon reinforcements who could properly handle this.

I'd made up my mind long ago to leave the raven token where it sat in my pocket. Pride, sanity, and common sense argued against summoning Jay and the Corbie Boys. They definitely weren't the solution I wanted. But it had taken me hours to get this far, and from the way the Grey Quarter acted, I doubted I had that much time left. If only I could use my phone… but this deep into the Gaslight, you never knew who or what might answer.

Had Jay known that it would come down to an awful choice between my principles and solving the case? I refused to let him win. No. I turned away from the window, determined to find another solution. I rounded the corner… and ran right into an outside patrol.

The fight was short but intense. I was outnumbered from the start, by professionals when it came to subduing the unwilling. I gave as good as I got, kicking and biting, struggling, using every dirty trick I'd learned over the years, but it only postponed the inevitable. Soon enough, I was battered, bruised, and bleeding, my hands bound behind my back. My captors forced me into the temple, giving me a final shove that sent me stumbling to my knees.

"Nat MacDonald. Your timing is impeccable, if inconvenient." I looked up to see who'd addressed me in such a cool, nonchalant manner. He was tall, skeletal-thin, and all sharp angles, without a trace of softness or kindness to be found. Like his colleagues, he wore drab grey, but on him, it somehow looked regal. His eyes were voids, reflecting nothing and completely dead inside. "I have any number of clients who could find a use for you. You'll fetch a nice bonus." There was something off about how he spoke, with intonation and emphasis placed a beat too soon or too late.

His eyes were too disturbing to look at for long, so I dropped my gaze to his hands. His fingers had too many joints, and moved in upsetting ways, never still for a second. I decided his face was safer than those writhing, twitching hands. "Who are you?" I asked. *Stall for time*, I thought. *Get a hand free, maybe I can get to the token after all.* Like it or not, I no longer had the luxury of sticking to my morals.

"I'm the Grey Quarter. Or the Grey Quarter is me. I grew every one of my employees from my own flesh and bone, after all. Take your pick."

"I'll call you Grey."

"Call me whatever you like. It won't matter for long. Within the hour, we'll be out of here, and you'll be on your way to somewhere new and exciting." His smile stretched much farther than necessary, like a death's head jack-o-lantern. "Nothing personal, you understand. It's just business. Our clients have needs, and we satisfy them. It's almost a pity our jobs put us at odds. I've always found the idea of private investigators to be so fascinating." He bent down to regard me on an equal level, bringing his dead eyes and Halloween grin just out of my reach. "Imagine, ferreting out secrets for a living. The power that could give you over people." He tilted his head, in wicked contemplation. "Would you perhaps be willing to work for me? Excellent pay, travel opportunities, and you'd meet the most interesting individuals."

A chill ran right down to my bones, as my body reacted on some instinctive, primal level to Grey's inhuman presence, calm delivery, and utter soullessness. I reached deep inside for a measure of courage. "I'll pass," I choked out. "Conflict of interest." Behind my back, I twisted my hands furiously, praying for any miracle that would let me escape.

None came.

"Very well." Grey summoned one of his men with a flick of the fingers. "Put Miss MacDonald somewhere out of the way. Don't damage her unnecessarily. I haven't decided what to do with her yet."

None-too-gently, I was helped up and shoved into a cage by myself. The door was slammed shut and locked with alarming finality. It looked like I'd have time to think over the many ways I'd fucked this one up.

Outside the cage, Grey and his people continued the last of their preparations with a businesslike efficiency. I'd ceased to be anything more than another item on their To-Do list. Fine by me. I resumed my efforts to wriggle free of my bonds.

Suddenly, I became aware of a presence behind me. Invisible, barely more than a suggestion, but familiar and welcome. A soft "Shhh" echoed by my ear as my bonds loosened, the rope falling away from my wrists. I jerked my head around and caught a hint of blue eyes and long blonde hair. "Rebecca!" I whispered with surprise. "How—where did you come from?"

"I—I don't know," she whispered back. She was little more than a shade, a flicker in the corner of the eye; I had to strain to make her out in the weird light of the room. "I mean, one minute I was in the office, convinced you'd gotten in trouble, and then I was caught up by a wind, and when I came to my senses, I was outside. I saw those bastards grab you, but I didn't know what to do. I didn't even know if I *could* help. I feel really weird, like I'm being pulled in a hundred directions. Less real and more real, at the same time."

"I've never been so glad to see you," I said. "It's time to summon some help and get this over with." Now that my hands were free, I could finally reach into my pocket and retrieve the blood-stained raven token. Keeping my movements as slow and unobtrusive as possible, I did just that. I drew it forth, unwrapping it with trembling fingers. Summon one devil to put rest to a second? Fine. The option was no longer unthinkable. I closed my eyes, and took a deep breath, as if to say farewell to my morals before taking that road paved with good intentions. I'd break the token. Jay and his people would arrive to save the day. There would be blood, and suffering, and death. It would be my fault. Oh, no one would blame me, but I'd always know.

I wondered if the blood on my hands would be real or metaphorical.

And then a sudden impact smacked the token from my hands. The Grey Quarter had snuck up on me with terrifying stealth, reaching through the bars with an inhumanly thin arm to thwart my efforts. "One uninvited guest was more than enough, Miss MacDonald. Though I see your ghostly girlfriend has come along as well. Very well." He snapped his fingers at a minion. "Fetch me a spirit jar for Miss Rice, so we can show her the appropriate hospitality. I know plenty of people who'd love a ghost in such fine shape."

"No!" I lunged for the token, but it had skittered just out of reach, falling outside the confines of the cage. Grey casually reached down for it…

… only Rebecca got there first, desperately wrapping her ethereal hand around the raven.

"Break it!" I screamed, throwing my entire essence down the link we shared, wishing her physicality and substance with every fiber of my being.

She did. The token snapped easily, releasing a burst of ancient magic. "Nat?" Rebecca said faintly. "I feel really funny—" And then she exploded into a million shards of blinding light.

"Rebecca!" Though my vision remained dazzled in the aftermath of the explosion, I could see *something* going on beyond the cage. Dozens of fireflies, which expanded into actual people. A shining host of newcomers. At their head was Polly, looking taller and more regal than ever, a statuesque goddess wrapped in white robes. Behind her, many others I recognized from the Gaslight District—shopkeepers and artists, bartenders and musicians. Those who had lost friends and family to the Grey Quarter. Those who had an interest in seeing order restored.

Things moved quickly after that, with Polly and her reinforcements making swift work of the Grey Quarter's men. They freed the prisoners, myself included, and set about finding clothes and blankets and hot drinks as necessary. The only one they didn't capture was Grey himself, who took one look at the odds, and stepped sideways into a hole in space, which immediately closed afterward. His last words hung on the air long after he'd vanished, as though waiting for me. "Now, Miss MacDonald, it *is* personal. Fare you well until the next time."

Rebecca pulled herself back together, seemingly none the worse for wear, and we went home, hand in hand, satisfied in a job well-accomplished. But we still had a loose end.

Jay Willoughby popped a crème egg into his mouth, without bothering to unwrap the foil first. After he'd chewed and swallowed, he gave me a look, somewhere between satisfied and sour. "You got the job done, but you screwed the pooch by calling Polly and her pals. I don't know how the hell you subverted my token like that, and I don't really appreciate it. I thought we had a deal, Nat."

I didn't tell him that I had no idea what had happened, that I suspected some other power—perhaps the Gaslight District itself—had taken matters into its own hands, using Rebecca as its pawn. Let him figure it out for himself. "You could have done better than Polly?"

"Grey wouldn't have gotten away, that's for sure. Shit, I really wanted to get my hands on him and his secrets."

I smiled, thinly. "Polly said that they're dismantling his network and returning everyone to their homes and loved ones. They even have a line on Grey's contacts and clients, and may, in time, be able to shut them down and rescue even more people. Tell me you'd have done all that. That you wouldn't have taken over his operation for your own ends."

Jay's expression told me all I needed to know. Oh, he'd likely have set the prisoners free. But he'd have made good use of the infrastructure. He slowly ate another egg, without breaking our locked gazes. Then: "Why are you still here? Our business is concluded. Fuck off."

"A pleasure." I couldn't help but put an extra strut in my step as I walked out, leaving him to the dubious pleasures of his dark, disturbing office.

We'd gotten lucky; whatever had worked through Rebecca had allowed us an unexpected kind of victory. Two villains thwarted in a single blow... but neither was completely out of the game, and both were upset with me. That was something to worry about.

And... that was the second time now that something mysterious and powerful had chosen to manifest through Rebecca, the first being the time we'd met, when she'd transformed into a ghostly stag to rout our enemies. Sooner or later, her benefactor might very well call in its markers for services rendered. Before that point, I wanted to know who—or what—we were dealing with.

At the end of the day, it always boils down to two things: questions and answers. Bring me the first, I'll give you the latter. Just be careful; there's always a price.

NAT MACDONALD is a lifelong native of Puxhill, the daughter of a blues singer and a sax player who made beautiful music together. A private investigator who deals in mysteries and secrets, she's an expert at handling the Gaslight District, Puxhill's oldest, weirdest neighborhood. She lives with her girlfriend, Rebecca, who is a ghost through no fault of her own. She enjoys good suits, fine whisky, and building houses of cards when business is slow. Her main piece of advice to tourists is to never stray from the well-lit areas after dark, but definitely do check out the Theatre of Dreams if at all possible.

MICHAEL M. JONES lives in southwestern Virginia with too many books, just enough cats, and a wife who knows where all the bodies are buried. His stories, many of which take place in this same setting, have appeared in anthologies such as *Clockwork Phoenix 3*, *D is for Dinosaur*, and *Fitting In*. The characters in "The High Cost of Answers" first appeared in "The Strange Case of Rebecca Rice," available in *Like a Mystery Uncovered: Erotic Detective Stories* (caution: adult material!). For more, visit him at www.michaelmjones.com.

the more
THINGS CHANGE

An account by Jaisy,
AS PROVIDED BY CAROLYN A. DRAKE

You know those gentrifying assholes that everyone loves to rag on? I'm one of them.

"You're buying this dump?" Mark wrinkled his nose and pushed his black-rimmed glasses back up the bridge of his nose. I had teased him countless times about his resistance to join the Dark Side and just get contacts, but to no avail. Mark was married to his glasses, just as I was married to my pink high tops and signature bedazzled jean jacket.

"You're not using your imagination!" My cloud of dark hair puffed out around me as I threw my gloved hands out, gesturing to the narrow two-story house before us. White paint peeled and freckled the entire exterior, and having already done a walkthrough with my relator, I knew the interior was no better.

The façade was still charming, though, in the way that only old colonials in cramped historical neighborhoods can be. The rest of Trenton was full of similar homes.

Of course, the rest of Trenton was also filled with empty warehouses, the highest unemployment rates in the state, and a rampant heroin problem. The days of "Trenton Makes, The World Takes" died around the same time the steel industry tanked, and all that remained of the capital city of New Jersey were these shelled-out houses scattered along the crumbling sidewalks, and the residents trapped inside of them.

"Fresh paint," I continued, ticking items off on my fingers, "new gutters, new windows—"

"A bulldozer would be cheaper."

"Mark, look at the neighborhood," I said, gesturing to the surrounding houses lining the rest of the desolate street. "Right now, yeah, it's crap, but two to three years from now? This place is on the fast track to being a hip paradise. The train to New York is five blocks west, and there's already a brewery three blocks down, right next to a cupcake boutique."

"Breweries are the sign of a place getting nice," Mark agreed, crossing his arms. "That still requires you to live here until this neighborhood is safe to walk around at night, though, if that ever even happens. Come on, Jaisy, you're a pharmacist, not a DIY Pinterest Queen. This place is going to need so much work just to be livable. Just get a normal person house. Or better yet, a condo, right next to mine."

"I'm not going back to Hoboken. I'm on the wrong side of thirty and still living on ramen three times a week just to make rent every month. Now that I have finally paid off my student loans, I can actually start my life," I said, turning to admire the home that would shortly be my legal property. "I'm going to make this work. And just wait, three years from now, when this neighborhood turns around—"

"What the hell is this?"

I twisted my head to see Mark reach into the overgrown weeds that passed for a lawn and use two fingers to lift a ribbon of tattered fabric. The material might have been white once, but time and mud had stained the cloth to resemble the color of smashed worms. Reaching forward, I fingered a broken and rusted metallic clamp at the end, frowning in thought.

"It looks like a restraint," I said.

"Restraint for what?"

"We use these on psych patients at the hospital."

Mark all but threw the strap down on the driveway, wiping his hands on his jeans.

"Ugh, I've got staph now," he sneered.

"It's probably not actually a restraint," I said, although I know my voice did not carry any confidence. "I mean, it's possible it is. The realtor said this place used to be a church."

"This was a church?" Mark lifted his eyebrows at the relatively normal looking residence before us. The windows were broken, but held no stained glass. And there was no belfry or steeple, only a small second story bedroom that I planned to make into a study.

"Must have had a small following," I shrugged, "it's been abandoned since the late nineties."

"Why would a church have crazy person restraints in its front yard?"

"Maybe they did work with the mentally ill or something on premises?"

"Let's just add 'possible former mental institution' to the long list of reasons for you not to buy this dump. There are plenty of *other* reasons on that list, too," Mark nodded to the yard of my soon-to-be next-door neighbor. An older, heavyset woman in a drab button-up collared shirt and sweatpants was planting a "Trump-Pence" sign in the lawn.

Mark and I exchanged wry grins.

"Nice try, but I'm still getting it." I punched his arm. "I already put an offer in. Just a matter of time before they accept. So get used to it, Sparky."

"Fine. But don't expect me and Daryl to visit until it's gentrified enough that we won't get stoned for holding hands walking from the train to your place."

There was no wind that day, despite how grey the fall weather was, and yet, the front door slammed shut at that exact moment.

Mark and I stared at the ramshackle house for a moment before looking back to each other.

"Bad hinges?" I shrugged.

Mark merely eyed the house warily and turned back toward his truck.

The next two months flew by in a whirlwind of paperwork, three separate trips to Ikea, and an unhealthy amount of pizza and beer.

Before I had time to even assemble my furniture, snow had begun to blanket my new front lawn, we had a new President, and I was officially flat broke from the down payment for my new house with no money left for Christmas presents.

Thankfully, my parents—still living "down the shore" near Cape May—were understanding of my predicament and signed my name to all of the gifts they had gotten for the Snyder Family Christmas Party.

The party went as anticipated: there were jabs at my withering uterus from my aunts, my dad and uncle got into a fight about politics, and I live-Tweeted the increasingly louder and drunker debate while downing Pinot Noir and dangling my keys over the bassinet containing my sister's third baby. Christmas, 2016 style.

Despite my mother's continued protests about how dangerous it was for a woman to live alone, I finally managed to slap together some furniture and unpack enough of my belongings for my new place to resemble a home sometime in January 2017.

That's when I realized that I was not, in fact, living alone.

Tuesday evening was winding to a close. I had just finished my allotted one glass of red wine per night and was flipping channels.

I landed and paused for a moment on *Home Alone*, smiling at the memories of my childhood this movie invoked. My thumb clicked on the remote and the channel flipped to The Food Network, but the cooking competition that was unfolding on screen just caused my stomach to rumble, and I was reminded that there was nothing in my fridge except questionable milk and leftover Chinese takeout.

Deciding that sleep was healthier than binging on leftovers, I turned the television off and stood in the dim room lit only by the last of the wick in my Christmas cookie candle.

I finished the last of my wine and turned away from the television... And then it turned back on.

"Kevin!" Mrs. McCallister shrieked behind me; I swung around, surprised. Blinking, I whirled my gaze about the room, but I knew that I was alone in my house. The remote control was untouched on the folding chair where I had left it.

I picked up the remote and clicked the television off once more. The black screen was paired with silence. I watched for a flicker of resurrection for several seconds, but the screen remained dead.

"Weird," I muttered, dropping the remote back on to the chair and turning back to the kitchen. I was not surprised, however, when the television clicked back on behind me.

"Oh, what the hell," I hissed and spun around once more on the empty room.

The thought occurred to me that a neighbor might have a universal remote and be on the same frequency as mine, but someone in this neighborhood owning anything other than an ancient pre-HD television seemed unlikely.

I held my elbows for a moment, staring at the television, before slowly walking forward, my bare feet chilled by the creaking wooden floor. With my face inches away from the screen, I reached a careful hand toward the power button and pushed, turning off the television. I stared at the blank screen, aware of my breath shaking as I inhaled, eyes locked on the monitor.

Nothing happened.

But I screamed when it did.

"What the shit!" I leapt backward when the bright light and squawks of the television filled the room.

My hands shaking, I lunged forward and yanked the cord out of the electrical socket, then half-ran to the kitchen, flipping on the light and stumbling across the linoleum until I could pivot and put my back to the kitchen counter. Too many horror movies had been seared into my brain for me to be even slightly practical about phantom televisions.

I stared at the screen through the archway of the living room, rocking on my heels, waiting, ready to grab my keys and run the fuck out of the house if it flipped back on. The air stayed blissfully void of any sound but my own gasps.

Then... creaking floorboards above me. Deliberate and slow, moving from one side of the room to stand directly over me, and then they stopped.

The sound of my heart hammered in against my eardrums. Hands shaking, I pulled out my cellphone and began to call 911, but in the silence, I suddenly felt like a moronic child. What would I say, "Help, my TV is possessed and my old ass house is making noises that old ass houses make?"

"Get a grip." I breathed through my mouth and out my nostrils in slow, steadying breaths. "You're a freaking adult, act like it."

Of course, that is when all of the appliances in the kitchen began going haywire.

"Fuck!"

My blender pulsed empty air; the dishwasher began a cycle; the fridge started rattling angrily and spitting ice out all over the floor; my microwave screamed that there was something ready for consumption inside of it; and the dial on the oven twisted all the way up to 450 degrees.

Needless to say, seconds later, my scantily clothed ass was on the sidewalk, shivering in the snow.

"You alright, Jaisy?"

Somehow, I managed not to have a heart attack at the sound of the voice coming from behind me. I spun around and found my neighbor, Mrs. Schweitzer, arms laden with grocery bags and her wrinkled brow drawn down in concern as she surveyed my gym shorts and bare feet.

Mrs. Schweitzer seemed to be a kindly older woman, but we had only exchanged tense pleasantries on a handful of occasions. Any time we ran into each other, her strained eyes were drawn to the rainbow flag flapping by my doorway, and I'm sure she noticed how my smile tightened anytime my gaze fell on the "Trump-Pence" sign still planted in her front yard.

Needless to say, our encounters were brief.

"The, the TV," I stammered, pointing to my house, my thoughts and emotions a blurred jumble. "It just turned on by itself. And then my kitchen, everything just… just…"

My brain struggled to find words to explain what had just happened, but when I turned back to Mrs. Schweitzer, her eyes were wide—not in surprise, but understanding. I felt that she knew what had happened in my home… and that she had been expecting this sort of thing to happen for some time now.

She made the sign of the cross and kissed the gold crucifix hanging around her neck.

"What—" I asked, utterly confused now, "why did you do that?"

Simply shaking her head, Mrs. Schweitzer continued walking down the decrepit sidewalk.

"Oh, come on!" I hissed as I watched her cross the front lawn toward her house. "You can't do cryptic shit like that and walk away!"

There was a strong gust of wind, and my hair flew about me. My hands worked furiously to warm themselves, and I turned back to face my dark home. The front door was still open and gaping. I listened, but there was no sound coming from the kitchen now.

All seemed quiet. Tentative, I took a step forward.

There was a sound like a hiss, or a whisper. Then the front door slammed shut.

"Oh, I am definitely feeling something here," Byron Tarrant all but moaned in my living room.

Hugging my arms around my middle, I clenched my eyes shut in an effort to kill the mental image of this ass-clown who dropped out of my pharmacy class three years before graduation to "find himself" exploring Western Europe on his dad's dime moaning anything, ever, in my presence again.

Topped with a beanie and some seriously stupid facial hair, Byron's head lolled about his shoulders as he wavered on his feet, like he was caught in an otherworldly wind. A graduate student who smelled like burnt coffee trailed behind and filmed Byron's trance, and both wandered around the corner into the kitchen.

"Sweetie," Mark whispered in my ear, "I'm saying this as a friend: moving to Trump country is rotting your brain."

"I don't know what else to do," I snipped, watching as the sun set outside and knowing that the madness would start soon. Lately, I had made a point to be out of my house before sunset and crash on various couches with a number of lies to ensure my friends outside of Mark never found out that I was afraid of the dark. "None of the other psychics and crap I contacted online replied, and I was panicking, so when he said he could help... I know this is really stupid, but I'm desperate. I poured everything I have into this place. I can't just up and leave."

"Jaisy, it's an old house, and you're living on your own for the first time in your life sans significant other, parents, or roommates. Plus, you've been so stressed with the move and work and... well, with everything that's going on in the world, it's understandable that you—"

"You think I'm imagining this?"

"I think your brain is filling in gaps."

"Trust me, I don't want to spend my only day off this week having Byron Fucking Tarrant traipse around my place finding reasons to sniff my underwear. If I could convince a priest to get in here and bless this place with so much holy water that I have to file for flood damage, I would, but apparently there's a protocol to getting holy men to do their exorcism magic nowadays, and I don't belong to any of their clubs!"

"I believe they're called 'churches.'"

"Okay," Byron's nasally voice interrupted. He stood back in the living room, hands before him, eyebrows raised condescendingly. "I am sensing a lot of negative energy coming from this room."

"Would it be better if we left?" Mark asked, his voice and features dripping with bogus sincerity.

Byron blinked once, lips unsmiling, before turning his entire frame toward me.

"Jaisy, you said in your email that you found some things out about the history of this abode. Would you care to share a bit more?"

"Sure," I nodded. "So, I told you the first bit—"

"Oh, uh, just, tell us everything," Byron interrupted, pointing to the camera. "And speak loud, if you don't mind. It's for Jamie here's thesis." The graduate student looked up at me and smiled tightly before putting her eye back on the eyepiece of the digital camera.

Mark snorted into his hand, somehow managing to fake a cough.

Cheeks burning, I pulled out my cellphone and opened the email I had sent Byron the previous week.

"I had a friend who does investigations into insurance fraud dig up some stuff on the neighborhood," I read aloud, squinting at the small text. "Turns out my relator lied to me about the name of the church. She said it was called 'Christ's Covenant,' but that was in 1994, before it was purchased by a breakaway sect called 'The Church of Divine Mercy.' This guy, Father Sadowski, founded the sect in the late eighties."

"Go on," Byron nodded, posing his hand to his chin and fixing me with a studious stare.

"The premise of this sect's belief was that all sins could be traced back to demonic influences."

"Oh, honey," Mark sighed.

"No, just, listen," I snapped. "This guy would perform mass, what he called, 'purges' on a regular basis. My buddy said the videos he found on the church's pre-Y2K website showed a tame version of *The Exorcist*, like some kind of monthly juice cleanse but for the soul. Certain people, though, he said had actual demons inside of them, and the only way they could be cured would be a full-fledged exorcism. He performed the exorcisms here."

"And you believe that one of the demons he exorcised is still hanging around?" Byron asked.

"One of the exorcisms went wrong. A thirteen-year-old girl—" I flicked my eyes back down to the email on my phone screen. "—Ashley Monroe, died in 1997, and Father Sadowski was arrested. He died in prison three years ago."

As if on cue, the curtains covering one of the living room windows fluttered, and my stomach dropped as I got a glance at the sky—it was blood red, no trace of sunlight anywhere. Nightfall was upon us.

The cabinets in the kitchen began to rattle. Around the corner, the bathroom door slammed shut, squeaked open, and then slammed shut again.

"Oh, oh!" Byron clapped his hands excitedly. "Quick, let's get this. This is going to get so many hits!"

He and the grad student hurried down the hall toward the bathroom.

"It's probably just a draft," Mark called after them, sounding bored.

And then, the television turned on. The cable box was not hooked up, so there was only white noise pouring through the screen and speakers.

Static filled the room as the lights overhead began to flicker.

My stomach began to sink, and I backed away, looking around warily.

"It's here," I said, and felt myself begin to tremble.

The bathroom door suddenly slammed shut again—this time, though, there was violent force behind the sound.

Byron's screams echoed down the hall. The grad student swiftly appeared at the end of the hallway, just outside the bathroom door, face white and mouth open in horror. She dropped the camera and sprinted toward us. Mark and I both leapt backward to get out of her way as she passed, our backs hitting the living room wall, and she all but scrambled out the front door on her hands and knees.

"Jesus fucking hell!" Mark yelled over the static of the television. I'll admit, I think we both considered running after her for the front door before we kicked into high gear and raced down the hallway. We reached the bathroom door at the same time and tried to open it, but to no avail.

On the other side, Byron's voice had reached high-pitched squeaks of terror and pain. From the sounds he was making, I pictured his guts being yanked out through his nostrils.

"Break it down!" I shouted to Mark, and we both threw ourselves against the wooden door. When that did not work, however, Mark—who had been a quarterback in college—pushed me out of the way, planted his back against the hallway wall, and kicked at the doorknob.

The door burst open, and Byron Tarrant fell forward, flat on his face, sobbing. His pants were yanked down around his ankles, and it looked like someone had drawn a smiley face on his pimply, pale butt cheeks with lipstick.

"Oh, gross," I cringed at the thought of my brand new lipstick on his ass.

Blubbering, Byron crawled away from the bathroom. Mark helped him to his feet and tactfully directed his gaze toward the ceiling while Byron yanked his pants back up before scampering away.

Within seconds, we heard the front door slam again, followed by the sound of a van peeling out. The rest of the house fell silent, as if the mission had been accomplished; the television turned back off, the lights stopped flickering, and the cabinets remained still.

Mark and I exchanged looks before he tapped the bathroom door open with his toe and we peered inside.

The light was on, although one of the bulbs in the overhead lamp had burst.

Below the lamp, written on the mirror, were words scrawled in more of my lipstick:

HA HA HA

And right underneath, it continued:

GET THE FUCK OUT

For the next few days, I stayed with my parents down near Cape May. I told them that the house had a bug problem and needed to be fumigated.

My mother immediately put me to work sorting through the

leftovers from my childhood scattered throughout the attic. As I sifted through all of my childhood accessories—my collection of Pogs, a Tamagotchi that was still somehow alive, and even a mess of Polly Pockets—I tried to also sort through my options for dealing with a demon.

Should I keep looking for new psychics?

Should I try to call an actual priest and start the arduous process of securing an exorcism? Exorcisms seemed to be what caused this...

Should I learn to simply live with a demon haunting me for however long it took to pay off a substantial amount of my mortgage?

Or, was my only option to just walk away from the house? Giving up the symbol of my adult life finally beginning was not something I was eager to do.

One thing was for sure, though: I could not stay with my parents in my childhood bedroom with the twin-sized bunk beds for the rest of my life.

"Mrs. Schweitzer?" I called from my parked car on the street. The old woman who I had been effectively stalking for several hours looked over her shoulder as she approached her house, groceries in hand. When her eyes landed on me, she turned away and quickened her shuffling pace up the driveway toward her front door.

Kicking my car door open, I jogged across the street, my pink high tops slapping the wet pavement, and up the lawn toward her. "Mrs. Schweitzer! Wait, please, I just need—"

She rounded on me, however, before I had the time to finish. Her pale blue eyes were fierce, and she held her shoulders back with pride, even though her hands were laden with two sets of heavy grocery bags.

"This was a decent neighborhood," Mrs. Schweitzer stated, chin held up high.

"I—" Frowning, I stood before her on the damp grass. "What?"

"We've all lived here for over twenty years," she continued. "This was a good place for families. It was a good place to grow old. No one is excusing what Father Sadowski did, but we are not all like that here."

My heart quickened at Father Sadowski's name.

"What do you know about the demons he exorcised?"

Mrs. Schweitzer sighed, and only then did her shoulders slump.

"There were no demons," she shook her head. "He only worked on teenagers. Certain *kinds* of teenagers. Like that man who comes by your house sometimes with his… friend."

"Mark and Daryl?" I asked, confused. "What does this have to do with them?"

"He thought they—the teenagers—were possessed by evil spirits. He was trying to free them, but—" She swallowed, seeming to slump down even further, as if all of the defiant fight that had been in her a moment ago was seeping out through her feet. "We could hear their screams, even from out on the street. He told us it was necessary to save their souls."

"What did he do to them?"

She cast her eyes down and did not reply.

My thoughts sprung to the restraints Mark found in the yard. "He… Did he torture them?"

"Hot coils on their hands, electricity to their… their privates—" She trailed off and clenched her eyes shut, shaking her head. "Besides the girl in 1997, there were also… others who did not take to the treatment. But they were not murdered. They ended up hurting themselves."

My mind worked slow, picking apart the massive ton of information I had just unpacked. "So, there was never a demon in any of the people he exorcised. All of those teenagers were just… gay?"

And just like that, as if someone had simply flicked on a light switch, all of my fear and confusion melted, replaced by hot fury.

"How could you let him do that?" My voice shook with self-righteous anger. "Why didn't anyone stop him? Why didn't you call the police?"

"You have no idea what it's like to live in a town that's dying. I know what you're doing here," Mrs. Schweitzer cut me off before I could ask what the hell economic disparity had to do with torturing gay kids. "You're waiting for us to get edged out, just like they did in Brooklyn, and Asbury Park."

Blinking and stunned by this sudden shift in who was attacking whom, I opened my mouth, but found that I had no words.

"You think we're all out of touch gay bashers, women haters, Nazis, whatever," she continued, her eyes hard but watering. "We may be a part of an older world, but we're not evil. We're just angry about not being listened to. When you're constantly getting ignored and then told that you're the problem, rage bubbles up. Rage forces you to become something ugly inside. It's a sickness. We're not like that around here. At least, we didn't used to be."

My mouth must have fallen open at some point, because I became aware that it was agape.

The elderly woman seemed to be lost in her own memories, however, and did not pay attention to me. Her eyes were on the brown dead grass beside me.

"That was all so long ago," she said softly. "But it never really stops, does it?" She finally lifted her gaze to me and opened her mouth to speak, but stopped herself. Instead, she turned around and began shuffling toward her front door.

"Wait," I said, my voice cracking. "If it's not a demon, what is it?"

Mrs. Schweitzer did not turn around or reply.

"What happened to the others?" I called after her as she began to unlock her front door. "The others who were exorcised and hurt themselves? The survivors?"

Mrs. Schweitzer cracked open the door and turned, looking back at me morosely.

Behind her, hanging on a wall coated in peeling wallpaper and lit by a mounted lamp, was a school photo of a boy who could not have been older than eighteen. In the photo, he was smiling and holding his diploma. A funeral card was tucked into the corner.

"There were no real survivors," Mrs. Schweitzer said before closing the door behind her.

"Think about it," I spoke over the noise of the bustling brewery around us. Everything seemed to echo against the exposed brick walls and oak bar. At one of the long picnic tables, a crowd scream-sang "Happy Birthday" while a baby cried and a bearded man who could have been anywhere from his mid-twenties to early forties blew out the candles on a gluten-free cupcake. There was a round of applause, followed by everyone taking a swig of their IPAs. Between Mark and I, our pint glasses sweated atop the oak barrel we had managed to snag for ourselves in the packed brewery.

"Slamming doors," I continued, "vandalism, and profanity. What, or rather, who does that sound like?"

"Uh—" Mark scrunched his face up in mock concentration. "— everyone from my high school?"

"Exactly. It sounds like a pissed off teenager. I think Mrs. Schweitzer is right. It's not a demon that's haunting my place."

"You think it's the ghost of the girl who died there?"

I nodded.

"Shit," he said, sounding genuinely intrigued. "So what are you going to do, call the Ghostbusters?"

Fidgeting with my glass, I hesitated. There was something that felt wrong about this. Yes, this thing—ghost—was a problem, there was no denying that. As things stood at the moment, there was no way she and I could both continue living in my house together. One of us had to go.

And yet, targeting the spirit of a murdered teenage girl who had been persecuted for her sexuality in life felt so wrong.

"We're just angry about not being listened to." Mrs. Schweitzer's voice whispered once more in my ear. Her words had been playing on repeat within my mind for days now, like a scratched record. *"When you're constantly getting ignored and then told that you're the problem... Rage forces you to become something ugly."*

"I want to try something else first," I replied at last and looked up at Mark as he adjusted his glasses. "You've got Amazon Prime, right?"

The house had been quiet and still when I arrived, although I attributed this to the sun sitting above the horizon. Once Ashley materialized from wherever she had been all day and found me back, I was sure there would be quite the racket. As such, I got to work immediately.

Three hours later, my heart hammering in my chest, I lowered myself into the creaking chair I had grabbed at a yard sale and watched the sunlight disappear from the second-floor bedroom window. I flipped on the overhead light, and the moment that the sun dipped entirely below the skyline, I cleared my throat.

"Hey, Ashley?" I called out, feeling stupid speaking to the empty space. "Sorry to kind of catch you off guard here, but I wanted to try something, if you don't mind."

On a small foldout dining table before me, I set a shining silver bell down.

"Ring once for yes, twice for no," I continued, folding my hands and looking around. "Can you do that for me?"

A few moments passed. The bell did not ring, although the door to the bedroom creaked and swayed lazily on its own. Goosebumps trickled up my arms, but I forced myself to continue in an even tone.

"I wanted to see if you would be interested in having this room." I stood up and gestured to the small bedroom, fit with a futon that I had covered with a paisley comforter that had once resided in my own childhood bedroom. Against the opposite wall was the television with a joint VHS and DVD player. Plastering the walls were posters of my favorite bands and movies from the 1990s; a Spice Girls collage nine-year-old me had painstakingly pieced together from cut-up magazines was on proud display on one of the bookshelves, which contained—among other movies—*Spice World*.

"I dug some of this stuff out of my parent's attic, so, apologies if it's kind of beat up. This—" I flopped down on the lavender blow up chair, smiling as the plastic squawked beneath me. "—was my faaaavorite thing in my room when I was your age. Mine got busted, but they still sell them on Amazon. Oh, and I wasn't sure if you were an N*Sync or Backstreet fan, so, feel free to tear down the one you're not a—"

The N*Sync poster was abruptly ripped off the wall. My fingernails dug into my palms from the violence of the reaction, but I could not help but emit a hiccup of a laugh. That was a very teenage response.

"Good choice." I nodded, trying to keep the fear out of my voice. "Justin's got the best solo career now anyway."

Standing again, I wiped the sweat off my palms onto my jeans and walked over to the bookshelf containing all of the DVDs I had found for five cents apiece on Amazon and Craigslist. I took *Home Alone* off the shelf and held the case aloft for any floating entities in the room to see.

"Figured you liked this one, if you kept turning it back on. Not sure if you ever used a DVD player, but they're super simple."

I popped open the DVD player and inserted *Home Alone*, then placed the remote on the small foldable dinner table set up next to the television. "I also brought back some old movies I loved. *Homeward Bound* is, of course, a classic. Feel free to watch whatever, though."

At this point, I knew that I was rambling, but there had been no sign of the afterlife other than the bedroom door creaking and the poster getting torn off the wall. I was starting to get nervous. What if I was wrong, and this was a demon I was blabbing away to?

To distract myself, I ran my fingers over the R. L. Stein books lining the second bookshelf flanking the television.

I remembered the hours I pored over these volumes. Summer after summer, chilling in my cut-offs and jellies, blasting Britney, sipping CapriSun straight from the pouch, unrolling a Fruit-by-the-Foot…

Immediately, my nerves were soothed, and I almost felt calm. At peace.

Nostalgia can be a hell of a sedative.

"All of this stuff." I plopped back down in the blow-up chair, fidgeting with my watch. "It brings me back to what I used to think were simpler times, you know? The nineties seem so wholesome and easy compared to what we've got now. But you're proof that nothing was great or perfect back then, either. All the same shit that's happening now was happening back then. It just wasn't happening in plain sight yet."

The chair across from me squeaked, as if someone had just sat down in it. For the first time since I had started speaking, I felt like I was having a real conversation with a living person, instead of empty air. I sat up straight, fixing my eyes on where I felt like a thirteen-year-old's head would be on the chair in front of me.

"I'm sure you don't want to be stuck in the spot you died in," I said, my voice quiet, "and I know this does not make up for what happened to you. I wish I could tell you that things are getting better, and that this kind of stuff doesn't happen to people anymore. But, I want you to know that I'm here, you know, if you ever want to talk."

I stopped speaking, and the chair across from me gave an uncertain squeak.

"I mean," I rushed on, "you know, we can probably find ways to communicate. Even if you just want to, uh, you know, I just want you to know—"

The bell rang once, startling me.

The edges of my mouth crept up into a smile.

"Cool."

A week later, after I helped Mrs. Schweitzer carry her groceries home from the convenience store on the corner, I threw together some leftovers and started to make my way to the couch to watch the news.

The house had been uneventful for seven days at that point, with only the odd creaks of floorboards and the loud electric hum of the television upstairs being used. There was one occasion that I awoke around three in the morning to the sound of canned laughter drifting down through the floorboards to my bedroom on the first floor. I thought I recognized the theme to *Saved by the Bell* before I drifted back to sleep.

As I entered the living room, I glanced out the window; the sky was just turning a vibrant red and orange hue, void of any yellow tints from the sun.

From upstairs, there was the telltale tinkling of the bell.

The pace was not urgent, but the sound was reminiscent of an impatient customer trying to get the attention of a clerk.

For a moment, I hesitated. I was still freaked out by this idea that there was someone else living in my house. Still, though, I managed to keep cool as I climbed the stairs with my plate of food in one hand and poked my head into the bedroom.

The bell stopped ringing. On the television, the first season of the *Buffy* home screen was static. The remote was on the little dinner table, in front of the rickety chair. The blow-up chair had been moved beside it, so that two people could watch the television side-by-side.

"Ashley?" I asked, glancing around the room even though I knew I would not see her.

The bell rang once, and the chair before the dinner table was pulled out for me.

"Oh!" I managed to keep myself from leaping backward and swallowed my shock. "T-thank you!"

I sat, and immediately, the remote control was scooted toward me. The "play" button clicked down on its own accord, and an episode of *Buffy* began.

Beside me, the blow-up chair depressed a bit, like someone small had just thrown themselves into it.

Feeling genuinely pleased by that thought, I smiled at the chair and stirred the leftovers on my plate.

"This is a good episode," I remarked around a forkful of lo mien as the first scene began.

The bell on the table rang once in agreement.

Born and raised in Cape May, New Jersey, **JAISY** attended St. John's University and graduated from the PharmD program with honors in 2011. Post-graduation, Jaisy completed a two-year residency with Bellevue Hospital and stayed on for an additional three years as a clinical pharmacist. In 2016, she accepted a position at Robert Wood Johnson University Hospital and currently resides in Trenton, New Jersey, with her spiritual roommate.

A Jersey Shore native, **CAROLYN** currently resides in Howell, New Jersey, where she works as a Promotional Review Editor for Bristol-Myers Squibb. Her professional work has appeared in a number of online publications, including HCPLive.com, where she was a regular contributor. In 2016, her first short work of fiction was published in the Three Rooms Press *Songs of my Selfie* anthology.

memories of
FARROWLEE BEACH

An account by Sandy H. Downing,
AS PROVIDED BY S. E. CASEY

owden was the last place that I ever wanted to return. The town assumed the personality of the stretch of coastline it sat on: toughened by the battering winds, suspicious of the storms that defied forecasting, and defensive from the corrosive ocean salt. It wasn't any single feature that triggered my loathing, but the particular mix that made it so repulsive. I had hoped never to return, but after more than a decade away, it was death that drew me back to its upswept streets and unlit doorways.

The death wasn't tragic; rather, it was a relief. Toremi Varney (Auntie T as she demanded we address her) died at one hundred and one years old. Born January 1890, assuming the family records were accurate, my great aunt on my mother's side had outlived her youngest sibling, my grandmother, by fifteen years. Being an equal fifteen years older, overall Auntie T managed thirty more years of life than her little sister.

The Varneys weren't native to Maine. They had immigrated from Australia or New Zealand or some place in between. The fact that they never committed to a definite country of origin was but one of their many eccentricities. My grandmother was too young to remember much of the family's exodus. Blue Granny (our nickname because of her eyes) rebuffed any questions concerning those days as being unimportant and unworthy of retrospection. My cousins and I wondered if there were some misfortune she didn't want to relive, or even better, if there were some nefarious doings in the family history that she didn't want to reveal.

Not many Varneys had left the confines of their out-of-the-way corner of the world. However, Blue Granny had fallen in love, gotten pregnant, married, and moved down the coast to Boston. Although I may not understand such things so well, no doubt her decision left its scars. Though never any overt displays of discord, there seemed to be an unspoken tension between the Varneys and us. While we were always treated with an abundance of politeness, there was no warmth. However, maybe this gives the Varneys too much credit in assuming they are capable of genuine affection in the first place.

After Blue Granny's funeral, we never expected to hear from the reclusive Varneys again. For the last fifteen years, we hadn't any contact. Thus were we surprised by the funeral invitations. My uncles made the decision that we should all attend.

I decided to drive up from Boston alone. It was easier to make the trip by myself instead of insinuating my way into a carpool with my cousins. It also made for less stress not having to endure the questions that would come with a four-hour drive. Whenever my cousins got together, they would recount their many shared tales of past adventure. I did like to listen to them—the inside jokes and braggadocio—but would rather they didn't attempt to include me in the repartee. During lulls in the conversation, I would suffer the same questions about my job, or if there were any *lucky* ladies in my life. Despite the barbaric jibes they traded with each other, I would be spared with supportive nods and mild encouragements.

We were offered use of the Varney guesthouse, generously afforded to us as long as we wanted. They didn't even require us to RSVP. My uncles decided we would accept their hospitality and meet at the coastal estate the day before the wake.

Located in eastern Maine, the deceptively wide state and its winding roads made for a demanding drive. December provided its unwanted companions as well: gusty winds, the crunch of road salt, and the sudden undulations of frost heaves. I had to memorize the number of the interstate exit as well. Even in a region filled with small towns, Sowden was so insignificant not to be listed by name.

The main street running through the town's center had only two stoplights. Wind beaten boards clung to skeleton frames of the small buildings and shops huddled close together. Nearing six o'clock, long after sunset this time of year, all offices and stores were closed. The dull, lightless façades offered no hint of life.

As a hobby when encountering a deserted place, I wondered how many days without mankind the empty streets presumed. The town could have been a study of what it would look like three days after a sudden human extinction. My exacting estimation was based on the qualities of being somewhat neglected and slightly unkempt. The only flaw in my assessment was the dogs. By the third day without people, they would have realized the free ride from the indulgent hand of man was over and would be roaming the streets in desperate packs. However, there was nary a trace of animal life, canine or otherwise.

I caught both red lights. They had long cycles despite the absence of traffic. Useless this time of year, they should have been shut off, but perhaps the town knew it wouldn't be considered otherwise. However, if Sowden had some redeeming quality that demanded attention, it remained well hidden.

The blank windows of the buildings were impenetrable, the pure interior darkness turning the glass into a mirror. In the reflection of my headlights, I saw myself behind the wheel, a soul-searing stare unintentionally turned back around to lance right through me. My heart jumped at the sight, an acute fear of being watched causing me to look away. I pushed down the fright as if I had been caught red handed committing some moral atrocity.

Keeping my eyes squarely on the road, I pushed through the dreadful cluster of shops and municipal offices. The Varney's estate was reachable by a single-lane road, which lay shortly past the town center. It was the only reason to take the poorly paved road. It had no branches, and no other places existed beyond, unless one wanted to drive straight into the ocean.

I hesitated at the turn. With no headlights behind me, I idled, contemplating my choice. If I were to be the first to arrive, what would be the proper etiquette in announcing myself? Was I obligated to offer the hosts condolences, or was it proper to wait for the wake? Would the Varneys even remember who I was? As one of Blue Granny's six grandchildren, maybe I would be unrecognizable to them without the presence of my five cousins.

I turned left, away from the coast.

A few miles down the road, a rustic house announced itself with a red, apple shaped sign reading, "The Fourth Little Piggy." I pulled into the gravel driveway of the bed-and-breakfast, taking the second to last parking space. Optimistically slinging my duffel and garment bags over a shoulder, I hurried through the biting December cold through a hibernating garden to the front door.

A middle-aged woman with red cheeks and kind eyes greeted me. With a radiant smile, she inquired if I would be dining or interested in a room for the night. Her eyes shifted to my luggage. She didn't make me answer.

"So it'll be a room then?"

I nodded.

"And it'll just be you... correct?"

I nodded again.

She tilted her head, her grin widening—sympathetic, not cruel.

I ventured downstairs at eleven. After breakfast and before lunch, it was the time when the dining room would most likely be empty. The rosy-cheeked woman from the night before greeted me merrily. She wore the same wide smile, apparently a permanent condition. Allowed to choose any table, I grabbed a corner seat by the window.

It was easy to tell how extremely cold it was outside. The grey grass stood stiff despite the wind. The rhododendron's leaves curled into tight cones in their evolutionary response to conserve heat.

The beaming woman, who had identified herself as the wife-half of the husband-and-wife ownership team, filled me in on the weather. The snowstorm that had been forecast had pounded southern New England overnight, Boston getting the worst of it. Not only was there more snow than expected, but it would linger for another day. She announced how fortunate *we* in Sowden were, the town far enough north and east to be spared even a glancing blow.

Considering the blanket of gunmetal clouds outside, she was certainly an optimist.

While waiting for my soup and sandwich, I contemplated the implications of the weather. My apartment snowbound, everyone would know that I had spent the night in Sowden. There would be no denying that I avoided both my family's company and the Varney's lodging offer. Furthermore, it looked like I would be stuck in Maine for another day.

I inquired about a room for a second night.

"Such a beautiful town, might as well make the best of it. So, here on business or pleasure?" she asked.

I told her the truth, leaving out names and specifics.

Forcing a tight smile of manufactured sympathy, her cheeks flushed even more. "I'm so sorry to hear. Is it someone from Sowden? We are such a small town that I didn't hear of any recent passings except, of course, for—"

Leaning back on her heels, she sized me up and down as if comparing my features to some loathed model. I couldn't help but to feel sorry for the Varneys. They weren't bad people, but intentional isolation draws hostility. Nonetheless, I was happy to have inherited the brown eyes and dark hair from my grandfather rather than the blue eyes and blond hair of my grandmother.

The hostess regained her composure, albeit her face drained of most of its red. Mumbling a promise to check the night's room reservations, she scurried away. I finished my lunch alone, enjoying the view out the window. While there was ample time before the wake, it was too cold for a walk. With nothing else to do, I retreated to my room. I considered calling my family at the estate, but didn't know the number. It was of no consequence. They wouldn't be worrying about me, and besides, I would see them soon enough.

Lying on the bed, I rehearsed meeting the Varneys, as well as my uncles and cousins, figuring what each may ask. Despite having plenty of sleep the night before, my mind began to drift. Drowsily, I found myself in a hazy dream world of sand and sun. Alone amongst a stand of tropical trees, I watched the balmy breeze blow the sail-like fronds above back and forth.

The soft sand made for poor footing. A sudden fear of sinking straight through the beach gripped me. I lay on my back, floating atop the snow-white surface that generously shared its stored heat. Soaking up the warmth of this secret place, the terror of sinking receded.

Watching the palm fronds wave back and forth, with nowhere to be, I enjoyed the sun, the breeze, the beach, and the best part, the fact that I had it all to myself.

There were no cars with Massachusetts license plates parked at the funeral home. With a clear view of the entrance, I waited for my uncles and cousins to arrive. However, after a chilly hour, I became paranoid that they somehow had slipped past my lookout. Not wanting to be the last to arrive, I headed through the cutting cold to the front door.

The room holding the wake wasn't hard to find. It was the only activity in the somber place. I was greeted by what seemed a thousand blue eyes leveled directly onto me. My uncles and cousins were nowhere to be seen. I cursed them as well as myself. If I had stayed at the guesthouse, this embarrassment could have been avoided.

The Varneys were a homogenous family, easy to tell they were related by their blue eyes, blonde hair, slight build, and angular faces. It was impossible to ignore how much I stood out. They even dressed in a separate fashion. While they too wore black, they had somehow found a darker shade.

Without the courtesy of a greeting line, there was nothing else to do but approach the closed casket. I lowered my head in respect, taking a few disguised deep breaths. The room expanded, no longer feeling so cramped and crowded. Thankfully, the circles of blonde-haired mourners turned their attention away from me, resuming their secretive whisperings. I silently thanked my Aunt for this respite.

Auntie T had no living brothers or sisters; with her passing, a generation had ended. From the experience of losing my own mother and father, I sympathized with her children now alone at the top of the hierarchy. They had no one left to look up to, and now took the spot of being the next in line to pass. I offered my condolences to each, although I couldn't remember names or in what order they were born. They welcomed me by name without any prompting.

Not having anything to talk about or anyone to talk to, I drifted to the back of the room, pretending to be interested in the tasteful, yet dull art. I was twenty-one the last time I was among the Varneys. Of course, I wasn't alone then. All roughly the same age, my cousins and I were the only young people on the estate, an agreeable arrangement as we didn't have to integrate anyone else into our clique. Fifteen years later, nothing had changed. The Varneys were a wasting family. Except for my grandmother, who somehow slipped free of Sowden to start a new genealogical line, there weren't any new beginnings here, the lack of children and young adults painfully apparent.

I was alone, and not the comforting alone of solitude, but that terrible alone under the judging gaze of others.

To my surprise, several of the Varneys initiated conversation. After talk of the snowstorm and unseasonable temperatures, they inquired why I hadn't stayed at the guesthouse the previous night. None of the questioning was accusatory or defensive. They seemed to be genuinely concerned for my cost and convenience. They urged me to take advantage of the lodgings for as long as I liked.

When I inquired for the whereabouts of my uncles and cousins, I received different answers. Some said they had stayed at the guesthouse the previous night, while others claimed not to have seen them.

I took a seat at the side of the room. Keeping my attention on the door, I watched for my family to come. However, no one entered. No one left as well. What was everyone waiting for?

The conversations in the room lapsed into prolonged stretches of silence. I could feel the attention centering onto me, the half-family interloper. Fifteen minutes before the scheduled end, I gave up hope for my uncles and cousins, and escorted myself out. I crossed the silent room. With no distractions to conceal my exit, the many blue eyes painfully bore into me again.

Only back in the hallway did I dare to exhale. Taking a moment to catch my breath, I thumbed through the guest registry scanning for surnames not Varney. Mine was the only one. The funeral director closed and locked the doors to the wake, all the Varneys still inside. Were they opening the casket to view the family matriarch one last time? I wondered if my lingering had delayed the ritual. However, my duty finished, it was of little concern. I turned away and hurried outside. The starless sky that stretched over the parking lot looked pregnant. Despite the expectant heaviness in the curtain above, so far there was no snow. It may have been so cold that the precipitation evaporated in the upper atmosphere, the moisture squeezed dry by the oppressive frigidity.

Passing the side of the building, my curiosity piqued. I pushed through the row of privacy bushes. The windows the room of the Varney wake started high on the wall, so I had to stand on my toes to peer inside.

I stifled a scream at my reflection, not immediately recognizing the leering face staring back. A wave of panic washed through me, the penetrating eyes meant for the Varneys instead gazing deeply into me. What foulness in my soul could they see? I quickly looked away before any loathsome revelations could be prised away. I never liked looking in a mirror, and to see myself as an ogling Peeping Tom only reinforced this minor phobia.

The lamps of the parking lot were faint, and so the brighter lights inside should have allowed me a clear view in. Had they been turned off? It occurred to me that if I couldn't see in, those inside could see out. The thought of all those blue eyes staring back at me from the dark drove the air from my lungs, leaving a circle of guilty condensation on the glass.

The fear gripped me again. I realized why I hated Sowden. It never let you see in, never allowed access to its secrets, but its reflections were always watching to snatch away mine.

Stumbling back through the prickly bushes, I jogged to my car, chased by the town's prying eyes. Since there would be no funeral, my business in Maine was mercifully finished. However, with the storm still raging at home, I couldn't leave. Furthermore, I hadn't been able to secure an additional night at the bed-and-breakfast. When checking out, the husband-half of its ownership team informed me that they were booked solid.

Driving out of the parking lot, I hesitated at the exit, considering my options. With the sinking, lingering fear twisting my gut, I took a deep breath and turned right toward the coast.

There were four cars with Massachusetts plates in front of the guesthouse. Part of me was relieved to catch up with my family, but now I would be the center of attention, barging in on whatever activity in which they were engaged.

I tarried in the car, contemplating if driving to the Varney guesthouse was indeed the best option. Unable to come up with a better scheme, I exited into the night's suffocating cold. Simultaneously, a side door of the addition built onto the end of the guesthouse opened, and an old man shuffled out. It wasn't an uncle or cousin, and it wasn't a Varney. His name was Holm.

While Holm wasn't related to the Varneys, he too had emigrated from Australia (or New Zealand or somewhere in-between). He served as the caretaker of the estate, seeing to all guests. There couldn't have been many, Blue Granny the only Varney I knew to leave this place. And besides family, who would ever be invited here?

And who, other than family, would ever accept?

"Greetings, Sandy, welcome back. We're happy to show you our hospitality once again," Holm said.

I winced at the mention of my name. However, it did have its history here, as Blue Granny had bestowed it on me. She insisted on naming all her grandchildren.

With a sweep of an arm, Holm ushered me into the guesthouse. No one was inside, although the living space was a mess. I crossed to the hallway lined with the dormitory style bedrooms. Strewn clothes, luggage, and toiletries could be seen through the open doors, but still there was no one. I smiled at a spent candy wrapper left on one of the nightstands, the sure sign of Uncle Seabury, the unrepentant sweet tooth of the family.

At a little past six o'clock, they were probably out to dinner, or maybe they had gotten lost on the way to the wake, circling the town in another quixotic adventure. I turned to head back outside, but came face-to-face with Holm, who had crept up behind me with my bags slung over a bony shoulder. I hadn't necessarily intended to stay, but to avoid calling him presumptuous, my decision was made.

"Here you are, Sandy, the second on the right. It has the best view of the beach. We saved it for you. Your grandmother would have wanted you to have it."

I always suspected I had been Blue Granny's favorite. The two of us could sit in the same room for hours without needing to speak, each of us comfortable not to have to fill the silence with empty words. While she had a rough edge and was always scolding my cousins for their lack of manners or good sense, she never spoke harshly to me. Although, I suppose I never gave her good reason to.

While Holm set my bags down, I inquired to the whereabouts of my erstwhile family.

"I'm sorry, but I'm not certain. I wouldn't worry, you will see each other soon enough," Holm answered.

Holm's ignorance was suspicious. He maintained ferocious vigilance over everything that happened on the grounds. In fact, he could be so prescient that I convinced myself all things here were intentional—the placement of each grain of sand, the timing of every seabird's call, the tides running at the estate's whim, independent of the moon.

Once Holm settled my things, I walked with him back to the front door. The freezing cold outside made the decision to stay a little more palatable. The old man didn't seem to notice the chill, hovering in the doorway—half-in, half-out.

"Good night, Sandy. We're glad to have you back. I'm sure everything will be as we always remember."

I nodded to him in a hurry to be alone so I could finally relax. However, after settling on the couch, I could only stare at the front door, expecting it to burst open at any moment. Impossible to unwind this way, I retired to my room, where I would have some warning to my family's return.

I lay on my bed listening, but the house remained quiet. The only sound was the murmuring of the waves lapping back and forth against the shore. In tune with this natural metronome, I began to relax. Slumping farther and farther into the soft mattress, I imagined the beach outside, alone in the dark and cold. There was no need for it to exert itself tonight, no one but me to hear it.

Still, in the moonless, loveless night, the waves continued to crash on the beach.

I awoke with the sun in my eyes, the window shade having been left open. By the angle of the light, it was well past dawn. I checked my watch, but it was dead, having stopped at two-thirty in the morning.

There was no sound outside my bedroom door, which I, too, had left open. Had my cousins drawn something on me or doused me with shaving cream as they were wont to do to each other? No, I was clean, spared once again.

Embarrassed that anyone could have looked in on me while sleeping, I searched for a mirror to see how bad I looked. There wasn't one in the room, so I settled to rake a hand through my hair.

But it was no matter, as the house was still empty.

I threw on a coat and ventured outside. Not a cloud sullied the brilliant turquoise sky, and surprisingly, the cold had lifted. The low-pressure system that had skirted to the south must have dragged some warm air in behind it. Walking to the far end of the guesthouse, I scanned the length of the snowless estate. With a view of all five other houses, there were no signs of life here either. Given the property's emptiness, I was compelled to begin my extinction game.

However, I struggled to make any estimate of how long mankind could have been dead. It could have been a day or it could have been years. The sight before me had an odd quality, maybe a lack of detail or perhaps a resurfacing of memories scrambling my morbid talent.

The grounds were conspicuously pristine. Tucked into garages, there weren't any vehicles outside to give away the general decade. There was also no machinery, gardening tools, or other gadgets left around to gauge a frequency of prior activity. There wasn't even evidence of electricity to prove the century, no wires or poles. The power-lines must have been diverted underground, a good idea considering the region's strong coastal storms.

I marveled at Holm's ability to keep things so orderly, but then again, the Varneys weren't a messy people. And of course, there were no children here, no toys or other clutter to pick up after. Without the chaos of the young, the homes were so well kept they could have been ready for immediate sale. It looked like they were fully prepared to move out at a moment's notice.

The climate added to the deception. The lack of snow or salt stains around the walkways didn't give away the season. If I were to take a picture, it could have been passed off as summer. However, and maybe this condition was what was so acutely disturbing, it wasn't a confusion of season, but an *absence* of such, a profound stagnation of time. I ended my usually merry diversion without a guess less out of frustration than an unnamed, rhythmic dread that crept into me.

The fear welled up again, that feeling of being under a soul-rending stare. My stomach wrenched as if threatening to turn inside out, my true self to be judged. But this was madness. There was no one here.

I shivered, but not from the cold. In fact, it was so warm that I took off my coat. The simple act broke the petrifying fear, allowing me to think rationally again. With no biting cold to drive me inside, my attention turned to the welcoming swish of the ocean. I walked to the beach for what would most likely be the final time.

The beach dominated the layout of the estate. In fact, it was the main reason the Varneys had settled here many years ago. Blue Granny confided that the family didn't emigrate to just anywhere, but researched many places to find the perfect spot: a mirror of the place they had left. And so thousands of miles from their Oceania origins, they found one in Maine. Blue Granny never elaborated why the topography was so important, and I never pressed her. I sensed she was telling me a great secret, reluctant to reveal as much as she did.

As if carved by a protractor, the crescent of yellow sand arced uniformly in contrast to the jagged coastline that typified the glacial dump of New England. Two sentinel-like granite formations stood at either end of the beach, framing the geometric bend. The soft concavity smothered the waves that fed into the bay from the ocean. During the summer, these trapping currents and the relative shallowness made the waters much warmer than other local beaches. In another regional aberration, there were no islands to be seen from the coast, the water falling off the horizon.

The estate's buildings weren't the usual New England cottage or saltbox structures. The hipped bungalows with open beach-facing verandas were more characteristic of those found in tropical locales. The trees spared from the initial clearing appeared out of sorts too. The trunks grew straight without limbs or leaves until fanning out at the top. Of course, at this time of year, they had lost most of their foliage and what remained weren't fronds or coconuts, but the stubborn needles and cones designed to survive the seasonal temperature swings and salt spray.

So did the Varneys find a veneer of their ancestral home, wherever exactly that was, whatever circumstances they had left. The landmark beach I'm sure once had an Indian name, but it was now known as Farrowlee Beach. I assume it was titled the same as its doppelganger on the other side of the world.

On the waterline, fragile spines of ice tinkled, pushed into each other by the languid waves. The bay's undercurrents were too active for it to have iced over this early in the winter, but the tidal pools of stranded water had frozen overnight. When the tide re-advanced, it broke the thin ice into needles, scattering them. Their life would be short in the extinguishing glare of the midday sun.

Wiping a bead of sweat off my brow, I couldn't help but to chuckle, knowing all the snow waiting for me at home.

Running a hand through the water, it was much warmer than I expected, the cove still conserving some summer heat. I removed my socks and shoes, compelled for one last, albeit quick, wade in the surf. This chapter of my life closing, it would be a fitting ode to Blue Granny, who was so proud of her family and the place she grew up.

Rolling my khakis to the knee, the water was less bracing than I anticipated. I waded deeper, each step more refreshing than the last. I tossed my sweater back on the beach so I could feel the sun on my bare arms and neck. Waiting for the cold to sink in, I enjoyed the determined back and forth pull of the water against my legs.

I swiveled to the guesthouse, scanning the windows for my family. What a sight I must have been! Me, knee deep in December's icy waters! It would give us a story to share and laugh, one where I would be the star. Surprisingly, the bright sun cast no glare over the windows, and I had a clear view inside.

But no one was there, the house empty.

I stepped out of my pants, one leg at a time, careful not to get them wet, and stripped off my shirt. Throwing both onto the beach, I waded deeper, up to the thighs and then to the waist, compelled by some dormant sense of adventure. Gritting my teeth, I plunged in.

The water was invigorating. I swam away from the coast into the middle of the bay.

The temperate waters made me doubt how cold it had been the day before. Peering into the depths below, the blue-green smears of kelp anchored to the seafloor waved back and forth to the soft rhythm of the undercurrents. The healthy color and easy motion gave away the kindness of this little bay.

I swam out to the cove's imaginary boundary line created by the beach's curve and its flanking rocks. Treading easily, I could feel the embrace of the azure waters pushing their warmth up to me. I dared to go no further, the grey ocean beyond undoubtedly cold and cruel.

I began the swim back, my arms and legs suddenly heavy from exertion. From this perspective, the beach looked far away. The concavity of the bay also appeared unreasonably deep, as if I was viewing everything through a fisheye lens.

Unlike the effortless crawl out, progress back to shore proved laborious. I corrected course to the south end of the beach, interpreting the complicated currents tilting this way. Still, it was a battle. My enthusiasm and energy flagged, but I was wholly determined to make it back.

And there they were! At the beach's southernmost point, I saw my entire family—three uncles and five cousins—waving to me. I cried out to them, eager to be in their company. It was mutual, their arms warmly waving back and forth beckoning me in.

On our last day on Farrowlee Beach, it was as Blue Granny would have wanted to see us: frolicking together in the sun and surf of this timeless place. My legs cramped and my arms spasmed. However, deciphering the swirling tidal currents for the easiest path to shore, I knew that even if I were simply to float, eventually they would deposit me at the exact point where my family gathered.

I sighted my buoyant Uncle Seabury, and behind his girth bobbed Uncle Shelley. My cousin Heather and her younger sister Coral floated to the side of each. They were all here, a little off the shoreline, under the surface, their bluish-purple arms waving.

Waving back and forth in the soft rhythm of the undercurrents.

Navy spots bloomed over the edge of my vision and my numb arms were leaden, but I was happy. My head ducked under the icy waters once and then twice, but there was no need to struggle against the cold weight, for I was no longer alone. I knew where I was going and where I belonged.

With my family on Farrowlee Beach.

Under sky and water, my vision tunneled and my lungs filled. Everything her color, same as her kind eyes, always and forever blue.

07/03/17- Obituary, *Boston Gazette*: **SANDY H. DOWNING** of Dorchester, Massachusetts, has been officially pronounced dead after a long time missing. Born in 1955, he is the son of Harold Downing and Marina (Hopewell) Downing, both deceased. Sandy went missing 12/12/91, the same day as the famous Hopewell family disappearance. The Hopewells, to whom Sandy is related, were lost without a trace on a day of an early season 1991 blizzard. While the mysterious Hopewell case was closed twenty years ago, everyone presumed deceased, a clerical oversight did not change Sandy's official status. There will be no service or funeral arrangements. Information on the charity auction of his unclaimed assets will be announced soon.

S. E. CASEY grew up on the coast of New England near a lighthouse. As a child, he always dreamed of smashing the lighthouse and building something truly vulgar with its rubble. This has become the writing method for his unconventional, grotesque stories. His broken down and rebuilt weird tales have been published in many magazines and anthologies, a listing of which can be found at secaseyauthor. wordpress.com.

about the
EDITORS

In addition to co-editing *Mad Scientist Journal*, **JEREMY ZIMMERMAN** is a teller of tales who dislikes cute euphemisms for writing like "teller of tales." His young adult superhero books, *Kensei* and *The Love of Danger*, are now available. He lives in Seattle with a herd of cats and his lovely wife (and fellow author) Dawn Vogel. You can learn more about him at bolthy.com.

DAWN VOGEL writes and edits both fiction and non-fiction. Her academic background is in history, so it's not surprising that much of her fiction is set in earlier times. By day, she edits reports for historians and archaeologists. In her alleged spare time, she runs a craft business, co-edits *Mad Scientist Journal*, and tries to find time for writing. She is a member of Broad Universe and an associate member of SFWA. Her first novel, *Brass and Glass: The Cask of Cranglimmering*, is available from Razorgirl Press. She lives in Seattle with her awesome husband (and fellow author), Jeremy Zimmerman, and their herd of cats. Visit her at historythatneverwas.com.

Made in the USA
Las Vegas, NV
11 January 2022

41089988R00195